PRAISE FOR

"K.P Gresham is one of the gutsiest authors I've ever read." Chilehead Adventurer Review

"K.P. Gresham plunks us directly into the Texas politics, the swagger, the TEXAS. We are there." Claymore Award Review

"K.P.'s books are easy to read and difficult to put down. (She writes) lots of twists to keep the reader guessing." Bookzilla

"K.P. Gresham injects powerful descriptive language into her story line, whether with character, dialogue or setting." Diane Donovan, Midwest Book Review

To learn more about K.P., check out her website at www. kpgresham.com where you can also sign-up for her newsletter!

FOUR REASONS TO DIE

A PASTOR MATT HAYDEN MYSTERY

K.P GRESHAM

Epiphany's
Flame

To my writing tribe:
Fellow Sisters in Crime authors Helen Currie Foster, Kathy Waller and Fran Paino; my editor Rachel MacAuley, my cover designer Elizabeth Mackey,

And the loves of my life,
Kevin and Bethany

CONTENTS

1. The Governor's Mansion — 1
2. The Inauguration — 10
3. A Good Ol' Texas Barbecue — 16
4. Stayin' Put in Austin — 26
5. Officially Missing — 35
6. Lambert Speaks His Mind — 44
7. After Hours — 48
8. The Tale of Two Breakfasts — 51
9. Lieutenant Gage — 58
10. Just the Facts, Ma'am — 66
11. It Smells Like Manure — 71
12. Mrs. Duff Arrives — 79
13. The Reverend David Duff — 87
14. Shelly Duff — 95
15. Hester Honeywell — 101
16. The Evidence Box — 110
17. Angie Arrives — 116
18. The Rumble in the Jungle — 119
19. Eating Crow — 127
20. Bishop Hamlin — 132
21. An Understanding Reached — 137
22. The Chase — 144
23. The Oak and Horn — 151
24. Fire! — 157
25. Plan B. Very Plan B — 164
26. The Hanging Man — 174
27. Gage Takes Charge — 179
28. Dessertus Interruptus — 188
29. Disaster Strikes — 195
30. The ICU — 203
31. A Corner Is Turned — 212

32. The Missing PowerPoint   218
33. The Sign of Four   223
34. Senator William J. Womack   229
35. The Crime Board   239
36. He's No John Wayne   244
37. The Wives Have Claws   249
38. A Bishop's Confession   257
39. He Parked Where?   268
40. Follow That Car!   274
41. Mum Has Her Say   282
42. Chief Aguilar   292
43. You Shouldn't've Done That   297
44. Danny Lee Ashe   304
45. Huntin' for the Homestead   311
46. The Rittenhouse Roadside Filling Station   315
47. Finally   318
48. Four Reasons to Die   324
49. The Senator's Son   332
50. So Sayeth the Father   343

About the Author   353
Also by K.P Gresham   355

1

THE GOVERNOR'S MANSION

MATT HAYDEN STOOD on the second-floor balcony of the Texas Governor's Mansion, taking in the sunny day and the crowds beginning to gather beyond the gates. Leaning on the white wood railing to take the weight off his weak leg, he could barely make out the pink granite dome of the Texas Capitol peeking through the oak trees. A breeze rustled his light brown hair, and he tugged at the unfamiliar collar around his neck. He hadn't worn it for months, but today's events warranted his pastoral formal attire.

"A beautiful day for an inauguration, don't you think?" he asked the man standing beside him.

"For now. Rain's on its way," came the doomsday reply.

Matt suppressed an impatient grimace. Pastor Lambert, visually unremarkable with mousy brown hair, heavy-lidded eyes and a down-turned nose, looked as depressing as his attitude.

"Not 'til sundown," Matt offered, hoping to lighten the man's dreary mood. "All the outdoor festivities'll be over by then."

Lambert shrugged, refusing to be roused from his sad-sack demeanor. It crossed Matt's mind that perhaps the man was not a supporter of the soon-to-be-sworn-in governor.

Yes, Matt felt a surge of pride. His best friend's son, Jimmy Novak, was about to become governor of the great state of Texas.

The door behind Matt opened and Jimmy's Chief of Staff, Deshawn Keegan, hurried over to Lambert. "Pastor, we have to leave for the Capitol soon, and there's still no sign of your boss."

That didn't sound good, Matt thought. Lambert was the assistant to Reverend David Duff, the pastor of a large San Antonio church. Reverend Duff was to pronounce the benediction at the end of the swearing–in ceremony.

Lambert sniffed. "Reverend Duff prefers solitary prayer before speaking publicly."

Deshawn's brow furrowed. "I'd appreciate it if you'd give him a call. In case he's lost track of time."

"As you wish." Lambert sighed as if he'd been asked to handwrite the Book of Genesis. "Excuse me." He pulled out his cell phone and walked to the end of the balcony.

Deshawn growled in frustration, and Matt tried his earlier observation to lighten the mood. "It's a beautiful day for an inauguration, don't you think?"

Deshawn's smile flashed. "You never know what you're gonna get for weather in January. I think the good Lord's happy we're inauguratin' Jimmy." He looked up at the sky. "Sunny. A little breeze. Might have some rain tonight, but that's nothin'."

"Don't say that to Elsbeth," Matt said, referring to Jimmy's mother. "She'll have a conniption if one hair on her head gets wet."

"With all the hairspray she uses, the water'll roll right off."

The two shared a grin. Elsbeth Novak, Jimmy's mother, was a bulldozer in heels. Now, with Jimmy still an unmarried man, the duties of First Lady of Texas fell to her. Matt wasn't sure whether to laugh, cry or spend the next four years in prayer for the great state's survival.

Lambert walked back to join them. "He didn't answer."

Deshawn breathed deeply. "Perhaps you could go and look for him?"

"Me?" Lambert looked surprised. "I've just walked all the way over from the prayer breakfast."

"Maybe he's still at Ms. Honeywell's?" Deshawn suggested.

Matt looked up sharply. "Hester Honeywell?"

Lambert slanted a slight frown at Matt. "You know her?"

"I've met her." And the lady had made quite an impression. Though well into her seventies, she had a knack for quick observation and a sharp wit. A mover and shaker in the state's upper political echelon, she'd been a valuable supporter of Jimmy's gubernatorial campaign.

Lambert sniffed. "She invited Reverend Duff and me to stay at her home last night. Unfortunately, hotel rooms were hard to come by."

Lambert's tone was stiff with disapproval, Matt noted. Probably because of Ms. Honeywell's ownership of the Midnight Cowgirl several decades back. Well, the bikini-clad barrel racers *had* drawn a crowd.

"You were at the prayer breakfast, but the Reverend...?" Deshawn let the question hang.

"He went to St. Gregory's Episcopal for some quiet meditation," Lambert supplied.

Deshawn's clap on Lambert's back was none too gentle. "Then I guess you know where to start looking."

The three men walked back into the mansion, around the boxes that held the exiting governor's possessions and down the grand staircase. Matt took the steps slowly, having forgone his cane for the day. By the time he reached the bottom,

Deshawn had pointed Lambert toward the service door behind the stairs.

"You doin' all right, Preacher?" Deshawn asked.

"Physical therapist said no cane was okay." Matt wiped a bead of sweat from his brow. "But perhaps it wasn't the best choice for today."

"We'll sit you down in the library." Deshawn motioned down the mansion's main hallway.

When Matt entered the high-ceilinged room, his face brightened. "James W.," he said to the tall, chunky man standing at the window. "How's the proud father?"

Sheriff James W. Novak turned. "Ridin' the gravy train with biscuit wheels." Matt noted the soon-to-be-governor's father was wearing his black funeral suit—the only formal clothing he'd allowed Elsbeth to purchase for him. James W. preferred wearing his khaki Wilks County Sheriff's uniform when he was out in public. He crossed the room in four strides, shook Matt's hand and then peered more closely at Matt's face. "You lookin' a little peaked there, Preacher. Best have a sit." He motioned to the pair of pink-and-green upholstered chairs flanking the library's white fireplace.

Matt pursed his lips. "Those look pretty fancy."

"*Everything* in this place looks pretty fancy." James W. grinned. "But it's gonna be Jimmy's fancy for the next four years."

Matt sat down gingerly, grateful for the respite. "Where is the soon-to-be governor?"

"Over at the Capitol having a transition meeting with Governor Huff. Official handoff, I guess."

Matt nodded. The soon-to-be-former Governor Huff had taken Jimmy under his wing years ago and mentored him through the hairpin turns of Texas politics. Jimmy was his chosen successor.

A familiar woman's bellowing voice in the hallway broke into his thoughts. "The grand stairway is original to the home's 1855 construction." Elsbeth, the Novak family matriarch, was giving a tour of the Governor's Mansion. "Note the marks on the banister? Those were caused by nails that Governor James Hogg pounded in to keep his children from sliding down." A murmur of chuckles followed.

Matt couldn't help but smile. "Sounds like she's lived here all of her life," he said, his voice low.

James W.'s nod was one of pride. "She's as happy as a hog in mud."

Matt, a native Floridian, sometimes found James W.'s repertoire of Texanisms confusing, but that's how his friend expressed his thoughts. In this case, James W. was not calling his wife a pig, but simply saying she was in her element.

James W. sat down in the low back couch nearest Matt and surveyed the library. "Haven't been here since I was a kid."

"A school trip?" Matt asked.

"Naw," James W. said, stretching his legs. "My daddy was a mover and a shaker in Texas politics. We came here for special occasions back in the day."

"That's right," Matt nodded, remembering. "Cash Novak."

"Probably one reason Jimmy went so high, so fast," James W. admitted. "The Novak name goes pretty far in some circles."

Elsbeth, cinched into a barn red suit and matching pumps, appeared in the archway. "And here we have the library—" Elsbeth shot James W. a glare. "Centered in the room is the Pease American Empire sofa gifted by the mansion's first residents, Governor Pease and his wife, Lucadia."

James W. jumped to his feet, looking like a child who'd been caught with his hand in the cookie jar.

"And the mantel"—now her frown focused on Matt—"is

flanked by a pair of bergère gentleman's armchairs acquired by First Lady Joe Betsy Allred."

Matt felt the heat rise in his face, and he pulled himself as fast as he could out of the chair.

James W. took him by the elbow to steady him. "They're serving Tex-Mex in the conservatory," he whispered.

The two headed out of the room and down the hall. Winded, Matt paused at the entrance to the state dining room to catch his breath. An oval mahogany dining table took up most of the room, a six-branch brass chandelier overhead. "I'll bet every item in this room has a story," he said. He kept his voice low, as two men were deep in conversation by the nearby sideboard.

"And if you give her a chance, Elsbeth'll tell you every one of 'em," James W. whispered. "She's spent the last two months studying everything she could lay her hands on about this place."

The two men—one white-haired, Santa-Claus-round and wearing a banded clergy shirt and the other broad-shouldered, square-jawed and immaculately groomed—apparently were so engrossed in their conversation they didn't realize they were no longer alone.

"You have to be at the Board of Director's meeting." The rotund clergyman sounded adamant. "That weaponry course of study is vital, but the Bambi lovers are puttin' up a stink."

The square-jawed man shook his head. "Gotta be in D.C. for a Senate vote—" He stopped talking when he saw Matt and James W. standing in the doorway. "Can I help you?"

"Just takin' a gander," James W. answered, backing out of the dining room.

Matt followed him down the hall to the conservatory, which had once been the mansion's back porch. The wide expanse of windows made the more informal room light and airy. A buffet table overflowing with food spanned the wall across from the windows.

James W., his eyes wide with delight, headed straight for it. "C'mon, boy," he said. "Let's get some grub."

Matt got in line behind his friend.

"Pastor Hayden. It's so good to see you."

Matt turned to find the elegant Hester Honeywell standing behind him. Shoulder-length silver hair was pushed back stylishly behind her ears, allowing her well-defined cheekbones and chin to take center stage. She was exquisite. "Ms. Honeywell. This is a pleasure."

"I've been following your recovery through Jimmy."

A line started to form behind them, so Matt picked up a plate.

"First the bullet you took in the head last August, and then the stroke at Thanksgiving?" She put a hand on his arm. "I'm glad to see you."

"Thank you." Not wanting to discuss the details of his recovery—or lack thereof—he turned back to the table. "Quite a spread, don't you think?"

"Fonda San Miguel is catering." She leaned in and lowered her voice. "Best Mexican brunch in Texas."

His brows rose in mock horror. "Them's fightin' words, Ms. Honeywell. You best be careful."

"Careful about what?" The Santa-sized clergyman from the dining room now stood in line behind Hester, his eyes steeled with animosity.

Hester's azure-blue eyes narrowed. "Hello, Robert."

The man reached a chubby hand toward Matt. "Reverend Robert Meade," he said, eyeing Matt's clerical collar. "I don't believe we've met."

"Matt Hayden." Matt shook the man's hand.

"And where's your church?" Robert Meade's question sounded more like a challenge than a polite inquiry.

Hester interceded. "Matt's the pastor at Jimmy's home church in Wilks."

That wasn't exactly true, Matt thought. He hadn't been able to resume his pastoral duties at Grace Lutheran since being shot. Considering the tension between these two, however, he decided not to correct her.

"Quite a spread here," Matt said instead. He turned to fill his plate but was interrupted once more, this time by Deshawn.

"Sorry to bother you, Pastor Hayden," he said, out of breath. "But we can't find Reverend Duff. And it's time for the inaugural speakers to head to the Capitol."

Matt stepped back so Hester could get her food. "What does that have to do with me?"

"We need someone to give the inaugural benediction."

Matt almost laughed. "There's plenty of other pastors here you can ask." He nodded toward Reverend Meade, who was obviously listening in on the conversation. "Ask him."

"Can't," Deshawn said. "He's giving the invocation."

"I don't have anything prepared," Matt protested. "Weren't there a bunch of preachers at the prayer breakfast earlier?"

Deshawn huffed in frustration. "You don't understand how political these things can get. The speakers, even the clergy, have to be vetted. Political views. Background checks. You can't ask just anyone."

Matt lifted his chin. "You're asking me."

"Because you're his home pastor." Jason spread his hands. "Nobody could object to that."

Matt felt his head begin to whirl. This was exactly the type of commotion his doctor had said to avoid. "How about Pastor Lambert?" he suggested. "The man you sent looking for Reverend Duff."

Meade sniffed. "He doesn't preach. He's a bean counter. 'Administrative Pastor' I believe is the term."

The man was officious, to say the least. "I didn't catch what church you're with, Reverend Meade," Matt said.

Meade's eyes widened, as if insulted that Matt didn't already know. "The Christian House of Love here in Austin."

Deshawn cleared his throat. "He and Reverend Duff lead the two largest nondenominational churches in Texas."

"Nonetheless, I'm sure you can put together a prayer better than anything Duff would come up with." Meade narrowed his gaze at Matt. "You're not afraid to speak to the Lord, are you?"

"I speak to the Lord all the time," Matt answered evenly. "Thankfully, he's pretty forgiving when I don't say things just right."

The two men's eyes met. Assessing. Deciding.

Meade spoke. "It doesn't need to be long. A few Scripture-inspired blessings." Meade's smile didn't reach his eyes. "You're familiar with the Scriptures, of course."

"*I* am," Matt replied.

"Great," Deshawn said. "Let's find a quiet space where you can write something up."

Reluctantly, Matt allowed himself to be led from the room.

"God go with you," Meade called after him.

Matt looked heavenward. "I hope so."

2

THE INAUGURATION

MATT STOOD in the Capitol's rotunda, anxiously looking at his watch. Color Guard members, inaugural officiants and reporters swarmed around him. So much confusion. His vertigo switched into high gear as he searched for a quiet place to review his hastily written benediction. None presented itself.

Then the crowd parted, and Jimmy, surrounded by family and staffers, cut a path through the melee. The governor-elect spied Matt and headed his way.

Matt extended his hand. "Congratulations, Governor."

"Almost." Jimmy winked and pulled him into a bear hug. "Thanks for stepping in, Preacher." He lowered his voice. "This won't be too much for you, will it?"

Matt was afraid of that very thing, but he managed a smile as photographers surrounded them. "I pray all the time. No problem."

Jimmy laughed. "I can always count on you."

James W. joined the two. "Heard you got roped into praying, Preacher." He slapped Matt's shoulder. "I take my eyes off of you for one second and look what happens."

"Let's get a photo of the three of you," a reporter called out.

The three posed: Jimmy's hand on Matt's left shoulder, James W.'s on his right.

"Pastor Hayden!" An aide waved at Matt from the doorway to the outdoor stage. "Time to go."

Matt was ushered through the heavy wooden exterior doors and down to his seat on the bunting-festooned podium. He settled into the padded folding chair, then gulped when he saw the huge crowd spread out before him. There looked to be thousands of people on the south lawn. Directly in front of the stage was a roped-off area for friends and family of the dignitaries. He spotted Pearl, the widow of James W.'s oldest brother, and her new husband, Bo Peveto, staring at him with open mouths.

He felt as stunned to be here as they looked to see him.

Matt had been given an aisle seat four rows up from the official family seats. He shuddered when he realized he was in the direct line of sight of the cameras and news crews mounted on a scaffolding halfway through the crowd. He surveyed the fifty or so folks that sat with him on the stage. Every one of them was spit polished, squeaky clean and conservatively attired.

Matt, however, feared he stuck out like a sore thumb. His suit was ill-fitting; he'd lost a good twenty pounds over the last few months. Then there was his hair. The surgeons had done a great job of putting a plate in his head to protect the exposed brain, but now his skull looked lopsided. He'd grown his hair long to try and cover the deformity. He must look like a hippie to some.

He decided to focus on the prayer he was about to give. He studied the paper, still in his hand. He read it through, then shook his head. He needed to add something about helping the poor—.

There was a movement to Matt's right, and he looked up to see Reverend Meade taking the seat directly in front of him.

"Did you write a good prayer?" Meade paused to ask.

"Best I could do in a pinch." Matt shrugged.

Meade nodded. "I'm sure it will be fine." He lowered his bulk onto the folding chair, and Matt's discomfort about his appearance abated. No one would be able to see him with the Santa-sized man sitting directly in front of him.

"Ladies and gentleman," came a deep male voice over the loudspeaker. "Please rise for the posting of the colors by the Texas military joint Color Guard."

Matt stood and put his hand over his heart, more to hide its pounding than to honor the flags that passed him by.

The white-uniformed Color Guard took its place in the aisle as the dignitaries were ushered in. They raised their sabers as the incumbent lieutenant governor and his family entered. Jimmy, Elsbeth and a very proud James W. followed. When all were settled, the Wilks County Boy Scout troop led the crowd in the Pledge of Allegiance. Standing to the extreme right of the stage, the University of Texas Longhorn Band played the National Anthem.

There was a roar off in the distance, and everyone strained their eyes to watch for the military flyover. The engines of the four planes rumbled deep in Matt's bones as they skirted the crowd and stage. Then a thought struck him. The benediction was at the very end of the program. Surely, Reverend Duff would hear those planes going overhead and show up now.

Matt bowed his head as Reverend Meade took to the podium and began his invocation. "Almighty Father, Creator of all things good, Giver of all things righteous..."

Matt realized his hands were shaking. His doctor had warned him not to get excited or upset. The last stroke he'd had was caused by exactly those precursors. He must take deep breaths. In one, two, three, four, five; out one, two...

He continued the process until he felt his insides calm.

Meade was still praying. "Strengthen these two good men whom you have chosen to lead your peoples and this great state to obey your will. In the name of Jesus, Amen."

Matt hadn't heard a word of the prayer, but he didn't care. His head was clear, and his hands were steady.

Next on the agenda was the swearing-in of the lieutenant governor. Matt had never met the short man with the slicked-back chestnut hair. In Texas, the governor and lieutenant governor did not run as a team, so Jimmy's entourage had never included the man standing at the podium with his hand on the Bible.

His acceptance speech ensued, and Matt felt his nerves start to quicken again. No Reverend Duff. Matt might have to do this after all.

Surreptitiously, he looked back at the benediction. *Bless our leaders with the gift of discernment that they may listen only to the guidance of those sworn to do Your will, not those of false prophets who have only their own interests at heart.* Yes, Matt thought. That one's dead-on.

His thoughts were interrupted when applause erupted after the lieutenant governor's acceptance speech.

Next came the main act. The Texas Supreme Court judge introduced Jimmy; he and his parents headed up to the podium. Elsbeth took center stage, holding the Bible for her son to take the oath; James W. stood behind Jimmy, the buttons on his suit straining to maintain their hold.

It always struck Matt how alike father and son were. They shared the same height, the same burr haircut, the same Czech blue eyes. But mainly, both shared their love of Texas: all of its bravado and all of its courage.

Jimmy put his hand on the Bible.

Panic slammed into Matt like a Mack truck. The benediction came right after Jimmy's acceptance speech. Breathe, Matt told himself, trying to still his shaking hands.

"So help you God?" The judge was prompting.

"So help me God," Jimmy said.

The crowd broke into wild applause as the judge shook Jimmy's hand. Elsbeth, then James W. hugged their son. Then, Jimmy went to the podium to deliver his acceptance speech.

"Please, God," Matt silently prayed. "Speak through me. Let it be you talking, not me. Give me peace." He prayed it over and over again, until Jimmy ended his speech.

Matt was called to the podium to deliver the benediction. Though his stomach was nervous, his steps were steady. He looked out over the crowd and felt the peace that "passes all understanding" fill him. "Let us bow our heads in prayer."

He waited for the crowd to settle, then began. "Spirit of the Living God, fall afresh on us..."

The prayer was a short one, and before Matt knew it, he was finishing with the last petition. "Seek first not the kingdom of plenty or the kingdom of political superiority but may our new governor and lieutenant governor humbly seek first the kingdom of God and His righteousness. In the name of Jesus Christ our Lord, we pray. Amen."

He was surprised when the audience applauded. Not overly so, but it was a prayer after all.

Jimmy came up to his side and shook his hand. "Thank you, Preacher."

Elsbeth's handshake was less enthusiastic, but then again, she'd never been much of a fan. James W., on the other hand, folded him in a bear hug. "Great job, son," he said.

Son. That said it all. James W. had always treated him like a son. Matt's own father up in heaven would approve.

Relieved and happy, Matt returned to his chair and was about to take his seat when Reverend Meade turned around.

His eyes were filled with rage.

Matt's smile dropped. "Is something wrong?"

Meade narrowed his eyes, and Matt could almost feel the sparks shooting his way. Meade leaned close. "I know who you are," he hissed.

"What?" Matt asked.

"I know who you are," Meade repeated. "And what you're trying to do."

Matt was stunned. "I beg your—"

"And you won't get away with it." Meade refused to let him finish. "Stay out of my way, or else."

Matt fell back in his seat, his head spinning, as Meade tramped back up the aisle.

3

A GOOD OL' TEXAS BARBECUE

TEN MINUTES LATER, Matt was still in his seat on the now-empty inaugural stage. The doings for the big barbecue were beginning to take shape on the Capitol lawn. Towers of scaffolding were replaced by chuckwagons and trailers filled with long, black grills. He was thankful that the activities gave him a few minutes of anonymous solitude. Despite his deep-breathing exercises, his heart still thudded and his hands still shook. The image of Reverend Meade's grim face and his fire-filled stare refused to dissipate.

Matt hadn't seen that much hate in a man's eyes since his days as an undercover cop on the Miami docks.

He felt a presence at his side and looked up. Bo Peveto, his friend and now James W.'s brother-in-law, stood there, his brows furrowed. Matt nodded. "James W. send you to find me?"

Bo, tall, lanky and dressed in a tailor-made suit of dark gray, grunted as he sat on the stairs. "He's worried about you. So are Pearl and me." He studied Matt's face. "What's wrong?"

Matt shook his head. "A little overwhelmed is all."

Bo sniffed. "If you don't want to talk about it, that's fine. But I've been a bartender way too long not to know when someone's bothered."

Matt took a deep breath, then let it out. "I need to sleep on it some."

Bo nodded. "Pearl and me have to head back to Wilks."

Surprised, Matt looked at his watch. It was barely noon. "Already?"

"Angie called. Said the Fire and Icehouse is packed. Guess the whole town is celebrating Jimmy's inauguration. It's more than she and the staff can handle without another bartender."

Matt understood. Bo had been given the day off to attend the inauguration as the newest member of the Novak clan.

Thinking of Angie back at the Icehouse brought a smile to his face. Somehow he, the small-town pastor, had managed to fall in love with the red-haired vixen who owned the Fire and Icehouse across the river from his church. The match hadn't gone over too well with some members of his congregation, especially since Angie was reputed to be an angel by day and a devil by night.

Now that he thought about it, however, maybe that was truer than people realized.

"I'm all for getting out of Austin," Matt said. "Let's go."

Bo helped him to his feet and up the stairs to the south lobby entrance. "Everybody's in the governor's office on the second floor. Elevators are across the rotunda. You good for that?"

Matt nodded. It took a few minutes, but they finally made it inside the elevator. Matt leaned against the paneled wall and wiped a drip of sweat from his brow.

Deshawn hurried over. "Saw you coming across the rotunda," he said, nodding to the second-floor balcony that circled the lobby. "Mr. Peveto, it's time for the family portrait." He

grabbed Bo's elbow and showed him through to the governor's...
Jimmy's...office.

Matt followed. The Novak clan was gathering in front of
the large room's deep blue curtains. Jimmy stood in the middle,
his mother and father on the right, beside the Texas flag, and
Pearl and Bo on the left, beside the United States flag. Matt
grinned with pride at his friend, Bo. After serving twenty years
for manslaughter, the gray-haired hippie now stood tall beside
his beloved new wife and smiled for the camera.

Pearl, on the other hand, was a tiny thing. Her short-curled,
gray hair was as dew on a rose with her pale face and smooth
skin. She had a small chin that gave the impression she was a
frail, timid woman, but she was far from that. Ask the man
she'd shot to save Matt's life last July.

Though Pearl and Bo were an unlikely pair, James W. and
Elsbeth were the perfect foils to each other. As the cameras
flashed, Matt studied the two of them. Both proud as could be.
Both singular personalities with outspoken opinions. And
somehow, both loved the other deeply.

Would he and Angie make as good a match?

Deshawn returned to the room, this time herding those
who had given speeches at the inauguration. To Matt's chagrin,
Reverend Robert Meade was among them.

"Thank you, family," Deshawn nodded to the Novak clan.
"Let's have the speakers now. Governor, you stay where you
are." Deshawn directed everyone where to stand. Meade bris-
tled when Matt was instructed to stand beside him. Matt
wasn't really happy about the configuration either. Though he
kept from directly looking into Meade's eyes, he could still feel
the heat of hatred emanating from the man.

Deshawn studied the tableau. "Pastor Hayden, please
stand in front of Reverend Meade. He's blocking you."

Meade's glare almost singed Matt as he walked to the front.

"Looks good," Deshawn nodded. "Okay, everybody. Smile!"

Jimmy's next group photo included Hester Honeywell. Matt sat down on a nearby chair to watch the Texas political bigwigs gather around Jimmy, Hester among them. How were they referred to again? Oh, yes. The Texas Philanthropic Society. And their philanthropy was devoted to preserving the Great State of Texas in all its glory.

As the cameras flashed, Bo and Pearl approached. "We need to get going, Preacher," Bo said. "You ready?"

"I sure am," Matt stood, a little more easily this time. "I'll let James W. know we're leaving." He headed for the far corner where James W. and Deshawn were looking at a clipboard.

"Sorry to interrupt," he said. "Bo needs to head back to the Icehouse, so I have to leave."

Deshawn's head jerked up. "You can't. You're sitting at the head table for the barbecue. All the dignitaries are."

Matt shook his head. "I'm no dignitary, only a substitute. Besides, I've had enough for one day."

"But Hester Honeywell specifically asked to be seated next to you."

Matt's eyes rounded in surprise. "You're kidding."

"I was going to put you between her and James W." Deshawn said quickly.

"C'mon, Preacher," James W. said. "I could enjoy myself if you were there."

"You'll be with Elsbeth."

Deshawn shook his head. "Jimmy sits in the middle, then Elsbeth sits beside Governor Burr, then Mrs. Burr, then James W., then you, then Hester, then—"

"What about Reverend Meade?" Matt interrupted.

"Reverend and Mrs. Meade will sit on the lieutenant governor's side. He's their home church pastor."

Well, shoot, Matt thought. "I really don't want to do this."

"You'll be doin' me a favor," James W. said. "This might give me an excuse to get back to Wilks tonight. Takin' you home and all. Hell, I have a county to protect."

"All right," Matt sighed. "But that's it. After the lunch, I'll head back to the mansion to get some shut-eye until you're ready to head for home."

"Thanks, Preacher." Deshawn headed for the center of the room. "All right, everyone! Let's get some grub!"

———

MATT WAS A FLORIDA BOY, born and raised. An undercover cop serving on the drug-infested docks of Miami, he'd seen violence and graft and gluttony and murder—including the assassination of his own father at the hands of a corrupt chief of police. Matt considered himself a man of the world, and after discovering he felt more inclined to show God's love to folks than to try to control his own anger in a damaged system, he became a man of the cloth. Between the reality of the world and plumbing the depths of his soul, he figured he was prepared for "most anything."

Nothing had prepared him for Texas.

From his view at the inaugural barbecue's head table, seventeen *thousand* people—at least, that was the number of tickets sold for the event—were taking their seats for the sit-down lunch on the Capitol's front lawn. The four city blocks of rolling grass were spread with tables and chuckwagons and servers and police. Music blared, echoing off the skyscrapers that cocooned the Capitol grounds. And the guests! Stetson-topped cowboys, Texas flag-diapered babies, big-haired women and silver-buckled businessmen all waited in anticipation of the feast to come.

James W. looked out over the crowd. "Take a peek at all those folks out there, Preacher. They're all here to celebrate my Jimmy."

Matt suspected some of them were there for the food, but he kept that under wraps.

"Mrs. Burr," James W. said to the woman sitting on his left. "This is Pastor Hayden."

The chic woman extended a petite hand. "That was a lovely benediction you gave. So refreshing."

"Thank you," Matt replied. *Refreshing?*

"Mrs. Burr and I go way back. Met each other back in freshman chemistry on the north forty."

Matt had been in Texas long enough to know James W. was referring to the University of Texas campus, only a few blocks north.

Mrs. Burr nodded. "Did you see that Elmer Wittig is going to be the new director of the chemistry department?"

"You don't say." James W. turned, and the two fell into deep discussion.

Matt looked back at the crowd. "How are they going to feed all these people?" he asked, not expecting an answer.

"Leave it to Eddie Deen," Hester answered beside him. "He's been doing this since 1995. *And* everyone'll be served in less than an hour."

Matt shook his head. "Impossible."

"I thought you believed in miracles." Hester's lovely lips pressed into an amused smile. She gestured to the waiter tasked with serving the head table. "The pastor here needs a Shiner," she said. "And so do I."

Matt kept a smile on his face, trying to find the words to decline the offer. His doctor would be very unhappy if Matt took a drink of alcohol.

Apparently, Hester saw his hesitation. "No tab, Pastor. The

head table's beers are on me. Shiner Bock was my sponsor when I was on the rodeo circuit, and I like to see folks have a good time."

Matt heard bottle tops popping behind him, and a beer appeared in front of him. Hester clinked her bottle to his. "Let the show begin." Knowing he shouldn't but not wanting to insult the elegant lady either, he took a swallow of the cold brew.

Doggone, that tasted good.

An elderly man moved up to a microphone at the side of the table and raised his hands to quiet the crowd.

"Who's that?" Matt whispered to Hester.

"The chaplain for the Texas Congress."

Matt bowed his head as the man said grace, all the while wondering why Deshawn hadn't asked this chaplain to step in and give the inaugural benediction for the AWOL pastor. Which reminded him. Was there any news about the missing Duff?

The celebration began. Platters filled with briskets and sausages and chicken appeared from the chuckwagons circling the gathering. Gallons of potato salad and coleslaw arrived like magic on the red-checkered tablecloths. Rivers of barbecue sauce flowed, sopped up by a couple of thousand loaves of plain white bread. Hoots and hollers and George Strait and laughter echoed off the surrounding business towers. The smell of onions and garlic and hot sauce mingled with the macabre sight of sauce-lined lips, orange-stained shirts and greasy licked fingers.

And true to Hester's word, everyone was served in less than forty-five minutes.

Matt wiped away the last bit of sauce from his chin, sated with some of the best barbecue he'd ever had. When he put down his napkin, he realized Hester was staring at him expectantly. Grinning, he inclined his head. "I stand corrected. That Eddie Deen fella pulled it off."

Hester nodded her approval. "I always appreciate a man who can admit when he's wrong."

Matt felt a motion at his side and looked up to see Deshawn leaning over James W.'s shoulder.

"Time for your interview with the *Dallas Daily News*." Deshawn slapped a large hand on James W.'s shoulder. "Ready for your close-up, Sheriff Novak?"

James W.'s scowl was good-natured. "Not particularly."

Hester winked. "You'll get used to it, James W."

"Elsbeth would be better at this than me." James W. shoved out of his chair.

Deshawn paled. "Yeah. Not so much."

The two men walked away, and Hester gestured to the waiter for another round.

"Not for me," Matt said. "One's enough." Then, maybe because he'd had a beer, he summoned the courage to ask her the question that had been on his mind since sitting down at the table. "I'm honored, but a little surprised you asked Deshawn to seat us together. Why?"

"You made quite an impression on me last year. It's refreshing to meet someone who is thoughtfully apolitical." She sipped her beer. "I loved your answer when we asked if you were Republican or Democrat."

"I don't recall—"

Hester nodded. "'I do. You said that 'Republicans get babies born, and Democrats get babies fed.' Or something like that."

Matt didn't remember the conversation exactly, but that sounded like something he would say.

"Plus, Jimmy's been singing your praises. Says you saved

him a couple of times when folks tried to pin him down about evolution versus the Bible."

Matt remembered the talks he'd had with Jimmy. "I'm only saying that God can create anything any way he wants."

Hester patted his hand. "And that's why I wanted to sit with you. You're an interesting man, Pastor Hayden."

"Not everyone agrees with you." Matt cast an eye down the table at Reverend Meade. He looked to be in deep conversation with the strong-jawed, strong-shouldered man he'd been talking with in the State Dining Room back at the mansion.

Hester followed his gaze. "You're talking about Meade."

"Apparently, he didn't like my benediction much."

"Take it as a compliment," she said. "Besides, I can assure you he would've disliked Reverend Duff's prayer even more. David Duff is"—her blue eyes twinkled—"shall we say, less circumspect than you are."

The mention of the missing pastor focused Matt back on the man's mysterious disappearance. He decided to leave the table in hopes of finding James W. If anyone would know if Reverend Duff had surfaced, it would be him. Besides, Matt didn't want to talk politics or hear another word about Reverend Meade. "This has been fun," he said, rising. "Thanks for the Shiner, Ms. Honeywell."

"Any time, Pastor Hayden."

He stood for a moment, surprised by the slight tilt of the world. He'd only had one beer, for Pete's sake.

Finding his balance, he headed up the sidewalk and into the Capitol. James W. was probably up at the governor's office. He headed across the crowded rotunda to the elevators. As he waited for the doors to open, he felt a poke and heard a flash go off behind him. He turned to find four reporters, their cell phones thrust toward him. *What in the world?*

"Pastor Hayden," a tall man said. "What was your agenda when you wrote today's benediction?"

A red-haired woman jammed her cell phone closer. "Word is that some in the clergy consider your views a call to socialism."

Matt felt like he'd been gut-punched and fought hard to keep his breath even.

A cameraman stood beside a man in heavy makeup. Matt could feel the lens zoom in on him as a microphone was thrust into his face. "You used the term, 'stand in solidarity with the poor.' Does that mean you intend to counsel Governor Novak that he should raise taxes?"

His head began to reel, and it felt like an elephant was sitting on his chest. The doctor had warned Matt that the worst thing he could do was get upset. Sweating now, Matt looked beyond the reporters to see if James W. or Deshawn or someone was around who could save him.

Then he spied Reverend Robert Meade against a far wall, standing with the square-jawed, broad-shouldered man. Meade's arms were crossed over his chest, a malevolent smile on his face.

To Matt, it was the smile of Satan.

The world tilted wildly. Matt hadn't realized he was leaning against the elevator doors to steady himself until they suddenly opened behind him.

Oh, no.

He was already far down the dark tunnel to unconsciousness when his shoulder hit the floor.

4

STAYIN' PUT IN AUSTIN

MATT WOKE to the sensation of a blood pressure cuff tightening around his arm. Next, he heard the blip, blip, blip of a heart monitor above and behind his head. He was semi-reclined in a bed, covered in sheets that were somewhat stiff.

Aw, heck, he thought. He was back in a hospital.

He remembered flashes of consciousness. A quiet argument taking place between James W. and Elsbeth. Being hoisted into an ambulance. The prick of needles in his arms.

The blood pressure cuff let out a gasp and relaxed its grip. He opened his eyes to find himself not in an actual hospital room, but in a glassed-in exam chamber. The nursing station beyond was bustling with staff and...

Oh, cripes. Dr. Ryan was staring straight at him from behind the desk.

She came around the counter, pushed a strand of dirty-blond hair around her ear and headed straight for him.

"Pastor Hayden," she said after she closed the door behind her. "You ignored my orders. I have half a mind to hand you your walking papers. You ignored my orders."

Matt knew she didn't mean it, but he also knew she was seriously upset with him.

"Did I not say don't let yourself get excited?" She settled her fists at her waist. "Did I not say you were not to over-exert yourself? Did I not say to avoid situations that would increase your blood pressure—"

"I know," he said. "But I didn't have a choice."

"I told you," she barreled on, "excitement boosts the flow of adrenaline. This allows the amygdala to send signals to the frontal lobe of the brain, which increases heart and blood pressure and..."

Matt felt like a schoolboy being chastised by the principal.

She held up his chart. "Then I got the blood work back." Her eyes narrowed. "You've been drinking."

He quelled under her fit-to-be-tied gaze. "I didn't want to insult—"

She held up a hand to stop his explanation. "We'll talk of this later when we're both calmer." She pulled up a stool. "The only reason I haven't admitted you is that the EMTs treated you with a clot buster on scene, and your vitals have been within range since you got here."

"You're not admitting me? I can go home?"

"Yes and no. I'm not admitting you, but I'm not letting you get in a car for an hour to ride back to Wilks, either." She folded her arms and glared at him sternly. "Not for at least a few days. You and I both know a small-town clinic is no place for you if another one of these episodes happens."

Matt did understand, but he didn't know where he could stay in Austin. "I'm not sure I can bunk with James W. The Governor's Mansion is—"

She shook her head. "James W. arranged for you to stay at Hester Honeywell's home. Her place is only a few blocks from the mansion, plus she has plenty of spare rooms and a staff that can keep their eyes on you."

"Hester Honeywell?"

"I want you to rest. The Governor's Mansion is no place for you right now. James W. agreed, and you're going to Ms. Honeywell's." She stood. "I'm putting together your orders and prescriptions. I'll observe you for a few more hours here, then let Ms. Honeywell know she can have her driver come and pick you up."

She shook her head at him one more time, then headed for the door.

"Dr. Ryan?" he called.

She turned.

"I'm sorry. I'll be good. I promise."

The corners of her eyes crinkled. "Your lips to God's ears, Pastor Hayden." She flashed a rueful smile, then left.

———

TWO HOURS LATER, Matt was loaded into a spotless, shiny, totally loaded black Suburban and driven away by a short, bald twenty-something with biceps the size of melons.

"Thanks for your trouble," Matt said from the back seat. He would've preferred sitting next to the driver, but the man had insisted it would be easier for Matt to get in and out of the back seat.

Matt turned his attention to Austin's descent into night. They passed the Capitol; the tables and chuckwagons and people were mostly gone. Neon signs lit up bars and restaurants, competing music pouring out onto the streets. The still-exuberant crowds swarmed down the sidewalks, debating where to start their night of carousing.

"Do you work for Ms. Honeywell full time?" Matt asked the driver.

The man, his face as clean-shaven as his scalp, looked at Matt in the rearview mirror. "I'm a grad student at UT. I help her out around the house, and she gives me free board in exchange."

"Smart," Matt commented. "What are you studying?"

"Law," he answered. "How about you, Pastor? Where's your church?"

Technically, Matt was still on medical leave and didn't have a church, but he gave the easy answer. "Wilks, Texas. A small town about an hour southeast of here. My name's Matt, by the way."

"I'm Connor. Connor Evans."

"Good to meet you," Matt said. "I appreciate the ride."

Connor's head bobbed. "You need anything while you're at the house, need to go somewhere, let me know."

They passed the Governor's Mansion, which was lit up like a Christmas tree. Matt figured everyone inside was gearing up for the inaugural balls later. Three in all, James W. had said. The Governor's Ball, the Republicans for Texas Ball and the UT Alumni Ball. Elsbeth had been delighted, trying on at least forty dresses in anticipation of the evening. James W. fussed that he had to wear a tuxedo.

Four blocks and a few turns later, Connor pulled up in front of a moss green Victorian mansion. A cream-colored porch stretched the width of the house's front, rounded a circular tower, and came to a stop halfway down the south wall. A steep roof featured three front-facing gables, their detailed millwork in pristine condition.

"Well, heck. I told him to park behind the garage," Connor said as he drew up behind a blue car.

"Excuse me?" Matt asked.

"Pastor Lambert. We must park the cars in the garage at night. Downtown neighborhood and all." Connor hopped out to help Matt descend from the tall Suburban

then guided him up the sidewalk to the house.

"Quite a place," Matt said, a little out of breath.

"Wait 'til you see the inside." Connor's strong arm went around Matt's waist as they approached the stairs. "We'll get you settled in the parlor and let you rest a bit."

Connor opened the leaded glass front door, then ushered Matt through the foyer into a high-ceilinged yet cozy parlor. The walls were Wedgwood blue with polished oak crown molding and window casings. At the parlor's far end stood a stone fireplace, its heavy wood mantel supported by short, masculine corbels. Two upholstered Queen Anne chairs book-ended the hearth. The room reminded Matt of a Victorian-era gentleman's smoking room.

Connor settled Matt on the embroidered blue settee. "I've got one more errand to run for Hester. Make yourself comfortable."

"Is Miss Honeywell home?" Matt asked.

"She's upstairs changing for the Governor's Ball." Connor pulled out his cell phone. "I'll let her know you're here." He finished the text, then headed out the front door.

Matt barely had a chance to lean back into the couch's soft padding when he heard heavy footsteps rushing down a stairway beyond the parlor's archway. A giant of a man, at least six-foot-six, with a stomach heading toward paunch and oil-slicked, ash brown hair, came barreling around the corner.

"Pastor Hayden, I'm so sorry to have kept you waiting." The man closed in, then bent, putting his hands on his knees so that he could study Matt's face. "Hmm, yes. You look like you could use some refreshment. Would you care for a brandy?"

Matt shook his head. After the scolding he got from Dr.

Ryan earlier, liquor was the last thing he wanted. "Water, please."

"Of course." The tall man straightened and headed for the archway, then turned. "I'm Lyle, by the way."

Matt heard a door open above him. "Lyle!" Hester Honeywell's voice called down the stairs. "I need you to zip me up."

"Be right there," Lyle called back. "Make yourself to home, Pastor. Look around. I'll be back in a jiff."

Matt stared at the archway, wondering exactly who Lyle was. An assistant, perhaps? The man had to weigh at least two hundred and seventy pounds, but he moved like a gazelle. That is, if a gazelle existed that wore a size fourteen shoe.

The doorbell rang. Matt looked around to see if anyone was coming to answer it. When no one came, he stood and went to the door to see who was there.

When he saw the familiar form of James W. on the other side of the leaded glass, he opened the door.

James W.'s face immediately lit up. "Son, you're a sight for sore eyes. How you feelin'?"

"I'm doing a lot better." Matt stepped aside to let James W. in. "Looks like I'm going to be in town for a few days. I have a follow-up appointment with Dr. Ryan tomorrow morning at nine." He led the way into the parlor.

"Matt, I'm sorry as can be that I made you stay on for the barbecue. I wanted to share the moment, that's all." James W. plopped a bag and cane on the floor as he sat down in the large wingback.

Matt returned to the settee. "No need to apologize. I'm a big boy. I should've insisted."

"And Jimmy feels lower than a gopher hole for guiltin' you into saying that prayer."

"Deshawn's the one who asked me."

"Cuz Jimmy told him to." James W. looked around at the

intricate woodwork, the leaded glass windows and the antique
furniture, then let out a low whistle. "Makes the Governor's
Mansion look like a mashed potato sandwich." He got a glint in
his eye. "Let's look around."

Matt shrugged. Lyle had said it was okay to make himself at
home. "I'm in."

James W. eyed him carefully as he stood up. "You're
looking a whole lot steadier on your feet. You doin' okay,
then?"

"Dr. Ryan wouldn't've let me out if I wasn't doin' okay."
Matt's lips quirked in a smile. "And to make sure, she's got me
coming in every day this week. I won't be going back to Wilks
until at least Friday. Earliest."

"Oh!" James W. picked up the bag he'd carried into the
house. "Here's some clothes for you. I figured you were pretty
much Jimmy's size. And one of Jimmy's aides got you some
skivvies and toiletries. Hope that's all right."

"Thanks." Matt nodded. "Leave 'em there. I'm not sure
which room I'm stayin' in."

"And I grabbed this for you." James W. held out the cane
he'd brought. "Doctor's orders."

Matt glared, but took it.

The two men walked through the archway, into the
spacious dining room. A glass cabinet on the far wall was filled
with china serving dishes and delicately etched crystal. A bay
window on the right allowed the last hints of sun to shine on
the polished ten-seater dining room table. On the left wall, a
wide staircase with a plush blue and silver Oriental runner
begged for thick pine garlands with red berries to adorn its
banister at Christmas.

Matt heard a familiar droning voice coming from a doorway
tucked behind the staircase. He peeked in and realized the door
led to a study, where Pastor Lambert, the dismal aide to the

missing Reverend David Duff, sat behind an ornate desk, talking on his cell.

"Tell George we'll go with the anthem from the first Sunday in November," Lambert was saying. He listened for a moment, then nodded. "And the same PowerPoint, too. Tell Pastor Steve to reuse the sermon he did at the Patriots Elder-care Center."

Again, there was silence. "It's only Tuesday. We've got plenty of time to make these changes." A pause. "Yes, I'll be in the office tomorrow morning. But get these items put in motion. No reason to leave things to the last minute."

"Who's that?" James W. asked, looking over Matt's shoulder.

Before Matt could answer, the doorbell rang again. This time, Lyle appeared at the top of the stairs. "Can you get that, Pastor Hayden? We're having an issue with Hester's hair."

"This place is crazier than the Governor's Mansion." Matt headed for the front door, followed by James W.

A man dressed in a dark navy uniform stood beyond the milky glass. Matt opened the door to a burly police officer with four stars on each collar point of his immaculately pressed shirt. "May I help you?" Matt asked.

"I'm Chief Aguilar. Is Hester home?"

James W. stepped forward, a surprised smile on his face. "Charles," he said. "Come in."

"James W." The round-faced police chief, a compact man with enough muscle to ward off thoughts of flab, broke into a smile. The two men shook hands.

"Chief Aguilar." James W. turned to Matt. "Let me introduce you to Pastor Matt Hayden."

Chief Aguilar extended his hand. "Great benediction, Pastor." His gaze darted around the parlor. "Is Hester here?"

"She's upstairs, changing," Matt answered.

"What's up?" James W. asked.

Chief Aguilar's lips pursed. "Your son has ordered his first mandate to the Austin Police Department. The special kind that skirts around protocol."

James W. looked taken aback. "What are you talkin' about, Charles?"

"Nothin' nasty, James W. It lit a fire under me, that's all." Charles gave a quick glance around the room. "Reverend Duff's been missing less than twelve hours, but Governor Novak wants him declared missing and our top priority until the man is found."

James W. blew out a breath. "I know he's been worried about the man all day."

"So I'm here to let Hester know what's up," the chief explained. "Since Duff was staying here at Hester's, this is where we've got to start nosing around."

"Makes sense," Matt said. "And Lambert, Duff's assistant, is still here tonight. You might want to start with him."

Chief Aguilar nodded. "First I'll talk with Hester. Then I'll check this Lambert out."

5

OFFICIALLY MISSING

ANGIE O'DAY SLAMMED down the phone located at the pass-through between the Fire and Icehouse's kitchen and bar. She ran shaking hands through her wavy red hair, then wrapped her fingers around her skull to keep from screaming. *Not again!*

Her cook, Dorothy Jo Devereaux, looked up from the onions she was chopping. "Something's happened to Matt." The short, heavy-set woman who had worked in the Fire and Icehouse since Angie was in diapers wasn't asking a question.

"That was Jimmy's chief of staff on the phone." Angie leaned back against the knotted pine wall. "Matt fell. Hit his head."

Dorothy Jo put down the knife. "Is he in the hospital?"

"Deshawn said they released him." Angie surveyed the crowded room. She couldn't leave to be with her fiancé, could she? Every citizen of Jimmy's hometown seemed to have come to her bar to celebrate his inauguration. The Fire and Icehouse had, at one time, actually been Wilks' firehouse. The bays for the trucks had been divided into two rooms. The front held the bar, complete with tables and booths and plenty of televisions. The back room was packed with pool tables, skeet ball shoots and pinball machines, as well as tables for teams to play trivia. Every table—hell, almost every wall space—was taken up by the revelers. Even with the cool night and threatening showers, customers spilled out through the patio doors and onto the party deck beyond. In the time it had taken for her to answer the phone and digest Deshawn's message, at least ten orders for drinks had spat out of the computerized ordering system. She picked up the oldest order, grabbed four shot glasses and lined them up on the counter.

"Do you need to go pick him up?" Dorothy Jo asked as the kitchen ordering system came to life. She ripped the paper off its printer.

Angie rimmed each glass with salt, then scooped ice into a cocktail shaker. "He can't come home. The doctor wants him to stay in Austin for the rest of the week. Just in case." She dumped some reposado into the shaker, capped it and began shaking.

"Where's he staying?" Dorothy Jo ladled a glob of queso into a bowl already filled with guacamole and chorizo.

"I don't know. The Governor's Mansion, I guess. Deshawn said it'd be best for me to wait and come tomorrow." She topped the shot glasses with wedges of lime and nodded to the waitress that they were ready to serve. "Matt's doing okay. What he needs tonight is rest."

Dorothy Jo scooped warm tortilla chips into a bowl and added it to the serving tray holding the queso dip. "Maybe. But it might do you a world of good. You're white as a sheet."

Maybe, Angie thought. Or maybe she needed a break from worrying about Matt.

Bo, loaded down with supplies, came hurrying through the kitchen's back door. He and Angie scrambled to restock the limes and ice and liquor that had been running low. Angie picked up the next drink order, grabbed two frosted mugs and set them under the Fireman's Four beer tap.

No. Dorothy Jo was wrong about her needing to see Matt. Tonight, all she wanted to do was make drinks, wash glasses and make some more drinks. A nonstop, don't-think-about-anything pace would keep her from worrying over Matt.

And from wondering why the last thing she wanted to do was be with him.

———

WITH THE NEWS that Hester was still getting ready, Chief Aguilar decided to take Matt's advice and talk with Reverend Duff's assistant, Pastor Lambert. So summoned, Lambert, his face looking more dismal than it had that morning on the Governor's Mansion's balcony, joined Matt, James W. and Chief Aguilar in the parlor.

"You wanted to see me, Chief Aguilar?" Lambert asked, refusing to sit.

The Austin Police Department head pushed off the mantel and walked over to Lambert. "I got a call from the governor. He wants me to look into the whereabouts of your boss."

Lambert's heavy-lidded eyes opened slightly. "Reverend Duff?"

Matt resisted the urge to roll his eyes. *Of course, Reverend Duff.*

Lambert held Aguilar's gaze for a moment, then nodded. "I'm concerned he may have run into trouble."

Curious, Matt thought. Lambert didn't appear concerned. Inconvenienced, perhaps. Something in Matt's gut stirred. A sixth sense that had developed inside of him when he'd been a cop. He looked over at James W., who sat in the wingback chair. The two of them shared a suspicious look but said nothing. This was Aguilar's turf.

"Why did the governor call you?" Lambert asked.

"He's the one who invited Reverend Duff to speak today, so naturally he's concerned that the man's missing. Plus, I understand the governor received a call from Reverend Duff's wife."

"Shelly?" Lambert lifted his shoulder in a half shrug. "She's been very excitable lately."

Aguilar's gaze sharpened. "Was there trouble between her and her husband?"

"Hardly. She's pregnant. Due any day now. That's why she didn't accompany Reverend Duff to Austin. Too long a drive. Our church is in San Antonio, you know."

"I understand you've been calling around, trying to find Reverend Duff. Have you learned anything?"

"No."

"When was the last time you saw Reverend Duff?"

Lambert sniffed. "I dropped him off at St. George Episcopal on my way to the prayer breakfast this morning. "

"Why?" Aguilar pressed.

"Reverend Duff likes to meditate before speaking to a large crowd. He knows the bishop at the church quite well and asked if he could take a few moments for silent reflection in St. George's beautiful sanctuary. The bishop said 'of course.'" Lambert shrugged. "I never saw him after I dropped him off."

Lyle appeared in the archway. "Sorry. That took longer than we expected." His gaze settled on Chief Aguilar. "Is something wrong?"

Aguilar ignored the question. "May I speak with Hester please?"

"She'll be down in a minute." Lyle surveyed the scene and must have noted the somber mood of the room. "May I get you some refreshments? Tea? Something stronger?"

"Water, maybe," Matt said.

Lyle's eyes rounded in horror. "Oh dear, I haven't gotten your water yet. And your soup! Oh, dear." He turned on his heel and headed for the kitchen. "Hester," Matt heard him call. "Chief Aguilar is here to see you."

"Chief Aguilar?" Hester's contralto sounded surprised. He heard light footsteps coming down the stairs, then Hester appeared in the archway. Matt sucked in his breath.

Hester, her silver hair swept up in a loose chignon, looked like a Mt. Olympus goddess. The iridescent ice-blue gown swept over her shoulders, tapered to her trim waist, then flowed into a sweep of lustrous layers that promised to glow and shift and scintillate across many dance floors that night.

For a moment, the men in the room could only stare. Chief Aguilar was the first to recover. "The governor's asked me to look into finding Reverend Duff."

She flinched. "You expect foul play." She closed her eyes for a moment. "What can I do to help?"

"I'd like to see his room, please. Where he stayed last night."

"Of course, Charles. Anything you need." She called through the archway. "Lyle?"

She turned back to the chief. "My driver will be here any moment to take to me the Governor's Ball. Unless you want me to cancel my plans for tonight?"

Aguilar's lips hinted at a smile. "Not if you'll allow me to escort you for the evening."

"Witness protection, hey?"

Matt's stomach lurched at Hester's words. He'd been in the Fed's Witness Protection Program for five long years. It was no joking matter.

Apparently, Hester saw his grimace. "Pastor Hayden. I didn't ask how you're doing."

Matt smiled. "Tired, but good enough not to be admitted to the hospital. I appreciate your putting me up for the night."

"For the week," she corrected him. "I'm sorry as can be that I bullied you into having that beer when I knew you were still recovering."

Matt straightened. "I'm a grown man, Ms. Honeywell. I could've said no."

"And I'm a hustler, Pastor Hayden. It's what I do best." She raised her chin. "You will call me Hester from now on."

He nodded. "And I'm Matt."

"Or Preacher," James W. interjected. "That's what we call him in Wilks."

"Good. Glad we got that settled." Her smile almost made Matt forget the lousy day he'd had.

Lyle appeared in the archway with Matt's water and set it down on the coffee table. "Yes, Hester?"

"The chief would like to see Reverend Duff's room. Show him up, please." She turned back to the parlor. "You'll excuse me, gentlemen. I must finish getting ready." In a swirl of ice-blue luster, she flowed out of the room.

Aguilar turned to Pastor Lambert. "I'd like you to come with."

Pastor Lambert huffed. "I have to be getting on the road. I want to be in San Antonio before ten."

Aguilar's gaze went flat. "I'd like you to stay in town tonight, if that's all right."

Lambert cleared his throat abruptly. "That won't be possible."

Aguilar's eyes bore into him. "Is there a problem?"

"With Reverend Duff missing, I must get back to San Antonio to take care of the church. We worship 17,000 people every weekend. I can't wait until Thursday to begin preparations for Sunday services."

"There's always the phone," Matt said, then immediately wished the words back.

Lambert stared at him, his eyebrows slanted angrily.

Matt shrugged. "Just sayin'."

Aguilar studied the two but let the moment pass. "Nevertheless, I need you available for questioning."

Lambert's chin went up. "If that's your final word, I need to call my staff and let them know I won't be at work tomorrow. My phone's over at the guesthouse. I'll meet you at Reverend Duff's room."

Aguilar waited for Lambert to leave, then turned to Matt. "What was that all about?"

Matt closed his eyes. He did not want to get involved in this. In fact, Dr. Ryan would have his head if she knew he was anywhere near a police investigation.

But a cop didn't hold back evidence from another cop.

"James W. and I heard Lambert down here making arrangements for Duff's absence right before you got here."

Aguilar looked at James W. "You heard that?"

"Yep. Said something about getting a pastor to preach a sermon that he'd done back in November. And something about the choir anthem?" James W. glanced back at Matt.

Matt nodded. "And the PowerPoint."

James W. pulled himself out of the wingback chair and hitched his thumbs in his belt. "If you're open to suggestions—" He let the words hang.

"Go ahead," Aguilar nodded.

James W. lowered his voice. "I'd secure Reverend Duff's bedroom as soon as possible."

"I hear you, though it may be too late. I've got crime scene tape in the car. What else?"

James W. slapped a hand on Matt's shoulder. "Pastor Hayden here used to be a cop. He's helped me on several murder cases. Has a sixth sense about how things go down. You'd be smart to listen to him if he comes up with anything."

Aguilar's gaze shifted to Matt. "You were a cop?'

Matt straightened. "Yes, sir. Four years. Special Investigations Department of the Miami P.D."

"What did you investigate?"

"I was undercover in the drug enforcement program."

Aguilar's dark eyebrows raised. "That takes some cojones, son." He looked down at Matt's cane. "Is that how your leg got busted up?"

"No, sir." Matt smiled sheepishly. "I didn't get shot until I became a pastor." Although not exactly the correct context, he needed to lighten the mood.

"Well, since you're stayin' here, keep your eyes open. Let me know if you see anything suspicious."

"Yes, sir."

"I'll get the tape." Aguilar started for the door, then turned. "Pastor Hayden, why don't you come upstairs with Lambert and me. I could use another set of eyes. Especially a preacher's."

"Sure." Matt listened for the front door to close behind Aguilar, then glared at James W. "You shouldn't've told him I was a cop. I'm not supposed to get excited about things right now."

"You don't need to get excited. You need to keep your eyes open is all." The cell phone in his pocket rang, and he pulled it out. He hung his head. "It's Elsbeth."

Matt's face paled. "Heck, James W. You're supposed to go to that Governor's Ball, too."

James W. nodded miserably as he answered the phone. "Hey, Elsbeth." He winced as Elsbeth let loose on the other end of the line. "Jimmy's not going to be there for another half hour." Matt could hear Elsbeth's high-pitched voice, though he couldn't make out what she was saying. "Yes, Elsbeth," James W. said. "I'll be right there, Elsbeth." She started to add something, but James W. cut her off. "Honey, the longer we talk on the phone, the later I'm gonna get to the mansion to change."

That seemed to do the trick, and James W. ended the call. "I gotta go."

"You think?" Matt tried hard not to chuckle. "Cheer up, James W. This is only gonna last four years."

James W. glared at Matt as he returned the phone to his pocket.

"Unless Jimmy gets reelected." Matt was having too much fun. "Come to think of it, Texas governors don't have term limits, do they? This could go on for decades."

James W. turned on his heel and headed for the front door.

"Of course, you could always—"

James W. held up a finger. "One more word, Preacher, and your flour sack's gonna be full of weevils."

Matt had no idea what that meant, but he bowed his head in surrender.

"That's better." James W. allowed a pleased nod, then hurried out the front door.

Feeling good for the first time all day, Matt sat down on the settee and finally had that drink of water.

6

LAMBERT SPEAKS HIS MIND

REVEREND DUFF'S room was across the backyard in Hester's guesthouse. Lyle explained that Hester had bought the house behind the Victorian mansion and connected the two abodes with a solarium. Now the Craftsman-style home was used to house the guests of bigwigs in town, including the governor.

And what a house. According to Lyle, the main floor of the home was dedicated to the art of socializing, complete with large halls, winding staircases and an industrial kitchen. Lyle led them to an elevator off the main foyer and held the door back for Matt and Aguilar to enter. "The guest suites are upstairs."

When they reached the second floor, Lyle led the way down a long hallway lined with doors opening to bedrooms beyond. "Reverend Duff's room and Pastor Lambert's room are across the hall from each other on the far end."

Matt resisted the urge to let out a low whistle at the elegant embellishments of coffered ceilings, plush carpeting and gilded mirrors. Narrow hall tables holding flowers and other knickknacks were spaced between the bedrooms. Chief Aguilar walked over to one and grabbed a tissue from an ornate box.

"Here we are." Lyle fished a key from his pocket. "I locked the room when I heard that the reverend had gone missing." He opened the door, which gave way to a good-sized suite. A king-size bed was centered in the lodge-themed room with an opened suitcase on top. A small desk was on the left wall, and on the right, a deep-cushioned chair was centered between two doors.

"Thank you, Lyle," Aguilar said.

"Here's the key." The giant of a man handed it over to the chief. "I've got a pie in the oven."

Aguilar stepped inside, gave the room a quick perusal, then walked to the open door on the room's right side. "Bathroom," he said over his shoulder. Using the tissue he'd grabbed, he opened the second door and looked inside. "Closet." He gave the space a once-over. "Pair of shoes. Golf hat. Raincoat." He turned back to Matt. "Anything strike you?"

"The desk seems wrong," Matt said. "No pens or papers. No Bible. When I go into a hotel room, I usually toss all kinds of junk on the desk." He turned to study the bed. "Wait a minute. There's a briefcase here by the bedstand."

Aguilar rounded the bed for a better look. "We'd better get it dusted for fingerprints before we open it."

Matt heard a door open down the hall, then Lambert appeared in the doorway. "Exactly what are you doing in here?"

Aguilar turned on his heel, his eyes hard. "What do you think we're doing?"

"Trespassing," Lambert, dressed in light blue pajamas with navy stripes, sniffed. "This is Reverend Duff's room."

"This is Hester Honeywell's room," Matt said quietly. He

immediately wished the words back, but dadgum, this guy got
on his last nerve.

Aguilar nodded. "We have her permission. Frankly, I'm
thinking we need to look at your room, as well."

Lambert's sulking eyes flared to anger. "You think I've got
Reverend Duff hidden away in my closet?"

"I think you're not lifting a finger to help us find your boss,"
Aguilar said. "And I get the impression you don't much care for
him, either."

"Of course, I care for him," Lambert said, but his eyes said
otherwise. "I have responsibilities to perform in San Antonio,
and I am *not* pleased I have to stay in this house one more
night."

Matt remembered Lambert had said something similar on
the Governor's Mansion's balcony this morning before anyone
realized that Duff was missing. "You're not upset because you
can't go back to San Antonio tonight. You're angry because you
must stay *here*. What is it about this house that has you so
riled up?"

Lambert's nose went up an inch. "Hester Honeywell is a
tramp. For all I know, this is a brothel when not used for official
state visits. Or maybe even during those state visits. She's no
high and mighty society lady. She's a pimp."

Matt could almost feel the hair bristle on the back of
Aguilar's neck, but the police chief kept his calm. Aguilar
pulled his cell from his pocket and speed dialed a number.
"Jeremy," he said when someone answered. "Send a squad car
over to Hester Honeywell's." A pause. "Yeah, between Eighth
and Ninth. I want 'em to seal off some rooms. And get the
crime techs over here. I need the place gone over."

Matt caught the word "rooms" and knew that Lambert had
indeed gone a step too far.

Aguilar ended the call, then dialed another number. "Hey,

FOUR REASONS TO DIE 47

Hester. Yeah, we're still over at the guesthouse. You go on ahead to the ball. I'm gonna wait for a car to come over. I want to seal up some rooms over here. Run some labs. You okay with that?"

She said something that made him smile. "I appreciate it. Yeah, I'll tell you all about it. Oh, and Pastor Lambert's going to need another room. You got anything over on your side where we can put him up?" He listened for moment. "That'll be perfect. See you in a bit." He hung up the phone.

"I'm moving?" Lambert asked.

"Yeah. I'm gonna have your room checked out too. Not to worry, there's a servant's bedroom over in the mansion where you can stay the night."

Lambert's jaw dropped, but Matt was happy to discover that, for once, the man had nothing to say.

"Grab your toothbrush, Lambert," Aguilar said. "Everything else stays in the room."

Lambert's mouth worked in and out like a goldfish, but still nothing came out. Finally, he turned to go into his room. Aguilar followed. "Only must-haves," he called from the doorway, then turned to Matt. "Gotta love that woman. She's putting her permission in writing. You and Lyle can witness it right?"

"Sure."

"Better head on over to the kitchen. She needs to get going."

"And you?"

"I'll make sure Lambert's tucked in nice and tight, then wait for the squad car."

Matt headed for the elevator. Lambert was an idiot, that much was certain. But did he have anything to do with Reverend David Duff's disappearance?

7

AFTER HOURS

ANGIE LOCKED the Icehouse's front door and turned off the exterior lights. "Finally," she sighed and leaned back against the door. She was so tired, she wasn't sure she could make it to the nearest bar stool to sit down.

Dorothy Jo's wrinkled face appeared in the pass-through window. "I could use a drink," she said.

"Me too," came Bo's call from the back of the kitchen.

No matter how hectic or how slow the day had been, the after-hours wind-down was a tradition for the three of them. Although Angie yearned to drop into her second-floor apartment's bed, she didn't want to disappoint her two best friends. "What'll it be?" she asked.

Dorothy Jo came through the swinging doors, carrying three shot glasses. "I've had a hankering for some of that Old Rebel Pecan Whiskey."

"Great idea." Angie rounded the bar and grabbed the bottle.

Bo appeared from the back, holding up a rag. "It's stopped raining."

They grabbed their jackets, and Angie turned out the interior lights. The three headed outside, and, after Bo wiped down the chairs at the closest table, they settled into their routine. Cigarettes were lit, whiskey was poured, and they silently breathed in the fresh, chilly night air. Angie slapped her leg and called Shadow, her burly old dog with the body of a German shepherd and the face of a bloodhound, to join them. He plodded over and dropped like a sack of potatoes onto the wooden porch.

"Don't know how that doesn't hurt," Dorothy Jo said, taking a drag from her cigarette. She picked up her glass. "To Governor Jimmy Novak."

"To Jimmy," Bo and Angie chimed in.

Silence prevailed a few more minutes, then Bo spoke up. "Any word on how Matt's doing?"

Angie dashed out the stub of her cigarette and reached for the pack of Winston's. "No. Only that call from Deshawn this afternoon. At least Matt wasn't admitted to the hospital."

"Ain't you gonna call him?" Dorothy Jo asked.

"He's probably in bed by now." Angie tapped out a cigarette.

"Maybe James W. would have more information," Bo suggested. "You could give him a ring."

Angie shook her head. "He's going to all those inaugural balls." She flicked her lighter and lit her cigarette. The flame illuminated the faces of the other two. They looked surprised. "What's wrong?"

Dorothy Jo cleared her throat. "Don't you want to know how Matt's doing?"

Angie took a puff and blew it into the cold night air. "Of course, I do."

"Then why aren't you in your truck and heading up to

Austin?" Dorothy Jo pressed. "You could be with Matt in less than an hour. But you're not. You're here."

"We've been goin' and blowin' all day," Angie snapped.

"It's not only tonight," Bo said quietly. "You and him. Well, you all haven't been the same since—" He stopped. Breathed in deeply. "Since he had his stroke in November. It's like you're his nurse now."

Angie slammed her whiskey on the table. Bo's words were too damned close to the truth. "What's going on between Matt and me is none of your business." She stood and slapped her leg for Shadow to get up. "Let's head upstairs, boy. I don't need this."

8

THE TALE OF TWO BREAKFASTS

MATT WOKE to the tantalizing smell of bacon and coffee. His bedroom was on the main floor of Hester's home—down the hall from the kitchen. It was not only a bedroom, but a suite —complete with a massive four-poster bed, a chaise lounge fronting a small white marble fireplace, a walk-in closet that was bigger than his dorm room at Wartburg Seminary and a bathroom with a jetted tub with fixtures he speculated might be gold-plated.

The night before, when Lyle had settled Matt in for the night, he'd explained the room had been the original master for the home. Hester, however, preferred her room upstairs, as it had a private screened-in balcony that made her feel like she lived in a treehouse.

Matt fought the urge to stay cocooned in the softest bedsheets he'd ever slept on, but knew he had a nine o'clock appointment to keep at Dr. Ryan's. He gave the pillow one last deep smell—lilacs, he thought—then swung his legs out of bed. A sudden stab of pain shot through his shoulder, and he tried to rub it away. It must've taken the brunt of his fall yesterday. Well, better that than his head.

His sleep-filled eyes worked to focus on the bedstand's alarm clock, then opened in horror. "Holy crap," he muttered. It was a quarter to eight. Forget the coffee he was beginning to long for. He had to shower.

He stood up and was greeted by the zing of unhappy nerves speeding through his leg. "Damnit," he said and reached for his cane. He hobbled into the bathroom, all the while thinking he felt way too old to be a man of thirty-seven. Only six years ago, he'd been chasing down drug runners on the docks of Miami. Now, he'd be outpaced by a snail.

When he finished his shower, he toweled himself off with the thickest, softest Turkish towel he'd ever used, wrapped it around his middle and limped into the bedroom. He stopped dead in the doorway.

Lyle—who else could it be?—had laid out Matt's clothes and left a tray complete with coffee service and muffins on the table by the chaise. As he dressed, Matt consumed two cups of coffee and a muffin, and was pleased to find himself ready to meet the world in plenty of time to make it to Dr. Ryan's office. Now all he had to do was figure out how he was going to get there. He set out for the kitchen to ask Lyle.

Connor, the chauffeur, sat at the breakfast nook table, chowing down on a plateful of scrambled eggs. Today, he wore a blue T-shirt that strained over his muscled frame, and his bald head showed a little bit of fuzz. Must've been a late night, Matt decided.

Connor raised his cup in greeting. "Mornin', Preacher," he said. "I'm your ride to the doctor's office. Just a few more bites." He forked up a large scoop of eggs.

Across the table, Lambert, his head down, stiffly took a bite of bacon. Matt wasn't sure, but it was almost like the man was pretending no one else was in the room.

"Hope you found the coffee I set out for you." Lyle stood at the counter, blotting a fresh batch of bacon with a paper towel.

"You're a gem," Matt said. "And those muffins were delicious."

"I figured you'd wanna sleep in. Quite a day yesterday. Have a seat, Preacher." Lyle brought the bacon to the table. "Munch on this before you go. Get some protein in you."

Matt took his place between Lambert and Connor. "Good morning, Pastor," Matt said. "Did you sleep well?"

Lambert hmphed, and Matt took that as a signal that the servant's bed had given him a bumpy ride.

Matt turned to Connor. "You had a busy day yesterday."

"No kidding." Connor gulped down more coffee. "I lost count how many trips I made to the airport. Why those editors couldn't have coordinated their flights a little better, I don't know."

"Cuz some of 'em can't stand each other," Lyle offered from the stove.

Connor grinned. "True enough." He waggled his eyebrows at Matt. "You should hear what folks say on their phones when they're being driven around. It's like they completely forget there's another person in the car."

Lambert finally looked up. "And I bet you feed every morsel you hear to Hester. Another little service—of the many services—you provide, I'm sure."

Connor's smile faded, as his eyes narrowed. "It's a good thing you brought your own car, then." He shoved away from the table. "I gotta run up to the apartment and get my keys," he said to Matt. "I'll pull around to the front. Come out when you're ready."

Jaw clenched, Connor marched to a door at the back of the kitchen. Lyle, his lips tight with worry, followed him out.

Lambert gave Matt a knowing look. "What do you want to bet that apartment only has one bedroom?"

The implication regarding Connor and Lyle's relationship was clear.

"Your Hester Honeywell tolerates all kinds of filth in her home." Lambert sniffed smugly.

Matt remained silent. He knew what he wanted to say but held back. He was not going to get upset today. He was going to stay calm. Even if it meant playing the wimp to this hate-filled man.

Lambert took Matt's silence as an opportunity to press his point. "The Bible is clear on the subject, of course." Lambert's chin went up. "Turn or burn. That's what I say."

Matt felt his heart begin to palpitate. He had to get out of this situation, and now, yet he couldn't let Lambert have the last word.

He grabbed his cane and got up from the table, then looked Lambert straight in the eye. "I'm a lot more worried about people who hate each other than those who love each other."

He turned and saw Lyle standing in the doorway. "Thank you," the giant man mouthed.

———

ANGIE WAS SITTING at her kitchen table, nursing a steaming cup of coffee, when her cell rang. She glared at it through half-slit eyes, then reached for it. "Hello?"

James W. let out a deep chuckle. "Did I wake you up?"

"No." She peered at the wall-mounted clock. "It's only ten o'clock. You know I closed last night. What d'ya want?"

"To make sure you were up to speed on Matt."

She reached down to pet Shadow's neck. "Saw him say the prayer on TV. Got a call from Deshawn around supper. Said Matt had fallen and been taken to the hospital, but they let him go. Is he at the mansion with you?"

"Too much goin' on here. He's over at Hester Honeywell's."

Angie's eyes opened on that. "Who is Hester Honeywell?"

"She's a seventy-five-year-old lady and good friends with Jimmy."

No competition then, Angie thought. "What happened?"

"Too many people asked him to do too many things, and it was too much for him. All I can say is there's a whole lotta guilt goin' around up here."

Angie finally sat up and rubbed her eyes. "Did he hit his head when he fell?"

"Lucked out there. His shoulder took the brunt of the fall, but his blood pressure was through the roof. Dr. Ryan gave him what for. I wish she hadn't done that. It wasn't his fault, really. So you comin' up here?"

"I figured I'd stay here and get his place ready for him." Then a thought struck her. Why was James W. calling her and not Matt? Was he in that bad of shape? "He's lucid and everything, right?"

"He's fine. I went and saw him last night. But he won't be home 'til after this weekend. Dr. Ryan said she wants him nice and close in case something jiggles loose in that brain of his."

"Well, I can't get up there until tomorrow. I gave Dorothy Jo the day off. She almost worked herself sick yesterday." In truth, Angie still wasn't ready to see Matt. Bo had been right. She and Matt hadn't been the same together since he had that stroke. She had a lot to think about.

James W. was silent, but she knew what he was thinking. Yes, if Angie really wanted to see Matt today, she could make it happen.

"Well," he said finally. "Jimmy lent Matt some of his clothes and stuff. I'm guessing he'll have enough to last until tomorrow."

"Good. I'll give him a call and see what I can bring up for him on Thursday."

"That works. I'm sure he'll be glad to hear your voice."

Angie took a deep breath. "Then why is it you who called me instead of Matt?"

Again, silence.

"I have to go downstairs and prep the kitchen." She got to her feet. "Thanks for the update."

———

MATT'S APPOINTMENT with Dr. Ryan went well. His blood pressure was still high, but not in stroke territory like it had been yesterday. When she'd asked him what he'd been up to, he'd circumvented the fact that Hester's home was ground zero for the investigation into Reverend Duff's disappearance. Instead, he talked about Lyle's excellent cooking. Which was no stretch. The chicken soup Lyle had made for him yesterday was the best Matt had ever eaten.

With orders to see her again the next day—and not to stray outside, he needed all the rest he could get—Matt returned to the mansion. He headed straight to his room to change into the sweats Jimmy had sent over. His plan for the day was to rest up, lay low and...

And call Angie. Right?

He was opening the bag of clothes James W. had brought over when a knock came at the door.

"Come in," Matt called, as he pulled out a pair of sweatpants.

Lyle entered, his eyes ready to pop out of his head and his

smile clownish with delight. He looked as if he'd found the golden egg. "Chief Aguilar sent a lieutenant here to do some follow-up questions. She'd like to talk with you."

Matt tossed the sweats on the bed. He'd make a better impression in his pastor's wear. "Lead the way."

Instead of leaving, Lyle, his excitement almost palpable, closed the door behind him.

"What?" Matt asked.

"Her name's Lieutenant Gage," Lyle said in a stage whisper. "Oh. My. God."

"What about her?"

"Straight out of *The Black Panther*. You know, the movie?" He put his hand on his heart. "A warrior princess. Right in our parlor. She could decapitate me with one slice of her hand, but I wouldn't care. She's gorgeous." He drew out the word with something close to ecstasy. "I want to marry her. As long as she doesn't kill me."

Matt was getting used to Lyle's penchant for dramatic flair. "She's a cop," Matt said.

"She's a goddess." Lyle's eyes closed in delight.

"Let's go, Apollo," Matt chuckled. He started for the door.

Lyle wagged his finger. "Unh, unh, uuuunnhh." He nodded toward the cane leaning against the fireplace. "I've been given strict instructions. No walking around without that."

Matt glared, but limped over and grabbed the cane.

Lyle led the way down the hall, past the kitchen, across the dining room and into the parlor. "Lieutenant? This is Pastor Hayden."

9

LIEUTENANT GAGE

MATT ROUNDED the parlor archway and stopped. Lyle was right, the tall woman was stunning. But what he noticed first and foremost was that she was an intense, no-nonsense cop. Maybe it was the steady stare of her wide-set eyes. Or the way her muscular build and stiff posture said, don't mess with me, I'm on a case.

"I'll be right back with some coffee," Lyle said. "What a nasty day out there. Thank goodness it was nice yesterday. You know what they say about Texas weather..." His voice trailed off as he headed for the kitchen.

Matt nodded. "Lieutenant Gage. What can I do for you?"

"Chief Aguilar wanted me to do some follow-up regarding Reverend David Duff's disappearance. Please have a seat."

Matt lowered himself carefully into one of the Queen Anne chairs fronting the fireplace and hooked his cane around the arm. "I'm not sure what good I can be to you. I never met the victim."

"I'm aware of that."

Water glistened on her black buzz cut hair and soaked the

collar of her blue turtleneck, Matt noted. She wore little makeup. She didn't need it.

Gage settled in the wingback chair. "The chief had the idea you were not satisfied when you went to see Duff's room."

"That's true," Matt nodded. "But I still can't put my finger on why."

"We'll go up there in a minute," she said. "Maybe a second look will jog your thought process."

Matt nodded. "We were a bit rushed. The Governor's Ball and all."

"First, let's get your details out of the way." She pulled her phone from her purse. "You don't mind, do you?"

"I'll do anything I can to help you."

She hit record on the phone, recited the date, time, her name and rank, then nodded to Matt. "Fill in your information, please."

"I'm Matt Hayden. I live in Wilks, Texas, at 311 Manor Street." Though Matt was no longer the officiating pastor at Grace Lutheran Church, the church council insisted that he stay in the parsonage until he was healed.

Or until Pastor Fred Osterburg decided he could no longer be interim. After all, it was a long trek for Fred to make between Houston and Wilks every Sunday morning.

"You're the pastor of Governor Novak's home church, is that correct?"

"I'm actually on medical leave, right now. I, uh, took a bullet to the head last July. My recovery has been up and down." Literally, Matt thought. Twenty-one hours ago, he'd definitely been down.

Gage raised a sculpted eyebrow. "You were shot? Why?"

"Some bad guys had been after me for a while. They finally found me."

"Why would someone want to shoot you, a pastor?

Matt squirmed in the not-so-comfortable chair. "My offense against them took place in Florida when I was a cop, not a pastor. My father was killed by some corrupt policemen. I was the witness that would put them in jail, and probably on death row."

"Is there any way that situation might have a bearing on Reverend Duff's disappearance?"

The question was straight as an arrow, and he was impressed. She'd cut right to the chase.

"I don't see how," Matt answered. "All the folks that wanted me dead are now dead themselves. Besides, there was no way of anyone knowing I would be Reverend Duff's substitute to pronounce the benediction. I certainly had no idea that was coming."

"Well, apparently you made quite a splash," she said.

"What do you mean?"

"I recommend you don't watch the morning news."

It took a moment for Matt to get her meaning. "The reporters in the rotunda." He felt his pulse quicken. Don't get excited, he told himself.

"Don't worry. They looked like the bad guys. Not you."

Lyle entered with a tray loaded down with a coffee service and glazed doughnut holes. "Is there anything else I can get you?"

Gage had to bend her head way back to look up at him. "Why don't you join us, Mr. Griffey. I need to get your statement."

Lyle swallowed audibly. "Of course." He put the tray down on the coffee table and took a seat on the settee.

Gage smiled in what Matt considered an attempt to calm a nervous witness.

Apparently, playing the good cop was not her forte. "You don't mind if I record this, do you?" She pressed the record button on her phone and again stated the date, time and place for the record. "You understand I'm recording this, Mr. Griffey?"

He shot Matt a nervous glance, then nodded. "Yes, I do."

Gage sat back in her chair. "Let's get the prelims out of the way," she said. "Name, address, occupation?"

Lyle cleared his throat. "Lyle Griffey. I live here, and I write grants for nonprofits."

Again, her sculpted brow lifted. "You live here? Are you related to Ms. Honeywell?"

He shook his head. "No, ma'am. I'm a 'domestique' for Ms. Honeywell in exchange for room and board."

"A domestique?"

He leaned forward, his face relaxing. "I love to cook, clean —I call it putzing." He waved a hand as if chores were pleasurable. "I pretty much take care of the house. Inside, I mean. Help her plan her parties. Since my degree is in accounting, I keep her books." He beamed. "I'm her Gal Friday, you might say."

Gage poured herself some coffee, then settled back. "Let's start with who was actually in the house yesterday morning."

"Well, Hester, of course. Pastor Lambert and Reverend Duff came the day before. Myself and Connor."

"Connor?" Gage asked.

"Sorry. Connor Evans. He's Hester's outdoor man. Lawn. Repairs. Chauffeur."

"So Mr. Evans lives here as well?"

"Yes, ma'am." Lyle glanced Matt's way. "We share an apartment above the garage."

Gage sipped her coffee. "Give me a rundown on yesterday morning's activities. Who got up when, who left for the inauguration when. That kind of thing."

"Hester, Connor and I had breakfast at 6:30. Hester

wanted to give Connor some last-minute instructions about when he was supposed to pick up folks coming in for the inauguration."

"What folks?"

"Hester owns the publishing company for several county and small-town newspapers. Her editors came in from all around the state for the day."

Matt's eyes widened. When he'd met Hester last summer in The Society Club's bar, he'd wondered why Hester was so powerful in Texas politics. A piece of that puzzle fell into place.

Lyle shrugged. "Then Connor left for the airport, and Hester headed into her study."

"What was in the study?" Gage asked.

"She reads through the newspapers from her various markets every morning."

"And what did you do?"

"Reverend Duff had mentioned the night before that he liked oatmeal." Lyle squiggled his shoulders. "I make the best oatmeal. Ever." He turned to Matt. "Want to know my secret ingredient?"

Matt couldn't help but smile. "Sure."

"Ricotta cheese. And Kashi cereal. You mix the Kashi with the oatmeal while it cooks, then pour the mixture over ricotta cheese. Oh, and figs. The dried ones, you know? The wet from the oatmeal plumps those figs up like flowers in bud."

Even Gage looked amused, Matt noted. "Back to what happened, Mr. Griffey."

"Lyle. Please."

Talking about food had apparently calmed Lyle's nerves. The large man relaxed into the settee and threw a giant paw over its back. "Pastor Lambert and Reverend Duff came over from the guesthouse around 7:30, I would say. I served them breakfast in the dining room. Hester joined them, of course."

"Did you catch any of their conversation?"

"Reverend Duff thought the oatmeal was delicious."

The way Lyle said it, Matt decided that Pastor Lambert had not.

"They talked about the schedule for the day, of course. Reverend Duff and Hester had a conversation about Bishop Hamlin up at St. George Episcopal Church. Apparently, the bishop and Reverend Duff had a relationship that went back years. Duff said he was going to stop by Hamlin's church that morning for some quiet devotion time. Hester said to say hello for her."

"Did Lambert have anything to say?"

Lyle's smile dropped. "He doesn't say much. He frowns a lot."

The sound of a man clearing his throat had Gage looking toward the archway.

"You're here about Reverend Duff's disappearance, I take it?" Lambert, dressed in his cleric shirt and suit, stood in the doorway, glaring at Lieutenant Gage. "I expected to be summoned when you arrived."

Matt kept his focus on Gage. He watched the sharp-eyed lieutenant size Lambert up. From the flat line of her lips, she didn't look impressed. "Pastor Lambert?"

"Yes."

"I'll be with you in a little while. Please wait for me in the kitchen."

"I need to get back to my parish in San Antonio."

"And I need to finish my interview with Mr. Griffey. I appreciate your full cooperation."

Matt decided if the pastor pursed his lips any tighter, he'd look like a dried prune. With a huff, Lambert turned on his heel and exited the parlor.

Gage returned her attention to Lyle. "What happened after Reverend Duff and Pastor Lambert finished breakfast?"

Lyle thought a moment. "Hester went upstairs to get ready for the prayer breakfast."

"Why would Hester go to the prayer breakfast?" Matt asked, then realized he'd interrupted. "Sorry. I thought the prayer breakfast was simply a pastor thing."

"Heavens, no," Lyle said. "There's no separation of church and state at that event. Politicians, lobbyists, movers and shakers and, of course, the clergy all attend. They hold it down in the big ballroom at the Hilton by the convention center."

"I see." Matt nodded apologetically to the lieutenant. "Sorry."

"Go on, Lyle," Gage said.

"Pastor Lambert and Reverend Duff left the house around 8:30. Lambert was going to drop Duff off at St. George Episcopal, then drive over to the Hilton."

"Whose car did they use?" Gage asked.

"Lambert's. He drove himself and Reverend Duff up the day before. They wanted to escape the morning traffic jam on I-35 coming up from San Antonio. Then Connor came to get Hester, dropped her at the Hilton and headed back out to the airport for his next pick-up."

"Do you know why Hester invited Reverend Duff to stay at her home?"

"Governor Novak—well, he wasn't governor yet—asked her to. Hester's house is the unofficial lodging for many a governor's out-of-town guests. We've been doing that for years."

Lieutenant Gage's phone rang. She paused the recording and looked at the display. "Excuse me. I have to take this." She hurried into the foyer.

Lyle looked at Matt anxiously. "How'd I do?"

"Great," Matt said.

Lyle leaned in. "I told you she was beautiful. Isn't she beautiful?"

Matt cast a glance toward the foyer and lowered his voice. "You know what I think is beautiful?"

"No, what?" Lyle's breath quickened as if he expected to learn a dirty secret.

"That oatmeal recipe you talked about. Any way you can whip that up for tomorrow morning?"

"Oh, Preacher," Lyle laughed. "You are a hoot!"

10

JUST THE FACTS, MA'AM

LIEUTENANT GAGE RETURNED to the parlor. "I've put through the search warrants for confiscating security camera footage, especially at St. George Episcopal."

Matt nodded. "Last place we're sure of his whereabouts."

"I need to see his room. You know which one was his?"

Matt lumbered to his feet and grabbed his cane. "Follow me."

He led the way through the dining room to the back hall. Lambert stuck his head out of the kitchen. "I'm in here."

"Good to know." Gage kept on walking.

"I believe I am next on your agenda," he called after them.

Gage barely looked over her shoulder. "You believe wrong." She followed Matt into the solarium and firmly shut the glass French doors behind her.

They entered the Craftsman-style home, took the elevator to the second floor and headed for the taped-off bedrooms.

"Here we are," Matt said, gesturing to the room on the right.

Gage broke the seal and motioned Matt inside.

To Matt, the room looked much as it had the previous night. Except for the dark smudges where fingerprints had been lifted and the absence of items like Duff's briefcase and suitcase, all was as it had been.

Gage took a paper from her pocket. "Here's the list of the items that were removed from the room for further testing." She handed it over.

"Good," Matt replied. "Does this include the items in the briefcase?"

"Why is that important?"

"I wish I knew." He scanned the list. Bible. Legal pad. Reading glasses. A large bag of peanut M & M's, a pink and a blue highlighter. Two blue pens and one green pen—apparently Duff preferred the Uniball variety. Two pencils. A pad of Post-It flags. A bottle of aspirin. Breath mints. A comb and small bottle of hairspray. Matt looked up. "Where's the laptop?"

"There was no laptop in the briefcase."

Matt's brow arched. "It's hard to believe, in this day and age, that he didn't use a computer. I looked him up last night." He pulled his cell from his pocket, punched in Duff's name and hit "images." A column of photographs began to load. He pressed the one that looked like Duff's official photo and expanded it.

A young man, was Matt's first impression. Forty at the most. No particularly interesting features. Thinning brown hair, clean-shaven, slim but not skinny oblong face. Green eyes, maybe? A solid nose between two slightly bony cheeks. He wore an Egyptian blue suit jacket with a matching shirt topped with a white clerical collar. A three-inch golden cross on a large-looped chain hung around his neck.

Matt went back to the lines of photos. Duff in a prayer circle, same shirt and clerical collar, same cross. Duff surrounded by children on a playground, wearing the same garb but adding a straw fedora with an Egyptian blue band. Duff in front of a church door pointing at a floral Easter cross. Again the hat was added to the shot along with what Matt concluded was Reverend Duff's normal wear. Then the photo he thought he remembered. He turned the phone and showed it to Gage. "See? Duff's working on a laptop and the caption reads, 'Writing Next Sunday's Sermon.' Let me see that list again."

Gage handed him the inventory of the briefcase's contents.

"It says here the legal pads in Duff's briefcase were blank."

"So?"

"No laptop and no handwritten notes. And he hadn't finished Sunday's sermon? We need to find that laptop."

"Well, for now, I've got Duff's background information you requested." Gage pulled out her own phone. "Five foot eleven. One hundred eighty pounds. In good health. Born in San Antonio. Attended River Walk Fellowship Church, where his father, Jesse, was head minister. Graduated Baylor, then went to seminary in Berkeley, California. Went back to River Walk Fellowship for his internship and subsequently was hired there. Became the head pastor after the sudden death of his father. Married five years ago to Shelly Elliott."

"Have you spoken with her yet?"

"Yes. I talked with her this morning," Gage answered. "She's coming here later today, even though it's against her doctor's orders."

"Is she ill?"

"She's pregnant. Very, very pregnant, apparently. Her doctor doesn't want her to travel, but she's insistent." Gage shrugged. "Can't blame her. How much bedrest can you get when your husband's missing?"

"Good point."

"Her mother's going to drive her." Gage's phone pinged, and she looked at the screen. A wicked smile spread across her face. "Time to talk with Lambert."

Matt nodded toward the phone. "What's that all about?"

"The search warrant to examine Pastor Lambert's car came through."

———

MATT AND GAGE headed back through the solarium to the main house. Connor was waiting for them, a white prescription bag in hand. "I picked up your meds, Preacher. "

"Thanks." Matt took the bag and turned toward his room. "I'll be with you in a moment, Lieutenant."

"Of course." She continued down the hallway to the kitchen.

Matt closed the door behind him and crossed to the bedside table, which held a carafe of water and a glass. Lyle, of course. Matt ripped open the sack and took his pills. More blood thinners, he thought with disgust. Perhaps he should avoid shaving for the foreseeable future.

He grabbed his cane, ready to head for the kitchen, when his cell phone rang. He pulled it out.

Angie.

She'd been by his side through the ups and downs of his recovery. No complaints. No harsh words. But lately, there'd been fewer words of any kind.

He brought the phone to his ear. "Hi, honey."

"Hey." There was a pause, then she asked. "How are you?"

"A lot better than yesterday."

"Good." Another pause. "I saw you give the prayer at Jimmy's inauguration. Did you overdo it?"

"I guess." But that was a lie. The prayer had gone well. It

was Reverend Meade's parting words that had set him on the downward spiral: *I know who you are. I know what you're trying to do.*

Matt shook off the memory. "I saw Dr. Ryan this morning. She said I need to lay low for a while."

"James W. said you can't come home until after the weekend."

"Yeah, I'm at this lady's house. Hester Honeywell. Apparently, she's the designated B&B for guests of the governor."

"I can't get up to see you until tomorrow."

Did she sound disappointed about that? Or relieved? "Whatever you say. You've got a business to run."

"Okay, then."

Hmm, Matt thought. Definitely relieved.

"When I *can* get up there," Angie continued, "what do you need? Your shaving kit? Clothes? Prescriptions?"

"All that stuff. As for the meds, bring the whole bag." Matt was on so many pills that he had to keep them in an old computer bag—which reminded him. "And my computer." It was difficult doing research on a cell phone.

"I'm not sure how long I'll be able to stay," she said.

Or wasn't sure how long she wanted to stay? Matt shook away the notion. What was wrong with him? "That's okay," he said, trying to sound cheerful. "I'll take you for as long as I can get you."

"I love you, Matt." Her voice was almost a whisper.

Were those tears he heard? "I love you, too."

"I gotta go. I gave Dorothy Jo the day off, so I'm running the kitchen."

"Angie," he said quickly. "I'm really glad you called."

"Yeah," she said. "Me too."

The phone went dead. He stared at it for a long moment, then headed for the kitchen.

11

IT SMELLS LIKE MANURE

LIEUTENANT GAGE, her eyes flat and her hands folded around a cup of coffee, sat across the breakfast nook table from Lambert. Her cell phone, plugged into a charging wire, lay on the table between them. Not wanting to interrupt Gage's interview, Matt took a stool at the island.

"For the record," Gage said, "Pastor Hayden has joined us in the kitchen." Her focus swiveled back to Lambert. "So how long have you been at River Walk Fellowship Church?"

"Ten years. I received my Masters of Economics from Criswell College in Dallas and was immediately called to River Walk Fellowship."

"And Reverend Duff arrived at River Walk Fellowship three years later?"

"The original Reverend Duff—Jesse Duff—had been at River Walk for twenty years, before his tragic car accident four years ago. David Duff is his son. He grew up in our congregation."

"Then went to college and seminary."

"Yes," Lambert said. "He attended the American Baptist

Seminary of the West in Berkeley, California. Much to his
father's chagrin."

Something there, Matt thought. Disapproval, for sure. And
a definite preference for the father.

"What was his degree in?"

Lambert's downturned nose flared. "I believe he earned a
Doctorate in Religion and Practice."

Lambert had only earned a master's, whereas the missing
Duff had a doctorate. Envy perhaps? Matt wondered.

"How did you feel about a younger preacher getting the top
job when you'd been there longer?" Gage asked.

Lambert let out a chuckle. "You're under the impression
that I would've wanted the job. I am not a preacher, Lieutenant
Gage. My skills are administrative in nature. You might say I'm
the business manager for the church. There are many pastors
employed at River Walk Fellowship. Our music director, our
school principal, the adult education director, the community
care liaison—all of us are ordained ministers. We have
answered the call to serve God using the talents and expertise
God has put in our hearts."

"That sounds like a very large church," Gage said.

"We worship seventeen thousand every Sunday. This
includes traditional and contemporary services, youth services,
a Spanish service, evening vespers—we have a very long reach."

Matt cleared his throat. "And Reverend Duff preaches at
all of them?"

Lambert nodded. "The high school service coincides with
the contemporary service. When it comes time for the sermon,
he preaches at one, and we project him on the big screen in the
other. And the pastor in charge of our Spanish outreach trans-
lates the sermon as Reverend Duff delivers it."

"Does Duff use the same PowerPoint for all the services?
The same songs?"

"Definitely not the same songs, of course. The PowerPoints are mostly the same; the Spanish service is translated, of course. And for the youth, we make it a little less formal."

"You say 'we.' Are you in charge of the PowerPoints?" Matt asked.

"I'm in charge of making sure they're done by the office staff and sent to the audiovisual people. I have little input as to what they say, of course. That all comes from Reverend Duff."

Now's my chance, Matt thought. "Does Reverend Duff do his sermons on the computer and send them out for Power-Point, or does he create the PowerPoint for you?"

"A hybrid of that. He composes his sermons on his laptop, then he highlights in yellow the items he wants put in the PowerPoint."

Matt kept his tone steady. "Did he send in his highlighted sermon for this coming Sunday before he came to Austin for the inauguration?"

"I'd have to check."

Matt studied Lambert's slightly pale cheeks and narrowed eyes. *He's lying.*

Gage sent an impatient look Matt's way. "Let's get down to yesterday morning. Give us a rundown of your movements between the time you came down for breakfast and the last time you saw Reverend Duff alive."

"We came down, I guess about 7:30 or so. Ate breakfast at the dining room table. Ms. Honeywell had already eaten, but she came to join us and had some coffee. We ate oatmeal—nasty stuff—finished up I'd say around eight, then went back to the guesthouse to get ready to leave. I'd say we left here a little before nine, got in my car and headed for St. George Episcopal."

"Where was your car parked?"

"In the garage," Lambert answered. "Connor insists that it

be inside. The neighborhood isn't quite safe, he said. The alley and all. And I'm sure you've noticed the area around here is, shall we say, in transition."

"Ms. Honeywell's home is three blocks from the Capitol, Pastor Lambert." Gage said. "Austin's downtown has grown up around it."

"It's no use trying to sugarcoat the realities of your town, Lieutenant." Lambert folded his arms across his chest. "There's a park between here and there that is a hangout for delinquents and drug pushers. The Travis County Courthouse is on the other side of that park, and its dumpsters are splattered with profanities and graffiti. Personally, I've been afraid for my safety ever since we drove up to this house." He sniffed.

"So the last time you saw Reverend Duff was?" Gage asked, ignoring the outburst.

"Around 8:45, maybe 8:50. I dropped him off at St. George then hightailed it to the prayer breakfast."

"Did you see Reverend Duff go into St. George's?" Gage asked.

"Yes. Bishop Hamlin had given Reverend Duff the code to the back door. I watched him disarm the door and walk in. The door closed, and I drove to the Hilton."

Gage frowned and sat back in the chair.

"For Pete's sake," Lambert said. "There are plenty of witnesses that will attest to the fact I was at the prayer service."

"I'm sure there are."

Matt studied Gage's face. Was there something behind that comment?

"Actually, Pastor Lambert," she continued. "I need to have a look at your car."

"What?" Lambert demanded.

She picked up her phone, tapped a few keys, then turned

the phone for him to see the screen. "I have a search warrant to inspect your vehicle. Is it still parked in the garage?"

Lambert's face turned redder than a tomato. "I object!"

Gage pushed away from the table. "Do you have your keys with you?"

Lambert's scowl was vicious as he fished them out of his pocket.

"Let's go," Gage nodded for Lambert to lead the way.

Matt followed them out the door. He kept his grin to himself, but inside he was enjoying the show. Gage was a force to be reckoned with. He made a mental note to stay on her good side.

———

LYLE ESCORTED MATT, Gage and Lambert to a long passageway behind the kitchen. "The garage door is at the end," he said, and went back to his work. The two doors on the right opened to a pantry and laundry room, respectively. The two on the left were closed.

When they reached the far door, Gage opened it, and the group walked down into the three-car garage. A blue Ford Focus was parked in the farthest bay.

"Stay here," she instructed Lambert, then approached the car. She walked around the small, four-door sedan, all the while recording the scene on her phone. When she was satisfied, she pulled on some latex gloves and opened the driver's side door. She pulled a penlight from her jacket and studied the interior. "Pastor Hayden, may I borrow you, please?"

"Yes, Lieutenant?" Matt went to her.

Gage nodded into the car's interior. "What do you see?"

The Focus was immaculate, as if it was fresh off the

assembly line, Matt thought. Gage opened the remaining three doors. "Not one gum wrapper, not one blade of grass," she said.

Matt looked back at Lambert. "Is this car a recent purchase?" he asked.

"I bought it two years ago."

"Looks like he doesn't drive much," Gage whispered, still on her knees at the passenger door.

"It's been wiped," he mumbled back.

She got up, walked around to the back of the car, inserted the key and opened the trunk. Matt hobbled over to look in.

The compartment, surprisingly large for such a small car, was completely empty. No jumper cables, no safety kit, no nothing.

Gage slammed the trunk closed. "Goodness, Pastor Lambert. Your vehicle is clean as a whistle."

"Cleanliness is next to godliness," he said smugly.

Leaning heavily on his cane, Matt limped around the car. The bumpers and grill were spotless, the tires shiny. He completed his circuit of the vehicle, then attempted to bend down to check out the back wheel wells. He'd found many a drug stash in the crevices of wheel wells. His head protested with a dizzying pounding that forced him to lean against the car so as not to fall.

"Pastor Hayden?" Gage asked. "You okay?"

"Wanted a look at the wheel wells. Bad idea," he said, waiting for his equilibrium to return.

Gage got down on one knee, focused the flashlight above the tire and peered in. Her sleek eyebrows shot up. She pulled an evidence bag from her suit jacket and reached up into the recess. When she brought her hand back, the bag was filled with dirt. She sniffed it, then held it up for Matt to get a whiff.

His brows lifted. "Manure?"

"And fresh enough to smell like it." Gage got to her feet, sealed the bag, then labeled it.

As she did so, Matt again studied the car's fenders, wheels and valance panels. They were spotless.

Gage finished labeling the bag. "I'm impounding your car, Pastor Lambert."

His droopy eyes widened in anger. "On what grounds?"

"Things aren't adding up, and my search warrant expressly covers any actions I deem necessary to take."

"This is ridiculous!" Lambert stepped forward. "I demand to see Chief Aguilar. Why are you making such a big deal out of my car? Is this your chance to finally prove yourself as a police officer?"

"Police *Lieutenant*," Gage corrected him. "And let's go over the chain of command here. The Governor of Texas asked the Austin Police Chief, who has over eighteen hundred officers under his command, to investigate the disappearance of an inaugural speaker. The chief chose me out of those eighteen hundred officers to comply with the governor's request. The governor's a big deal. You are not."

Lambert blew out an angry breath. "Are you done with me?" he demanded.

You wish, Matt almost blurted.

"I'll have more questions for you later, but we're done for now," Gage said. "Besides, Mrs. Duff is on her way here. I'm sure you will be a great comfort to her."

At the mention of Mrs. Duff's arrival, Matt watched Lambert's face go from cherry red to ghostly white. Gage missed it because she was already headed into the house, but Matt hadn't. Pastor Lambert looked scared spitless that Mrs. Duff would be arriving on the scene.

"When is she getting here?" Lambert sputtered as he stepped into the house.

"Mid-afternoon," Gage answered.

Lambert turned on his heel. "I'll be in my room if you need me."

As Lambert hurried away, Matt saw him pull his cell phone from his pocket. Who's he going to call, Matt wondered. And why was he upset Mrs. Duff was coming?

Gage interrupted his thoughts. "I've put in a call to the garage to pick up the Ford Focus. While I'm waiting, I've got another case to consult on."

Matt nodded and decided to head to his room and put his feet up for a bit. This could prove to be an interesting afternoon.

12

MRS. DUFF ARRIVES

MATT WAS AWAKENED by a knock on his bedroom door. He rolled his feet off the chaise and sat up slowly. "Yes?"

Lyle peeked in. "Oh, dear. You were asleep. I'll come back later."

Matt looked at his watch, and his eyes rounded in surprise. "It's almost two o'clock." He waved Lyle in. "I better get up, or I won't sleep tonight. What do you need?"

Lyle came in and shut the door behind him. "Hester and I have a problem and wondered if you could help us out."

"Sure." Matt reached for his cane and stood up. "What do you need?"

"Mrs. Duff is going to stay with Hester while the police look for her husband. Apparently, she's very pregnant. And, well," he shrugged, hands out. "She can't climb steps, and she's supposed to be on bedrest. Something about preeclampsia—whatever that is."

"You need her to stay in this room."

Lyle breathed a sigh of relief. "Yes. But not to worry, Preacher. We've got a plan for where you can stay."

Although Matt would miss the elegant surroundings of the former master suite, his main concern was where he would go. He knew there was at least one more bedroom on the floor with Hester's master suite, but the only way up was via the staircase —an absolute no-no, according to Dr. Ryan's strict instructions. Obviously, there were rooms over at the guesthouse, but he enjoyed the hustle and bustle of the main house. Well, beggars can't be choosers. He was lucky to have a place to stay at all.

"I'll start pulling my things together." Matt hobbled to the closet to retrieve the gym bag that James W. had brought over.

"I'll strip the bed while you get your things," Lyle said.

"I won't be long." After all, Matt had very few things to pack.

Lyle was bundling up the used sheets and pillowcases when Matt returned from the dressing area. "Follow me." The large man led the way out into the hall.

They crossed through the kitchen and back down the hallway that led to the garage. Lyle tossed the linens onto the floor of the laundry room, then opened one of the doors on the left that had been closed earlier.

To his surprise, the door was an entrance to a small elevator. "I didn't know the main house had an elevator."

"This was the lift to the servants' quarters up on the third floor." Lyle motioned Matt to get in first, then squeezed himself into the remaining space. He pressed the top button on the panel. "The elevator can stop on the second floor, but Hester refuses to let anyone use it. She says using the stairs is as good an exercise as a person can get. She's shoved a bookcase in front of its door."

Matt hugged his gym bag close, since Lyle took up most of the enclosure. Matt realized it would be a snug fit for the large man even if he was the car's only occupant. The elevator rose slowly—very slowly—and the air inside became dense. Matt wasn't claustrophobic, but in these circumstances, the higher the elevators rose, the more the walls seemed to close in on him.

Finally, the upward motion stopped, and Lyle opened the door into a narrow hallway with three doors all in a row across from the elevator. "Lambert's room," he explained, gesturing to the closed door on the right. "The bathroom," he opened the door directly across, to a small, white-tiled lavatory. "And your room on the left." He led the way to the last door and opened it.

Matt entered, and a smile immediately spread across his face. "This is..." he searched for the word. "Charming."

Awash in teal, white and gray-striped wallpaper, the cozy room looked like something one would find in an old English country cottage. There was no ceiling, only white exposed rafters and the gray-painted underbelly of the roof. To his right was a gabled nook, its window looking out over the front yard and a window seat from which to enjoy the view. Straight ahead, the Victorian home's tower room was set up as a comfy-looking reading nook, rimmed in leaded glass windows. On his left, a white iron twin bed trimmed with vintage brass finials was piled with several down comforters begging for someone to drown themselves in them. An armoire and slatted rocker with tufted cushions finished off the room's furniture.

"This is great." Matt put his gym bag on the bed.

"I'm afraid you'll need to share the bathroom with Pastor Lambert." Lyle bit his lip. "I hope that won't be a problem."

"Lambert's staying in the other room?" Matt nodded over Lyle's shoulder into the hallway.

Lyle lowered his voice conspiratorially. "His is much smaller."

"Well, this will do fine," Matt said. "In fact, this is perfect." To be honest, Matt had been a little overwhelmed with the opulence of the first-floor master. *And* he'd still be in the thick of things here at the main house.

"Great. Now I have to go ready the room for Mrs. Duff and her mother." Lyle headed for the door. "We're taking out the chaise and bringing in a twin bed for the mother. Apparently, she's very protective of her daughter. Are you coming back down?"

Not wishing to repeat the cramped experience of riding with Lyle in that elevator, Matt shook his head. "I'll be down in a bit. I want to settle in first."

"Sounds good. Since you slept through lunch, I put aside some macaroni and cheese for you. When you're ready I'll warm it up."

Matt nodded as the door shut behind Lyle. He wouldn't be long. One thing he'd learned in this house was that Lyle could definitely cook. He hung up his clothes, decided to keep his sundries items in the bedroom with him and headed out to call the elevator. As he waited, he peeked into the bathroom. No more than six feet across, the room was cozy. A claw-footed bathtub rested beneath the dormer window at the far end of the skinny room. Next came the toilet, then a pedestal sink beneath a silver-framed mirror. Across the room from it was an open white metal shelf unit stocked with towels, soaps and toilet paper, with an old-fashioned cast iron wall vent at its side.

When Matt heard the elevator rattle to a stop, he returned to the hall. To his surprise, the door opened before he had the chance to reach for the handle.

Pastor Lambert stopped short when he saw Matt standing in the hallway. "What are you doing here?" he demanded.

"I was—"

"Were you going through my things?" Lambert shoved past Matt and went straight to his bedroom door.

"I was not in your room."

Lambert swiveled back. "You're not a cop. No search warrant gives you the right—"

Matt rounded on the man. "I said I was not in your room. They've moved me up here because Shelly Duff needs to be on the first floor."

"That woman is going to stay here? Overnight?" He said it as if a poisonous snake was being loosed in the house.

"She's pregnant, as you should know."

Lambert cackled. "It's a good thing she's staying on the main level, or your Hester Honeywell would have to reinforce the floors."

Ignoring the jibe, Matt continued. "And she wants to stay in Austin until her husband is found."

At that, Lambert's jaw clenched, but he said nothing.

"Meanwhile," Matt jerked a thumb over his shoulder at his new bedroom. "You stay out of my room, and I'll stay out of yours. Got it?"

Lambert's eyes leveled, but he gave a curt nod and huffed into his own bedroom, slamming the door behind him.

Matt shook his head. What was up with this guy? Whatever it was, Matt wasn't going to trust him further than he could throw him.

He studied the door to his new digs. He didn't have anything in the room that he wanted to keep secret. Heck, most of the stuff in there was borrowed from James W.'s son.

Still.

Matt pulled a hair from his head, opened the door and laid the hair across the latch bolt. Carefully, he pulled the door shut and headed for the elevator.

———

AN HOUR LATER, Matt sat in the parlor, thoroughly sated from a late lunch of the silkiest macaroni and cheese he had ever consumed. This time, Lyle informed him that the secret ingredient was cream cheese.

Though he'd not yet seen Hester today—she was out doing her political thing now that the new governor and legislature had been sworn in—she'd sent word through Lyle that she'd appreciate it if Matt could welcome Mrs. Duff and her mother when they arrived at the mansion.

Matt couldn't refuse, not that he'd want to. Somewhere inside he felt a little bit of pride that Hester had picked him to play host in her home. With Lambert hiding in his room upstairs, Lyle and Connor getting the downstairs master ready and Lieutenant Gage checking out the security cameras at St. George Episcopal, Matt settled into the wingback chair to read the paper until the guests arrived.

He hadn't even gotten a chance to look at the front page when the doorbell rang. He pushed himself up from the chair and went to greet Mrs. Duff and her mother. He opened the door, and his eyes bulged in, what? Shock? Fear?

The younger woman—the one with the county-fair-winning pumpkin bulging through her open wool coat—nodded. "I know. I'm huge."

Only when he attempted to speak did Matt realize his jaw had dropped open. "I'm so sorry," he said. "Won't you come in?"

"No apologies," the young woman said. "I have the same reaction whenever I look in the mirror." She stepped into the foyer. "I'm Shelly Duff." She turned to the woman behind her. "And this is my mother, Mum."

"I'm Matt Hayden." He helped the mother into the foyer.

"It's getting a bit nippy out there," Mum said, with a hint of a British accent. "I'm glad we got here when we did."

Matt hung each woman's coat on the hall tree. Mother and daughter shared the same frame, maybe five foot two, maybe a hundred and ten pounds—when the baby bump was absent from the equation—and the same delicate face. The difference, of course, was in how they wore their hair. Mum—was he really going to call her that?—wore her gray hair short and straight. Shelly's blonde waves flowed around her shoulders.

"Won't you come in," he said, remembering his host duties. He gestured Shelly toward the wingback chair, calculating it was the one seat that he could count on not to collapse beneath her. Mum sat down on the settee.

"Thank you." Shelly attempted a smile that never made it to her sad, brown eyes. "Is there any word about my husband?"

"Not yet, but I assure you, the police are turning the city upside down looking for him. At Governor Novak's strict instruction," Matt added.

"Yes, he's called twice to keep me posted on the investigation." A tear escaped down her cheek and she wiped it away. "It's difficult to adopt the appropriate legal terminology when this is such a personal matter."

Despite the tear, Matt sensed the woman was made of sturdy stock. When he glanced at Shelly's mother, her face was stolid, but her eyes watched her daughter like a hawk.

Like mother, like daughter, Matt decided. Solid.

"Perhaps you would like some coffee? Tea?" he asked.

"Tea would be lovely," Mum said. "Decaf, of course. The little one doesn't need to kick her mum any more than she does already."

"Of course." A job for Lyle, to be sure. "And you're parked out front, I assume?"

"The Nissan Rogue," Shelly said.

"I'll get someone to unload your things." And that duty would fall to Connor.

So far, so good on the host thing.

"I'll be right back." He headed for the archway, then

paused. "Would you like me to let Pastor Lambert know that you're here?"

Shelly blanched, while her mother's eyes flashed.

"Absolutely not," Mum said.

"Yes, ma'am." He headed for the kitchen, his eyebrows raised. Whatever the conflict between Pastor Lambert and Shelly Duff concerned, it was deeply felt on both sides.

H stopped and swiveled when he heard a moan behind him, only to find Shelly Duff bent over, her eyes squeezed shut and her arms wrapped around her stomach.

Mum was immediately at her side. Matt looked at her nervously. "Is she gonna be okay?"

Mum's face was creased with concern, but her voice was light and efficient when she spoke. "Perhaps we'd best get her settled in before having that tea. Once she gets her legs up, she'll be right as rain."

"Of course," Matt agreed. "I'll make sure your room is ready."

He headed back through the archway, and as soon as he felt he was out of sight, he and his cane went into high gear. He hurried down the hall, getting to his old room as Connor and Lyle were coming out.

"Is everything ready for Mrs. Duff?" Matt demanded.

Lyle's forehead puckered. "Preacher, are you okay?"

"I'm fine. But unless you're into birthing babies, we need to get that woman to bed right now."

"On our way," Connor said. He and Lyle hurried toward the parlor.

Having passed the baton, Matt leaned back against the wall to catch his breath. Who knew? He'd moved pretty quickly with that cane. Maybe he could give those drug dealers a run for their money after all. That is, if the perps were over eighty years of age.

13

THE REVEREND DAVID DUFF

MATT SAT at the kitchen island, watching Lyle prepare a lasagna for the night's dinner. The giant, sporting a waist apron covered in watermelons, was grating a large ball of mozzarella into a bowl. Matt winced as Lyle's enormous fingers moved treacherously close to the box's grate. "I thought folks put ricotta cheese in lasagna," Matt said.

Lyle shook his head, never taking his eyes off his task. "Fresh, grated mozzarella. That's my secret ingredient." He smiled proudly. "That, and a few other tricks."

Matt's phone buzzed and he answered it. "Matt Hayden."

"Sorry I'm so late in getting back to you," came Lieutenant Gage's reply.

Matt was taken aback. Did the chief investigator think she owed him an apology? "No problem," he said. "Any leads?"

Lyle stopped grating. "Who is it?" he mouthed.

"Gage," Matt mouthed back.

Lyle slid the grater, bowl and cheese closer to Matt and leaned over to listen in.

"No new leads and now a defunct old one," she answered,

sounding tired. "I was over at St. George's this afternoon. Like
Lambert said, he dropped Duff off at the church, was there
until Duff punched through the security system and entered
the building, then drove off. Fifteen minutes later, Duff left the
church."

"Could Lambert have been waiting for him somewhere?"

"I checked out the security cams at the Hilton. Lambert
entered the prayer breakfast at 9:10 a.m. and was in full sight of
the cameras for the next hour and a half."

"Damn," Matt said.

An exhausted chuckle came across the line. "You said it,
Preacher, not me."

"What's your next move?"

"I need to interview Mrs. Duff. Has she arrived there yet?"

"Yes, she's here. Hold on." Matt nodded at Lyle. "Do you
think Mrs. Duff is up for talking with the lieutenant?"

Lyle raised doubtful eyes. "I'll check." He wiped his hands
on his apron and hurried out of the room.

Matt spoke back into the phone. "The trip up from San
Antonio was pretty rough on her. For a minute, I thought she
was going to give birth right here in Hester's parlor. She went
straight to her room to lie down." He checked his watch. "It's
four o'clock now. I'd say she got here about an hour ago.
Lyle's checking to see if this is a good time for you to talk
with her."

"Thanks."

"Are there any leads on where Duff might've gone after he
left St. George's?" Matt asked.

"We're putting together a list of security cams around the
church. He was heading northeast when he walked out of
range of the church's security system."

"I'm not familiar with the area. How far is St. George from
the Capitol?" Matt asked.

"It's about a fifteen-minute walk to the Governor's Mansion."

"So he was heading in the right direction at least."

"There's a good side and a bad side to that," Gage said. "There are plenty of cameras around that area due to the proximity of the state grounds and some large businesses on the way. The bad news is, there are a whole lot of cameras we have to check."

Lyle came back in. "She's sound asleep. Mum said she'd prefer not waking her until it's time to eat."

"I heard that," Gage sighed. "Ask him what time dinner will be over."

Matt started to repeat the question, but Lyle held up a hand. "I heard. Hester said she'd like dinner to be served at six o'clock. She has one last committee meeting for the day at seven."

"I'll be there at seven, then," Gage said. "That'll give me time to go back to the office and start writing this up."

"I'll let Mrs. Duff know you're coming when she wakes up," Matt offered.

"I'd like you to sit in on that interview," Gage said. "She might need some moral support from a preacher."

"Always glad to help. See you then." Matt tucked his phone in his pocket, then looked again at his watch. Almost two hours before supper. He could get a lot done on this Duff investigation if only he could access the internet from a decent-sized monitor. "I don't suppose I could get my hands on a computer to look up a few things," Matt said. "I'm not getting mine until tomorrow morning."

Lyle was at the stove, poking at a boiling pot of something. "What's tomorrow morning?"

"My fiancé is coming with my things."

Lyle turned from the stove, his grin wide. "Why Pastor

Hayden, you never said anything about being engaged. Congratulations!"

Matt offered a weak smile in return. "We're going through a rough time. I think."

He didn't quite know what was going on between him and Angie. He had hopes that tomorrow might bring some answers.

"Well, if it's a computer you need, I've got one you can use."

Matt perked up. "Are you sure?"

"Sure. I keep all my business accounts—you know, my grant writing projects, Hester's books—on a Surface. It's not a large screen, but you're welcome to use it." His eyes twinkled. "Unless you're planning on looking at something nefarious that I'd rather not have on my search list."

"Nothing like that. Just trying to find some answers about Reverend Duff's disappearance."

"Anything I can do to help that sweet lady down the hall. I hate to think her baby might be born without a daddy." Lyle turned off the gas stove's burner. "I'll run upstairs and get it."

Fifteen minutes later, Matt sat down on the parlor's settee. With a cup of hot tea at his side, he settled back and powered up the Surface.

His first priority was to get an understanding of where the pertinent points of interest in the investigation were in relationship to each other. A pentagon came to mind as he studied the downtown Austin map. At the top of the pentagon, or the northernmost point, were the Capitol grounds. The northwest point was Hester's house. The southwest point was St. George Episcopal Church. The southeast point was the Hilton by the convention center. Nothing of relevance took up the remaining northeast point, but the pentagon shape still worked for him.

So Lambert had driven eight blocks south to get from Hester's to St. George's. After dropping off Duff, Lambert had to drive another eight blocks, this time straight east, to the Hilton. Duff, on the other hand, would have had to travel north by northeast, through the heart of downtown Austin, to get to the Capitol grounds—approximately a twelve-block trek as the crow flies.

Next, Matt gave a harder look at River Walk Fellowship Church in San Antonio. Instead of returning to the church's website, he went to the San Antonio newspapers and searched for the death of David Duff's father, Jesse Duff. It didn't take long to find what he was looking for. The senior Duff's death had made quite a splash in the *San Antonio Express-News*.

REVEREND JESSE DUFF, senior pastor at River Walk Fellowship Church, and his wife Edna were killed Sunday morning in a three-car wreck on the southbound I-35 lanes near the Ratama exit. Two other people were killed in the accident, including the drunk driver who was driving northbound in the southbound lanes.

MATT HAD TAKEN a moment to consider how devastating that must have been for their son, David. And for the congregation to lose a head pastor after twenty years? Jesse Duff had been there long enough to baptize and then marry an entire generation.

He searched for more information and found it in the *Southern Christian Texan*. The article contained the same information about the accident but went into much greater detail as to Jesse Duff's ministry.

. . .

*THE ENTIRE CHRISTIAN community grieves the loss of
Reverend Jesse Samuel Duff, an amazing man of God. We take
heart in the fact that Jesse's ministry will continue in and
through his son, Reverend David Duff, who upon hearing of his
parents' deaths, by the grace of God, was able to preach of the
magnificent saving grace of our Lord, Jesus Christ, to his father's
congregation. His words of discipleship, humility and God's love
are a tribute to his upbringing and a tremendous comfort to all
those who grieve the passing of his father.*

MATT WAS IMPRESSED to read that David Duff could
preach within hours of hearing the news of his parents' deaths.
That took guts. When Matt's father, Michael, had died—
murdered by the police chief who would soon come after all
three of Michael's sons—Matt had been a rage-filled mess of
hate for months. Only by the grace of God had he found the
peace that would allow him to get on with his life.

The last items he searched were the two seminaries from
which Lambert and David Duff had graduated. The difference
between the two institutions could not be overstated. Lambert's
college seminary was a very conservative institution. The seminary's website emphasized its adherence to strict interpretation
of Scripture. Duff's seminary, on the other hand, was part of a
consortium of theological schools that included Episcopalians,
Jesuits, Lutherans and even Unitarian Universalists. Its website
emphasized ecumenical partnerships, as well as the individ-
ual's search for faith.

By six o'clock, Matt's head was spinning, and the scent of
garlic and tomatoes and all things lasagna told him enough was
enough. And was that fresh-baked bread?

When he entered the kitchen, Lyle was on the phone.

"No problem," said the cook, his face red from the steam

coming off the lasagna. "You gotta do what you gotta do." He punched off the phone and looked up at Matt. "That was Hester. She won't be home for dinner after all."

"Anything wrong?" Matt sat down at the island.

Lyle shook his head. "She needs to show up at a happy hour over at the Driskill."

Matt had heard that name before. "That's a hotel, right?"

Lyle smiled deliciously. "Oh, honey. You have no idea. She's the Grand Dame of Austin. We'll need to get you over there some time."

Connor came in from the mud room. "Getting pretty chilly out there." He rubbed his hands, then sniffed. "Lasagna?"

Lyle nodded. "And the focaccia bread should be ready." He leaned down to look at the smaller of the two ovens. "Looks good." He pulled on his mitts and opened the oven.

"Great," Connor said. "I'll have a chance to eat before going to class tonight."

Class? Then Matt remembered. Connor had said he was a law student at UT.

"I'll go let Pastor Lambert know it's time to eat." Connor headed for the back hallway.

Five minutes later, he returned to the kitchen, his lips pursed and his eyes troubled.

"Everything okay?" Lyle asked.

"Lambert says he'll eat his supper in his room," Connor answered.

Lyle snickered as he cut the lasagna. "I count that as a good thing."

Matt studied the shorter, muscular man, who was rubbing his bald head. "You're troubled about something."

Lyle looked up. "Did Lambert say something mean to you?"

"No. Not to me, anyway." Connor leaned a muscled arm

on the island. "I got off the elevator and was about to knock on his door when I heard him talking on the phone."

"What did he say?" Matt asked.

"He was mad. First I heard him say, 'I've been trying to get a hold of you all day. I thought maybe you'd already thrown your phone away.'" Connor looked up at Matt, confusion in his gaze. "Then Lambert said, 'What the hell did you do to my car?'" Connor shook his head. "The cops have his car, right?"

"They do now." Matt's brow furrowed. "But they didn't have it yesterday when Reverend Duff went missing." He thought back over the scene between Lieutenant Gage and Lambert in the garage this morning. Lambert had seemed surprised when Gage had mentioned the car was squeaky clean.

Matt's eyes locked with Connor's. "Which means someone else may have been driving Lambert's car yesterday."

14

SHELLY DUFF

LIEUTENANT GAGE ARRIVED PROMPTLY at seven o'clock, her close-cut hair sprinkled with rain and her long fingers gloved. "This cold front's taking its time coming in," she said, doffing her coat. "Precipitation could play hell with the evidence—if we ever find any."

Matt waited for her to hang her jacket on the coat rack. "You need to speak with Connor. He overheard Lambert asking someone on the phone about his car."

"We haven't released it yet." Gage let out a sigh. "But we haven't even proved a crime has been committed. I have to return the car to Lambert."

"You should talk to Connor first," Matt said.

"Okay. Where is he?"

"Unfortunately, he's not here. He has a class at UT tonight."

"Tomorrow then," Gage said. "Let's head on to Mrs. Duff, then."

"Any sightings of Reverend Duff on security cameras?" Matt asked, leading the way back to Shelly Duff's room.

"We think we've got him going into the Hobby Building's parking deck." She wiped the water off her hair and dried her hand on her suit pants. "But nothing on him coming out."

"Are there any interior cameras in the parking deck?"

"None that work."

The two shared a look, then Matt knocked on the bedroom door. "Mrs. Duff? It's Pastor Hayden. Lieutenant Gage is with me."

Almost immediately, the door opened. Mum studied the lieutenant a moment, then extended her hand. "I'm Shelly Duff's mother. Call me Mum."

"Lieutenant Gage." The tall woman shook the mother's hand. "May we come in?"

Shelly Duff, her head slightly elevated, lay in a twin bed by the white marble fireplace. Matt cast a questioning glance at Mum and nodded toward the king bed centered in the room.

"It's too tall for her to get in and out of," Mum explained.

"Lieutenant Gage, you said? Please have a seat." She motioned to the desk chair by her pillow. "I'm Shelly Duff. Do you have any word on my husband?"

"I wish I did, Mrs. Duff." Lieutenant Gage sat down. "But I can assure you, we've got a whole lot of people looking for him." She pulled a small notebook from her pocket. "Are you up to answering a few questions for me?"

"Anything you need." Shelly looked at her mother. "Why don't you have Lyle bring in some more chairs for you and Pastor Hayden."

As soon as Mum was out the door, Shelly turned a stern gaze on the lieutenant. "It doesn't look good, does it?" She narrowed her eyes. "Don't lie to me, Lieutenant. I'll be able to tell."

"All right." Gage put down her notepad. "We know your husband went to St. George Episcopal yesterday morning, and that he left fifteen minutes later. We have footage of him on security cameras walking into the Hobby Building parking garage. And that's the last time anyone saw him."

"He never came out of the parking garage?" Shelly asked.

"Not that we can see."

"So he's been kidnapped." Shelly didn't put it as a question.

"Mrs. Duff, we're not sure of anything right now."

"It's Shelly, please. Thank you for telling me the truth." Shelly extended her hand to the lieutenant.

"And I'm Naomi." Lieutenant Gage took Shelly's hand and held it for a moment.

Trust, Matt thought. And Lieutenant Naomi Gage had just sealed it with Shelly Duff.

Mum returned, loaded down with a tray bearing glasses of water and a bowl of peanut M&M's. "Lyle will be right along with the chairs."

Shelly reached for the candy and popped one in her mouth. "That man's a sweetheart. When he was settling me in, he asked about my cravings." She crunched down on the chocolate-covered peanut. "Perfection."

"What did I miss?" Mum asked.

"We're getting started on some background questions." Gage aimed a pen at her notebook. "When did you last see your husband, Shelly?"

"Monday afternoon. David and Pastor Lambert left our house mid-afternoon, probably around two o'clock?" She sent a questioning look at Mum, who nodded her head in agreement.

"And the reason you didn't come with him?"

Shelly patted her belly.

Gage nodded. "I figured as much. Have to dot all the I's."

"She's supposed to be on bed rest," Mum put in. "Her doctor's not exactly pleased we drove up from San Antonio today."

"Like he could keep me away," Shelly said.

"Why did your husband and Pastor Lambert stay here at Hester Honeywell's? Did your husband know her from before?"

Shelly shook her head. "David was supposed to deliver the benediction at the inauguration. Governor Novak's chief of staff made the housing arrangements for all of the visiting dignitaries."

For the next few minutes, Matt listened as Lieutenant Gage walked Shelly through the basic background questions about Reverend Duff. Finally, Gage put down her pen and looked Shelly in the eye. "I have one last question for you, Mrs. Duff. Can you think of anyone who would want to harm your husband?"

Shelly laid her head back on her pillow and studied the ceiling for a long moment. "Harm him, no," she said, then raised her head. "But shut David up? That could be a long list."

"Why?"

"My husband is a fiercely loving man." Shelly smiled at Gage's confused expression. "He believes, truly believes, that God is love. And David can be fierce when calling out the preachers and politicians who call themselves Christians but teach nothing but hate and privilege and fear."

Something clicked inside Matt. "Is Pastor Lambert one of the folks that would like to 'shut your husband up,' to use your words?"

Shelly rolled her eyes. Mum sniffed.

"David's father could be somewhat rigid," Shelly said carefully, and Matt could tell she was trying to be gracious in her description of her deceased father-in-law. "He always had to be in control. He could never 'let go and let God.' You know what I mean?" She directed this question to Matt.

"Yes. It's difficult to understand God's grace if you spend

FOUR REASONS TO DIE   99

your time judging others and yourself."

Shelly's eyes narrowed. "That is exactly what I mean." She fell back on her pillow to catch her breath, then looked at Matt. "Since David has taken over River Walk Fellowship, he's committed his life to preaching about God's love. Its inclusivity. Its caring."

"What does this have to do with Pastor Lambert?" Gage asked.

"River Walk Fellowship is quite different now than when David's father was in charge. We've started food pantries, a thrift shop, sponsored mission trips. Heck, we've added a Hispanic ministry that worships over two thousand people. All of this and more. But it all costs money. More staff added. More buildings needed. Lambert keeps the books. Our people are giving more and more, but there are several ministries that cost a disproportionate amount of money. Sometimes we go in the red."

"A cardinal sin, I assume," Matt said.

"Lambert and David are not on the same page when it comes to money. And another thing. Because some of our older members tend to think those outreach ministries are a door to socialism, they are leaving the church. Those are big-money donors walking out the door, and that makes Lambert very unhappy."

"I think we've gone down that road enough for tonight," Mum said. She went to her daughter's side, picked up Shelly's wrist and checked her pulse. "Your heart's beating like a rabbit's."

Gage cleared her throat. "You've been very helpful, Shelly. If I have more questions or news, I'll come back tomorrow."

She stood, but Matt leaned forward in his chair. "A quick how-things-are-done question. Nothing to do with what you were talking about."

Mum glared, but Shelly nodded for him to continue.

"Did David have his sermon finished for this Sunday when he left San Antonio?"

Shelly chuckled softly. "He barely has it finished before he gets in the pulpit. He gets the basics down, of course. He's starting a new sermon series before Lent begins. It's all been outlined. But he'll be working on it until the last minute."

"I see. What, generally, is the deadline for David to get his sermon's PowerPoint content to your media department?"

"Wednesday," she answered. "Why?"

Matt smiled. "My secretary's always on me to get her my PowerPoint by the Monday before."

Shelly snickered. "David's secretary would sing the *Hallelujah Chorus* if she could get David to have it to her by Tuesday."

Matt nodded victoriously. "I thought so."

Gage and Matt said their good evenings and left the room. When they were almost to the kitchen, Gage put her hand on Matt's arm and stopped him. "What was that all about? The PowerPoint thing?"

Matt didn't answer, but instead asked his own question. "Any chance I can see the evidence you removed from Duff's bedroom last night?"

"Sure. When?"

He did a quick calculation. If Angie was working tonight, she wouldn't leave tomorrow until noon to come to Austin. "Tomorrow morning, after my doctor's appointment? Say around ten?"

Gage chuckled. "You don't let any grass grow under your feet, do you? Tell you what. I'll stop by to talk with Connor tomorrow morning and then take you over to the lab myself. And you're looking for what?"

"Following up on a hunch."

15

HESTER HONEYWELL

MATT TUCKED the day's *Austin-American Statesman* under his elbow, ready to catch up on the latest news. The mansion had quieted down for the evening, but he resisted the idea of heading upstairs to his bedroom. Spending a couple of hours down the hall from Lambert sounded anything but restful. The solarium that connected the main house to the guesthouse was all glass and would provide little opposition to the cold wind blowing outside. He headed for the parlor, but it was dark. He felt along the wall for a light switch.

"Can I help you?" Lyle called from the kitchen, where he was wiping down the counters.

Matt turned. "Not ready to go upstairs yet."

"Need a place to kick up your feet? Read your paper?"

Matt chuckled. "On the nose."

"Step into my study, said the spider to the fly." Lyle's eyes twinkled with mischief as he came around the island.

"I thought that poem said parlor," Matt said.

Lyle shrugged. "You've already seen the parlor."

He led the way to the study's French doors, nestled

beneath the grand staircase. "I'll put a fire in the stove, and you'll be snug as a bug in a rug." Lyle flipped a wall switch and the desk lights turned on.

Matt stood at the doorway. "Are you sure it's okay to be in here?"

"Absolutely."

Still Matt hesitated, not wanting to invade Hester's private study. He'd only gotten as far as the doorway the other night when he and James W. discovered Lambert talking on the phone. The desk where Lambert had been seated was centered on the left wall and reminded Matt of something one might see in the Oval Office. Behind it was an oil painting of a beautiful woman in full rodeo gear riding a chestnut horse around a barrel. Matt knew in an instant the stunning rider was Hester.

Matt stepped inside. The walls were covered in a dark, intricately carved linenfold paneling. Several plaques and awards were displayed around the room. To his right, he was surprised to find a small cast iron potbelly stove, probably the same vintage as the wall grates in the third-floor rooms. In front of the stove sat two very comfortable-looking recliners separated by a small Mission-style table.

Lyle grabbed a match from a brass box on the table, then opened the stove's fire door. He lit the wood already inside. "That'll get it started." He straightened. "Would you like some tea? Chamomile, maybe?"

"That would be great."

"I'll adjust the fire when I get back. The dang thing's smaller than a three-gallon jug, but those little wood burners can put out a lot of heat." He gestured to the oversized chairs. "Make yourself comfortable."

Matt settled down in one of the leather recliners, leaned his cane against its soft arm and flipped on the table's art deco reading lamp. The newspaper's front page was plastered with stories of yesterday's inaugural festivities. After a careful scan of the article describing the inauguration itself, he breathed a sigh of relief. No mention of his benediction or of his taking a dive in the elevator. Well, of course not, he chided himself. You're no big deal.

Next, he flipped through the paper looking for photos of the inaugural, keen to see if James W. or Elsbeth had made it onto the page. Elsbeth would be thrilled if it were so.

Hester's low voice came from the doorway. "Care for some company?"

Startled, Matt reached for his cane. "I'm so sorry. Lyle said it would be okay—"

"Stay where you are, Preacher. Fact is, I'd like to spend some time with you." Hester, dressed in navy linen slacks and a matching loose-knit sweater, settled into the recliner opposite Matt's. "How are you settling in?"

"My doctor was very pleased with my blood pressure this morning. Your letting me stay here had everything to do with that. Gorgeous house, by the way. And Lyle makes everything perfect. Thank you so much for inviting me."

Hester tilted back the seat, and the footrest popped up. "Lord knows I've got the room." She sent him an apologetic smile. "I'm sorry we had to move you out of the downstairs bedroom. I hope you'll find the tower room comfortable."

"I'm sure I will. It's a lovely room."

"And I'm sorry you have to be on the same floor as that pain-in-the-neck pastor. I had to let him stay here, though. They took his car." She leaned over and whispered. "Your room's a lot nicer." She nodded toward the newspaper on his lap. "What are you reading?"

"Looking at the photos. I'm hoping Elsbeth Novak— Jimmy's mother—made it into the paper. If so, she'll be more likely to forget that James W. made her late to the Governor's Ball."

"Oh, she's in there all right. Check out the second page of Section B."

Matt flipped open the paper, and sure enough, Elsbeth and Jimmy grinned out at him. The caption below read "Our New Governor and First Lady of Texas." Oh, yeah, he thought. James W. was completely off the hook. "Did you get a chance to talk with Elsbeth?" he asked.

Hester hooted. "She had so much to say, I didn't have to talk much."

Lyle arrived, carrying a tray loaded with tea and cookies. He placed it on the table separating the recliners. "I took the liberty of bringing a cup for you, Hester."

"Well done, my friend." She picked up the teapot. "How do you take your tea, Preacher?"

"One sugar cube, please."

She poured him a cup. "Lyle, I can handle things from here out. Go get some rest."

"You've had a long day, Hester. I can lock up."

"Good night, Lyle," she said sternly.

"You're the boss." He bowed slightly. "Good night."

Matt started to fold the newspaper when his eyes landed on the picture of a familiar face from yesterday. He held the paper up for Hester to see. "Who's this man?" he asked, pointing to a photo of the square-jawed, broad-shouldered man standing with a younger, smaller man. Both wore oversized cowboy hats, bolo ties and matching large brass belt buckles.

Hester glanced at the picture, then rolled her eyes. "That is Senator William J. Womack and his son, Hogg Womack."

"Hogg?"

She chuckled. "Named him after Governor James Steven Hogg, the first Texas-born governor of our great state." She poured cream into her cup, then lifted the teapot. "Texans have weird ways of naming their kids, but Senator Womack's boy got off easy. Governor Hogg named his daughter Ima."

Matt raised a brow. "He named his daughter Ima Hogg?"

"At least he didn't name her sister Ura." She smiled at her own joke. "But make no mistake. Ima Hogg was a great lady to this state. Philanthropist. Patron of the arts. Sponsored the Houston Symphony. Activist in the civil rights movement. School board member. I want to be like her when I grow up."

Matt allowed that comment to sink in, then returned his attention to Womack's photo. "William Womack's a state senator?"

"Oh no, my friend. He is a U.S. senator. Conservative extraordinaire."

Ah, Matt thought. He knew he'd seen the man before. Though the shot to his head occurred more than six months ago, his memory still held cobwebs that needed to be swept away.

Matt remembered Womack standing next to the Satan-eyed, Santa-Claus-sized Reverend Meade when the reporters had attacked him in the rotunda the day before. "Womack seemed to be pretty tight with Reverend Meade. Every time I turned around, they were together."

Hester picked up a cookie. "Of course. They're joined at the hip. Meade's sermons raise a lot of donations for the Senator's campaigns. 'William Womack will take back our country from the devil's clutches.' Sure." She waved her cookie at Matt. "Tell people what's wrong with our country and who's to blame. Rally 'em around your righteous cause and all their troubles will disappear. Such bullshit."

"Hester!" Lyle's voice called down the hall. "You're supposed to be taking it easy!"

"And you're supposed to be done for the night!"

No reply was forthcoming, but Lyle's interruption had done the trick. Hester sat back in her chair and smiled apologetically at Matt. "Sorry. Sometimes I get on my horse and ride it a bit hard."

Matt spared one last look at the photo. "They sure don't look like father and son."

"Hogg got his mother's looks and his father's mean. He's goin' to UT and racking up quite a reputation. There's this 'brotherhood' thing that he and his daddy belong to. Now what is its name?" She searched for the word, then shook off the effort. "Whatever. A bunch of hunters formed it right after World War II. You have to be invited to get in, and initiated, too. Hogg got arrested last year for almost killing a kid during hazing. Rumor is Hogg was the one pouring the liquor down that poor boy's throat. He got off without even a hand slap, of course. Daddy made sure of that." Hester sipped her tea. "Sorry. My hackles go up when that kind of privilege gets thrown around."

"Sounds like this kid's pretty spoiled."

"You'd be wrong about that. Hogg Womack is a disappointment to the senator in every way. Not smart enough. Not good enough. That boy would do anything to get his father's approval. And I mean anything. Stay clear of that family. They're bad news."

Matt took that in and wanted to ask more, but Hester looked as if she was getting upset. He decided to change the subject. "Is this hunting group a sanctioned fraternity at UT?"

"Absolutely not." Hester sounded offended. "They're only a bunch of men who sit around a fire, talk big and drink beer, if you ask me. But it's a big deal for some." She gave a dismissive wave of her hand.

Matt sensed her change in mood. Her eyes sunk into worry, and her smile disappeared. "Hester?"

She looked at him, deciding something, he thought. Then she leaned in. "What do you think has happened to Reverend Duff?"

A cut-to-the-chase question, Matt decided. That was the kind of person Hester Honeywell was. And she deserved a straight answer. "The longer he's missing, the more I'm concerned we're not going to find him alive."

"Talk to me."

"The best possible spin that could be put on this is that he had an accident of some kind that knocked him out." Matt checked his watch. "It's now thirty-six hours since he was last seen. By now, he should've regained consciousness, or at least been found by somebody who would've taken him to a hospital. All the medical facilities have been alerted to watch out for him."

"Surely there are other possibilities," Hester said.

"Assuming he didn't want to disappear?"

Hester frowned. "His wife is going to have his baby at any moment."

Matt decided not to mention that when someone goes missing, the family is the first to come under the scrutiny of the law as the culprits. Instead, he said, "The other possibilities are very dark."

She swallowed hard. "Tell me."

"He may have been kidnapped."

She looked him straight in the eye. "Or murdered."

"I'm afraid so."

"Oh, God." Hester bowed her head and went very still.

Matt glanced around the room for something to change the subject and saw the oil painting above the desk that captured the action of the beautiful horse and rider racing around a barrel. The horse's chestnut mane and woman's golden hair flared in the wind while dirt and sand spit from beneath the horse's hooves. It was as if the two were fighting the very air to cut closer and go faster. He stood and nodded toward the artwork. "Is that you?"

Hester turned in the chair. "A million years ago." She got up to join him. "It was a gift from the Wranglers National Finals Rodeo Committee commemorating the fortieth anniversary of my last championship."

"It's beautiful," he said.

"A Tim Cox original," she said, a hint of pride in her voice.

"You said your last championship. You won more than one?"

"Three." She gestured with a thumb over her shoulder. "Those are my buckles hanging on the wall."

He studied the shadow boxes holding the carved pewter buckles. Each was engraved with an image similar to the oil painting behind the desk—a woman and horse speeding around a barrel.

"I bet you've got some stories to tell," he mused.

"Preacher, you have no idea." Her laugh was short. "Course, that part of my life ended with my accident. Broke my back barrel-racing in Houston the next year. Worse, we had to put my horse down. Shattered leg and broken hip. I'm not sure I would've competed again, even if I could. I messed up the angle going into the barrel. That poor horse did the best he could. Old Brick had the biggest heart of any animal I ever rode."

"I really was trying to perk up the conversation." Matt returned to the table and reached for a cookie. After one bite, he did a double take. "Delicious. Not only sweet. Kinda savory."

Hester's smile returned. "It's Lyle's secret recipe, but I'll tell you the secret because he will anyway. He puts cardamom in 'em. Calls them 'tea bites.'"

Matt nodded his approval. "He sure can cook."

"He made 'em yesterday but wasn't about to share his 'good stuff' with Lambert. My God, what a judgmental little scum. Given his attitude, I wouldn't be surprised if Lambert's the one who orchestrated Reverend Duff's disappearance."

The cop in Matt knew not to respond to her comment, despite the fact that he thought the exact same thing.

"Well, I think I'll head up to bed," he said. "I've got a doctor's appointment in the morning—Dr. Ryan's ordered daily updates on my vitals. And my fiancé's coming up to bring me some of my things."

The corner of Hester's mouth turned up. "I wondered when you were going to mention her. Angie, isn't it?"

"Yes." Matt jammed his hands in his pockets. "You've heard about her, then?"

"James W. told me all about you two. The angel by day, devil by night bar owner and the preacher."

Matt's face reddened. "Well—"

Hester gave a dismissive wave of her hand. "Not to worry. He also told me Angie is his half-sister, and he was as happy as...how did he put it?" She looked heavenward, searching for the memory. "Ah, yes. He said if he felt any happier about your relationship, he'd drop his harp plumb through the cloud."

Matt gave a lopsided grin. "That sounds like something he would say." He grabbed his cane. "Thank you again for letting me stay here."

"Good night, Preacher. I'm looking forward to meeting your Angie."

"Good night."

Matt sighed as he headed for the back hallway elevator. Hopefully, his reunion with Angie would go smoothly. When he said his prayers tonight, that would be the first one.

16

THE EVIDENCE BOX

MATT, Lyle and Connor were finishing their breakfasts when the front doorbell rang. Lyle got up to answer the door and came back with Lieutenant Gage in tow.

"I didn't mean to interrupt your breakfast," she said. "But I did want to speak to you, Mr. Evans, about something you overheard last night? Something about his car?"

Connor shot a glance at Matt, who shrugged. "You know I had to tell her."

"Have a seat, Lieutenant." Lyle pulled a chair out for her. "I'll get you some coffee."

Gage sat down and removed a notepad from her suit jacket pocket. She nodded at Connor. "Go ahead."

Connor repeated to her what he'd told Matt last night. He'd gone up to Lambert's room to tell him supper was ready and overheard part of the pastor's conversation with someone on the phone.

When he was finished, Gage studied her notes. "'What the hell did you do to my car?' Those were his exact words?"

"Yes, ma'am," Connor nodded.

Lyle placed a cup of coffee in front of Gage and sat down in the remaining empty chair. "I wanted to tell you something as well," he said, shoving a plate of blueberry muffins toward her. "I hadn't remembered it until Connor and I were talking last night about what he'd overheard."

Matt perked up. This was the way it worked in investigations. A witness would give as full a statement as they could in the original interview, but something later would trigger them to remember another piece of information.

"You asked me when I first saw Lambert the morning of the inauguration," Lyle said.

"And I told you that Lambert and Reverend Duff came over from the guesthouse for breakfast around 7:30."

"That's right," Gage agreed. She flipped her notebook to an earlier page, checked her notes, then nodded for Lyle to continue.

"I saw Lambert before that. He came over earlier, maybe around 7:15 or so. I was preparing breakfast. He had to walk through the kitchen to get to the garage. I said good morning. He nodded and said he had to get something out of his car."

"Then what?"

"I assume he went to his car.," Lyle answered. "When he came back, he was carrying a phone charger. Then he headed back to the guesthouse." He leaned forward, his eyes dancing conspiratorially. "But."

Gage looked up from her notes. "But what?"

"That wasn't the only reason he went to his car."

"How do you know?"

"Because when he came into the kitchen, he was carrying a bag—a paper bag that looked pretty heavy. He had to use both hands."

"And?"

"And when he came back in from the garage, he didn't have the bag." Lyle leaned back, a triumphant look on this face.

That could mean anything, Matt thought to himself. Maybe Lambert was bringing down some garbage. Maybe dirty clothes. Still, it was something to consider.

"And when was the next time you saw him?" Gage asked.

"When he came over with Reverend Duff for breakfast," Lyle answered.

Lieutenant Gage nodded and tucked her notebook back into her pocket. "That's excellent, Mr. Griffey." She turned to Connor. "Has your garbage been picked up this week?"

He shook his head. "They come on Friday."

Gage nodded at Matt. "I'll check the garbage, and then we can go."

Hester walked in as Gage left for the garage. "Lyle, we're having guests for dinner this evening. Will six-thirty work for you?"

"Sure. How many?"

Hester went to the counter and poured herself some coffee. "Probably seven, which includes the preacher and me and Shelly Duff and her mother."

"No problem." Lyle buttered a streusel-covered muffin. "But Mrs. Duff's doctor wants her to avoid spicy foods, seafood and beef products. What do you know about your guests' preferences?"

"I imagine they'll eat most anything." Hester poured cream into her cup. "They don't look like they've missed many meals."

"Who's coming?" Connor asked.

"Governor Novak and his parents."

The muffin in Lyle's hand stopped halfway to his mouth. "I beg your pardon?"

"Governor Novak called to ask us over to his place for dinner so he could meet with Mrs. Duff, but I explained she's on bedrest. So I suggested they come over here." Hester looked at Matt. "They'll probably be happy to see you, too."

Well, James W., anyway, Matt thought. "It'll be a fun evening," he said instead. "And she's right. James W. and Elsbeth aren't picky."

"Something special that can be fixed in a day. And I don't want to make anything they've had lately." Lyle's brow furrowed. "I could do a rack of lamb, maybe."

Matt shook his head. "We had that on New Year's Eve."

Lyle bit his lower lip. "A ham?"

"Christmas Day," Matt said.

"How about turkey?" Lyle asked. "We're not too close to Thanksgiving."

"Not to worry." Matt's mouth twitched. "They didn't have turkey for Thanksgiving."

Lyle's eye rounded in horror. "No turkey on Thanksgiving?"

"Theirs was stolen."

There was a moment of silence while everyone took that in, then Hester said, "Turkey it is. Especially yours, Lyle. Nobody fries a turkey like you." She winked at Matt. "It's the moistest bird you'll ever eat."

Lyle rubbed his hands together. "Wow. Cooking for the governor." He stood and faced Hester. "I'll make you proud, Boss. This'll be the best dinner party you've ever thrown." He turned to Connor. "Finish up those pancakes. We've got to go shopping!"

———

TWENTY MINUTES LATER, Gage ushered Matt into a small, windowless room located in Austin's forensic headquarters on the east side of town. The room was furnished with one metal table and two chairs. He sat down in one of them and hooked his cane on its back.

Gage cut the seal on the first of the two boxes on the table. "Here you go," she said, shoving it toward him.

The items inside the box mirrored the list that Gage had shown him the night before. Pens, pencils, highlighters, Post-It Flags, some sundry items. He'd check those out in a moment, but right now he was intent on the Bible and legal pad. He pulled both from the box.

The Bible had a blue hardcover and bookmarks grouped in the book's center. Matt flipped through the pages and saw that it was a red-letter edition that highlighted Jesus's words. He frowned, gave the pages a more thorough investigation, then laid it on the table.

"What's wrong?" Gage asked.

"Did you fingerprint the Bible?"

"Yes. Why?"

Matt didn't answer, but instead pulled the legal pad out of the box. He studied the binding at the top of the yellow pages. "This is a brand-new pad," he said. "No pages have been torn out yet."

He handed the pad to Gage, who studied the lightly perforated top page. "You're right," she said. "This is the original first page."

"And you fingerprinted this as well?"

"Yes," she answered, her voice impatient. "Why?"

He dumped the rest of the contents on the table and grouped the office supplies together.

"Mrs. Duff said last night that her husband worked on his sermon right up until the last minute, right?"

"Yes."

"He brought all of these pens and highlighters and flags for that purpose, right?"

"Right."

Matt held up the Bible. "Then why does it appear this Bible has never been used for study purposes? Why is there not one highlighted verse, not one dog-eared page, not one minute mote of soil in this pristine, what appears to be brand-spanking-new, Bible?"

Gage's mouth went slack.

"And this legal pad. Never before used. Not even an imprint of anything on the top page."

"You're right."

"Mrs. Duff said he had yet to send his PowerPoint script to the secretary for this Sunday's sermon. There should be notes somewhere."

Gage gestured for the Bible, and Matt handed it over. "See how those bookmarks are all clumped on the same page? They haven't even been separated yet. That is not a pastor's study Bible." He swept his hand over the office supplies. "He must use all the highlighters and flags or why would he have brought them?" He shook his head. "We need to find Reverend Duff's real Bible and the laptop his wife says he brought. When we do, we'll be a lot closer to finding out what happened to him."

17

ANGIE ARRIVES

GAGE DROPPED Matt off at Dr. Ryan's office on her way back to Austin's police department's downtown headquarters. When Connor picked him up twenty minutes later, Matt had a smile on his face.

"Looks like you got some good news," Connor said, as Matt climbed into the front passenger seat.

"My blood pressure's down to 140 over 85." He snapped his seatbelt in place. "And I gained a pound. I have Lyle to thank for that."

"Wait 'til supper tonight." Connor pulled away from the curve. "Turkey, duchesse potatoes, red wine cranberry sauce, cornbread stuffin' muffins—you're in for a treat."

Knowing Lyle, that was probably an understatement. "Anything healthy on that menu?"

"Green beans," Connor answered. "If you don't count the fried onion rings, of course." He turned onto the street. "Mind if I run a few more errands before I take you back to the house?"

Matt looked at his watch. It was ten o'clock. He wasn't expecting Angie for another two hours. "No problem."

Matt watched the streets of Austin whiz by, then noted the darkening clouds coming from the north. "Are we expecting rain?" he asked.

"Worse," Connor answered. "A cold front. We might get some ice out of it. That's one reason I wanted to head out to the farm now. Those country roads can get pretty slick, pretty quick."

"Country roads? Where are we going?"

"Poultry farm out east of town. Lyle ordered up a hen turkey for supper. The stores don't stock such big ones after the holidays."

After a thirty-minute ride to the farm, Connor parked in front of a barn-sized store and got out. He returned a few minutes later, a large, white-wrapped parcel under his arm that he put into an ice chest on the truck's backseat floor. He hopped back in and started the truck.

"One more stop before home." Connor pulled out of the gravel driveway.

The Grassville Co-op Store was another fifteen minutes out of Austin. Connor hurried inside and came out bearing three gallon jugs of oil in each hand.

When Connor opened the door to jump back in the cab, Matt shivered. "It must've dropped twenty degrees since we left Dr. Ryan's place."

Connor slammed the driver-side door behind him and started the engine. The dashboard thermometer read forty-six degrees. "If they're expecting sleet, it's still got a ways to go."

Forty-five minutes later, Connor pulled into the mansion's garage. He turned to Matt. "Go ahead on in, Preacher. I'll get the stuff inside."

Matt climbed out, grabbed his cane from the backseat, and

headed for the kitchen. "We're back," he said to Lyle, who was slicing onions.

Lyle glanced up, a worried look on his face. "Your fiancée's waiting for you in the parlor."

"Angie's here, already?"

"She's been here for over an hour." Lyle lowered his voice. "And not too happy that you weren't here."

"She knew I had a doctor's appointment." Matt hobbled through the kitchen and into the dining room. "Angie?" he called.

She appeared in the parlor archway. Her long red hair flamed about her like something the angel Gabriel himself would unleash in the final battle. She stood, feet apart, fists on waist, her green eyes flashing with anger. His beautiful, sexy Angie looked like a dragon ready to shoot flames at her enemy.

He swallowed hard, realizing at this moment *he* was the enemy. "Hi," he said.

She drew herself up to her full five foot eight inches "Don't 'hi' me," she spat out, the power of her rage forcing him to step back. He found his balance when his backside hit against one of the dining room chairs.

"Where the *hell* have you been?" Her words echoed off the paneled walls and into the surrounding rooms.

There was the sound of rapid footsteps above him, and Matt turned to see Hester standing on the second-floor landing. "He's been a guest in my home." She proceeded down the stairs, never taking her eyes off Angie. "And I don't cotton to anyone yelling at my guests, especially in my home." When she reached the bottom step, she crossed her arms over her chest. A quiet rage simmered in her azure blue eyes.

Matt glanced back at Angie and saw the flames of fury in hers.

Lord help me, he gulped.

18

THE RUMBLE IN THE JUNGLE

THE GOOD LORD apparently heard Matt's prayer and, in His or Her benevolence, sent a miracle down from heaven.

The doorbell rang.

For a moment, everyone froze. Then Lyle, ever the gal Friday, hurried forward. "That must be Bishop Hamlin," Lyle said brightly. "He called to say he would stop by this afternoon to visit Mrs. Duff and her mother." Lyle stopped halfway through the dining room—a distance that happened to be the midpoint between Hester at the bottom of the stairs and Angie, who stood in the archway—but he spoke to Matt. "Preacher, I bet you could use a pot of tea after such a chilly morning. Why don't you take your fiancée into the study, and I'll bring in a tray with some cookies for you." He turned to Angie. "I consider myself a bit of a baker, but I'm sure your skills in the kitchen far outpace mine. The preacher tells me you own your own restaurant."

The doorbell rang again, and the big man smiled. "Head on into the study. I'll be right with you."

He proceeded to the front door, but Hester interrupted his

escape. "Put three cups on that tray, Lyle."

He stopped but didn't turn around. His shoulders sagged. "Yes, ma'am."

——————

ANGIE WAS FURIOUS. Yes, she knew she shouldn't have yelled in this woman's house. Yes, she knew that she had caused a scene. But she had good reason to be furious with Matt. How dare he go against almost every order his doctor had given him? And the fact that complete strangers had witnessed her explosion only made her angrier.

The old lady led them through some fancy French doors into a room tucked under the grand stairway. What was her name again? Hester somebody. She certainly had money, Angie realized. The diamond broach she was wearing on her black cowl-neck sweater was huge. And from the looks of the house, this woman didn't accept anything but expensive. Hester headed straight for a desk that looked bigger than two horse troughs and sat down stiffly in the leather chair behind it. She nodded briskly at the tandem leather reception chairs fronting the desk.

Matt sat first, leaning his cane on the chair. Angie plopped onto the remaining chair and lifted her chin defiantly toward the home's owner. "What I have to say to Matt doesn't concern you."

"Then you shouldn't have yelled so loud that everyone in the house heard. I'm Hester Honeywell, by the way. And you are?"

Matt cleared his throat. "Hester, this is my fiancée, Angie O'Day."

"I can speak for myself," Angie snapped at him.

"That much is obvious," Hester smiled wryly. "But do you

have anything of value to say?"

Angie's face went scarlet—she wasn't sure if it was from shame or fury. "I have plenty to say."

"That wasn't my question." Hester leaned her elbows on the desk. "I'm talking value. What exactly is your beef, Ms. O'Day?"

Fine, Angie thought. Matt wasn't lifting a finger to defend her or to get rid of the arguably elegant woman. She turned in her chair and stared bullets his way. "On Tuesday, I watched you say a prayer on the front lawn of the Capitol. On TV."

"Now, Angie," he said.

"Thousands were in the audience, hundreds of thousands could've seen it on TV. And I said to myself, is this what Dr. Ryan had in mind when she told you not to get roused up about anything? That excitement is the last thing you need?" Angie jabbed a thumb at her chest. "I'm the one who watched you suffer a stroke last December in the middle of your sermon. *I'm* the one who nursed you through your paralysis, your confusion, your feeble health situation. But no. On Tuesday, there you were, speaking in front of a crowd of thousands. And what was the phone call I got two hours later? Oh, yeah. You had another stroke!"

"I did not have a stroke," Matt said.

"That's not what Deshawn said on the phone." She felt her eyes begin to fill with tears, and she fought them off. "It wasn't until hours later that I learned you'd been released from the hospital and sent here."

"I'm sorry it happened that way."

"Me, too!" This time, a tear did slip out, and she swiped it away. "I called Dr. Ryan's office Wednesday morning to get the real scoop."

When Hester's eyes rounded at the news, Angie huffed. "Don't get on your high horse about HIPAA. Matt gave me medical power of attorney way back after he got part of his skull blown off last August." Her eyes flashed. "Oh, yeah. That happened. He's got a plate in his head, did he tell you that? Trying to get all the blood vessels back to work around that foreign object is hard enough. Add high blood pressure, acceler-ated adrenaline and other chemical reactions from stress, and you have a high risk of stroke." She lasered a fierce look back at Matt. "She assured me you didn't have a stroke, although your blood pressure and heart rate were through the roof. But no. No stroke. At least not yet. No, the reason the ambulance was called was because you fell. *And you didn't have your cane with you.* Oh, and the fact you had alcohol in your system might've had something to do with the fall. Alcohol?" She demanded. "What the hell were you thinking?"

Out of the corner of her eye she saw Hester's cheeks redden, but brushed that aside when Matt started to speak. "Angie, I didn't have a stroke. I admit that the day was a little overwhelming, but things were out of my control."

"I have spent the last six months of my life taking care of you. I have driven you to Austin for physical therapy, then worked you through all the exercises they gave you. I've been with you at your doctor's appointments and lab tests. I've taken care of sending in all your insurance stuff and played footsie with the hospital and doctors' billing departments. I have made sure you've had your meds, food, clean clothing—whatever you need. And the first time I let you out of my sight, you're telling me you couldn't man up and take control of your own well-being for one lousy day?"

She felt a twist of nausea in her gut and stood up to walk it off. "Then today. I got here early—a quarter after nine, I think—because I heard an ice storm is heading this way. I was informed you were at your doctor's appointment. No problem. That Lyle guy settled me in with some coffee and blueberry muffins. Then ten o'clock came and went. Ten thirty. At ten forty-five, I called the doctor's office. They said you'd left an hour earlier, and they didn't know where you'd gone." She stopped to glare at him. "Why the hell didn't you come straight back here? You're supposed to be resting, not gallivanting around town." Tears steaked down her face. "I can't do this anymore, Matt. I can't. I will not live my life in fear, especially when you don't follow the doctor's instructions."

She turned to Hester. "Was that of any value to you? Because it sure was of value to me!"

Angie stumbled for the door and opened it, just as Lyle was heading through the dining room with the tea tray. She allowed him to enter, then turned back to the study. "I'm going for a walk. After all, I don't want to waste anyone's time by saying something that has no value."

———

MATT BOWED HIS HEAD. He had deserved every word that had come out of Angie's mouth.

"Preacher." Hester's voice was soft. Calm. "The circumstances you were faced with—"

"No. She's right." The severity of Angie's words were only now beginning to set in.

She'd said she couldn't do this anymore. Couldn't do what? Take care of him? Be with him?

Couldn't love him?

Lyle set the tea tray on Hester's desk. "I'm so sorry, Preacher. I should've let her know you were with Connor. But she didn't ask—well, she might've come looking for me, but I had to go up to the attic to get the turkey fryer and all that stuff. I was so busy preparing tonight's dinner that I didn't give her a second thought."

Matt leaned forward on his elbows on the chair's armrests. His heart was racing, and he felt the dreaded pulse echoing in his skull. He knew what that meant. He had to go upstairs and get some meds to calm him down. "I think I'll go to my room for a while. Take it easy."

"I've already taken the things she brought for you upstairs," Lyle said. "I can bring some tea up to you. It's already made." He gestured at the tray.

"No. Thanks. I think I'll lie down." Matt pushed himself off the chair and wrangled his cane from the armrest.

Lyle, his face hangdog, turned his attention to Hester. "Mrs. Duff asked if it would be okay to have Bishop Hamlin stay for lunch in her room. I'm making a tortellini salad— there'll be plenty to go around."

"Of course," she said. "If that's not too much trouble for you."

Bishop Hamlin, Matt thought. Perhaps he had some ideas on Reverend Duff's disappearance. "When he's done, could you give me a call on the cell? If I'm up to it, I'd like a quick word with him."

"Sure thing, Preacher," Lyle nodded.

Matt had little energy for the walk to the mudroom. When he entered the elevator, he leaned back against its wall as it ascended. All the while, the fear of losing Angie spread through him like the sudden onset of the flu. His stomach roiled. His head ached.

His eyes watered.

The elevator opened to the third-floor landing, and he headed left to his tower room. He closed the door quietly behind him and shuffled over to the bed. He sat down, not sure he even had the strength to lift his legs onto the mattress, and tried to even out his breathing.

"What do you mean, no?"

Matt started. Where was that voice coming from?

"I have a right to know what's going on," it continued.

Lambert, Matt realized. His voice was muffled, as if coming through a tube. *"This is not what we agreed to."*

There was a moment of silence, then a strident, *"Shit!"* Footsteps, pacing. Echoing.

The sounds were coming from behind the slatted rocker across from the bed. Matt stood as Lambert began talking again. *"He hung up on me. That brat hung up on me!"*

Matt moved to the rocker as he heard the sound of the toilet flushing. He quietly pulled the chair aside. That's when he saw it. The antique cast iron wall vent.

On the wall shared with the bathroom.

Matt heard the familiar beeps of a cell phone, then *"Reverend Meade, please."* Lambert's voice was clearer now. *"Pastor Lambert."*

Reverend Meade? The Santa Claus pastor with the Satanic eyes? Matt wanted to sit down in the rocker to have a closer listen but didn't dare risk the old chair squeaking.

"What do you mean he's busy? You tell him this is important. I cannot stay in this house one more minute."

Water ran in the sink, and Matt assumed Lambert was washing his hands. Then came the rustle of a towel being pulled off a rack.

There was a pause, then Lambert's desperate voice. *"Robert, you have to get me out of this house. These people are crawling down my neck."*

A moment of silence, then Lambert again. *"Keep an eye on things? They think I have something to do with Duff's disappearance!"*

Another gap, then, *"Not for this long!"*

Pacing footsteps started up again.

"I can't go home. The police still have my car. That idiot kid—"

The pacing stopped. *"I am calm! Tell me what's going on!"* A pause, then another *"Shit!"*

Matt looked at the grate, dumbfounded. Meade was involved with Duff's disappearance? Lambert was supposed to keep an eye on things? What things? The investigation trying to find Duff? And who was this "kid"?

The door to the bathroom opened, then slammed shut. A similar pair of sounds occurred moments later at the far end of the hall.

Matt pulled his cell phone from his pocket, checked his "recent" list and tapped one of the numbers. The phone rang only once.

"Preacher?" came Connor's voice over the cell. "Is everything okay?"

"I need something, if you have the time," Matt answered.

"Sure. I've already wrapped all the bushes and brought the plants into the solarium. The ice storm, you know. What do you need?"

"If Pastor Lambert leaves the house, could you follow him maybe? See where he goes?"

"Sure," Connor said. "You think he's up to something?"

"I don't know. But keep this under your hat, okay? Don't tell anybody—well, unless Hester asks."

"You bet, Preacher."

Matt moved to the bed, took his meds and sat down, his thoughts turning back to Angie. Where had she gone and when would she come back? *Would* she come back? She could have gotten into her truck and headed straight back to Wilks.

He kicked off his shoes and struggled to get his legs on the soft, inviting comforter. It was long moments before his meds kicked in and he fell into a fitful sleep.

19

EATING CROW

ANGIE'S WALK took her to the Governor's Mansion, around the Capitol building, then back toward Hester Honeywell's home. With each step, the weather turned chillier and her temper cooled. By the time she reached Hester's front door, Angie's soul was filled with regret. She never should've yelled at Matt. She never should've yelled at all. She must seem like a piece of trailer trash to everyone who witnessed her despicable behavior.

The front door was locked, so she was forced to ring the doorbell. Great, she thought. Exactly what she wanted to do. Rouse the household. Again.

A few moments later, Lyle opened the door. "Sorry," he said. "I was washing some vegetables for tonight." He stood back to let her pass.

"Thanks." She shrugged out of her jacket and hung it on the hall tree. "Where's Matt?"

"Up in his room," Lyle answered. "But Hester asked to see you when you got back."

Hester was the last person Angie wanted to see, but why put off the inevitable. The woman deserved an apology.

She followed Lyle to the study. He gestured her in, then headed for the kitchen.

"Come in, Miss O'Day." Hester sat in one of two leather recliners in front of an old potbelly stove. "I thought you might be chilly when you got back," she explained. "Lyle's going to bring us some hot chocolate."

Angie moved to the empty recliner but didn't sit down. "I owe you an apology for my behavior. I'm sorry I disturbed you and your household." She lowered her eyes. "I'm sorry I yelled at Matt."

Angie felt Hester's gaze on her, and there was silence between the two for a long moment.

"Let's talk," Hester finally said.

Angie looked up. "I don't think I can deal with a lecture right now, although I deserve one. I need to talk with Matt."

Hester held up a hand. "No lecture intended. Just a simple conversation while you warm up and we have our hot chocolate."

Reluctantly, Angie sat down. The stove gave off a surprising amount of heat, which felt good. She rubbed her hands: they were colder than she'd realized.

Lyle entered with a tray of steaming cups and small cookies. "Tea bites," he explained. "With a hint of cardamom." He passed a mug to each woman, then left.

Hester sat back in her chair and blew on her cocoa to cool it. "Do you know why so many men are misogynists?"

The question caught Angie totally off guard. "You mean women haters?"

Hester nodded. "Because they are afraid of women."

Angie set down her cup, afraid she would spill it. She

wasn't sure whether to laugh or to humor an old woman who was obviously going senile. "Afraid?"

"Because we're better than them," Hester answered. "We're smarter. We have a physical allure, a pull on them that they can't control. We carry babies in our wombs and birth them. They are intimidated by our power."

Angie's jaw slackened. "You're serious."

Hester smiled. "Of course I am, my dear." She sipped her chocolate. "We are the reason they've survived this long. If not for us, they would've killed each other by now." Hester lifted her chin. "That's why God created us, you know. Us women, I mean. We were to be a "helpmate" to man. How can you help someone if you're not wiser than them? More resilient? More insightful? As for the mate thing, well, that's obvious. To survive, God's human race needed to make babies. He created a bait— women—that men couldn't refuse."

Was this heresy or clarity? Angie couldn't decide. "So," she said slowly. "You..." she didn't want to say hate, "...don't care for men?"

"Of course I do. I'm simply not intimidated by them. And I realize I have a power they can't understand." Hester smiled. "I see I've given you something to think about. At least, I hope you will. But here's one more thing I'd like you to consider."

Oh God, Angie thought. What next?

"Then there are the men who conquer their fear and fall in love with us. And we become even more important to them. It takes a very strong, courageous man to love a woman. And when he does, she is everything to him."

"What is your point?"

Hester put down her mug and looked intently into Angie's eyes. "My point is, you hold great power over your fiancé."

Angie thought for a moment. "You're saying I need to be more careful in how I deal with him."

"There is that." Hester's smile was wry. "But how you see him is a huge influence on how he sees himself."

"I see him..." she stopped. "I see him the way he is." Her brows furrowed. "Truthfully."

"Ah, yes. Truth." Hester chuckled. "Quid est veritas?"

Now Angie was totally confused. "What?"

"John 18:38. 'What is truth?' Jesus said that."

Angie chuckled. "Now, you are so over my head."

"May I be honest?"

"Sure. Why not."

"Your truth is that Matt is an invalid. He's been shot, he's had a stroke—well, you know the drill. Am I right?"

"Yes. Exactly."

Hester leaned forward. "My truth is very different from yours. In the short time he has been in my home, he has been observant, decisive, witty and caring. On top of his game, as it were. Sure, he moves a little slow, but he is of strong mind and driven to work for justice."

Angie was taken aback, then shook it off. "You've only known him for what? Two days?"

"And I am telling you what I saw. And there's something else."

"What?"

"The minute you started yelling at him, he changed into a shadow of the man he's been. His shoulders slumped. He limped more. He became introverted and wounded."

Angie felt like she'd been slapped.

Apparently, Hester picked up on Angie's reaction. "I'm not trying to scold you. I'm trying to tell you that you have an incredible power over Matt. You've been looking at him as a patient for so long, you've stopped looking at him as a man. Your man. The man you used to be in love with."

The truth of those words, the fear she had been denying for

months, slammed into her. Angie felt the blood drain from her face. "I still love him," she whispered, desperately wanting it to be true.

"Of course you do," Hester said gently. "But you've been so stressed taking care of him, I think you've forgotten that you are in love with him."

Angi leaned forward, elbows on knees, head down. "Maybe. I hadn't thought about that."

"I understand." Hester stood and patted Angie's shoulder once. "You know, I like you, Angie."

Angie raised her head. "What?"

Hester headed for the study door. "I wanted you to know that." She closed the French doors behind her.

20

BISHOP HAMLIN

A TAP on the door woke Matt. "Yes?" he called, his voice hoarse with sleep.

"It's me, Preacher." Lyle came in and closed the door behind him. "You wanted me to let you know when Bishop Hamlin was ready to leave."

Matt gingerly swung his legs out of bed. "You didn't need to come up here. You could've called me."

"I wanted to make sure you were okay."

Matt rubbed his eyes. "Yeah. I'm okay."

"Then may I suggest you head for the solarium? I've turned on the heat lamps. It's quite beautiful out there when it snows."

"Snows?"

"Well, sleets, anyway. When you're done with the Bishop, I'll bring you some food."

He turned to leave.

"Lyle," Matt said quickly. He was afraid to ask the question, but he had to know. "Did Angie come back?"

"Yes. About a half hour ago."

"And she's still here?"

"She's in Hester's study."

"Thanks. I'll be right down."

The door closed, and Matt let out a sigh of relief. Okay, she's here. That was a good sign, right?

———

THE POT BELLY stove's flame had turned to glowing embers before Angie was ready to leave the study. Hester saw a different man when she looked at Matt. Could Angie?

She pushed through the double doors and headed for the kitchen. She found the person she was looking for peeling potatoes. "Hey, Lyle," she said by way of greeting. "Any idea where I might find Matt?"

"He's in the solarium with Bishop Hamlin." Lyle wiped his hands on a towel. "After their visit, I was going to bring the preacher a sandwich. Would you like one too?"

"That would be nice. Thank you."

He led her down the hall. When they got close to the master bedroom's door, Lyle put a finger to his lips. "That's where Mrs. Duff and her mother are staying. She's on bedrest." They shimmied past a wheelchair pushed against the wall. "Hopefully, she'll be up to joining us for dinner."

When they reached the solarium's double glass doors at the end of the hall, Lyle started to open them, but Angie shook him off.

"I'll take it from here," she said.

He sent her an understanding nod and headed back to the kitchen.

The solarium, is that what he called it? It looked more like a fancy greenhouse to Angie. Artificial grass stretched across the floor of the glassed-in, thirty-foot-long structure. Along the way were plotted flowers, bricked planters filled with shrubs and, if she wasn't mistaken, an elevated, circular herb garden in the center. White wrought iron lawn furniture was arranged in conversation-inducing patterns down the twelve-foot-wide expanse.

Matt, distinguishable by his unkempt sandy brown hair, sat in a chair facing away from her. Another man, elderly with gray hair encircling a shiny pink bald spot, sat beside Matt. Must be the bishop Lyle had mentioned, she surmised.

She studied Matt for a moment, noting his back was straight, his gestures strong. What had Hester said earlier? *On top of his game.* Angie saw the truth of Hester's words now. Had he been this forceful before and she simply hadn't noticed?

She cracked the door open to hear what had him so animated.

"Reverend Duff was going to leave you some papers when he came to St. George's to pray on Tuesday?" Matt asked.

"Actually, I think his 'quiet meditation' was more of a ruse to get the papers to me. He was very secretive about the whole thing." The elderly man had a high-pitched voice, almost child-like in its tenor.

"Why not give it to you personally? You said you expected to see him after the inauguration."

"Yes, but we would've been surrounded by other pastors. He wanted my advice on four upcoming sermon series, and it was important to him that no one know its subject matter."

"What were these four series supposed to cover?"

The elderly bishop shrugged. "When I returned to St. George's that afternoon, there was no envelope pushed under my office door. I never received whatever it was he wanted me to comment on."

Angie studied Matt as he questioned the bishop. His voice

was firm. Commanding, even. His train of thought, sharp as an arrow. What were they talking about anyway?

Then it hit her, and the knowledge almost bowled her over.

Matt was on a case.

The cop in her fiancé had surfaced, and Matt had come alive again.

The man with whom she had fallen in love had returned.

———

THE BISHOP WAS HOLDING something back, Matt realized. He had sidestepped Matt's question.

"I understand Reverend Duff was a determined man."

Bishop Hamlin chuckled. "He was a man on a mission. God's mission, to be sure."

"And that mission was?"

"I couldn't say."

Definitely holding something back, Matt decided. He tried a different tack. "What do you know about Reverend Meade?

Meade's face relaxed. "Big church. Incredible influence, not just in Austin, or even in Texas. He sits on several major Evangelical College Boards of Trustees across the country."

"Yes," Matt said. *Time to play a hunch.* "I got the impression that he and Senator Womack were very close."

The question made Bishop Hamlin shoot out of his chair. "Joined at the hip," he said abruptly, then glanced at his watch. "I really must go. It's getting late."

"Of course." That was an unexpected knee-jerk reaction, Matt thought. He stood to shake the man's outstretched hand. "I know how important it is to have another pastor— a close friend—to consult with when faced with a spiritual dilemma. You said that you and Reverend Duff have talked many times about your beliefs, your concerns. Surely you have some idea what Reverend Duff thought his mission for God was."

Bishop Hamlin glared as he considered his answer, then finally spoke. "He wanted to set the record straight." With that, he gave a quick nod and turned toward the door.

And there stood Angie.

21

AN UNDERSTANDING REACHED

ANGIE SAW the transformation in Matt the moment he set eyes on her. He lowered his head; his shoulders slumped. The man he had been moments before turned into a discouraged-looking, beaten-down patient.

And it was her fault.

She went to him, pushed his shoulders back, wrapped her arms around his neck and kissed him.

Matt was stunned. He dropped his cane, pulled her to him with one arm and raised his other to clutch her flowing red hair. He deepened the kiss. *My God,* he thought. *It's been so long.*

The sound of squeaking wheels seeped through Angie's lustful fog and she pulled back, breathless.

"I'm sorry," came Lyle's voice from the doorway. "I brought lunch, but—"

"No, that's okay." Her eyes locked on Matt's. "My cop here needs to get some food in him. He's working a case."

They ate their lunch as Lyle hovered. Finally, Angie pushed away from the table. "Those po' boys were delicious. What did you put in the mayo?"

Lyle winked. "It's remoulade sauce. With smashed garlic."

"Wow. Thanks for the tip." She winked back.

"Oops! I almost forgot." Lyle pulled the last plate from the cart and removed its lid with a flourish. "Dessert." He put the plate of thick, marbled brownies on the table. "Let me know if you need anything else." Lyle pushed the cart out of the room.

Angie waited for him to close the door before she pulled her chair closer to Matt and took his hand. "I'm sorry I yelled at you," she said, giving it a squeeze.

Matt smiled sadly. "Everything you said was true."

"From the point of view of a nurse, maybe. But I'm not a nurse, and you're not a patient. I'm sorry I've treated you like that. I'm sorry I've forgotten who we," she squeezed his hand again. "—who *we* are."

Matt shook his head. "It's hard to remember that kind of thing when you're emptying your beloved's catheter bag and cleaning his ass as needed."

"That was only for a little while. Because you worked hard to get better." She lowered her eyes. "I haven't given you credit for how strong you've been. Instead, I've beaten you down by reminding you of your weaknesses." She squared her shoulders. "Those days are over. When I saw you talking to that bishop guy, I saw the strong, motivated man I fell in love with. And I realized where I'd gone wrong."

Matt leaned back, studying her.

She continued. "You've always fought a battle inside your-self. Are you a cop who doles out justice or a preacher who doles out love? And suddenly I got it."

"Got what?" He chuckled, but there was no humor in the sound. "You figured out which person I am?"

"The truth is, you're both." She lifted his hand to her lips and kissed it. "You have to *be* both to be *you*."

"And you realized this how?"

"When you were talking to the bishop, I knew immediately what had brought the cop in you back. You're on a case. And for the first time in months, you looked whole."

Matt drew a deep breath. He hadn't really thought of Reverend Duff's disappearance as a "case." He simply wanted to know what happened to the man whose vanishing act had forced Matt into the predicament in which he now found himself.

"You can't deny it, Matt. You were using every weapon in that cop arsenal of yours to find out what the bishop was keeping from you."

Angie's beautiful smile was smug. He hadn't seen that slyly sexy look on her face for a long time.

"Fill me in," she continued. "What are you investigating and how is it that you're involved?"

A familiar feeling of belonging swept over him. This is what he and Angie did. They talked. About everything.

Including murder.

He settled back in his chair. "It started the morning of the inauguration. I was up on the Governor's Mansion's balcony..."

He told her how he'd been pressed into giving the benediction, renewed his acquaintance with Hester at the BBQ, then was backed into the elevator by a crush of unfriendly reporters. He gave her a timeline of what they knew of Reverend Duff's movements the morning of the inauguration, including his visit to St. George Episcopal where Bishop Hamlin presided, then brought her up to speed on the suspicious actions of Pastor Lambert, Reverend Duff's assistant. He made sure he emphasized it was James W.'s suggestion that Matt keep an eye on things at Hester's home, and how that got him involved with the police. "And the longer this drags on without finding him, the darker things look. I can't imagine what Mrs. Duff is going through. She was already having a difficult time with her pregnancy. Preeclampsia. Now her husband has been missing for almost three days. I don't know how she's dealing with it all."

"That's a whole lot of stuff happening right here in this house," Angie said.

"I know. I know." He gave her a rueful smile. "I'm supposed to be resting."

Her lips twitched. "I meant you're in a perfect position to see every angle. Sounds like divine intervention to me." She reached for a brownie and took a bite. Her eyes widened in delight. "This is delicious."

Matt grinned. "The food here is pretty amazing." He picked up a brownie; it was still warm. He broke off a piece. "Caramel?" he asked, as a gooey string of gold oozed from the chocolate confection.

"And dark chocolate chunks." Angie's eyes closed as she savored the taste. "Who is this Lyle, anyway?"

"He's Hester's accountant and chief cook and bottle washer. He and his partner, Connor, live above the garage in an apartment. Connor's the chauffeur and handyman around the place, when he's not going to law school. Hester depends on them for everything."

Her cell phone rang, and she pulled it from her jeans pocket. She looked at the caller ID. "It's Bo," she said.

Matt sighed. Bo probably needed her back at the Icehouse. He didn't want her to leave.

"That bad?" Angie asked into the phone. Matt came instantly alert. She saw his worried expression, then waved her hand that nothing was seriously wrong. "How long has it been sleeting?"

Matt shot a look outside at the lawn but saw no signs of ice.

"What's the forecast say?" She listened on the phone for a moment, then blew out her cheeks. "Well, heck. You don't have much of a choice. Shut her down." She looked out the solarium windows. "No, we're getting nothing here. It's cloudy. And getting colder. But no ice. Not even rain. Not yet, anyway."

Matt's mouth curved into a smile. She wasn't going to leave after all. He munched on Lyle's brownie as Angie and Bo talked a little more business. Finally, she hung up. "Guess I'm staying in Austin tonight."

He smiled and lifted the plate of brownies toward her. "Guess you have time for another."

"Guess I do." She took one. Bit into it. "The missing preacher's what had you so upset at the inauguration?"

Matt frowned. "Who told you that?"

"Bo. He said that after the ceremony was over you were upset about something. He asked you what it was, and you said you had to think on it. I was surprised to hear him say that. On the TV you looked fine when you said that prayer."

"I was okay with the prayer. I thought it went pretty well." No, it wasn't the prayer. It was Reverend Meade's reaction to it. *I know who you are, and I know what you're trying to do.* Matt felt the chill of the man's hate seep into his soul. He remembered the podium. The thumbs-up from James W. after the prayer. Returning to his seat. And that hateful, satanic glare of the well-respected clergyman.

"Matt, what's going on?"

He forced himself back to the present. "What do you mean?"

"You've turned into a nervous wreck right before my very eyes. Your face has paled, your eyes aren't focused. Your wringing your hands like you're covered in ants. What's this all about?"

He looked down at his hands and realized Angie was right. "It's nothing."

"Matt, you've gone from confident and relaxed to a ball of

nerves in less than two seconds. Whatever you were upset about on Tuesday is obviously still bothering you."

Of course it was the Reverend Meade thing. Matt brought his hand to his forehead and tried to scrub away the memory of the man's words.

"Matt. Talk to me."

He shook his head. "I'm being paranoid." he said. "Sometimes that comes with depression. It's nothing."

"Does it have anything to do with Reverend Duff's disappearance?"

"I didn't think so. Not until a little while ago." He forced his hands apart and rested them on the chair's armrests. "You remember I told you I overheard Lambert's phone calls today?"

"You said it sounded like he was talking to people who knew something about Reverend Duff's disappearance."

"And one of them is this man. Reverend Meade. Leads the largest nondenominational church in Austin. Very connected."

"And he's upset you?"

How to explain the gaping wound Meade had left in Matt's heart? "When I was a cop, I expected people to hate me—you know, hurt me or worse. I wasn't prepared for a man of the cloth to look at me like that."

The double doors opened behind them, and Lyle walked in.

"Sorry to bother you, Preacher, Angie. Connor called. Hester needs him to run some errands, and he was wondering if you could take over his watch on Lambert."

"Wait. What? Lambert left the house?" Matt started.

"He took a cab over to a bar on Fifth. Might've had a few. He was in there long enough. Then the taxi driver took him over to the Christian House of Love. Lambert went inside a few minutes ago. Connor's stickin' around to see if the cab brings Lambert back, but he can't stay. Angie, you've got a car, right?"

"A truck," she answered.

"Any chance the two of you can take over for Connor?"

Matt looked at Angie. "You game?"

"Sure." Angie picked Matt's cane off the floor. "I have to find someplace to hang tonight anyway."

Matt was already on his feet. "What exactly is the Christian House of Love?"

"It's a church over off Highway 360," Lyle answered.

"Whose church?" Matt asked, but he had a feeling he already knew the answer.

"Reverend Meade's."

Bingo.

22

THE CHASE

WITHIN MINUTES, Matt and Angie were driving southwest of Austin's downtown, heading out on the increasingly hilly Bee Caves Road. "How far out is this place?" Angie demanded, zooming around a chugging delivery truck.

Matt studied his cell phone screen. "Pretty far. Those restaurants back at the turn look like the last sign of commerce for miles."

"I'm not sure I want to be driving these roads when the ice storm hits."

Matt's cell rang. "It's Connor. I'll put him on speaker." He held the phone toward Angie so she could hear. "Hey, Connor," he said. "Angie and I are on our way to you now. We've crossed over 360 and are heading up toward Bee Cave."

"You've got a good ten minutes to go," Connor replied. "Still no sign of Lambert coming out of the church."

"That's good, I guess. The cab still there?"

"Still here."

Matt nodded. "Give me the rundown. What's happening?"

"I was lucky. Lambert called for the taxi from the kitchen,"

Connor answered. "I had plenty of time to get in the SUV to follow him."

"Did he go straight to Meade's church?" Matt asked.

"No." Connor chuckled.

"Where'd he go?"

"A bar. Over by the convention center. He was in there awhile. Came out looking pretty angry about something."

Angie lifted an eyebrow. Matt shrugged. "I guess he needed a drink?"

"Maybe," Connor said. "I think he was waiting for someone."

"What's the name of the bar?" Matt asked.

"The Oak and Horn. Sounds like a pub but looked more like a hunting lodge. Pretty derelict, though."

"Then he headed out to Meade's church?"

"Yep. Got here about a half hour ago. Been inside ever since."

"Where are you parked?"

"There's a barbeque place across the street and up the hill. I've got a bird's-eye view of the church from here. The restaurant's driveway is right across from the church's main entrance. The restaurant's parking lot is up the driveway. Perfect view overlooking the road below and the church."

"We'll be there ASAP." Matt disconnected the call.

"Why's Meade's church in the middle of nowhere? There's nothing out here," asked Angie.

"Pretty barren," Matt agreed. "Hardly any buildings, no bus stops, I haven't seen a gas station for a coupla miles." He took note of the steep incline on the left and the rugged hills on the right. "I never understood before why they say Austin is the start of the Hill Country. Now I get it."

Angie nodded to the gathering black clouds. "Storm's

coming in." She flipped on the truck's headlights. "How far to the church?"

"We should be able to see it once we clear the next hill." He studied the map on his phone more closely. "According to this, Westlake is only a few miles down the road from the church."

"Westlake?" she asked.

"Very high end. Lots of money. Jimmy had several fundraising events there for the governor's race." Matt nodded. "I guess that's where Meade gets a lot of his parishioners."

Angie turned her face toward him, but her eyes never left the road. "Who is this Reverend Meade? You and Bishop Hamlin were talking about him. Now Lambert's gone to see him. What's he got to do with Reverend Duff's disappearance?"

Matt snorted. "I wish I knew. But I know he doesn't like Reverend Duff, and I know he doesn't like me."

"Doesn't like you? How do you know that?"

"He told me." Matt straightened. "Hey, I think that's the church. Yeah. The Christian House of Love," he read off the wayside pulpit.

Ahead, built on the steep slope to the left of the road, a huge limestone structure cantilevered over the cliff. At first glance, the building, which had a footprint about a quarter of the size of a football field, appeared to be an auditorium of some sort. As they drew nearer, however, Matt could see the foundation-to-roof tall stained-glass windows on the structure's exterior walls. As they continued around the corner, a magnificent front edifice arched skyward, a stained-glass mosaic spanned the entire wall depicting a huge cross with a blindingly gold and silver dove at its center.

Angie let out a low whistle. "That took some money."

Matt was so busy gawking at the church, he almost forgot to

look for the barbeque restaurant's driveway. "Turn right," he said, pointing.

The gravel road had an almost straight-up incline, but they soon crested the hill. Sure enough, to the left of the log-cabin-styled restaurant was an empty parking lot, save for one black, luxury SUV parked at the far rail. Matt nodded. "That's Connor."

The SUV's driver-side window opened, and an arm came out to wave them over. Angie pulled up beside the vehicle.

Matt rolled down his window. "Thanks for following Lambert," he said.

Connor nodded. "No problem." He reached on the seat beside him, then handed a set of binoculars across the open window to Matt. "In case you need them." He looked around Matt toward Angie. "Lyle called. He said Hester has plenty of room at the house if you need a place to stay."

Angie leaned forward. "I don't want to impose."

"No imposition," Connor said. "Matt can tell you."

Matt nodded absently. His focus was on the church parking lot below. So far, no sign of Lambert. "Lambert's taxi is the silver Bronco?"

"Yep. Can you see the driver?"

Matt focused the lenses. "White male. Glasses. Talking on a phone. He keeps slapping the steering wheel."

"That's him," Connor said. "I think he's ticked off at Lambert. Probably wasn't expecting such a long haul."

Matt watched the driver get out of his car, the phone still close to his ear. He began pacing the length of the Bronco. "I see what you mean."

Connor leaned forward to continue his conversation with Angie. "Hester said to let you know that she's hosting a dinner party tonight for the governor and his parents."

"James W. and Elsbeth?"

Matt noted that her voice cracked a little. Though James W. and Angie had gotten along splendidly since finding out they were half-siblings, Elsbeth had never embraced Angie as a family member. Far from it.

"We weren't sure if you knew them," Connor said.

Matt offered a lopsided grin. "Everybody knows everybody in Wilks."

"Then I'll tell Lyle to put another plate on the table." Connor checked his watch. "I'd better get going."

Matt nodded. "Thanks again for your help."

"Anytime." With a wave, Connor put the SUV in reverse and drove away.

Matt focused the glasses back on the scene. First on the sculpted brass front doors of the church, then following the path over to the Bronco. The driver had now resorted to flailing his arms as he talked on the phone.

"I don't have any clothes to wear to a dinner party," Angie said. "I'll stay in my room."

Matt brought down the binoculars. "You know that would hurt James W.'s feelings. Besides, the poor guy has been stuck with Elsbeth for three straight days."

Angie pouted. "He lives with her, doesn't he?"

"And makes sure he puts in a full day's work plus overtime."

She ground her jaw. "I suppose I could pick up a pair of slacks somewhere."

"That's the spirit." Matt brought the binoculars back up to his eyes. After a moment, he heard her punching something into her phone. "What are you looking for?"

"The nearest Walmart." A few more taps. "Found it. Not too far from Hester's. I'll head there after we finish tailing Lambert. Which reminds me. What was the name of that bar Lambert went to?"

Matt paused. "The Oak and...something?"

Angie nodded. "The Oak and Horn." Again, she tapped into her phone. "I found it. Right across from the convention center like Connor said. I'll go to the website." A moment of silence, then. "He wasn't kidding. What a dive. It makes the Icehouse look like a four-star restaurant."

"Hold on," Matt said quickly. He adjusted the lenses on the binoculars. "That's him. Lambert's coming out of the church."

Matt and the glasses moved as one as he followed Lambert to the silver Bronco, where he handed the driver a large wad of cash. The two of them got back in the car, and Matt heard the Bronco's engine roar to life. The cab driver pulled a U-turn and gunned it toward the parking lot exit.

Angie slammed the truck into reverse, backed up, then made a beeline for the graveled driveway. They got to the bottom of the hill in time to see the silver Bronco turn onto Bee Caves Road and head toward Austin.

Ten minutes later, with the storm clouds overhead roiling with menace, the Bronco careened down Cesar Chavez Street toward the convention center. Angie did her best to follow the speeding car but still hang back far enough not to be noticed. So far, much to Matt's relief, Lambert had not turned around in the Bronco's back seat to check if he was being followed.

The Bronco sped through a yellow light, and Angie was forced to stop at an intersection only blocks from the convention center. She rolled her shoulders and took a deep breath. "Can you see him?" she asked.

Matt nodded. "It looks like he turned left at the second light down."

"Dang," she said. "I should've run the red."

"No. You did the right thing."

The light turned green. Angie gunned her truck down the street, then turned left at the second light, her wheels screeching.There was no silver Bronco in sight. "I lost him." She slapped the wheel with her hand.

Matt's focus, however, was drawn to a shabby, brown building down the street. "I think we found the bar. Pull over."

Angie pulled over and squinted at the sign hanging precariously over the door. "I can't make it out."

Matt picked up the binoculars and studied the faded paint on the sign. "The Oak and Horn. There's man's image carved on it. Looks like he has horns—"

Before he could say anymore, Lambert came banging out the front door and took an immediate right up the street. He turned at the corner.

Angie pulled forward in time to catch Lambert walking up to the silver Bronco waiting for him at the curb. The driver gestured to Lambert as he climbed in the back seat. It wasn't a wave of hello. The Bronco sped off.

"We're good," Matt said, as Angie reached for the stick shift. "I know where they're going."

"How?"

"That driver's had enough of Lambert for one day. They're going back to Hester's."

23

THE OAK AND HORN

MATT WAS right about Lambert's destination. As the Bronco stopped to let Lambert out at the front of the mansion, Angie drove around to the back, where Matt went in through the garage. Her next stop was the nearby Walmart, where she found a pair of black slacks, a sweater and a few toiletries needed for her unplanned overnight stay. When she walked out of the Walmart, a gust of wind and roar of thunder greeted her. The ice storm was coming, but she had one more errand to run before heading back to Hester Honeywell's.

The front of the Oak and Horn was anything but inviting. Besides the faded sign that hung precariously above the door, the building's brown siding was rotted and the windows behind the iron bars were filthy. No cars were parked in the empty street out front, but Angie noted an opened, rusty-gated driveway to the building's side. Maybe the regulars parked in a back lot.

Angie hurried through the ice-cold rain to the front door, shoved it open to the sound of creaking hinges and took in the dark interior of the Oak and Horn. Two dust-covered, cobwebbed antler chandeliers cast a yellowish light on the ripped-up, plaid-upholstered chairs and couches spread around the room. A ten-foot-tall stuffed stag reared on its hind legs, guarding the lone window to her right. Directly ahead and spanning the fifteen-foot width of the building was a well-worn bar, its surface scratched and stained. Above the bar, a mounted water buffalo's head on one side and a twelve-point elk's head on the other, was a bronze plaque engraved with the image of a man with antlers growing from his head and a horn pressed to lips.

The bartender, a muscular twenty-something woman, was the only person in the place. She turned from watching a TV mounted in a far corner. Her eyebrows shot up at the sight of Angie. "You want somethin'?"

Angie headed for one of the tattered leather stools fronting the bar. "A Lone Star." Though the comment seemed casual, it was a determined choice. First, Angie had no desire to drink anything out of a glass for fear it hadn't been washed in six months, and God only knew what the icemaker was spitting out. Besides, a long-neck bottle could make for a heckuva weapon if things went south.

The bartender pulled the beer from a fridge, popped off the cap and set the drink in front of Angie. Fast service, Angie noted. A closer inspection showed the woman's face was clean with modest makeup, her blonde hair swept out of her face with a blue bandanna. Her orange V-neck T-shirt was freshly washed, though a few sizes too small, and except for the vine-like tattoo sneaking down between the woman's breasts, Angie figured she'd have no problem finding a better place to tend bar than this dive.

The bartender was studying Angie just as closely, so Angie decided to make some conversation. "Women's volleyball?"

"The guys are gone, so I get to watch what I want."

Angie looked around. "This place seems pretty empty. That cuz of the weather?"

"No. They're all headin' out to the Homestead."

Angie wondered what that meant, but thought it was too early to press. Instead she took a swig of her beer. Ice cold. Nice.

"What are you doin' here?" the bartender asked.

Angie pulled her cell phone from her back pocket. "Gotta make some calls to find a place to bed down tonight." She made a show of calling up her phone directory, but in reality turned on her video to record their conversation. "I was up in Killeen visiting some friends. Listenin' to the radio on the way back, they said 71's closed between Smithville and Bastrop. I live on the other side of Bastrop. Decided to pull off the road and stay in Austin." She took another slug. "I'm Maeve, by the way." For some reason, she'd chosen to use her mother's name.

"Monica," nodded the bartender.

Angie decided to dip a toe into the information-gathering waters. She pointed her bottle at the bronze relief above the bar. "What's that?"

"Kinda like our logo. The Oak and Horn."

"Looks like the guy tooting the horn has horns growing out of his head. Or maybe branches from the overhanging tree?"

"No. That's Herne the Hunter." Monica chuckled. "A bunch of guys from around here have this like lodge-thing going. Formed this brotherhood of hunters based on a legend about a ghost who haunts a forest in Windsor, England."

Angie put down her beer. "That sounds totally weird."

"It is. They are." Monica tried to keep a straight face, but finally had to chuckle. "They are so into themselves. It's hysterical." Her eyes narrowed. "But they pay really well. They've run off a lot of bartenders, so they have to."

"Why haven't they run you off?"

"Cuz I'm tougher than them."

Angie glanced at Monica's well-toned biceps and nodded approvingly.

Behind her, the front door opened and slammed shut.

"Where are they?" a male voice demanded.

"The call came in around two o'clock. Harold snagged a buck."

Angie fought the urge to turn around. Instead, she started playing with her phone, pretending to tap in a text.

The man was at the bar in two loud strides. "Damn it. I've been in a mock trial all afternoon."

A law student, Angie decided. Probably at UT.

"Who are you?" He demanded.

It took a moment for Angie to realize the man was talking to her.

"Maeve." She turned to look at him. "Who are you?"

"What are you doing here?" He was only looking for answers. Not giving them.

Angie put the guy in his early twenties. Brown hair. Unremarkable features. More of a clerk's build than an outdoorsy type. Was he a member of this "lodge" Monica had talked about?

"She was on her way to Bastrop, but they closed down the roads," Monica intervened.

He still wasn't satisfied. "There's a lot nicer bars to land at than here."

"I'm not into nice bars," Angie said. "I drove by several of 'em. This place suits me fine." She decided to play one of her favorite cards. "Cuz I know good lookin' men—*real* men— hang out in these kinda places." The roof should open up and a lightning bolt from heaven strike her for telling such a lie. But from the look on the man's face, he was buying it. "What's your name, sugar?" she asked him.

"Hogg," he answered.

It took all of Angie's will not to burst out laughing.

"You better get your gear and head out to the Homestead, or you'll get iced in," Monica said.

"I'm going. But first, has a guy named Lambert been in here today?"

"Wearing a clerical collar?" Monica snorted. "Twice. Lookin' for you."

"Twice?"

"First time around two o'clock, second time around four. He was one angry puppy. What'd you do this time, Hogg?"

"That SOB called my father. My father! And he talked to Meade too. Do you know where Lambert's staying?"

"He said something about a honeycomb. No. That's not it. Well, honey something."

"Honeywell. Hester Honeywell. I should've figured that." He headed for the door but turned at the last minute. "Hey, darlin'."

Trying not to cringe, Angie turned around. "Yeah, sugar?" But her heart stopped when she saw the wall of pictures surrounding the door. Over a dozen photos of men, all hunters considering their camos and guns, who were grinning at the camera with...was that blood running from their mouths? And in their hands—what the hell were they holding?

"Stop by when you come back into town. I might be around," the guy was saying.

"Sure thing, sugar." *Not a snowball's chance in hell.*

He opened the door to leave and was slapped with the sting of sleet. He cursed under his breath and let the door slam behind him.

Angie turned back to the bartender. "Hog? Like a pig?"

"He's a pig all right," Monica said. "But Hogg is his real name."

"Geez." Angie shook her head. "What kind of parent would name their kid that?"

"Don't ask."

Angie took another sip from her beer, then poked a thumb over her shoulder. "What's up with all the photos back there?"

"Proof," said Monica.

"Proof of what?"

"Doing the deed."

Angie wanted to ask a follow-up, but Monica's gaze jerked to the TV. "Dadgum," she said. "Lousy ref."

Enough, Angie decided. Any more questions and the bartender would get suspicious. At least Angie would if their roles were reversed. She picked up her phone as if she was getting a text, then smiled broadly. "All right. I got a place to stay." She nodded at Monica, whose gaze was fixed on the TV, laid a five-dollar bill on the bar and headed for the door.

The closer she got to the photos, the more gruesome they looked. She had to show this to Matt. She raised her phone and did her best to focus on one or two in a close-up.

"Hey, whatcha doin' there?" Monica's voice had lost its friendly tone.

"Callin' up my GPS." Angie looked at the screen as if studying her map. "Congress Avenue is that way?" She pointed east, purposefully choosing the wrong direction.

"No. Back the other way." Monica's voice calmed slightly.

"Thanks." Angie gave her a wave and opened the door to a face full of sleet. "Stay warm," she called back to the bartender and jogged toward her truck.

24

FIRE!

MATT HADN'T REALIZED fresh cranberries popped open when they were cooked. Neither had he known that red wine, honey and ginger root were critical ingredients in making a cranberry sauce. After today, he had a much greater appreciation for the chemistry of cooking. "It's getting pretty thick," he called to Lyle, who was working at the island.

Lyle wiped his hands on his apron and came over to check the simmering glob Matt had created. "Looks good. Turn off the heat and stir in the black pepper." Lyle turned to Connor, who was chopping onions. "It's time for the stuffin' muffins to come out."

Connor hurried over to the double ovens. "Muffins coming out." He reached in for the casserole dish. "Brussels sprouts going in. And the bottom oven's ready for your potatoes." He checked his watch. "A quarter to five. The oil should be hot enough for the turkey." Connor hurried out the back door.

Lyle returned to the island, picked up the pastry bag filled with the Duchess potato concoction and began piping the potatoes into perfect circular swirls. "Preacher, that sauce goes in that bowl," he nodded to a thick cut glass vessel, "then put it in the freezer."

"Won't that melt the frozen stuff?"

"Gotta be chilled down. We won't leave it in there long."

"Lyle, I need you," called Connor from the back door.

"Be right back." Lyle almost trotted to the back door.

Matt did as he was told, then turned to survey the war-torn kitchen. Chaos had erupted a half hour ago, when Hester received a call from the governor asking if they could move dinner from six-thirty to five-thirty. Lyle had been in a panic ever since.

Matt pressed his lips together. Four forty-five? Where was Angie? He went over to the island to admire Lyle's handiwork. The Duchess potatoes, loaded with cheese and garlic and nutmeg, were works of art.

The front doorbell rang.

Matt wiped his hands on his apron—Lyle had insisted he wear one—and went to answer it. A surge of relief passed through him when he opened the door to find Angie standing on the other side. He took one look at the Walmart bag in her hands and nodded. "You should have enough time to get changed. Where've you been?"

"Hello to you, too." She hung her jacket on the coat rack. "What's the rush?"

"Change of plans. Jimmy needs us to eat at five-thirty. Hors d'oeuvres at five. He's gotta get on a call or something."

Angie shook the ice from her hair. "Oh."

"Lyle said your bedroom's upstairs, last door on the right."

"Preacher!" Apparently, Lyle had returned to the kitchen. "Where are you?"

"I'm in the parlor. Angie just got back," Matt hollered back.

"I need help plating the anti-pasta!" Lyle was sounding more rattled by the minute.

"On my way!" Matt kissed Angie's cheek. "I've got to get back to work."

"Wait a minute," Angie called after him. "I've got some stuff to tell you."

"Matt, please?" Lyle called.

Angie held up her hands in surrender. "Go. I'll tell you later."

———

ANGIE WAS TOUCHING up her lipstick when she heard the downstairs doorbell ring. She hit off the bathroom light and headed back into her assigned bedroom to put her boots back on.

Hester had given her a lovely corner suite on the second floor. The walls were papered in a hunter green pattern, the furniture white, the linens in light sage and white patterns. She loved the tower sitting room niche, and the view out the front window made her feel like she was living in a treehouse; the side window overlooking the alley, not so much. She zipped up her boots, pulled the pant legs over them and headed for the door.

A flash behind her stopped her in her tracks. She ran to the side window and looked down into the alley.

Fire!

A four-foot flame was shooting skyward from a steel pot positioned on the driveway leading out to the alley.

She tore out of the room and down the grand staircase. She heard voices in the parlor to her right but headed straight for the kitchen. Lyle was at the island, plating hors d'oeuvres.

"Fire!" she kept her voice low, but intense. "Where's your fire extinguisher?"

"Fire?" Olives flew across the island. "Where?"

"In the driveway. A big pot—"

"My turkey!" Lyle rushed toward the back door.

———

CONNOR WAS PUTTING the last of the glassware on the bar he'd set up in the parlor when the front doorbell rang. "Preacher, can you get that?"

"Sure." Matt placed the last knife and spoon on the dining room table and hurried to open the front door.

"Preacher!" James W. took him in a bear hug. "You're a sight for sore eyes."

"Elsbeth?" Matt whispered.

"You have no idea." James W. loosened his grip and stepped back to let Elsbeth inside. "Let me get your coat, dear."

"Jimmy," Matt extended his hand. "How's the new job?"

The new governor winked. "Well, you know, the first few days are kind of slow."

Hester appeared in the archway. "Welcome, everyone."

As hellos were shared, Matt became aware of a commotion coming from the kitchen. Apparently, Connor heard it as well. He frowned, then motioned for Matt to come over to the bar. "Stay here," Connor whispered. "Keep things calm." Then he was out the door in a flash.

Calm? What was going on?

"I'm sorry for moving up the schedule," Jimmy was saying to Hester. "The ice isn't too bad in the city, but out in the rural areas—well, there are a lot of electric lines down, closed roads. I'm getting a status report at six-thirty."

The Novaks had come dressed for the cold. James W. and Jimmy both sported V-neck sweaters over plaid shirts and dark pants. Elsbeth wore moss-colored knit tunic and matching slacks. For her part, Hester looked elegant in a black, calf-length sweater dress. Matt felt woefully underdressed in jeans and a long-sleeved polo.

"No problem." Hester's smile was confident. "I'm glad you're here, so I can finally have a nice chat with your adorable mother. Mrs. Novak, welcome to my home."

Elsbeth beamed. "Thank you for inviting us. Call me Elsbeth, please."

"Shall we have a cocktail?" Hester looked around, and for the first time noticed Connor was nowhere in sight.

Matt stepped up. "That bar's stocked." He grabbed a glass. "James W., you're a bourbon man, right?"

———

OUTSIDE, Lyle tossed the useless extinguisher aside. "It's empty!" He reached for the water hose.

"No!" Angie bellowed. "It's a grease fire!" She ran to the fryer's lid. "We have to cut off the oxygen."

"You can't get close enough to put that on." Lyle began turning the spigot.

"Stop!" Connor appeared from the garage and immediately assessed the situation. "Hold on." He ran back into the garage and came back wielding a rake. "Hook the lid on this!"

———

"HERE YOU GO, ladies. Two champagne cocktails." Matt handed the flutes to Hester and Elsbeth. Thank goodness he'd remembered how to make one.

Mum, dressed in light gray pants and silk blouse, appeared around the corner. "Am I too late for cocktails?" she asked in her clipped British accent.

"Not at all. The bar's open," Matt smiled. "Would you like a champagne cocktail?"

"No, thank you." Mum nodded toward James W.'s glass. "I'll have what he's having."

Hester took over. "Mrs. Novak, this is Mum, Reverend Duff's wife's mother. She and her daughter will be joining us for dinner tonight." She looked beyond Elsbeth. "Governor Novak, Sheriff, this is Mum."

"A pleasure to meet you all," Mum said.

"Mum?" Elsbeth frowned. "What's your real name?"

"I prefer to be called Mum."

Elsbeth's back straightened and her chin went up. "I'm afraid I'm not comfortable addressing a total stranger so casually."

Matt heard the rustle of stubborn snootiness enter Elsbeth's tone. He glanced over at James W. in time to see him gulp his bourbon. Beside him, Jimmy sighed heavily.

Here we go, Matt thought.

———

THE SOOT-COVERED turkey hung from a chain hooked to the rake. Ice sizzled as it hit the beads of oil and ash that dripped on the pavement and swirled around Lyle's feet. He stood in the middle of the smoky morass, his only focus on the black carcass of tonight's main course.

"My turkey," he said in disbelief.

Angie had never seen such anguish on a grown man's face before. This giant, wearing an apron that she suspected was actually two aprons sewn into one huge piece, was the picture of devastation. His stare was blank. His skin, pale.

She had to act. Dinner was to be served in twenty minutes. As far as she knew, she was the only other person on the premises who could cook. And Hester— the woman who had been so supportive of Angie despite her horrible outburst earlier—well, Hester's reputation as a hostess was at stake. Elsbeth would tell anyone who would listen.

"Lyle?" she asked.

He only had eyes for the burnt turkey.

"Lyle." She gave his arm a shake.

Finally, he looked down at her.

Good, Angie thought. He might still be of some help. "Did you make gravy?"

———

THE PARLOR WAS SILENT. Elsbeth and Mum were in a stare-down. Matt, James W. and Jimmy stood by the fireplace; it made for a fast exit route through the dining room if things got ugly.

Hester offered an elegant smile, as if unaware of any tension in the room. "Mum, how is your daughter feeling? Will she be able to join us for dinner?"

Distracted, Mum answered. "She's looking forward to it. Thank you so much for inviting us to your dinner party."

"Yes. Our first social event since the inauguration," Elsbeth butted in. "It's so important to learn people's names when you're in my position. Jimmy's not married, you see, and he's asked me to help with his social responsibilities."

That was a bald-faced lie, Matt knew. Elsbeth had made that decision before Jimmy ever put his name on the ballot.

"What is your name?" Elsbeth fixed a stare on Mum. "Really."

Mum looked Elsbeth straight in the eye. "Boudicca Winterbottom-Glasscock."

25

PLAN B. VERY PLAN B

ANGIE, Lyle and Connor, along with the bird still hoisted on the rake, had moved to the garage to escape the pelting sleet. Angie studied the turkey more closely and came up smiling. "I think we're in luck," she said.

"How do you figure that?" asked the very dejected Lyle.

"Check this out." She pulled out one of the wings and peeled back its skin. The meat below the scorched skin was white and moist, perfectly cooked. "We'll slice the meat into medallions, artfully dribble your gravy on top, and we'll be good to go. You've got the sides already done. Right? The potatoes and stuff?"

Lyle, who had been looking happier, suddenly yelped. "The potatoes!"

———

IN THE PARLOR, Matt frowned. Did he smell something burning?

"Very British," Mum was saying in answer to Hester's

inquiry. "My mother, only ten years old at the time, was sent to America to escape the Blitz. My father came a month later and settled in the same community. Neither of their parents survived the war."

"How dreadful," Hester said.

Matt listened to the conversation with only half an ear, quietly making his way toward the dining room. With each step, the smell of burnt food became more pronounced.

"And my first name is the name of my mother's mother..."

When Matt was out of sight, he picked up his pace and hurried into the kitchen. Smoke was seeping out around the oven door.

At that moment, Lyle ran into the kitchen, Connor right behind. In two strides, Lyle was at the oven door and pulling out the pan.

Matt's eyes widened in horror when he saw that the beautiful swirls of potatoes that had gone into the oven were now black as coal.

"My God," Lyle said. "My Duchess potatoes. They look like excrement emojis."

Angie took one look at the potatoes and grimaced. "Kinda. Yeah." She turned to Connor. "You have a pantry?"

He nodded toward the back hallway. "First door on your right."

She disappeared into the back hallway.

"Where's the antipasto?" Matt asked. "I've got to get back in there."

Connor retrieved the platter of hors d'oeuvres from the refrigerator and handed it over. "Here."

Matt grabbed the platter. "Can we do anything about the smell?"

"Oh. Right." Connor followed Matt to the kitchen doorway, then closed two pocket doors that Matt had not even realized were there.

"Oh my God, the green beans!" Lyle's hysterical wail was the last thing Matt heard before the doors closed.

———

BY THE TIME Angie returned from the pantry, Connor had opened all the windows and positioned fans to draw in the fresh air. Things were going to get very chilly, very quickly, she surmised. She dropped the boxes she'd taken from the pantry on the counter by the stove, then headed straight for the refrigerator to survey its contents. "Good," she nodded. "I can make this work."

"Make what work?" Lyle was staring at the two ruined dishes on the island. His voice was barely above a whisper.

"Dinner." Angie began pulling items from the fridge. "Gruyere cheese? Great."

Lyle picked up one of the boxes she'd put on the counter. "Potato flakes? Absolutely not. You are not serving the Governor of Texas potato flakes!"

———

"WHEN MY DAUGHTER WAS BORN, I finally was called a name that I loved. Mum." Mrs. Duff's mother smiled sweetly at Elsbeth. "Understand?"

Elsbeth nodded politely. Message received, Matt decided. Score one for Mum. He set the food on the far end of the bar and smiled brightly. "Hors d'oeuvres, anyone?"

James W. immediately headed over. "What have we here?"

Matt thanked the good Lord in heaven he'd been in the

kitchen when Lyle had prepared the food. "A little antipasto. Olives, cheese—."

"And pickled ginger! My favorite!" James W. headed straight for the platter.

"I understand your man is quite the cook," Elsbeth said to Hester as she followed her husband across the room.

"Lyle? He's wonderful." Hester said proudly. "Wait 'til dinner. He makes the best Duchess potatoes ever."

———

"NO WAY." Lyle clutched the box to his chest. "I only keep potato flakes around to thicken sauces."

"You have to have potatoes. You've got gravy and turkey." Angie put the water on the stove to boil. "Which, by the way, you need to start scraping the ash off of."

"And we don't have a vegetable." Connor nodded to the now green bean twigs.

"Oh, my goodness." Lyle grabbed his cheeks. "We have to have a vegetable. I didn't make a salad."

"There's carrots in the fridge." Angie picked up the chunk of Gruyere cheese and began grating it.

Connor pulled a cutting board from beneath the island. "I'm on it."

———

MATT HANDED MUM A PLATE, then extended another to Hester. "You have such a lovely house, Hester," Mum was saying. "Is this your family home?"

"Yes," Hester answered. "The Honeywells built it back in 1890. We're ranchers, of course. Have a big spread out in West Texas. But when my people come to town, we like to live in style. I live here full-time now. My brother's in charge of the ranch."

"My daddy had a ranch," Elsbeth said enthusiastically. "Not too far outside of Wilks. We raised cattle. Had a bull one time…"

As Elsbeth took center stage, Hester sidled over to Matt. "Do I smell smoke?"

"A small grease fire. Nothing to worry about." He plastered a smile on his face.

Hester's brow arched. "Is that a fib, Preacher?"

The plastered smile almost faltered, but Matt held on. "Not to worry. Everything's under control."

———

ANGIE DUMPED a stick of butter into a pan as she stirred the thickening potato flakes. "Have you got the carrots done?"

Connor looked up from the cutting board, two fresh Band-Aids on each index finger. "Almost."

"Dump 'em in as soon as the butter begins to foam up." She turned to Lyle. "How are the medallions coming?"

Lyle looked up from a pile of scraped, charred turkey skin and a smaller pile of salvaged turkey. "I think I've got enough for eight servings."

Angie added a cup of butter cubes and garlic powder to the now boiling water. A thought struck her. "Connor, did I see you slicing onions earlier?"

"They were supposed to be fried and used as the garnish on top of the Brussels sprouts."

"Great. Once you get the carrots in the butter, get out another pan."

———

"I'D BETTER SWITCH TO WINE," Jimmy said to Matt. "Got a call in a little while."

"We have a Pinot Noir and a Shiraz," Matt answered, showing the bottles.

"Pinot. Please." Jimmy tipped his head closer to Matt. "Any word on Reverend Duff?"

Matt checked to make sure Mum was involved in conversation. She and Hester were studying some knickknacks in a glass case. "Not a one. It's like he's fallen off the face of the earth." He poured the dark red liquid into a delicately etched glass and handed it to Jimmy.

"What's your take?" Jimmy sipped his wine.

Matt breathed deeply. It had been too long for him to conclude anything else. "I think he's dead," he whispered.

———

ANGIE FOLDED the Gruyere cheese into the potatoes, then nodded to Connor. "Give those onions one more minute, then add them to the potatoes."

Lyle was plating thin slices of turkey on a platter. Dark meat, white meat, dark meat, white meat. "That looks great," Angie said.

She moved over to check on the carrots. "Perfect" She reached for the bottle of bourbon Connor had brought to her, poured in two jiggers, then lit a match to the concoction.

"Haven't we had enough fire for one day?" Lyle asked.

"The onions are going in," Connor called. Angie came over, gave the mixture a taste, added some salt, stirred it around, gave it another taste. She smiled at Connor. "Give it a try."

Connor took a quick bite. "Wow. Hey, Lyle. I can cook!" He took a spoonful over to Lyle.

The big man's eyes rounded in surprise. "They'll never know they're flakes. What do you call this?"

"Kitchen sink potatoes," she said. "All right, the muffins should be warmed up nice. Check the gravy in the microwave." She huffed in frustration. "I feel like we're missing something." She shrugged. "Oh, well. Connor, let Hester know we're ready to serve."

———

MATT CHECKED HIS WATCH. In five minutes, they were supposed to eat. He glanced into the dining room. No food was on the table, but he was relieved to see Connor hurrying toward the gathering.

"Excuse me," Connor said. "This would be a good time to bring Mrs. Duff to the table. Do you need some assistance, Mum?"

"I may indeed." Mum nodded to the group. "This should only take a minute."

"Of course." Hester nodded to the dining table. "I see our wineglasses are in there." She didn't say "empty," but Matt knew she was surprised. "Perhaps we—"

"Sorry. My bad," Matt said. "That was my job." Which was a total lie. "I'll take care of that." He went to the bar and grabbed two bottles of Chardonnay from the ice bucket.

"We'll leave the end of the table nearest the hallway for Shelly. Her mother there," Hester nodded. "Governor, would you like to sit at the head of the table?"

"An honor, ma'am, but you are our most excellent hostess. I'll sit next to Matt." Everyone shuffled around to a seat, and Matt began pouring wine.

———

"LOOKS like we're ready to serve," Angie announced.

Lyle nodded as he surveyed the spread laid out on the island. "Everything looks beautiful...Oh, shoot!" Lyle's eyes widened. "The cranberry sauce. In the freezer." He rushed over and opened the door, then pulled out the deep cut glass bowl. "It's frozen."

Connor appeared in the doorway. "Mrs. Duff is at the table. Where's the food?"

Angie nodded to Lyle. "Put that in the microwave. Connor and I will start serving." She nodded to Connor. "Leave the turkey for Lyle to bring out. He deserves that honor."

———

MATT FELT a flood of relief when Angie and Connor entered carrying food.

Elsbeth's reaction was swift when she saw Angie. "I didn't know *you* were here."

"I couldn't resist watching a chef at work. Where did you find Lyle?" she asked Hester, as she took her seat beside Matt.

"I stole him from the Austin Social Club. Made enemies of several of the members as I recall, but I didn't like them much anyway."

Angie leaned into Matt. "When you say the prayer, make it a long one."

Matt obliged. He thanked the good Lord for Hester, then James W. and Elsbeth, then Jimmy, then Angie, then the strong bond between Shelly Duff and her mother. He continued on by asking God to bless and nurture Shelly and her soon-to-be-born baby, then the governor, then the great state of Texas. He was running out of things to pray for when, finally, Lyle appeared in the doorway, carrying the platter filled with turkey. Relieved, Matt finished with a quick amen, and Lyle placed the turkey in the center of the table while Connor snuck the bowl of cranberry sauce between Angie and Matt.

Hester kept her smile in place, but Matt could see behind it to the questions that were flying through her mind. "Lyle, this looks lovely," she said, only a hint of confusion wisping around her words.

"Angie was a great help," he said, then bowed. "Enjoy." He turned for the kitchen.

"And Lyle?" Hester called after him. "Don't forget to take a plate up to Pastor Lambert."

———

MOST OF THE food was gone in less than thirty minutes. Matt had no idea how Lyle and Angie had pulled it off, but everything was delicious. Except for the occasional "this is so good" and "I want that potato recipe," conversation had almost ground to a halt as the guests enjoyed their dinner.

Elsbeth had given him a start when she noted it smelled like something was burning, but Angie handled the comment smoothly when she revealed the carrots had been flambéed.

Toward the end of the meal, Lyle entered quietly and headed over to Matt. "Preacher, can I borrow you for a minute?"

"Sure thing."

Matt pushed way from the table, but Hester motioned for him to keep his seat. "Everyone, this is Lyle, the preparer of our feast."

"Well done," Jimmy said. He raised his glass. "To Lyle."

Lyle's face reddened at the governor's toast, and but he nodded appreciatively. "Thank you, but it was a group effort."

Angie shooed away his praise. "Nonsense, I was in the presence of a chef."

"You needed me?" Matt stood and followed Lyle to the kitchen.

Connor was waiting for them at the doorway and slid the panels shut once they were inside. Lyle headed straight for the island and leaned against it heavily.

Connor came up behind him and rubbed his shoulders. "You're gonna be okay. Do you want me to go up with you?"

Lyle shook his head and pushed off the island.

"What's going on?" Matt asked, concerned at Lyle's sweaty pallor.

"You'll see." He didn't look at Matt but led the way to the elevator. The two men got on and the journey to the third floor began. With each passing creak of the elevator, Matt had a growing feeling this was not going to end well. When the elevator opened, Lyle led the way to Lambert's room. He opened the door and stood back for Matt to look in.

Pastor Lambert's limp body hung from the light fixture centered in the ceiling, an overturned chair on the floor below his dangling feet.

26

THE HANGING MAN

JAMES W. STOOD in the doorway of Lambert's bedroom, his hands fisted on his hips. "Did you go in here?" he asked Matt.

Matt stood at his side. "I didn't. But Lyle did. He brought Lambert's supper up. When Lambert didn't answer his knock, Lyle opened it, saw the room was pitch black and turned on the light. As soon as he saw Lambert hanging there, he skedaddled down to get me."

"Lyle's fingerprints will be on the doorknob and the light switch, but that should be it."

"Yep."

James W. surveyed the room. "Looks like Lambert had to move the bed to get under that ceiling light."

Matt nodded. The bed was similar to the one in his room: a wrought iron twin with knobs at the four corners. And as James W. noted, it had been pushed up against the dresser on the far wall. "I wonder whose fingerprints we'll find on those posts."

"Besides the obvious"—James W. jerked his head toward the dangling body—"anything strike you as off?"

Matt nodded. "For one thing, I didn't consider Lambert a drinking man. That wine bottle tells a different story." He pointed to the dark green bottle lying on its side next to an open Bible and a few other sundries on the dresser top. "No beverage cups anywhere. Suggests he drank it straight from the bottle. Forensics will tell that story."

"Didn't approve of a recreational sip now and then?"

"He barely approved of breathing," Matt answered.

"Anything else?"

"Doesn't look like there was a struggle of any kind. Shoes neatly placed by the overturned chair." He nodded toward the desk. "An orderly stack of books and notepads. Of course, all of that could be staged. We won't know 'til crime scene gets here."

"Did you call this in?" James W. asked.

Matt heard disapproval in his friend's question. "I sent for the closest law enforcement officer that I could find to secure the scene. You."

James W. gave him a sideways glare. "Why did you really wait?"

Matt drew in a long breath. "I'm coming to the conclusion that Reverend Duff has been murdered. It's a hunch, but the more we look into the case, the more suspicions I have. I think Lambert had something to do with it, or at least he knew something. If he did commit suicide, it's a very convenient turn of events for several folks he ticked off." He looked James W. square in the eye. "I need your take on all of this. I need you."

James W. stared at him for a moment, then nodded. "Okay. But we've gotta go by the book." He pulled his phone from his back pocket. "I'll call 911. You call the cop who's handling Duff's disappearance."

Matt got out his cell and dialed Lieutenant Gage's number. He sighed when the call went to voicemail. Hopefully, she would check her messages soon.

The sound of the elevator creaking up the shaft had his attention. Was Lyle coming back up? Matt had suggested Lyle corral everyone in the solarium for dessert. Maybe being in the back of the home would shield them from the rush of EMTs, CSIs and cops who were about to descend upon the mansion.

When the elevator door opened, however, it wasn't Lyle who walked out.

"Angie," Matt said. He stepped between her and Lambert's door to block her view. "What are you doing up here?"

"I've been trying to talk with you all night. It's important." Her brows arched when she saw James W. "What's going on here?"

Matt didn't answer but steered her toward his bedroom doorway. "What do you want to tell me?"

"I went to that bar—The Oak and Horn that Lambert went to?—and did some snooping."

Matt felt his face flush. "You did what?"

"I got it all on video." She held up her phone. "And I saw that guy who Lambert was trying to find."

Matt pulled her into his bedroom. "What about him?"

Angie looked around the room, taking in the front window and the tower nook. "I must be right beneath you," she said. "I've got a little circle seating area just like yours."

"Angie, about the man?"

She turned back to him, her look apologetic. "Sorry. His name was Hog and—"

Matt's hand shot up. "Stop. You said Hogg?"

She nodded. "He was a total jerk. Pissed as hell that Lambert was trying to find him. He said Lambert even tried to call his father—"

"Enough!" Matt's head was spinning, but not from weakness. He was remembering his conversation with Hester the other night. U.S. Senator William Womack had a son named

Hogg. So...Lambert was looking for the Senator's kid, and when he couldn't find him, Lambert called the Senator? Womack and Reverend Meade had been thick as thieves at Jimmy's inauguration, and Lambert had gone to Meade's church this afternoon and come out madder than heck. Then he'd headed to the Oak and Horn...looking for the Senator's son?

And now Lambert was dead.

"What's James W. doing up here?" Angie broke into his thoughts.

Matt cast a glance at the door. "You're going to find out anyway," he said. "Lambert's dead. James W.'s making sure the scene is secure."

Angie stepped back. "He's been murdered?"

It sure looked like suicide, Matt thought, but... "I'm not sure." His phone pinged, and he looked at the display. "That's Lieutenant Gage." He answered it. "Thanks for calling me back. Lambert's dead. Apparent suicide by hanging. You need to come to Hester's right away." He listened for a moment. "Agreed. It could have been staged. I called 911. How soon—" He stopped when Gage interrupted him, then said, "We're up on the third floor of the mansion. Lyle or Connor will show you where the elevator is. I'm staying up here to keep the scene secure."

Matt turned to Angie, who was staring over his shoulder at Lambert's doorway. "Are you all right?" he asked.

"Yeah. Wow." She forced herself to breathe deeply. "What can I do to help?"

"Ask Hester to serve dessert in the solarium. That'll keep the cop cars and ambulances out of their view. I don't know if Gage will want to talk with everyone who was here or not."

Her eyes rounded. "You mean Lambert did this when we were all downstairs?"

Matt had no desire to get into the specifics of postmortem

details, but the bodily fluids soaking Lambert's pant legs still appeared to be damp. "It's possible."

The clank of the elevator had them both looking at the hall-way. "That might be the EMTs," he said. "Things are about to get pretty crazy up here." He turned to her. "I know Gage is going to want to talk to you about what happened at the Oak and Horn, but it might be a few hours before she gets to you."

Angie nodded. "I guess that Hog guy is a little more impor-tant now."

"Maybe." He thought for moment. "We need to shield Mrs. Duff as much as possible. The last thing she needs is to hear any more bad news."

"I'll do my best." She handed him her phone. "I'd feel better if you held on to this."

He pocketed the cell, then took her hands in his. "I'm really, really glad you're here."

"Me, too."

When she got up on her tiptoes to kiss him, Matt closed his eyes and deepened the kiss, reveling in the knowledge he wasn't alone anymore.

27

GAGE TAKES CHARGE

EXPECTING to find an uproar downstairs equal to the uproar in her stomach, Angie was surprised that all was quiet when she entered the kitchen. The only person in sight was Connor, who was calmly loading the dishwasher.

"Where is everyone?" she asked.

Connor put the last plate on the bottom rack. "Lyle's helping Mum get Mrs. Duff settled for the night, and Hester's showing Mrs. Novak the guesthouse."

Angie sat down on a stool at the island and put her head in her hands. "Any chance of some coffee?"

Connor turned to look at her. "You okay?" Then understanding dawned. He lowered his voice. "Did you see him? Lambert? Lyle said it was awful."

"Matt made sure I didn't see anything." *Thank God.* She looked up. "Does everyone down here know Lambert's dead?"

"Only Hester. And Lyle, of course." Connor moved to the coffeepot. "Lyle already put on a fresh pot for dessert. Cream or sugar?"

"Black. Very black."

He filled a mug and handed it to her. She took a sip. "Perfect."

Connor poured himself a cup and took a seat across from her. "Thanks for bailing Lyle out tonight with dinner. You've made a lifelong friend." He gave her a wink. "Two, actually."

Lyle entered. "Mrs. Duff is all snuggled in. I'm worried, though. She looks worse now than she did before dinner."

"She probably should've stayed in bed." Angie set her mug down. "But I don't blame her for wanting to be among people. I can't imagine what's she's going through. Maybe she thought the break would do her good."

Lyle went to the fridge and pulled out a gallon of Blue Bell vanilla ice cream. "I'll let that soften up a bit," he said, removing the lid. "Thank goodness my dessert plans are still intact."

Angie perked up. "What are we having?"

"Bananas Foster. Connor, can you fetch me some banana liqueur and dark rum? And then we need to set the table in the solarium."

Angie pushed away from the counter. "Where are the plates? I'll get started on the table."

The front doorbell rang. "I'll get that." Lyle hurried out of the room and came back almost immediately, followed by a striking woman wearing over-the-knee black leather boots and coat. "Lieutenant Gage, this is the preacher's fiancée, Angie O'Day."

The woman peeled off her coat and offered her hand. "Matt has been very helpful this week."

"I'm pleased to meet you," Angie heard herself say.

"This way, Lieutenant." Lyle led the way back to the elevator and returned moments later. His eyes were large. "Isn't she gorgeous?" he whispered.

"Gorgeous? Yes," Angie said.

And intimidating.

———

MATT BREATHED a sigh of relief when the elevator doors opened, and Gage walked out. He'd hoped she would be the first responder on the scene. "You made good time," he said.

She nodded, then saw James W. standing at the door. "Who are you?"

"Sheriff James W. Novak. I was on premises for Hester's dinner party." He pulled out his ID and handed it over. "Matt came and got me. We both hail from Wilks."

"A dinner party?" Gage repeated.

"The party was for Governor Novak. James W. is his father," Matt explained.

Gage nodded. "Okay. Where is the body?"

"In here." James W. stood back to let her enter.

Gage scanned the room. "Has anyone been in here?"

"Lyle," Matt answered. "When he brought up Lambert's supper, Lambert didn't answer the door. Lyle opened it and hit the overhead light switch. When he saw the body, he ducked out as quick as he could," Matt answered. "That's when he came and got me."

"Lambert wasn't invited to the dinner party?" Gage asked.

"I'm not sure. But I suspect he wouldn't have accepted the invitation anyway," Matt said. "He wasn't very social."

"He certainly didn't seem very friendly when we interviewed him." Gage took some rubber gloves and paper covers for shoes from her suit pocket and put them on. "Have you gone in the room?"

Both men shook their heads. "Not beyond the threshold," Matt said.

She stepped in and focused on the multi-shaded green

carpet. The pile had a fluffy shag consistency. "Something might've dropped in here, but footprints won't show." She took out her camera and began photographing the scene. Little by little, she advanced around the room.

She stopped when she saw the toppled wine bottle on the dresser, then moved to the desk. Her eyes rounded when she saw the notepad. "*I didn't know*," she read out loud. She straightened. "Didn't know what?"

"Interesting," Matt said.

She studied the overturned bottle of wine, then the floor. "Floor's dry," she said. "We need to find out if this bottle was full." She squinted to read the label on the smaller clear bottle. "Vinegar?"

Matt suddenly understood. "Maybe this is a suicide, after all."

"Why do you say that?" Gage asked.

"Wine mixed with vinegar. It's what they gave Jesus to drink during the crucifixion. Only, he refused to drink it."

Gage came around the bed. "There's plenty here for forensics to check out. Looks like the bed's been moved to make room for the chair he supposedly kicked out from under him."

She moved to the closet and opened the door. It was empty. She furrowed her brows, then searched the far side of the room that was blocked from view by the bed. She picked up a small traveler's suitcase. "He packed his clothes before he killed himself?"

"That isn't inconsistent with suicide," Matt said. "Folks are known to have cleaned their houses, done the laundry—that kind of thing—to make sure everything's in its place when they go."

"True. Which means this was not something he did on a whim."

"Perhaps not," Matt said. "But some folks might be glad he's out of the way."

"What do you mean?" she asked.

"Angie and I did a lot of footwork today. I have quite a download for you."

The elevator rattled behind Matt. "Looks like we've got company."

The door opened, and two large EMTs spilled out into the hallway. Matt and James W. stepped back to get out of their way.

James W. lowered his voice. "Give me some background here. What does Lambert have to do with Reverend Duff's disappearance?"

Matt led the way to the turret sitting area and gave James W. the lowdown. The last time Reverend Duff had been seen by a witness was when Lambert gave Duff a ride to St. George Episcopal Church. Though they had Lambert on surveillance tape, both driving away after Duff entered the church and then attending the prayer breakfast for the next hour, Lambert had no explanation for why and when his car had been cleaned and vacuumed, wiped of all fingerprints, etc., save for a dung-smelling splotch of dirt in the back wheel well. Matt recounted what he had overheard of Lambert's outburst when "some kid" had hung up on him, as well as Lambert's call to Reverend Meade. Finally, he told James W. about how he and Angie had spent the afternoon following Lambert around Austin, including a trip to Meade's church and two stops at a dive bar where Lambert was apparently looking for someone.

When he was finished, James W. shook his head. "Sounds like there were weevils in his flour sack, that's for sure."

"Preacher?" Gage called out for Matt. "I need you for a sec."

Matt and James W. headed for the hall. Gage stood in the hallway, hands on hips.

"What can I do for you?" Matt asked.

Gage turned. "Is there another way up here besides the elevator?"

Matt scratched his ear. "Now that you mention it, I don't think so."

"Go down and get Hester for me, would you please?"

"Sure thing."

James W. nodded. "I'll go down with you. When forensics gets here, they won't need me in the way." He punched the elevator call button.

A familiar chime had Matt checking his cell. He pulled it out. "That's my ringtone, but not my phone."

Gage shook her head. "It's not you. It's coming from the suitcase." She hurried in, fetched the bag, then brought it out to the hallway. "I was waiting to open this until forensics got here..."

"I'll document it for you." James W. pulled out his phone as she placed the suitcase on the floor.

Sure enough, when Gage opened the suitcase, the cell phone, placed on top of neatly folded clothes, was ringing.

"You'd better answer it," Matt said. "We don't know the password for his cell."

Gage had a thought. She aimed the phone toward Matt. "You do the talking. You're a preacher. So was Lambert. Maybe they'll think you're a colleague." She hit the answer button and put the phone on speaker.

Matt cleared his throat. "Hello?"

"Yes, hello," answered a man's voice. It had a slight accent to it. "Who is this, please?"

"I'm Pastor Matt Hayden."

"I'm looking for Pastor Lambert, please."

Hispanic? Matt wondered. Very polite. And very calm. "I'm afraid he's not available right now. May I take a message?"

"Sure. I am Pastor Cesar Garcia from Reverend Duff's church in San Antonio. I had a question about Sunday's Power-Point for the Hispanic service. I know Reverend Duff is ill, but Pastor Lambert may know what I'm supposed to do."

Ill? Matt looked from James W. to Gage. Is that what the folks at Duff's San Antonio church had been told? "Do with what, exactly?" he asked.

"I turned in the PowerPoint for Sunday's service today to the AV people, and they said I have the wrong one. I said, these are the notes Reverend Duff gave me before he left for the inau-guration—" Pastor Garcia stopped abruptly. "You said you are Pastor Hayden? You are the one who gave the benediction on Tuesday in Reverend Duff's place."

"I'm afraid so."

"No, my friend. You did a good job. I know Reverend Duff would approve."

"That's very kind," Matt said. "About the PowerPoint?"

"But now I understand Lambert has changed the service for Sunday. This is a *very* big deal." Garcia stretched the word "very." "Reverend Duff was kicking off a huge sermon series that was to go through the rest of the year. Very powerful stuff. Surely, Reverend Duff will insist on giving his sermon. Even if he has to do it from a hospital bed."

Something buzzed in Matt's head. The missing computer. The untagged Bible. The bare legal pads. "You know what he was going to say?"

"Of course. It helps me translate for him at the Hispanic services if I know what he's going to say. He gave me a copy of his sermon before he left for the inauguration. I have it. Word for word. How else would I know how to make the PowerPoint?"

Matt leaned back against the wall. Could this be the missing link as to why Duff had to be silenced? "I know Pastor Lambert made the choice to switch out the sermons on Tuesday night. Nobody told you?"

A sad chuckle came over the line. "I'm afraid that sometimes our Hispanic service is...forgotten...by members of the staff."

"By Lambert, you mean?"

"And others. But yes. This situation is not a surprise to me."

Matt nodded, remembering what Shelly Duff had said. Lambert resented having a Hispanic ministry at the church. It brought in little money and had cost the church several high-dollar donors. "May I ask a favor of you, Pastor Garcia?"

"Of course."

"Could you email me a copy of the sermon?"

"Yes." But there was hesitation in Garcia's voice. "I don't have it here at the house. It's in my office at the church. Can I send it to you tomorrow morning?"

Dagnab it, Matt thought. That sermon could be the key to everything. "Yes, of course. Tomorrow morning sounds great." He rattled off his email address for Garcia to write down.

"In the meantime," Garcia said, "what do I do about the PowerPoint?"

Matt considered. "I suggest you be prepared for either sermon. As I remember, Pastor Lambert said that this Sunday's sermon would be a repeat of one that was given in November?"

"Oh." Matt could hear Garcia's voice brighten. "I will check. That would make things much easier. Gracias, Pastor Hayden."

"And thank you, Pastor Garcia."

"You will speak to Pastor Lambert about this?"

"If I get the chance. Thanks again." Matt nodded to Gage,

and she clicked off the call. His eyes met hers. "That sermon might be what Duff's disappearance is all about."

Gage nodded. "But will it explain why Lambert is dead—or is something else going on?"

"I won't know until I see that sermon," Matt said. At that moment, the elevator clanged back into action. "That's probably the crime scene techs. We'd better clear out and make some room up here for your people to work."

The elevator arrived and the door opened. Three people in white paper cover-ups carrying bulky cases walked out. Matt and James W. stood back to let the crime scene techs by, then got into the elevator.

As the doors closed, Gage called out, "Don't forget to tell Hester I need to see her!"

28

DESSERTUS INTERRUPTUS

LYLE WAS SLICING bananas when Matt and James W. entered the kitchen. "I'm getting dessert ready. Will you be joining us? I'm making bananas Foster."

James W. grinned. "My spirits just rose like a corn cob in a cistern."

Matt's lips quirked as he observed Lyle's confused expression. "That means he's looking forward to it. Where is everybody?"

"Mum's settling Shelly in their room. Hester took Mrs. Novak over to the guesthouse to distract her from all the hoopla over here," Lyle answered. "The governor's still on his call in the study. Connor and Angie are setting up the solarium for dessert."

"We'll go over to the guesthouse, then." Matt grabbed James W. by the elbow. "You've got to see this place."

"Do me a favor," Lyle called after them. "Let 'em know dessert's almost ready."

Matt and James W. headed to the solarium. "Mrs. Duff and

her mother are staying in here," Matt nodded at one of the hallway doors.

James W. lowered his voice. "She sure didn't look good at dinner."

"No. She didn't."

Matt and James W. headed into the solarium.

Angie smiled. "I was hoping you'd make it for dessert." Her smile faded. "How are things going upstairs?"

"The crime scene techs have arrived. My guess is they're close to taking Lambert down." Matt immediately regretted his words when Angie paled.

James W., however, didn't notice. He was too busy gawking at the solarium. "Looks like a crystal palace in here," he said, then gave Matt a studied look. "This Hester lady runs with the big dogs." James W. turned to Connor, who was carrying a white filigreed chair across the expanse. "How come the windows aren't steamed up? It's nice in here but iced out there." He nodded to the frost-covered lawn.

"Special venting and special windows," Connor explained. "When Hester wants somethin' done, she gets it done." He pushed the garden chair under the white wrought iron table.

"C'mon," Matt said. "You've got to see this before dessert." He hurried to the far end and opened the French doors that led into the Craftsman-style home, James W. close behind. The two men stepped into the guesthouse's great room, its stone fireplace stretching two stories to the pine-gabled ceiling.

James W. let out a low whistle. "When can I move in?"

Elsbeth's bellowing voice echoed forth from the kitchen at the end of the great room. "A catering kitchen! Perfect for a party." She and Hester appeared in the doorway. "How many can you serve?"

"How many do you want to invite?" Hester said. Her gaze fell upon Matt, and he could've sworn he saw relief in those tired blue eyes. He could relate. Elsbeth had a way of wearing down the staunchest of spirits.

"Excuse me, ladies," Matt said. "Lyle's ready to serve dessert."

Elsbeth clapped her hands together. "I can hardly wait to see what he's cooked up this time."

Sure enough, the iron lattice table centered in the solarium was set with two candelabras and delicate gold-rimmed china. Angie and Mum stood at the far end, sipping coffee, while Lyle and Connor busied themselves with the serving cart.

"Mum," Hester said. "I'm so glad you could join us. Is Shelly all settled?"

"She fell right asleep," Mum said.

Lyle motioned to the table. "Everyone take a seat. We have coffee, tea, liqueurs, brandy, and a rather fine port. What would you like?"

Mum sat down beside Angie. "I'd like another Irish coffee, please."

"Make that two," Angie grinned.

"Plain coffee for me," Matt said.

Connor hurried into the mansion to fill the liquor orders, while Lyle lit the Sterno beneath the chafing dish. Good, Matt thought. It seemed Elsbeth and Mum had no idea that death was upstairs.

"James W.," Elsbeth said, "Hester has offered her home to any guests we need to host. Isn't that marvelous?"

James W. nodded. "Very gracious indeed."

Hester smiled. "It's what I do. Consider this your guests' home away from home."

"That is so thoughtful," Elsbeth gushed. "The Governor's Mansion is so confined. Almost all the areas are open to the public, and there aren't that many spare rooms."

"Which is one reason I bought the Craftsman home I

showed you," Hester said. She nodded as Connor entered with a tray of drinks. "Someone needed to provide special accommodations for the guests of Texas."

Elsbeth watched Connor pour a splash of Grand Marnier into her coffee. "Hester, between tonight's marvelous dinner and your incredibly gracious offer, I wish I could do something for you in return."

Ah. Now they were on a first-name basis, Matt noted.

Elsbeth sipped her coffee and gave a little cough. "My, this is good."

Matt suppressed a smile as he sipped his coffee wondering if Elsbeth had ever before tasted Grand Marnier.

"Did you watch any of my phone's video yet?" Angie whispered beside him.

"Not yet. But don't worry." He patted his pocket. "It's safe and sound."

Elsbeth suddenly put down her coffee. "I know!" She turned to Hester. "Are you a member of Austin's Junior League?"

Lyle and Connor exchanged a roll of their eyes behind Elsbeth's back.

"Not exactly," Hester said through a forced smile. "But I'm familiar with their group."

In other words, Matt thought, she had no desire to associate with them.

"Mrs. Meade informed me at the inauguration barbeque that, as First Lady of Texas, I'm automatically on the Board. Its membership is *very* exclusive. Tomorrow, I'm going to their luncheon at The Society Club near the Capitol. Have you heard of that?"

Matt almost choked on his coffee. Hester *was* The Society Club.

"Yes." Hester leaned back as Connor placed a crystal glass of port wine in front of her.

"Well, they're having an auction of some kind tomorrow. Perhaps I could introduce you to some of the ladies?"

"What a gracious offer," Hester nodded, then reached for her port. She downed it in one swallow.

Matt had an idea. "Sounds like a fine group of ladies," he lied. "Who's in this league?"

"Well, Mrs. Meade, of course. Everyone who's anyone," Elsbeth said. "Politicians' wives, charity leaders—the upper crust, as you can imagine. They do all sorts of fundraisers for those who are less fortunate."

She began listing the projects supported by the group, but Matt tuned her out. Reverend Meade's wife and Elsbeth had been sitting together at the head table for Tuesday's barbeque. Perhaps Mrs. Meade intended to introduce Elsbeth around to the members—showing that she and the first lady were the best of friends would be to Mrs. Meade's political advantage...

And he needed more background on Reverend Meade.

And Hester was going to kill him.

"Elsbeth, what a gracious invitation," Matt beamed. "Hester, what a wonderful opportunity for you to meet more of the movers and shakers of Austin."

Hester's eyes widened, but not as hugely as those belonging to Lyle, who stood behind Elsbeth. Beside him, Connor's head snapped around so sharply, Matt worried he could've slipped a disc.

"I'm not sure I'm open on Saturday," Hester managed

"Well, you should check," Matt pushed. "I wish I could be a fly on that wall. So many interesting people and inroads to learn about."

Hester held out her glass for more port as she studied him,

trying to figure out what he was up to. "I could check my calendar," she said slowly.

"Good," Matt nodded, his eyes promising an explanation to her later on.

"If you all are ready for the dessert—" Lyle carefully poured the rum into the bubbling banana mixture and then, with a flourish, ignited the rum. There was a spattering of applause as he shook the pan back and forth, basting the bananas until the flame died.

Thank God, Matt thought. Something that Lyle had prepared was finally being served.

Lyle ladled the bananas and syrup over bowls of ice cream, and Connor placed them in front of each diner.

Hester picked up her spoon, a signal to all that they could dig in, and scooped up a good-sized mound of ice cream, banana and goo. She brought it to her lips, anticipation glowing in her eyes, when her face suddenly froze. She dropped her spoon. "Shelly!"

All eyes turned to the French doors, where the very pregnant Shelly Duff stood, one hand holding onto the door sash, the other under her belly. "There are flashing lights outside," she gasped out. "Have they found David?"

Matt pushed away from the table. Damn. The last thing the woman needed was excitement. "No," he said, fumbling for his cane.

"Then why are they—" Her last word was choked off as she grunted and doubled over. Almost immediately, a puddle formed on the floor beneath her nightgown.

Mum ran to her daughter. "Her water has broken!"

Hester, halfway to the moaning woman, lasered a look at Lyle. "Call 911!"

"No!" Matt said. "Get the EMTs from upstairs."

Lyle almost leapt over Mum—a sight to behold—in his rush to the elevator.

Shelly had sunk to her knees. "Why are there EMTs here?"

Mum, holding her daughter's shoulders, looked up. "Yes. What are they doing here?"

"Pastor Lambert isn't well," Hester said.

"He might need them more than me," Shelly coughed out, then doubled over again.

"No," Matt said firmly. "You're the priority now."

Shelly let out a wail and collapsed on the floor.

Mum looked desperately at Hester. "The preeclampsia! We need help. Now!"

"They'll be here as soon as the elevator allows," Hester said. Matt saw in her eyes the concern that her very, very slow elevator might prevent the EMTs from getting there in time.

Finally, Shelly relaxed against her mother's chest. Had her episode of agony been a labor pain or something worse? Matt wondered.

As she caught her breath, she looked at him. "Lambert's dead, isn't he?" she panted. "That's why they can take care of me. He's dead. Tell me the truth."

"Yes," he said quietly.

"How did he die?"

Matt swallowed hard. "We're not sure."

"He knew," she said. "He knew what happened to David. I could see it in his eyes. My husband's dead."

She began to shake. She looked at her mother, then her eyes rolled back into her head. Drool ran down the side of her cheek as she convulsed.

29

DISASTER STRIKES

THE EMS TEAM moved Mrs. Duff from the hallway to the parlor so they had more room to do their ministrations. Matt looked on from the dining room, Angie at his side. Beside them, Elsbeth clutched James W.'s arm, her face twisted in horror.

For five minutes, the EMTs worked on Shelly Duff. Despite the tech's lowered voice, Matt knew she was in trouble. Her face was going from pale to gray, and her hands shook as if she was going into shock.

"She suffers from hypertension," Mum said, tearfully answering the tech's questions. "And possible preeclampsia. Her doctor advised against this trip, but I couldn't stop her."

By the time they loaded her on a stretcher and headed for the front door, Brackenridge's Trauma Center was on alert and an ob-gyn surgical team was being assembled. Mum climbed into the ambulance's front cab, and they were off.

Once the front door shut, Hester and Connor hurried out the back door to the garage. Mum would not be at the hospital alone. Which left Matt, Angie, James W., Elsbeth and Lyle in the dining room. They looked at each other in disbelief.

The study doors opened, and Jimmy hurried out. "What in the world is going on out here?" the governor demanded.

"Shelly Duff has gone into labor," Angie said.

"Oh!" He brightened for a moment, then saw the concerned looks on everyone's faces. "Oh."

James W. nodded at his son. "Your call went all right?"

"Yes," Jimmy said, shrugging. "It should've only taken a half hour, but everyone wanted to impress the new guy"—he pointed his thumb at his chest—"with their experience in dealing with ice storms."

"Who is Pastor Lambert?" asked Elsbeth. She looked as if she was rising from a deep fog.

"He's the assistant to Reverend Duff, the pastor who's been missing since Jimmy's inauguration," James W. answered.

She looked at Matt. "His absence was why you gave the benediction."

Matt nodded. "And nobody's seen him since."

Elsbeth looked at the front door. "And that poor woman is giving birth to his child?"

She pulled out a chair and sat down. "Oh, my. I hope that baby makes it."

Matt watched James W. put his hands on his wife's shoulders and slowly massage her muscles. Yes, Elsbeth could be difficult at times. But when push came to shove, she had a heart of gold. And James W. knew that and loved her to her very soul.

"Excuse me," Lyle appeared at the dining room doorway. "Lieutenant Gage wants to speak with you, preacher."

Matt nodded and headed for the kitchen.

"I'm coming with you," Angie said, falling into step beside him.

He gave her a surprised look.

"If I have to push 'Play' myself, you're going to watch the

video I made at the Oak and Horn this afternoon. And I think Lieutenant Gage will want to see it too."

WHEN THEY ARRIVED at the third floor, Matt told Angie to wait in his room, then he headed for Lambert's room. He returned almost immediately with Lieutenant Gage.

Angie saw right away that Lieutenant Gage was all business. Her dark eyes were penetrating, studying her notes as if they held the secrets of the world. She was dressed in all black, looking more like a cat burglar than a cop, but Angie decided it was her preferred choice of wear. Why bother choosing a spiffy wardrobe when there was a case at hand? Nothing about the woman struck Angie as superfluous or vain. She was the real thing—a cop from head to toe who put up with nothing but perfection.

"Why is Lambert still up here?" Matt asked.

Gage finally looked up. "Do you see any stairs up here?"

"Now that you mention it," Matt looked around. "No."

"Fire code violation number one. No emergency egress from this floor." Gage snapped her notebook shut. "Fire code violation number two. Elevator undersized and way out of code."

Angie tried to envision getting a dead body down in the elevator. A stretcher in an upright position? But the body would slump, wouldn't it? So someone would have to hold the body in place? She grimaced.

Gage must have been watching her. "Your fiancée seems to have grasped the problem, at least. We'll have to take the vic out the window—your window, by the way. Lambert's windows are too small."

"Okay," Matt said. "Is that why you wanted to see me?"

Gage shot Matt a wry look. "Let's have a little chat." She gestured to the tower space that had been furnished as a sitting room.

When all three were settled, Gage took out her recorder. She fed in the names of those present, the place, the date and the time.

Good heavens, Angie thought. Was it only seven o'clock? So much had happened since she'd walked in the front door only over two hours ago.

"All right, Preacher," Gage began. "Tell me why you decided to follow Lambert this afternoon, where he went and what you learned."

"Things actually started getting interesting before that," Matt said. "After Connor and I came back from getting the supplies for tonight's dinner party, I came upstairs to take some meds."

Angie swallowed. *Which he needed after I threw my tantrum in front of everyone.*

Matt continued. "I overheard Lambert talking on the phone in the bathroom." He pointed to the cast iron grate that shared a twin in the bathroom. "He was very upset with the guy he was talking to. He said he had 'a right to know' what was going on. I don't know what the other guy said, but Lambert came back with, 'This isn't what we agreed to.'"

"How do you know it was a guy on the other end of the line?" Gage asked.

"Because when the guy hung up on him, Lambert said, 'He hung up on me. That brat hung up on me!'"

"Those were his exact words?" Gage asked. "You're sure?"

Angie wanted to throttle Gage for doubting Matt. He'd been a cop, for God's sakes!

Matt seemed unruffled. "I'm sure. Then Lambert made

another call, and this time it was to Pastor Meade. I know that because I heard him ask for Meade by name."

"Go on," Gage said.

"It took a bit for Lambert to get Meade on the phone, but eventually Meade agreed to talk with him."

"About what?"

"Lambert wanted out of this house—Hester's house— immediately. He said, 'these people are crawling down my neck.' Apparently, Meade told him he needed to stay here."

"Why?" Gage again.

"Because he wanted Lambert to 'keep an eye on things' for him. Lambert went ballistic. Then I think Meade indicated that if Lambert didn't want to be here, he should go home. That's when Lambert told him the police still had his car and then said, 'that idiot kid.'"

"That idiot kid what?"

"I don't know. Meade hung up on him."

A knock sounded on the door, and a tech stuck his head inside. "We're done in there. You need anything else?"

"No. You can go."

Ten minutes later, Matt finished his rundown of the afternoon's events, ending with Angie and him watching Lambert go into the Oak and Horn and come back out almost immediately. "We followed him back to Hester's, and that was the last I saw of Lambert alive."

Gage looked at Angie. "Have you anything to add?"

Angie held her hand out to Matt. "My phone, please."

Matt's expression turned sheepish. "Sorry. I forgot."

Angie settled back in her chair. "After I dropped Matt off at the mansion, I had to run some errands. For me. I wasn't expecting to stay here overnight. And on my way back, I decided to stop by and take a look at the Oak and Horn. I mean,

Lambert had gone there twice in one day to find whoever he was looking for."

Angie cued up the video, hit play, then set the phone on the table between Matt and Gage. When the young man entered the bar, Gage sat forward in her chair.

"He called my father. My father!" the man was saying.

Gage looked up at Angie. "Can you stop it for a moment?"

"Sure." Angie hit pause.

Gage looked at Matt. "You know who that is?"

"His name was Hog," Angie said quickly. "Like a pig."

"Not exactly," Gage said. "It's Hogg. Two g's. He's named after a former governor of Texas. And his father is Senator William Womack. *U.S.* Senator William Womack."

Matt nodded. "And Lambert called Senator Womack, looking for his son, Hogg."

"And the son is a total jerk," Angie added. "Ready?"

Gage nodded, and Angie hit play on the phone. When Hogg left the bar, Gage signaled Angie to turn off the video. Angie watched the tape run for a little longer, frowned, then turned off the phone. "There's something else, too. I videoed it, but it's too dark for you to see."

"See what?" Matt asked.

"It was weird," Angie said. "I think there's some sort of cult thing going on there."

Gage's perfectly shaped brow arched. "Cult?"

"I got the impression that the hunters that frequent that bar were all at some sort of ritual. You heard the bartender say something about Herne the Hunter? And that some guy had shot a buck, and everyone was going out to 'The Homestead'?"

Matt shrugged. "Probably a beer party around a fire for the guys."

Angie shook her head. "It didn't show up on the tape—too dark, I guess—but there were photos on the back wall of guys holding something. I don't know, meat maybe? And there was blood dripping down their faces, on their clothes, all over the place. When I asked the bartender what that was all about, she said they took the pictures to show 'they'd done the deed.' Doesn't that sound weird to you?"

Matt considered. "It does. But we can determine two things from their conversation. That gathering is taking place as we speak, and we know Hogg Womack intended to go there." He looked at Angie. "You up for going back with me to the Oak and Horn tomorrow?"

"Has to be early. I have to get back to Wilks to work the night shift at the Icehouse," she said.

"Fair enough," he nodded, then looked at Gage. "Before that, though, I'd like to head over to your evidence lab and look at those street cam shots you have of Lambert dropping Duff off at St. George Episcopal."

Gage shrugged. "Sure."

"Great. And can you get me a wire?" Matt asked.

"For what? Or should I say, for whom?"

"I want to put one on Hester tomorrow when she goes to the Junior League with Mrs. Novak."

"Excuse me?" Gage asked.

"Elsbeth Novak was invited to the Junior League by Mrs. Meade, Reverend Meade's wife. I'm sure Hester is up to the challenge of learning about Meade's comings and goings. I'd like to know if he's at this bonfire tonight and what his relationship is with Senator Womack. The two seemed to be thick as thieves at the inauguration, and Hogg Womack and Lambert's phone calls have certainly tied them together in this business as well."

Gage nodded approvingly. "You have a devious mind, Pastor Hayden. I like it."

There was a knock on the door, and this time Lyle poked

his head in. "The fire department's hook and ladder just pulled up," he said.

He turned to leave, but Gage stopped him. "Did you see Lambert when he got back to the house this afternoon?"

"Yep. And boy, was he upset. His face was white, like he'd seen a ghost, and he looked like he was going to cry."

"Did you talk with him?"

"Sure did. He asked for a bottle of wine. I asked what kind, and he said, 'Does it look like I care?' Then he asked if I had any vinegar. I said of course, so I went to the pantry and got a bottle of apple cider vinegar and a nice Chardonnay." Lyle's phone buzzed, and he looked at the screen. "Oh, dear."

"What's wrong?" Gage asked.

"Preacher, you're wanted at the hospital."

Matt's heart sank. This couldn't be good news. He stood up.

Gage held up a hand. "Before you leave, I have to let you know you have to move downstairs."

"What?"

"Fire code," she answered.

Lyle's phone buzzed again. His eyes teared up as he read the message. "The baby was stillborn. A little girl." The big man's voice trembled, but he pulled it together. "Apparently, Mrs. Duff isn't doing very well either."

"Oh, dear God," Angie whispered.

The blood drained from Matt's face.

This time, Lyle couldn't control his tears. "Hester said you'd better come. Right away."

30

THE ICU

MATT TOOK the time to change into his clerical shirt and collar before heading out. He knew people sometimes found a minister's garb off-putting. But sometimes the collar brought a sense of calm. As he hung his cross around his neck, he offered up a silent prayer that Shelly would still be alive when he got to Brackenridge Hospital.

Angie was waiting in her truck, parked outside the front door. Due to the slippery front sidewalk, Lyle walked him out to the Dodge and helped Matt up into the cab. "Give my love to Mum," he said, his voice cracking on the last word. He abruptly turned and headed back into the mansion.

The drive to the hospital was silent. When they arrived, Matt was surprised that Angie turned into the parking lot.

"You can drop me off at the main entrance," he said.

Angie shook her head. "Hester's had a heckuva day. She can't stay here with Mum all night. I can." She drove up the ramp, pulled into a parking spot, grabbed her overlarge purse and climbed down from the truck's cab.

Matt got out, came around the truck and gave her a hug. "This might go south," he cautioned.

"Yeah. I figured as much."

The two walked down the ramp and into the parking entrance of the hospital. Matt checked in at the front desk. The receptionist nodded and provided the directions to ICU.

"Is there a chaplain on duty?" Matt asked.

"Yes. Would you like me to call him?"

"I'm not from Austin and don't have all my things. Could you ask him if he'd mind loaning me his communion set?"

"Of course."

He and Angie headed to the elevator.

"Communion set?" Angie asked after they got in.

"You never know what the family wants in situations like this."

When they arrived at the fifth floor, the way to the ICU waiting room was well-marked. They rounded the corner to find Hester and Mum sitting alone in the lounge. When Mum saw them, she pushed off the blue vinyl couch and headed toward Matt, her arms outstretched. "Thank you for coming," she said as she hugged him.

Matt held her for a long moment, then loosened his hold. "What do you need me to do?" he asked quietly.

Angie went to the couch to comfort the exhausted-looking Hester, and Mum pulled Matt toward the chairs facing the couch. "The placenta ruptured when they took the baby out," she said. "It's called placenta previa. They didn't know Sarah had it. They didn't have the right instruments to handle the emergency."

"Or the right surgeon," Hester put in. "Sarah's blood loss is significant. They thought they had it under control..."

"It's been an hour since she left surgery, but she's not getting any stronger." Mum wiped at her wet cheeks. "The doctor said it's not looking good." Her control cracked. "My baby," she sobbed. "My beautiful baby."

Matt felt his own eyes tear but willed himself not to let them fall. Mum was thinking of a baby, all right, but not the stillborn infant that had been lost. She was seeing herself holding her own baby daughter, probably only minutes after Shelly was born. And thinking of her now-grown daughter fighting for her life.

A stooped man dressed in a wrinkled suit came into the waiting room. He caught sight of Matt and walked to him. "Pastor Hayden?"

"Yes?" Matt met him halfway across the lounge.

"I'm Father Benjamin. You asked for a communion kit?" He pulled a small leather case from his suit pocket and handed it over. "Drop it off at the front desk when you leave."

"Thank you, Father."

Matt turned to head back to Mum's group, not sure of the best way to comfort the grieving mother and grandmother. But as he approached, he heard Angie's low, husky voice. "The Lord is my shepherd. I shall not want..."

Matt studied the woman he loved. He was supposed to be the "religious" one. But now, here, Angie was the faithful one.

He walked to their circle, as Hester's lips moved to the beloved psalm. Matt took Mum's hand and the two of them joined in. When Mum's voice faltered, he squeezed her hand. At the last verse, Mum looked heavenward, her face streaked with tears. "And I will dwell in the house of the Lord forever."

Mum retrieved a hanky from her purse and blew her nose. "Thank you," she said.

Matt's eyes found Angie's, and he offered her a slight nod. Thank God she had insisted on coming to the ICU with him.

The double doors at the far end of the lounge opened. Two women dressed in scrubs headed for the group.

"Mrs. Glasscock?" said the younger, freckled woman. It wasn't until Mum stood up and walked toward them that Matt remembered that was Mum's last name.

"This is Dr. Boya," the nurse continued. "She is the specialist we called in to look after your daughter."

Dr. Boya, a slightly built woman with tan skin, extended her hand. "I'm an ob/gyn oncologist."

Hester stood abruptly, a hand to her heart.

Dr. Boya put up a quick, practiced hand. "No, Shelly does not have cancer. Because of our training, ob/gyn oncologists are often called in to perform delicate procedures."

"Delicate procedures?" Mum echoed. "What delicate procedures?"

"We believe your daughter is experiencing a slow bleed. We think the fluid in her belly is pressing against the leak, keeping her from...experiencing heavier bleeding—"

Bleeding out, is what she is thinking. Matt did his best to keep the alarm from his face.

"—So, we need to go in and close that leak," the doctor finished.

Mum swallowed hard, and Hester was quick to put an arm around her shoulders.

Mum mustered her strength. "Can I see her? Before you... take her away?"

The doctor considered. "She's intubated, so she can't talk to you, but you can go in. Only for a moment, you understand."

Mum turned to Matt. "I noticed that man gave you something. Was it a communion kit?"

Matt was startled she knew what was in the small, leather box.

Mum smiled. "My father was a lay canon in the Church of England. I still have his kit."

"Mrs. Glasscock?" prompted the nurse. Dr. Boya had already left the lounge.

"Please come," Mum said to Matt. "I want to have communion with her."

Matt nodded. He'd been trained for such an occasion at Wartburg Seminary, where he'd studied to become a pastor. He would dip a portion of the Host—mostly likely a small, thin disk of wheat flour—into wine and touch it to the patient's lips. He hoped Shelly would be awake enough to satisfy Mum's need to share this with her.

The ICU was dark, a central nurses' station surrounded by curtained-off, eerily lit cubicles. Once again, his senses were confronted with the smell of antiseptic and coffee, along with the sounds of beeping machines and hurried footsteps. For a moment, Matt was swept back to the days and nights he'd spent in this very ICU after being shot in the head last August.

Unaware of his thoughts, the nurse hurried them to the nearest cubicle and pulled back the curtain.

Shelly lay on her back, her eyes closed, her face pale. Wires and IVs protruded from beneath the sheet that covered her, while a bag filled with blood sent its life-giving fluid into the top of her hand. A tube was inserted into her mouth, her nostrils penetrated by the clear, plastic, two-pronged nasal cannula.

The intimidating sight didn't stop Mum, however. She went straight to her daughter's side. "Shelly? Can you hear me? It's Mum."

Shelly's eyes remained closed, but Matt saw movement behind the heavy lids.

"I've brought Pastor Hayden with me." Mum motioned him closer to the bed. "He's going to give us communion. Can you open your eyes?"

With effort, Shelly's eyes slit open. She opened her hand

for her mother to take, then looked up at Matt. Her eyes widened slightly, and a smile whispered around the tube in her mouth. She pointed at his chest.

Matt looked down. Besides the black, clerical, tabbed shirt he wore, the only other thing on his chest was his cross. "This?" He held the three-inch long brass pectoral cross his mother had given him upon his ordination.

Shelly touched it, and her eyes glistened. She looked at her mother.

Mum seemed to understand. "David's cross was very special," she said.

Shelly nodded, and her eyes grew wistful.

"We'll find it, darling." Mum blinked away her own tears. "I'll bring it to you."

Shelly looked at the nurse who stood at the bottom of the bed. The freckled young woman also seemed to know what Shelly wanted. She went to the bedside table and handed Shelly paper and a pen.

Shelly wrote on the pad, handed it to Mum, then closed her eyes in exhaustion. Mum read it and handed it to Matt.

Bury us all together, it read. *With his cross.*

Matt couldn't—wouldn't—give in to the emotional gut-punch of those words. Instead, he opened the communion set. "Let's begin."

He recited the Words of Institution, performed the intinction of the body into the blood and held up the Host. "In the Apostle's Creed, we confess our belief in the communion of saints. Today, right now, at this bedside, the saints are gathered around us. Those who have gone before us and those still on this earth."

Mum turned to look at him, and Shelly opened her eyes.

"Shelly, your daughter is in the arms of"—he shifted his focus to Mum—"*your* husband, Mum. They are partaking of this very feast. At this very moment, we are all at the same table, sharing this incredible communion with our Lord, Jesus Christ. Remember this. Always. And do it often, in remembrance of Him who saved us."

He touched the Host to Shelly's lips, then gave that Host to Mum. He raised his hand and gave the sign of the cross as the orderlies came to take Shelly into surgery.

When the room was clear, Mum leaned into Matt and finally gave in to the tears that she'd been holding back. Feeling helpless, there was nothing left for him to do but embrace her sobbing body.

———

A HALF HOUR LATER, it was obvious that Hester had to go home. As Matt inserted the key into the ignition of Angie's truck, he looked her over. The bags under Hester's eyes had darkened, and her shoulders, the ones she always held ramrod straight, slumped.

The engine roared to life, and Matt headed out of the parking lot. Their trip across town to the mansion should be a quick one, he thought. It was almost midnight, and the icy streets were empty.

Hester finally broke the silence. "Angie's a good woman," she said. "A firecracker to be sure, but a good soul."

Matt offered a smile, but he kept his eyes on the slick road. "Yeah, I lucked out on that one."

"I take it she goes to your church?"

This time, Matt chuckled. "Hardly. She was born and raised Roman Catholic. She goes to mass a couple towns over."

"How'd that go over with your congregation?" she asked.

He shrugged. "I think some are more upset that she owns the bar across the river from the church."

"Ah," Hester said, as if she finally understood something. "Elsbeth."

Matt smiled. "Never a dull moment with Elsbeth."

They rode in silence for a few more blocks before Hester spoke again. "Do you think Shelly's going to make it?"

"I don't know. I'm praying that she will. For Mum's sake." He gave a quick sideways glance at Hester. Her face was turned toward the truck door's window, but he had a feeling she wasn't looking at the passing storefronts. "You okay?"

Hester swallowed hard and turned to look at him. "Shelly —" Her voice cracked. "Shelly named the baby Boudicca."

It took Matt a moment to understand why the odd name would have any significance. Then his brow arched in understanding. "Mum's real first name."

Tears welled in Hester's eyes. "They let Shelly hold the baby. 'Beautiful Boudicca.' She kept saying it over and over, Mum said." Hester leaned her elbow on the passenger door's armrest and brought her hand to her eyes. Her quiet sobs were more heart-wrenching than if she'd been wailing. "They let Mum in, after it was all over. To be with...them. Mum said the baby was beautiful, despite the...the discoloration. But Shelly, Shelly wouldn't let go. She kept saying 'Beautiful Boudicca.'" This time, Hester did sob out loud. "No more," she gasped out. "I can't..." She turned away.

Matt looked from Hester to the road and back at Hester. There was nothing he could say or do to help Hester. Or Mum. Or Shelly. The thought of the beautiful, dead baby in her mother's arms—.

Then something inside of him tightened. His helpless sense of gut-wrenching sorrow began to morph into something much more potent. More dangerous. More powerful.

The baby. Boudicca Duff. Dead.

He felt the anger of it, the injustice of it, fill him. And with it came resolve. Purpose. Fury.

"I'm going to find out who killed that baby, Hester," he said. "I don't know what's happened to Shelly's husband. I don't know if Shelly's going to make it. I don't know why Lambert is dead. But I know one thing. Shelly never would have made the trip to Austin if her husband hadn't disappeared. She never would've had to endure the worsening stress every passing minute her husband was missing. She never would've gotten out of that bed tonight if we hadn't found Lambert hanging from a rope in his room."

He gripped the steering wheel hard. "Someone is behind all those things that killed that baby. And I'm going to find out who."

31

A CORNER IS TURNED

MATT'S BRAIN turned on at six-thirty the next morning. Though he knew he should roll over and try to get some more shut-eye, he was just as sure sleep would elude him. He had a murderer to catch.

He grabbed a shower, threw on a navy turtleneck and a pair of jeans that Angie had brought for him and headed down the hallway to the second-floor elevator. Before he'd returned to Hester's last night, Connor had removed the bookcase that blocked the elevator from opening to the second floor. Apparently, Hester had ordered the deed done when she'd been forced to move Matt off the third floor due to fire code violations. As soon as the first-floor doors opened, he smelled fresh coffee and something delicious.

"Morning, Preacher." Lyle looked up from the Bundt-shaped coffee cake he was drizzling with a white goo. "Help yourself to coffee."

Matt poured himself a cup. "Any word on Shelly Duff?"

"Angie texted that Shelly made it through the night, but it's still touch and go." Lyle spooned up another glop of glaze.

It was no surprise that Angie had texted Lyle instead of him. Her last words were that Matt was to go straight to bed and get some solid sleep.

"We've got a schedule worked out," Lyle continued. "Angie's going to stay at the hospital a few more hours, then head back to Wilks to work at the Icehouse. I'll go over and stay with Mum so Angie can hit the road. One of Mrs. Duff's friends is coming over from San Antonio. She should be here by noon."

"I'm supposed to be at police headquarters at eight. Maybe I'll run over to the hospital before that."

Lyle shook his head. "Angie said to tell you not to come 'til later. Mum was finally sleeping."

"I'll head over there after I'm done at the cop shop, then."

Hester appeared in the kitchen doorway. "Well, everybody's up, I see." She moved slowly over to the coffeepot. Matt figured she must've slept about as well as he had. She filled her cup, sniffed appreciatively at the rich aroma and took her first sip. "Ah," she said. "Hazelnut."

"And cinnamon coffee cake." Lyle placed the coffee cake on the kitchen nook table, which was already set for four. "Would anyone care for scrambled eggs?"

Both Hester and Matt nodded as they took their seats. Steam rose as Hester cut into the glazed confection. She placed a slice on a plate and handed it to Matt.

He forked up a bite, and his eyes went round. "This is delicious," he said, his mouth still full. "How did you make it so moist?"

"Sour cream," Lyle said, as he whisked the eggs.

Matt smiled. "Your secret ingredient."

"I wish I had a secret ingredient for healing Shelly Duff." With a sigh, Lyle dumped the egg mixture into the skillet.

Hester looked up. "Is there any word on how she's doing?"

"I texted with Angie earlier," Lyle answered. "She said Shelly made it through the night."

Hester looked relieved. "Thank goodness. I was thinking I'd take some lunch over to them later."

Matt put down his fork. "I thought we'd decided you were going to the Junior League auction with Elsbeth."

"Oh. I'd forgotten about that." She leveled him a stern stare. "And why am I going with *that* woman to an event with *those* women?"

"Because I think Pastor Meade knows a whole lot about what's happened to Reverend Duff, and I need to know a lot more about Meade."

"You want me to what? Cozy up to Mrs. Meade?"

"And wear a wire."

Hester's eyes widened.

Matt continued. "I need to know what Meade's been up to since the inauguration. Before that, for that matter. Has he been in contact with Senator Womack? Do the Meades know Senator Womack's son? Did they know Lambert?"

"You think I can get any of that information?"

Matt looked her straight in the eye. "Hester, I think you can do anything you set your mind to."

She leaned back, studied Matt, then nodded. "All right. I'm in."

———

AFTER A SHORT VISIT to Dr. Ryan for a check on his vitals —which had gone up again—an hour later, Matt drove Angie's truck over to the Austin crime lab building.

Gage met him at the door and ushered him down the hall-way. "I'll introduce you to the sergeant in charge, then I have to hit the road."

They entered through a door marked "Evidence Lock-Up" and headed straight to the reception counter. A short, heavy-set man greeted them.

"Sergeant Mathison, this is Pastor Matt Hayden," Gage said. "He's been cleared to see anything he might ask for regarding the Duff disappearance. Consider him my second set of eyes."

"Yes, ma'am," Mathison replied.

Gage turned to Matt. "No photos, and nothing can be removed from the premises. Clear?"

"Clear." Matt nodded. He and Gage had already discussed the arrangement but stating the terms aloud would assure Mathison all was in order. "I need one more thing before you go."

Gage's eyes took on a suspicious glint. "What now?"

"I need to wire up Hester Honeywell for a luncheon she's going to around eleven."

Gage's perfectly curved eyebrow arched. "For what purpose?"

"She's having lunch with Pastor Meade's wife. We need to know what he's been up to the last few days."

She sighed. "We won't be able to use it as evidence."

"No. But we'll be able to use the information," Matt replied.

"Maybe." She blew out a breath. "Have you ever rigged anyone up before?"

Matt suppressed a laugh. In his undercover days, he'd been wired up so many times, he'd almost felt naked without the equipment on. "I can handle it."

"All right then. Check at the front desk before you leave. The stuff will be there."

"Thanks."

She left, and Sergeant Mathison cleared his throat. "What

do you want to see, Pastor?"

"We'll start with the footage taken from St. George Episcopal's security cameras."

———

ANGIE RETURNED from the hospital cafeteria to find Mum wide awake. "I had to get something to eat," Angie explained and set a to-go box on the coffee table. "Enough for two," she said, opening the box and grabbing a sausage and egg biscuit.

"Thank you," Mum said. "The growling in my stomach woke me up." Mum reached for an éclair.

"Any word yet?"

"Only that she's stable." Mum took a delicate bite from the pastry.

"That's good. Very good," Angie said. She glanced toward the lounge door, hoping the doctor would soon appear with an update. She and Mum were running out of things to talk about.

Mum studied the éclair in her hand. "The last time I ate anything, I thought it was going to be my last communion with my daughter." Her gaze turned thoughtful. "But your preacher showed me another way to look at it."

"Was Shelly able to take communion?"

Mum nodded. "The preacher called it 'intinction.'" She smiled. "Shelly was certainly taken with his cross. Do you know how it came to be his?"

With her mouth full, Angie merely shook her head.

"Most of the crosses have a story. David's does."

Angie swallowed the bite. "Reverend Duff?"

"It was his grandfather's cross. Also a Reverend Duff. As was his father."

"It passed down from generation to generation?"

"Oh, no. It belonged only to Grandpa Duff. It was his gift

to David when David was ordained." Mum's lip curled. "If it had been a gift from his father, I doubt David would've worn it very often."

Angie looked up. "David and his dad didn't get along?"

"It was an odd, generational thing. Great Grandpa Duff and David's father were preachers of the law. Grandpa Duff and David preached grace." Mum's face paled. "Oh, dear. I said that in the past tense. As if I believe he's dead."

Angie put a hand on hers. "Matt and Lieutenant Gage are doing everything they can to find him."

"I know." Mum drew in a fortifying breath. "But when they do find him, and...if he has passed on...I hope they find his cross. It was a beautiful heirloom. It would mean a lot to Shelly to have it."

"Matt's cross looks like a braided rope. What does David's cross look like?"

"It was hand-forged steel. With a diamond at each point and a ruby in the center."

The ICU doors opened. Angie and Mum stood as soon as they saw Dr. Boya come through the door.

"How is Shelly?" Mum asked.

Dr. Boya smiled. "I think we've turned a corner."

32

THE MISSING POWERPOINT

MATT PUSHED BACK from the APD monitor. He'd been studying the confiscated security tapes for hours—first those that showed Lambert dropping Reverend Duff off at St. George Episcopal at precisely eight-fifty-two, and then Duff leaving the church at nine-sixteen. He switched to the Hilton Grand Ballroom footage, which clocked Lambert walking in at nine-oh-four. Which meant Lambert had a clear alibi when Duff disappeared. Matt fast-forwarded to the end of the prayer breakfast and watched Lambert leave the ballroom at ten-twenty-seven with several other pastors, and street cameras documented his trek to the Governor's Mansion where Matt first met him.

Next, he ran the tapes of the traffic and business footage, which showed Duff entering the parking deck halfway between the church and the Capitol at nine-twenty. He studied every tape that showed an exit from the parking lot. Duff never emerged. Somewhere in that parking deck, Reverend David Duff disappeared.

Wait a minute. Matt sat up straighter in his chair. Lambert drove to the convention center, right? So why didn't he drive over to the Governor's Mansion—or at least to Hester's to park his car? Did he leave his car at the convention center the entire day?

Matt stood and went to the door. "Sergeant Mathison?"

The graying, pot-bellied man looked up from his desk. "Yes, Pastor?"

"Did Lieutenant Gage request any exterior convention parking security footage?"

Mathison shrugged. "I'll have to look."

"If she didn't, I guess she'd have to get a search warrant to get anything further," Matt said, more to himself than to the Sergeant.

"I doubt it," Mathison said. "The convention center is owned by the city, and the Hilton is always cooperative. When it comes to safety, we work together pretty well."

Matt's phone chimed. "I'd appreciate it if you'd check to see if it's already here."

"No problem."

Matt pulled his cell from his pocket. The caller ID read *River Walk Fellowship Church*. Matt clicked on the call. "Pastor Hayden."

"Good morning, Pastor," said a slightly accented voice. "Pastor Garcia here. We spoke last night?"

The pastor who led the Hispanic service, Matt remembered, *and* translated Duff's sermon outline for that Sunday's PowerPoint. "Of course," Matt said.

"Well, I have some good news and some bad news," said Garcia. "The bad news is I can't find the PowerPoint I translated for Sunday's service. I saved it on the church's computer, but the file is gone."

Matt's lips firmed. He didn't believe in coincidences when it came to crime. "And your good news?"

"I do have my handwritten notes from my conversation

with Reverend Duff about the overall focus for this year. Would you like me to send them to you?"

"Yes." Matt pinched his nose. "I know Spanish." Cuban Spanish from his cop days in Miami, but maybe—

There was a chuckle on the other end of the line. "You're in luck there," Garcia said. "I wrote them in English. How about I scan them into a PDF and email it to you?"

"That would be great."

"I'll go to the copy machine now. What's your email address?"

Matt gave Garcia the information, then thanked the man again.

"No worries," Garcia said. "Meanwhile, I'll try to find out what happened to Sunday's PowerPoint."

As Matt returned his cell to his pocket, Mathison came into the evidence room. "It's a no on any exterior footage, but I'm sure if Lieutenant Gage put in the request, we could have it before end of work today."

"Thanks." Matt turned back to the evidence box on the room's lone table. "I still have to go through the materials they found in Reverend Duff's room. Then I'll be done."

Mathison offered a knowing smile. "For now."

Matt nodded. "For now."

———

ANGIE BREATHED a sigh of relief when a robust, middle-aged woman came into the hospital lounge and made a beeline for Mum. "Darling," the woman said, taking Mum in an all-encompassing hug. "I'm so sorry."

Mum held the hug for a long moment. "Delia, thank God you're here."

The woman held Mum at arm's length to look her up and

down. "I feel terrible that you had to go through all of this alone. Why didn't you call?"

Mum turned to Angie. "I haven't been alone. Delia, this is my new, very good friend, Angie. Angie, this is my Bible Study leader and very good friend, Delia."

Angie and Delia shook hands as Mum sat down on the vinyl couch. "Take off your coat, and I'll tell you everything."

Delia shook out of her parka, straightened the sleeves on her sweater and took Mum's hand as she sat down. "I'm yours."

With relief that Mum's friend had arrived, Angie realized she was now free to go back to Wilks. She stepped out into the hallway and pulled out her cell. Her first call was to her cook, Dorothy Jo, at the Icehouse.

"We're good until two o'clock," Dorothy Jo said in answer to Angie's question. "Callie Mae and Devin are staying on past the breakfast shift. After that, we could really use your help. Bo's running on empty at the bar."

"I'll be there," Ange said firmly. "Tell Bo he's an angel."

Angie's next call was to Matt. "Hi, babe. How's it going?"

"I haven't learned anything new about Duff's disappearance." Angie heard frustration in his voice. "Everything's as Gage said. Duff went into a parking deck and never came out."

"I'm sorry." And she was, for both the missing Duff and Matt. She'd hoped, for his sake, he would find something to spur the investigation on. "FYI, Mum's friend has arrived, and I'm needed at the Icehouse. I'm thinking it's time for me to head back to Wilks."

"All right." There was a pause. "Tell you what. I'm waiting for the surveillance equipment for Hester to wear at that Junior League Auction. As soon as I get it, how about I come to the hospital, see Mum for a quick visit, then drive you back over to the mansion so you can grab your things and I can wire up Hester?"

"Sounds good."

"But here's the deal," Matt continued. "I need you to go to the Oak and Horn with me before you leave town. Just to get me in the door. I'm hoping that bartender you met yesterday will be on again."

"I'm good with that, but I can't stay long."

"No problem. While I'm headed your way, give James W. a call and see if he can join us at the Oak and Horn, say..." another pause, "eleven-thirty? He knows more about hunting than I do. That way, he can drive me back to Hester's, and you can head straight on out to Wilks." A beep came over the phone, and Matt said, "Hang on. An email I've been waiting for just came in."

There was a long pause, and Angie quickly ran through her schedule. Once Matt picked her up at the hospital, they'd go to the mansion, where she'd catch a shower. Then they'd head to the Oak and Horn. Something haunted her about that place. The photos on the back wall were gruesome.

"Pastor Garcia sent a PDF of his notes about Duff's upcoming sermon series," Matt said. "I want to stop by St. George Episcopal Church. I think Bishop Hamlin knows a whole lot more about this business than he was willing to talk about yesterday."

"Okay."

"I'll call when I leave there so you can come down. I'll visit Mum later this afternoon. Do you want me to gas up your truck?" Matt asked.

"No, I'll fill it up on my way out of town."

"Thanks. I'll see you soon."

Angie signed off the call and stared at her phone for a moment. What could possibly have been in that PDF from Pastor Garcia?

33

THE SIGN OF FOUR

ST. George Episcopal's limestone edifice towered over the busy street, only a few blocks from Hester's home. A Gothic design, the three-story tall sanctuary lined with stained glass windows dwarfed the two auxiliary buildings on either side. Matt followed a small brass sign that read "Office" to the one-story building on the left.

A bell rang above the door as he entered the reception area. The office beyond looked like something out of the fifties, surrounded by thin wood sliding cabinets and green steel desks. The only modern appointment in the room was the IBM industrial-sized copier that chugged away in the corner.

A harried woman stood at the copy machine, stacking the bulletins as they spit out. The sound of the copier's machinations were loud enough that they might have drowned out the bell, so Matt cleared his throat and said, a little more loudly than usual, "Good morning."

The woman turned, her pleasant face round, and her gray hair permed. She smiled easily when she saw Matt's collar.

"Sorry, didn't hear the bell." She clicked off the machine. "May I help you?"

"I'm here to see Bishop Hamlin."

Her smile faded a bit. "I'm afraid he works on his sermon on Friday mornings. He doesn't like to be disturbed."

Matt nodded. "Unfortunately, I have some sad news about a man we both knew, and I thought it would be better to hear it from me than on the TV."

"I see." She nodded in understanding. "What's your name, and I'll go let him know you're here."

"Pastor Matt Hayden."

"I'll be right back."

Matt watched her leave, hopeful that the hook that someone was dead would be enough to get him through Hamlin's door. At their parting yesterday, he had the distinct impression that Hamlin would not want to speak with Matt again any time soon.

The woman returned. "He'll see you, of course, but asks that you please keep it short."

She led the way down the hall, then motioned Matt inside the Bishop's office.

Bishop Hamlin's round, polished face was creased in annoyance as he sat behind his rather ornate desk. Matt noted that he didn't stand.

"Pastor Hayden. I didn't expect to see you again."

So soon, would've been the polite way of greeting. Matt noted that the bishop neither extended his hand for a hand-shake or indicated that Matt should sit in the needlepoint-upholstered chair opposite the desk.

"I'm afraid the news I have for you may be disturbing," Matt said.

"So Mrs. Williams indicated." The bishop tapped his fingers impatiently on the desk.

"Pastor Lambert committed suicide last night in his room at Hester Honeywell's."

Bishop Hamlin's jaw dropped, slackening his fat cheeks so that his face looked like a popped balloon. "When?"

"The coroner will be the judge of that. The last anyone saw him yesterday was around four o'clock and his body was discovered at six-forty-five."

The bishop stared at Matt for a solid five seconds before asking, "What happened?"

"He hanged himself."

Hamlin pushed himself out of his chair and began pacing against the far wall. "That poor soul," he said finally.

Matt felt the wall that Hamlin had put up between them fall away with every step. "Sir, I'm afraid I have more bad news."

The bishop stopped pacing. "They've found Reverend Duff?"

"No. It's Reverend Duff's wife. She miscarried the baby last night. It was stillborn. And Mrs. Duff is very, very ill."

"Is she going to make it?" Hamlin's question was more a plea.

"She lost a great deal of blood. I haven't heard the doctor's report from today yet."

"My God," Hamlin said. He sat down heavily in the chair next to Matt. "This has got to stop."

"What exactly must stop?" Matt asked.

The bishop worried his hands, obviously debating something internally.

Matt leaned forward, his voice gentle. "What's going on?"

Hamlin cleared his throat.

"Did Robert Meade and David Duff have a falling out?" Matt suggested.

Beads of sweat began forming on Bishop Hamlin's forehead. "What do you know about Pastor Lambert?"

"I know he worked at Reverend Duff's church. He was ordained, but not to preach. To administer churches."

"That's right. He was called to River Walk Fellowship Church in San Antonio straight out of seminary. Reverend Jesse Duff—David's father—was the head of the church back then. The older Duff was like a second father to Pastor Lambert." Hamlin paused, then breathed heavily. "You see, Lambert's own father had died when he was a child." He looked up at Matt. "Suicide. By hanging."

"The elder Duff and I had long discussions about Greg—Pastor Lambert's first name is Greg. Jesse was a...conservative, to say the least. Every act he performed, every word he spoke was based on a literal reading of the Bible. For Greg Lambert, that was water to a man dying of thirst. The elder Duff was solid. Assured. Everything Lambert was not." Hamlin shook his head. "Now to his own son, David, Jesse Duff's ramrod law-and-order version of Christianity was a curse. David was more a New Testament kind of guy, but his father—"

"More of a Leviticus kind of guy?"

Hamlin almost chuckled. "You could say that. When Jesse passed so suddenly, Lambert was a lost soul."

"But he stayed on at River Walk, even when David started a—shall we say—new direction for the church?"

Hamlin cleared his throat uncomfortably. "Lambert was coaxed into staying."

"By whom?"

"Reverend Meade."

That took Matt by surprise. "Why?"

"Meade likes to have eyes and ears everywhere. *Everywhere*," he emphasized, and gave a quick look at his closed office door. "He's climbing the ladder, as they say. And he's not only involved in the ecumenical world. He's into politics, as well. He has no intention of letting an upstart take him down."

"That's what Meade thought David Duff wanted to do? Take him down?"

Hamlin's smile was part fear and part admiration. "That's exactly what Duff wanted to do. What he felt he was called to do."

"To do what?"

"Call out the Pharisees and hypocrites. And in David's opinion, Meade was one of them."

"For example?" Matt asked.

"David Meade lives in a multimillion-dollar mansion. When Jesus died, his only possession was the robe they cast lots for beneath the cross."

"Tell me about the paper David Duff wanted you to look at —the paper he was supposed to drop off before the inauguration, but you said never showed up?"

Hamlin's head snapped up. "I didn't lie to you. There was no paper on my desk, in this office, on my secretary's desk, anywhere. Believe me, after he didn't show up at the inauguration, I was desperate to find it."

"Okay," Matt held up his hands. "What was it supposed to be?"

"His sermon for the following Sunday. Apparently, he was kicking off a year of 'setting the record straight'—his words exactly. I never saw the document."

"Speaking of documents," Matt pulled his cell from his pocket. "I got a PDF about Duff's sermon series for the year from someone at Duff's River Walk Fellowship Church." Matt was not going to get Pastor Garcia involved in this mess. "The four points that David Duff was going to preach on for the entire year were as follows:

"First, the life of Jesus.

"Second, the Eleven Commandments—an interesting count, I thought.

"Third, the Parables.

"Fourth, the Sermon on the Mount." He watched the bishop's face.

Hamlin let out a half-chuckle. "He was really going to do it."

"There's more to the PDF. Some of the main points he was going to cover. From what I could tell, Duff was going to emphasize the difference between what Jesus taught and did compared to what many so-called Christian pastors are saying from the pulpit."

Hamlin nodded. "David often said that some conservative zealots would be scared out of their wits if they ever read the Beatitudes, much less the entire Sermon on the Mount. And if I'm being honest, he might have been right about that."

Matt checked his watch. "I have to go. I borrowed someone's truck and I've got to return it."

Bishop Hamlin stood, held out his hand. "I don't know what's happened to David, but between Lambert's suicide and Shelly's loss, this has got to stop. Would you be free to get together again tomorrow night, after our Vespers service? That's really the earliest I can get away. We have a large funeral tomorrow."

Matt shook his hand. "I'll be here."

He headed for the door, but Hamlin called after him. "Please leave the hospital information for Shelly with my secretary. I want to go see her."

"Of course."

Matt hurried from the church to Angie's truck, a sickening realization growing in his stomach. Things were worse than he thought. People were dying...in the name of God.

34

SENATOR WILLIAM J. WOMACK

ANGIE HURRIED down Hester's grand stairway, her hair still wet from her quick shower. When she rounded the corner to the parlor, Matt was waiting for her. "Sorry I'm late," she said, then stopped mid-step when she saw how he was dressed. "You cannot wear that."

Matt looked down at his polo and khakis. "What's wrong with this?"

"You're going to a redneck bar, for Pete's sake, not a country club." She bent to her bag, opened it and pulled out a T-shirt. "Lose the polo. Wear this."

Matt studied the faded white shirt touting a "Don't Mess with Texas" logo. "That won't fit—"

"It's my night shirt. Too big for me, but probably okay for you." She watched a frown crease his face. "It's clean. I obviously didn't sleep in it last night."

"I don't—"

"You, of all people, should appreciate that it's not wise to stand out like a sore thumb when you're reconning a location." She narrowed her eyes.

He made a face. "Should've thought of that." He turned toward the archway, where he almost ran into Lyle. Matt grunted out a "sorry" and kept going.

"I need to get Hester's coat. And mine," Lyle said, his eyes wide with excitement.

"What are you so happy about?" Angie asked as she repacked her bag.

"I've been recruited." He opened the closet door.

"To do what?"

Lyle leaned back and looked back at Angie. "You know Matt fitted Hester with a microphone—super-glued it right into the brooch she's wearing—"

Angie's eyebrows shot up.

"Don't worry." He waved his hand. "It's only costume. Anyway, while she's in the banquet room downstairs, I'm going to be right above her in a second-floor card room, taping her conversations!"

The man looked so delighted she couldn't help but smile. "They couldn't have found a better man for the job."

His cheeks turned pink, then his smiled faded. "You're heading back to Wilks?"

She nodded. "Gotta get back to work."

"Don't be a stranger, Angie. You saved my butter last night." He brightened. "And next time, I'll cook for you."

"You are so on," she said. Her temper tantrum yesterday may have been forgiven and forgotten. Thank heavens, she thought. She had a feeling she was going to be seeing a lot of the little family here at Hester's as long as Jimmy was in the Governor's Mansion.

"This better?" Matt's voice came from behind her.

Angie nodded her approval when she saw he had changed into the prescribed T-shirt and jeans. "Much."

Angie and Matt shrugged into their jackets and headed for

the door. Angie paused to give Lyle a light peck on the cheek. "I'm looking forward to that dinner."

"You're on."

As they left the mansion, Angie hooked her arm into Matt's. "The ice is almost melted," she said.

"Safer for you to get home, anyway." Matt held up her keys. "You wanna drive?"

"You go ahead. I'll be on the road plenty this afternoon."

When they were settled in the truck, Angie took one last look at the mansion. "That's the fastest, longest twenty-four hours I've ever spent." She sighed. "How can you get so close to people when you've known them for such a short time?"

"Bad times have a way of bonding good people together." Matt pulled away from the curb. "How do you think Mum's holding up?"

"She's got Delia now. And the doctor's report was—what's the term? 'Cautiously optimistic'—about Shelly's prognosis."

"I'll stop by there later this afternoon."

They rode in silence for a few blocks, then Angie said, "Mum talked a lot about Shelly's husband this morning."

"Anything that would shed light on his disappearance?" Matt asked.

"Not really." She ran through the conversation with Mum in her head. "She talked a lot about David and his father, and his grandfather, for that matter." She continued to roll through the conversation in her head. "You know that cross you wear? When you're making calls and stuff?"

"Sure."

"Where'd you get it?"

"My mom gave it to me when I was ordained. It means a lot to me."

Angie nodded. "The cross Shelly's husband wears was given to him by his paternal grandfather. In fact, the way

Mum told it, the cross originally belonged to that grandfather."

"Interesting," Matt said.

Angie looked at him. "What?"

"That the grandfather gave it to his grandson, and not to his own son."

"I suppose." She shrugged. "Anyway, it was pretty fancy. It had four diamonds, one on each point, and a ruby in the center."

"That *is* pretty fancy." He pulled up to the curb across the street from the Oak and Horn. "James W.'s already here."

James W., adorned in a Gimmie cap, a camo T-shirt, jeans and rubber boots, walked toward them.

"See? You would have looked like a city slicker next to him. He knows what hunters look like."

"Okay. I get it. Don't make your point a blunt instrument, woman."

Smiling, Angie jumped down from the truck. She'd forgotten what it was like to kid around with Matt. Yes, things between them were getting back to normal.

Thank God.

———

MATT SMILED. He and Angie were back to joking around with each other. Thank God.

James W. nodded toward the bar across the street. "Guess this place doesn't serve food," he observed. "No lunch crowd."

"I'm not sure you'd want to eat it if they did," Angie said.

James W. fixed a glare on Matt. "I've been tryin' to get a hold of you for an hour. Where you been?"

"The morning's been non-stop," Matt said.

"Y'all, let's get this show on the road. I have an hour's drive to Wilks." She started to cross the street, then stopped. "You should know, I told the bartender yesterday that my name is Maeve." She looked down to kick the slush off her boots before going in, then saw Matt's shoes. Her head jerked up. "Take a seat at the bar as soon as we go in. You're wearing patent leather shoes, for Pete's sake."

"They're the only shoes I brought," he said defensively.

"Before we go in, y'all need to know I did a little homework with some of my hunting friends about this place. Got some skinny."

"Make this fast, James W.," Angie prodded.

"My buddy told me some pretty tall tales about the Oak and Horn. I wanna throw some of 'em against the wall and see what sticks." He looked at Matt. "Suck it up, son. You're the dumb, cynical Generation X'er. I'm the good ole boy."

Matt nodded. Cop hat time.

Angie pointed at her watch. "I'll get you in, then I gotta hit the road."

Matt inclined his head toward the door. "Let's go."

James W. led the way inside, followed by Matt and Angie. The place was indeed empty, Matt noted, not even a bartender in sight. Country music played on an old radio mounted behind the bar, and cigarette stink filled the room. Guess the no-smoking laws hadn't made it through the front door, Matt thought.

He gave the room a quick look-see, mindful of Angie's order to sit at the bar as soon as he got in. Lit only by two dust-covered, elk-horned chandeliers, the interior of the small bar was dark—which was probably a good thing. The plaid, cloth-upholstered chairs and sofa probably hadn't been cleaned since Nixon's resignation, the year Matt was born.

Ahead stood the bar, which ran the width of the building. Centered above the bar was the bronze image of a man standing beneath a tree, surrounded by animals and under-growth, and holding a horn to his lips. A water buffalo's head and many-pointed buck flanked the bronze relief.

Angie nodded to the wall behind them. "The photos," she whispered.

Matt squinted, trying to make out the pictures through the dark haze, when he heard a sound in the back room. Heeding Angie's admonishment, he turned and headed straight for one of the worn leather stools at the bar.

A woman with muscled arms and dishwater blonde hair pulled back with a red bandana came around the corner carrying a rack of washed glasses. She hoisted it onto the counter, all the while giving the newcomers a once-over, then recognized Angie. "You're back."

Angie nodded, took the stool beside Matt. "Good to see you. Monica, right?"

The bartender nodded, but her eyes were trained on James W. and Matt. And they weren't friendly.

Not looking for customers though the place was empty, Matt noted.

"Brought some friends with you," Monica said, scrutinizing the two men.

"These are the folks that put me up last night. Jim here," Angie nodded at James W., "is the hunter in the group. I thought he'd like to see the place."

"And you?" Monica asked of Matt.

"Along for the beer." Matt said. "Got a Shiner handy?"

"Make that two," James W. said.

Angie sniffed. "Make mine a Lone Star."

Monica pulled the bottles from the cooler, snapped off their tops and put the beers on the bar. "You hunt around here?" she asked James W.

"Down south of Bastrop mostly," James W. answered. "Got

a deer lease in Wilks County." Still standing, he kicked his boot up on the brass footrest and looked around. "You've got a lot of history here." He gestured with his beer toward the ten-foot-tall stuffed stag rearing from the corner. "Any idea who shot that bad boy?"

"Earle Lee Ashe," Monica supplied. "About forty years ago."

James W. banged his beer on the bar. "Naw. Any relation to Danny Lee Ashe from Benedict County?"

Monica's face relaxed. "His grandfather. You know Danny Lee?"

"We've been pigeon-shooting a few times. His old man had a place outside of College Station. Course, he's passed now." James W. picked up his beer and took a thoughtful swallow. "Those were good times." He nodded toward the back wall. "What about those photos back there?"

Finally, Matt thought. He had a reason to turn around and look at the pictures that had so bothered Angie.

"That's the wall of fame," Monica said. "Bunch of the guys from here kind of have a club."

James W. walked over to get a closer look. "What are those boys eating?" He turned back to Monica, a sly smile on his face. "Don't tell me. Herne the Hunter. Well, that fits about right with Danny Lee's daddy."

Matt was frustrated that he couldn't get up for a closer look at the pictures, but even from where he sat, he could tell there was a dark substance smudged and dripping from the men's grinning faces. "Herne the Hunter?"

"Some say it's a folktale," James W. said. "Others say you can hear Herne's hounds and him blowing his horns the night before national disasters or assassinations."

Angie looked up at the bronze plaque above the bar. "You mean that guy?"

Monica nodded. "That's Herne. Saved by Satan after being gored by a stag, only to be damned to grow those stag's horns from his own head for eternity."

Matt guffawed and took a slug of his beer. "Fairy tales. What a bunch of idiots."

Angie glared at Matt, then slipped off the stool. "Time for me to get on the road."

Not yet, Matt screamed silently. Monica wasn't hooked yet. And they needed an opening about—"What about that guy you said made eyes at you last night when you were here?"

Angie caught on quickly. He saw it in her eyes.

She sneered. "The one who was wearin' more money than you'll make in a year? He's off with those hunters, right?" Angie nodded at Monica. "What did you say last night? They're having a bonfire or somethin'?" She turned back toward Matt. "A bunch of men who could take you out with one shot, you pile of wuss."

"By golly," James W. broke in. He had wandered over to the side wall and was studying the trophies and certificates mounted there. He pointed at a long-barreled handgun that looked like something a pirate would've wielded. "You got a muzzleloader here."

Monica may not have cared for Matt, but her smile was genuine when she looked at James W. "If you can shoot a deer with that, you're welcome to join the group."

"Well, I'll be." James W. shook his head. "Is that what the bonfire's all about?" he asked. "Someone made the kill yesterday?"

Monica nodded. "Exactly. The hunter who made the kill eats the heart raw. That's the photos on the back wall. Proof you're in the club."

"That's sick," Matt said. "And one of them is the guy who made a pass at my girl last night?"

"I'm not your girl," Angie snapped.

"You sure acted like it last night between the sheets," Matt snapped back.

"I'm outta here." Angie headed for the door. "I'm sure one of you gentlemen will pay for my drink. Oh. Jim, I guess that means you." She stormed toward the door.

"Boy," James W. sauntered over to Matt. "If a duck had your brain, it would fly north for the winter," he chuckled.

Matt watched in the mirror as Angie reached for the door, but it opened before she could grab the knob.

A tall man silhouetted against the sunny outside stepped back as Angie pushed past him. "Now that's a nice lookin' little filly," he said, as the door closed behind him.

Annoyed, Matt studied the tall, broad-shouldered man in the mirror. He wore creased jeans, a starched white shirt and a butter-smooth suede jacket. His matching cowboy hat cast a dark shadow across his face. Something about him looked familiar, Matt thought, but he couldn't quite place him.

"Any of the boys back from the Homestead yet?" He walked inside and wrestled out of his jacket.

"Not yet." Monica, apparently knowing the newcomer's order, reached for a glass and a bottle of Jamesons. "Heck, you know that bonfire goes dusk 'til dawn. They're probably all still sleepin' it off."

The man tossed his jacket on a chair, revealing a large, oval belt buckle. "Wish I could have been there," the man said. "The vote in D.C. took forever." He straightened and rubbed a kink from his neck, giving Matt a closer look at the buckle. Deeply engraved into the silver was a man's head with antlers growing from it—the same pattern as the buckles mounted on the back wall.

"I expect somebody'll call pretty soon to say they're on the way back," Monica said, shoving the glass forward.

"When they get close to Lampasas, the cell service'll kick back in."

"Probably right." The man placed his hat on his jacket then turned to pick up his whiskey, giving Matt his first good look at the square-jawed man's face.

Matt swallowed hard. That square jaw and those broad shoulders belonged to U.S. Senator William Womack, father of Hogg and friend to Reverend Robert Meade.

Womack saw Matt's face in the mirror and his thick brows furrowed in confusion, but when he looked over at James W., recognition dawned. "Sheriff Novak," he said. "Hello."

To Matt, it sounded more like an accusation than a greeting.

"Was that pretty little redhead with you?"

"She's my sister." James W. eyes were steady, his mouth set in a line. "Hello, Senator."

Womack looked at Matt. "You gave the benediction at the inauguration."

Matt nodded, keeping his own face void of emotion. "Senator."

With the three of them staring each other down, Matt felt like he was standing under the high noon sun at the O.K. Corral.

Womack glared at Monica. "How long they been in here?"

"Maybe ten minutes." Wide-eyed, her face pale, the woman looked scared to death.

"I'll take care of your drinks, boys," Womack said. "Don't let the door hit you in the backside on the way out."

35

THE CRIME BOARD

The Crime Board

MATT CLIMBED into the passenger side of James W.'s Chevy quad cab, then blew out a low whistle. "If looks could kill," he said, "I'd be dead right now."

"Not a cheery fellow," James W. agreed. He jammed his key into the ignition. "FYI, Jimmy told me the senator never congratulated him on his gubernatorial victory."

"Really." Matt considered. Where was all this anger coming from? Meade's words to him at the inauguration—*I know who you are and what you're trying to do*—and now a U.S. senator kicking the governor's father out of a hole-in-the-wall bar. "And what's up with this Herne the Hunter thing? Eating a dead animal's raw heart? Bonfires that last all night?"

"It's a brotherhood," James W. said, pulling away from the curb. "When I talked to Danny Lee last night, he said the members are thick as thieves. His dad belonged to it, but

Danny Lee refused to join. He's a U.S. district attorney for the Western District of Texas, now. The group stays under the radar, but there've been rumors..." James W. shrugged.

Matt shook his head. "A brotherhood of Herne's Hunters. A missing, and I presume dead, pastor. A stressed wife and stillborn baby. An assistant pastor who commits suicide. A mega-church preacher and a U.S. senator with hate in their eyes. I can't get my head around it." He turned to James W. "What do you have on for the rest of the day?"

"Not much 'til 5:00. Another to-do, this time with the Young Republicans. Why?"

Matt's lips firmed. "I could use your help. It's time to set up a crime board."

———

WHEN THEY PULLED up to the mansion, Connor was outside, trimming the bushes fronting the porch. He straightened as James W. and Matt climbed from the truck. "How'd it go?" he called as the two headed up the sidewalk.

"Informative," Matt said. He nodded to the shears in Connor's gloved hands. "A little chilly for garden work, don't you think?"

"The firemen and medics made a mess here last night. Can't blame 'em, of course, but still." He aimed the shears at a nearby broken twig, "Lyle left some sandwiches for you in the fridge. And there's tomato bisque waiting for you on the stove."

"Thanks," Matt said, then stopped. "Do you guys have anything like a bulletin board or chalkboard I can use for a few days?"

Connor nodded. "There's a whiteboard upstairs in our apartment that Lyle uses during tax season to keep his clients straight."

FOUR REASONS TO DIE

That's right, Matt remembered. He'd forgotten Lyle was an accountant. "That'd be great, if you're sure it'll be okay with him."

"I'll text him and ask. Go get some food."

———

BY THE TIME they finished lunch, Connor had set up the whiteboard in the guesthouse library located beyond the first-floor great room. He'd also opened an armoire that held a computer and printer and pulled out the antique walnut writing desk's drawer to show them where all the office supplies were.

James W. did a three-sixty as he admired the shelves filled with books—all leather-bound—the deep-cushioned wingback chairs and the Tiffany lamps scattered around the room. "Never worked a case in such tall cotton before." His phone beeped, and he pulled it from his pocket. "Elsbeth texted me."

"What did she say?" Matt was already at the computer, punching in the password Connor had given him.

James W. held the cell a full arm's length away and squinted. "Happiest day of my life," he read. "Having lunch with Hester, the senator's wife and Reverend Meade's wife. I'm at the big girl's table!"

Matt suppressed a grin. James W. would never hear the end of this.

James W. sighed, then tapped in a reply.

"What'd you say?" Matt asked as the computer screen came to life.

"Can't wait to hear about it." He jammed the phone back in his pocket.

Matt couldn't wait to hear the recording from the "big girls" table.

James W. nodded at the papers Matt had put on the writing desk. "What are those?"

"Stills from the security footage I watched this morning. Let's get to work."

Within a half hour, the whiteboard was crowded with notes and photos. In the center was a church photo of David Duff, dressed in Egyptian blue clerical shirt and suit and wearing a matching blue banded Panama hat. Matt studied the photo closely. Around Duff's neck hung a heavy bronze pectoral cross with diamonds at each point and a ruby in the center. Ah, he thought. The cross Mum had described to Angie.

To the right were Duff's Riverwalk Fellowship connections. Matt included a photo of Shelly Duff, Pastor Lambert and Pastor Garcia—all taken from the church's directory. Next to Lambert's photo, he wrote "Administrative Pastor," "Disapproved of David Duff," "Desperate to talk to Meade," "Desperate to talk to Senator's son" and, finally, "Suicide." Next to Garcia. he listed "Hispanic Minister," "Missing PowerPoint Translation" and "Duff Confidante."

He stepped back to study the board, then focused, once again, on David Duff. The hat. The bright-blue suit jacket and shirt. The cross that, according to Mum, meant so much to him that he wore it all the time.

Wait a minute.

Matt hurried over to the writing desk and sorted through the screen shots he'd taken off the videos at Cop Central this morning. He pulled the St. George Episcopal photos and took them over to a Tiffany floor lamp to get a better look. The first one he'd copied was Duff getting out of the car. The camera was mounted on the corner of the building, the angle providing only a back view of Duff punching in the security code for the door and going inside. Nothing there but a view of Duff's back.

It was the next photo, though, that brought a small, slow

smile to Matt's face. "Take a look at this, James W." He handed the photo over.

"He's leaving the church. So?"

"Take a look at what you printed off," Matt said.

James W. sifted through the photos. "So?"

Matt pointed at the cross Duff wore in all of the newly printed photos. "Mum says he always wears his cross." He held up the security photo. "He's not wearing his cross in this photo."

"I'm not following you."

"Duff's on his way to give an inaugural prayer in front of thousands, and he's not wearing his cross? I don't think so." Matt turned the photo to give James W. a closer look.

"You're saying—" James W.'s eyes widened.

"I'm saying that man is not David Duff."

36

HE'S NO JOHN WAYNE

ANGIE WAS five miles past Bastrop when she saw the flashing lights of a police car a good half mile behind her. She squinted to look ahead in the now bright sunshine to see if there was an accident up ahead, but she was heading up a hill and had no idea what was on the other side. The traffic around her slowed, and she did the same.

The Department of Public Safety troopers' car was coming up quickly. Must be an accident, she thought. *Gosh, I hope no one's hurt.*

To her surprise, the DPS car swerved directly behind her, and the squawk of the "pullover" horn almost had her jumping from her seat.

"What in the world?" She hadn't been speeding. Bastrop had a reputation for speed traps, and anybody who drove Highway 71 through town knew to take care. Angie looked at her rearview mirror.

The trooper on the passenger side was staring straight at her. With a jerk of his thumb, he motioned her to move to the side of the road.

Confused, she did as he instructed. She slapped on her turn signal, slowed and cautiously made her way onto the gravel-covered shoulder. She removed her car registration from the glove compartment, grabbed her license from her purse and put them on the dash, then settled her hands on the wheel. Though she kept her head facing forward, her eyes were fixed on the rearview mirror. The two troopers were just sitting there, staring back at her.

What in the world was going on?

Ten minutes later, the same deputy got out of his car and walked up to Angie's truck. Dadgum, she thought. He had John Wayne's stooped shoulders, the lopsided gait, the imposing stature. The bravado.

She gulped, then rolled down her window. "May I help you, Deputy?"

"License. Registration."

Definitely not John Wayne, though. The wannabe's voice was a raspy tenor. She soberly handed over the items. "Is there a problem, Deputy?"

"We'll see."

He looked at her license and back at her, then chuckled.

To Angie's ears, that chuckle sounded very menacing.

His eyes met hers and his lip curled in a sneer. He tapped her license against his hand, then headed back and got in his car.

Angie desperately wanted to call James W., but her phone was in her purse on the passenger's side floorboard. She was too afraid to lean over to retrieve it. These morons might think she was reaching for a gun.

Another five minutes passed before the John Wayne wannabe opened his door and sauntered up to her truck. "Where you headed?" he asked when she rolled her window back down.

"Work," she answered. It was taking all her strength not to lay into him about the time.

He studied her license one more time, then her face. "You sure look familiar to me."

Angie shrugged. "I own a bar not too far from here. Maybe you've stopped by."

"Well, ain't that special."

As he said this last bit, the other trooper got out of the car and headed for the passenger side of her truck. He was built like a scarecrow, complete with straw-colored hair sticking out from below his hat.

The hair on the back of her neck began to prickle. "Deputy, what's this all about?" she asked.

The Wayne wannabe snapped his fingers then pointed at her. "I remember now. You're Sheriff Novak's sister. The father of Governor Novak."

Now, how in the world would he know that?

"What's it like having your nephew in the Governor's Mansion?"

He was talking nicely, but his glare was anything but. "We're all very proud of him," she answered.

The Wayne wannabe looked across to the scarecrow deputy, who now stood at the truck cab's other window. "What do you know, Terry," he said to the scarecrow. "We got a celebrity here."

"Terry" pushed his hat back on his head and let out a low whistle. "Sure is a pretty little thing."

This was getting creepier by the minute, Angie thought, but she kept the fear from her face. "Why thank you, Deputy." She batted her lashes. "Is that why you pulled me over, fellas?" she said in her flirtiest voice.

Wannabe let out a chuckle. "We were on the lookout for a truck matching your vehicle's description." He hooked a thumb in his oversized police belt. "You said you had to get to work?"

"Yes, I do." And she was a half-hour late thanks to these bozos.

"Tell you what, Ms."—he looked at her license again—"O'Day. Hey, why ain't your last name Novak? You married?"

"No. Engaged."

"I don't see a ring on that pretty little finger." The John Wayne wannabe leaned on her door. "You sure you're engaged?"

"I'm sure." The closer he got to her, the more Angie wanted to throw her truck into drive and get the hell out of Dodge.

"Too bad," the deputy winked.

"I do need to get to work. If you all are finished—"

The deputy straightened. "Tell you what. We'll escort you to your—what did you call it? Bar? We'll make sure you get there nice and safe."

"You really don't have to—"

"It's no trouble at all. In fact, we'll keep our eyes on you from now on. To make sure nothing happens to you. That would be such a waste of a pretty redhead."

Angie's heart skipped a beat, then another. Was he threatening her?

He turned to walk away, then stopped. "And make sure you tell that sheriff brother of yours that we'll be watching you, day and night. And the rest of his Wilks family too. Including his former sister-in-law Pearl and that brand-new husband of hers. Bo Peveto, isn't it? And he works at your bar, if I'm not mistaken."

Her mouth went dry.

"Yep. You tell your brother that he can be sure we'll take care of his family. You never know when a political nut might try to harm one of the governor's kin if your nephew ever crosses a line that upsets folks. You wouldn't want anyone you care about to get hurt, would you?"

"No, sir." *Get me out of here, God!*

"We'll pull around so's we can get you to your Fire and Icehouse lickety-split." He tipped his hat. "You make sure you tell your brother what I said now." He nodded for Scarecrow to join him back at the squad car.

Angie's heart was in her throat. He'd threatened her. A DPS trooper. Who had that kind of pull, to get a DPS trooper to threaten the governor's family?

The squad car pulled around, paused long enough at her window for both deputies to give her tooth-filled grins and thumbs up, then pulled ahead. Only when she was back on the highway and a few miles down the road did she realize she'd never told them the name of her bar or where the Fire and Icehouse was located.

37

THE WIVES HAVE CLAWS

The Wives Have Claws

LYLE BURST through the library's double doors. "Omigosh, omigosh, omigosh," he said, carrying the audio recorder and wires over to the writing desk. "You've got to hear this. Hester really got those old biddies to talk." He sat down on the fragile-looking antique chair behind the desk and began arranging his notes.

James W. and Matt shared a concerned look over the ability of the chair to hold Lyle's mass, but it seemed to be holding up.

"You had a good signal in the building?" Matt asked. He'd been worried the Austin Social Guild building's limestone walls would hamper the wireless connection.

"Everything worked great," Lyle said. He plugged the recorder into the wall, straightened a few wires, then tapped on a legal pad he'd set down. "I marked down the time code when things got interesting."

James W. pulled one of the wingback chairs around to face the writing desk. "Hester got them to talk?"

"Couldn't shut 'em up once they got started." Lyle's expression froze. "Not your wife, of course."

James W. snickered.

"Where is Hester?" Matt asked.

"Taking a shower. Said she had to wash off all the bullshit." Lyle picked up his legal pad. "Okay. I'm set up. What do you want to hear first?"

Matt considered. "Did Reverend Meade and Senator Womack's wives talk about their husbands?"

"That's about all they talked about. It was like their entire identity."

Matt sat in the other wingback chair. "Anything that might tell us why they didn't like David Duff?"

"I'm not sure," Lyle said. "Do you think Reverend Duff would have disapproved of their school?"

"What school?" Matt asked.

Lyle smiled. "That's where we'll start." He checked his notes, then forwarded the recorder. "This should be it." He hit play.

"It sounds like you and Mrs. Womack have been friends for years." Elsbeth's forceful contralto voice was easily recognizable.

"At least thirty years," came a mealy-mouthed, nasal reply.

Lyle paused the tape. "That's Mrs. Meade, the reverend's wife." He hit play again.

"We were sorority sisters at UT," came another voice, this one a smooth falsetto with a Dallas accent.

Lyle mouthed the words, *Mrs. Womack*.

"Delta Delta Delta," supplied Mrs. Meade. "You went to UT, didn't you, Hester? Did you belong to a sorority?"

"I was a rodeo girl," said Hester. "If I wasn't studying, I was riding."

"Oh," Mrs. Meade replied. "How nice."

"Mrs. Novak?" This from a new, perky, female voice. "May I steal you away for a moment? I'd like you to meet our Junior League president."

"Of course." Elsbeth dragged the word "course" into five syllables. "If you ladies will excuse me for a moment. Duty calls."

James W. winced.

"You met your husbands at UT?" asked Hester. Good job, Matt thought. Bring the conversation back to family.

"Robert and I attended the same church," said Mrs. Meade. "We met as teenagers in Bible Study."

"I met William at UT. He was a political science major, then went on to UT law school." Mrs. Womack tittered. "The man bleeds burnt orange."

"Our children grew up together. We secretly hoped my daughter, Deborah, and Charlotte's son, Hogg, would marry." Mrs. Meade sighed. "But Hogg went to Rolfe after high school, and Deborah met Kenny at Baylor."

"Rolfe?" This from Hester. "I don't believe I know that school."

"Rolfe Evangelical School of Trade and Technology," supplied Mrs. Womack. "That's where Hogg got his certification as a pharmaceutical assistant."

"It's a wonderful school," Mrs. Meade gushed. "Beautiful West Virginia campus. It's associated with the local community college so the students can graduate with professional certifications and associate degrees."

"That's the route Hogg used to get into UT. He wants to become a JD in Healthcare Law." Mrs. Womack's genteel accent sounded a tad forced. Sensitive subject, Matt decided.

"Both our husbands serve on Rolfe's Board of Directors." Mrs. Meade continued. "In fact, my husband attended a very important meeting there two days ago."

"The day after the inauguration?" Hester sounded surprised. "But I saw you both at the inaugural ball the night before. He's lucky to have grabbed a flight that would allow that."

"Oh, the church bought my husband a plane. But actually," Mrs. Meade's voice lowered, "Senator Womack uses it more than the Reverend, with all those quick trips to D.C."

"Maggie!" Mrs. Womack's voice was sharp.

There was an awkward silence, then Hester broke the tension. "You said Rolfe Evangelical is a technical school? What do most of the students study?"

"Rolfe offers a wide range of studies," Mrs. Womack's voice had returned to Southern sweet. "Some get certified as electricians, plumbers, car mechanics. Others study computers—coding and that type of thing. And of course, the medical certifications."

"More importantly," Mrs. Meade jumped in, "they graduate with a good Christian core. Chapel every day. Strict enforcement of dress code and, of course, no alcohol or smoking on campus. I wish the board had passed the new program that my husband proposed. It would have, too, if the senator had been there."

"The senator had to be in D.C., and you know it," Mrs. Womack countered. "His vote was key in stopping that gun control bill from getting out of committee."

"Still, Rolfe needs a course of study in hoplology," Mrs. Meaded insisted. "We have graduates in all sectors of the country except the military. Think how quickly the Army or the Marines would snatch up people with that certification!"

"What in the world is hoplology?" Hester asked.

"The science of arms and weapons of offense and defense, human and bestial," Mrs. Meade recited. And sounded quite proud as she did so, Matt thought.

"I'm not worried about the Rolfe Board of Directors, though," she continued. "The board members can't say no when our husbands are both there. Together, they're unstoppable."

"Ladies," this from Elsbeth, who sounded a bit out of breath. "It looks like they've opened another table for the silent auction. Shall we take a look?"

Murmurs of assent and the sound of scuffling shoes and moving chairs came across the recording. Matt looked up at Lyle. "Is that all?"

"There's more, but that's the main stuff on Reverend Meade and Senator Womack," Lyle answered.

"Turn it off for now please," Matt said.

Lyle did as he was told, then stood to stretch out his back. "I need a snack. Anyone else?"

James W.'s face lit up. "Absolutely."

"I'll see what I can find. I'll bring some iced tea, too." Lyle headed out the door.

Matt turned to James W. "What do you think?"

"I think I want to learn more about that school. What kind of courses would be taught for hoplolology...hoplopology, heck, whatever it's called?"

"Weaponry," Matt's brow furrowed. "Ballistics, probably."

"Bomb making." James W. shook his head. "I don't like the sound of it. Especially after we got a look-see at those Herne's Hunters this morning." He looked up Matt. "Where do we go from here?"

"We need another look at those security cam videos from this morning." Matt pulled out his phone. "I'm calling Lieutenant Gage. We have to go back to the crime lab."

———

ANGIE MADE sure her walk was steady as she crossed from her truck to the Icehouse's kitchen door. The squad car, its lights still flashing, was parked by the dumpster, and the two deputies inside watched her every move. When she reached the kitchen door, she fixed a bright smile on her face and waved at the squad car. "Thanks, guys!"

She opened the door, relief washing over her that she'd gotten home safely, when John Wayne's voice followed her inside.

"Anytime, Maeve."

The name shot through her like a bullet, but she had the presence of mind to make sure the door was shut behind her before her knees buckled.

"Angie!" Dorothy Jo stood only a few feet away at the walk-in fridge. "What's wrong? Are you sick?"

Angie sat back against the door, her heart slamming against her chest, forcing the air from her lungs.

Dorothy Jo was beside her in a second with a wet cloth. "You gonna pass out, honey?"

Angie buried her face in the washcloth. The cold water slapped at her senses, chasing away some of the terror that tore through her. She wiped down her face then looked up at Dorothy. "I'm okay."

"What in the world—" Dorothy Jo's question was cut off by the sound of crashing glass and Shadow barking at the front of the restaurant.

Shadow never barked inside the Icehouse.

Angie pushed off the floor and ran to the swinging doors separating the kitchen from the bar. "What's he barking at?" she demanded, pushing through.

Shadow stood on his haunches, barking at the window and

looking like he intended to lunge through it. "Shadow, down," Bo ordered, skipping around the broken glass of two beers he had apparently dropped.

The dog didn't budge, but his bark quieted to a slow, sinister growl. Bo ran around the bar and grabbed him by the collar. "I said down!" Bo pulled Shadow away from the door and the dog finally put all four paws on the floor.

Out of breath, Bo looked up at Angie. "There was this squad car outside. Cruising real slow. Shadow went ballistic."

Shadow's presence at the front door was a staple in the Icehouse. His oversized dog bed was in the far corner at the front, between the door and the bar's cash register. He greeted customers and wagged his tail at delivery men. Angie had never, ever seen him go ballistic in her bar.

But she understood why he had done so now. He had the face of a bloodhound and the body of a German shepherd. He could smell bad a mile away and bring his muscles to bear to kill it.

She went to her dog, kneeled down to meet him eye to eye, tousled his ears and said, "Good boy."

"What's going on here?" Bo demanded.

"She came in the back, white as a sheet." Dorothy Jo stood at the swinging doors, a revolver in her hand.

"Back in your bed, Shadow," Angie ordered. She got up and stared out the window. The DPS car was gone. *Thank goodness we don't have any customers right now*, she thought. She checked the back parking lot and the street that ran beside the bar. No squad cars. Nothing out of place.

But they were out there.

Bo had a shot of whiskey waiting for her at the bar. "We've got trouble," she said, tossing back the shot. "That squad car. We're being watched."

"By who?" Bo demanded. "James W. is the sheriff, for Pete's sake. His son's the governor!"

He was right, of course, Angie knew. The fact that the deputy had called her "Maeve," however, told her this had everything to do with the Oak and Horn, which meant it involved Reverend Duff's disappearance and, maybe, Lambert's suicide.

She turned to Bo. "You're off the clock. Go out to the farm and get Pearl. You two are staying at Jimmy's tonight."

Jimmy's home was the old Wilks mansion off the town square. He'd given permission for the family to use it as they saw fit while he was living in the Governor's Mansion.

"What are you talking about?" Bo demanded.

"Tell her to pack a suitcase. I want you both in town until this all gets settled."

"But—"

"You two live twenty miles out of town, in the middle of nowhere. You're an easy target. Those deputies are connected to something or someone extremely powerful who wants to keep Jimmy in line. Or James W., maybe. Or both. And threatening one of us might persuade Jimmy to do just that." She nodded at Dorothy Jo, who still clutched the revolver to her chest. "That includes you, so keep that gun close."

"Okay," Bo said. "Does James W. know about this? Jimmy?"

Angie shook her head. "Not yet..." She saw the concern in Bo's eyes and the fear in Dorothy Jo's. Though Angie had been scared to pieces only minutes ago, she had to be strong now. "Rest easy, everybody. James W. will get this squared away."

38

A BISHOP'S CONFESSION

A Bishop's Confession

MATT CLICKED off his cell and tossed it on the writing desk, then jammed his hands in his pocket. "Lieutenant Gage isn't available for another hour," he said to James W. "But her assistant said they weren't going to get the convention center's parking garage feed until then anyway."

"You know how these investigations go." James W. snorted. "Compared to most, we're going like a house on fire."

Matt inclined his head toward the computer. "Time enough to look up that Rolfe school the wives were talking about."

They were interrupted by the sound of heavy footsteps coming toward them down the marble hallway.

James W.'s face brightened. "Snacks!"

Lyle appeared around the corner all right, but he wasn't

carrying snacks, and he wasn't alone. Bishop Hamlin followed behind.

"Excuse me, Preacher." Lyle shrugged apologetically. "Bishop Hamlin insisted on seeing you."

The bishop's shiny bald head was bowed, his fedora in one hand, a briefcase in the other. "I visited with Mrs. Duff earlier," he said. Beneath bushy brows, his eyes raised to meet Matt's. "We need to talk."

Matt inclined his head. "All right, Bishop." He turned to James W. "This is Sheriff Novak, our new governor's father."

As Hamlin and the sheriff shook hands, Lyle breathed a sigh of relief. "I'll fetch the tea and brownies."

Matt gestured Hamlin to the wingback chair that faced away from the crime board. "Would it be all right if I took some notes, Bishop?" Without waiting for permission, Matt sat at the antique writing desk and picked up a pen. James W. sat on the opposite wingback.

Hamlin placed his hat on the side table and his briefcase against the chair, then looked at Matt. "Where to begin," he wondered out loud.

"You said you'd been to see Mrs. Duff?" Matt prompted.

To Matt's surprise, Hamlin's eyes teared over. "She, or should I say her mother, showed me a photo of Mrs. Duff holding her," he cleared his throat, "deceased daughter."

Matt hadn't known that such a picture existed.

"Apparently, Mrs. Duff asked her mother to take the photo." Hamlin's voice cracked.

"She wanted to remember—" At this, he pulled a handkerchief from his suit pocket and broke down. "I'm sorry."

"Take your time, Bishop," Matt said gently. He couldn't blame the man for reacting to the pain that Shelly and Mum were experiencing.

When Hamlin had somewhat composed himself, he blew

his nose and returned the hanky to his pocket. He leaned forward on his knees and stared at the floor. "This has got to stop," he said.

"What has to stop?" Matt asked.

"This...profanation!"

James W. looked questioningly at Matt.

"What is being profaned?" Matt asked by way of clarification.

"The very heart of Christ's teaching. On both sides," Hamlin answered.

"Bishop," Matt said. "Does this have something to do with Reverend Duff's disappearance?"

Hamlin's head snapped up. "It has everything to do with David's disappearance. This whole situation has turned vicious. Since Senator Womack got involved, it's all become ugly." He looked heavenward. "But the clergymen, Duff and Meade, they should have known better. They answer to a higher authority. *I* answer to a higher authority."

Hamlin's shaking fingers kept scrubbing at his plump chin. Then, as if making a decision, Hamlin gripped the arms of his chair.

"Now, David Duff was probably right in his interpretation," Hamlin said. "I know that. I've known that for years." He looked pleadingly at Matt. "But there's a way to discuss Scriptural interpretations that can lead to productive outcomes. Finger pointing seldom induces resolution."

"I'm not following you," Matt said. "You said this has been going on for years. What has been going on for years?"

"I'm not making sense, I know." Hamlin blew out a breath. "May I have something to drink?"

"Lyle's on his way with some tea."

"I was thinking of whatever's in that decanter behind you," the bishop said.

James W. pushed out of his chair and went to the vintage brass bar cart behind Matt. He picked up the ruby-red cut-glass decanter, gave it a sniff, nodded approval and poured the bronze liquid into three matching ruby glasses. He brought the first glass to the bishop, who took it gratefully and sipped. "Leave it to Hester to have a single malt at the ready," he said.

James W. put a glass in front of Matt and then, his own glass in hand, resumed his seat.

"You have to understand," Hamlin began. "We all accepted our calls to Central Texas at about the same time, give or take a year. I wasn't a bishop back then, of course, but I've been at St. Gregory's for over twenty-five years. Jesse Duff, David's father, came next in San Antonio. Then Chuck Schmidt accepted the call to St. Paul's Lutheran in Kyle, right about the same time Jeff Kaffee began at the Presbyterian Mission Church in San Marcos. Yes, I think Robert Meade was the last to join the group. The original group, I mean. Back then, his church was over on Austin's east side, before they built that mega-building on Highway 360."

Matt looked up from the notes he was scribbling down. "The group?"

"The I-35 Five," Hamlin chuckled. "Of all things, we met at an inauguration day prayer breakfast. Of course, our members have changed over the years. Pastors have left to take other calls, new ones want to join. We've had a couple of Southern Baptists, several Methodists. Even had a Roman Catholic priest for a few years. But the three of us—Meade, Duff and myself—we always stayed constant."

"What exactly was the mission of the"—Matt checked his notes—"I-35 Five?"

"A prayer group." Apparently more comfortable giving a history lesson, Hamlin sat back. "As *you* probably know, Pastor Hayden, being a religious leader is a very lonely experience.

You have to take on the burdens of your flock, but *your* burdens are yours and yours alone. Sure, there are other clergy members in your denomination who you can talk to, but they're often far away and sometimes even involved in what's bothering you. It's nice to have an ecumenical group of devoted ministers whose sole purpose is to lift each other up in prayer and support each other."

"I wouldn't mind being a part of a prayer group like that," Matt said.

"And Bible study. And, to be honest, a social group. There's an IHOP in San Marcos, fairly central for most of us, has a nice little nook off to the side that affords privacy. We're regulars there."

"You still meet, then."

"Every Tuesday at eleven. Early enough to beat the crowd. Of course, not last Tuesday. The inauguration and all." He raised his glass. "To your son, Sheriff Novak."

James W. nodded, and the two sipped their whiskey.

Matt did not join in the toast. Instead, he studied his notes, then put down his pen. "You mentioned Senator Womack became involved in the group. Tell me about that."

Bishop Hamlin put his glass back on the table. "Apparently, Reverend Meade and Senator Womack had been friends since their college days at UT. When Womack was elected to the U.S. Senate—oh, ten years ago maybe?—Robert Meade invited him to join the I-35 Five for lunch one day. Then again, a month later. By the next spring, the senator was a regular at our prayer meetings."

"He's not ordained," Matt pointed out. "How did you feel about that?"

"True, but he was a devout Christian. Very conservative. Well-versed in his Bible, could quote it better than a lot of clergy members I know. I figured he needed our prayers as much as anybody. And everyone seemed fine with the idea. I never raised any concerns about it."

Matt studied Hamlin's face. "But you had some concerns."

Hamlin breathed in deeply. "I began to notice that our group was not as...ecumenical as it once had been. The more progressive members began dropping out. More right-leaning pastors began expressing an interest in joining us. The three of us who were original members—myself, Jesse Duff and Robert Meade—allowed the number of participants to grow to seven total clergy, then nine. And Senator Womack, of course. Our meetings became more intense, more...righteous. Then the senator told us about a new school he was supporting up in West Virginia."

Matt and James W.'s gazes collided.

Matt forced his voice to remain steady. "What school?"

"John Rolfe Evangelical School of Technology and Trade. It's up in Pocahontas County, West Virginia."

"Pocahontas?" James W. finally spoke. "The Indian lady?"

"Yes. The woman who saved John Smith's life back in the Jamestown colony. John Rolfe was her husband—the man who evangelized Pocahontas and eventually married her."

Matt decided this was a moment when he needed a sip of good whiskey. And yes, Hester knew what to stock, that was for sure. His head cleared, he slowly put the glass back down and returned his gaze to the bishop. "And why did this bother you?"

"Because I realized then that Senator Womack had a much broader plan for the power of Christian conservativism."

"Did the other members understand what was going on?"

"No. They bought it. Hook, line and sinker. Train up the next generation to carry the torch. This was our mission for the future of our beliefs. Return to Christianity." Hamlin shook his head. "The fundraisers began, the sermons became more dogmatic, church memberships exploded. People wanted to

hear about the good old days. Wanted to go back to them."
Hamlin took another sip of whiskey. Grimaced. "The more
rules, the happier we'd all be. The lessons of love from Jesus
were supplanted by the laws of man."

Again, James W. broke in. "There's plenty of laws in the
Bible, Bishop."

"Actually, that's one that David Duff got right." Hamlin
looked straight at Matt. "There are eleven commandments in
the Bible. Period. Generally, we don't refer to the New Testament one given by Jesus on Maundy Thursday as a commandment, but that's exactly what it is."

Matt was torn between the desire to explore that statement
more and the cop in him that wanted to find David Duff. Right
now, with Duff's life possibly in the balance, he had to be a cop.
"So the I-35 Five took Womack's lead and went all in for the
school."

"And the belief system behind it. Humankind needed to
live by rigid laws to be Christian. And worse. Those that
weren't of the same mind could never be Christians." Hamlin
blew out another deep sigh. "And I said nothing."

"But David Duff did not go along with that belief system,"
Matt coaxed.

"When Jesse, David's father, died in that crash, and it
became clear that David was going to take his father's place as
head of the River Walk Fellowship Church in San Antonio, we
—the I-35 Five, which by that time was more like the I-35
Twenty-Five—invited him to our prayer group. He joined us a
few times, then started asking questions—biblical questions—
about what we were professing."

"He left the group?" Matt asked.

"Oh, no. If only he had." Hamlin chuckled humorlessly.
"The other members who disagreed with what was going on

had simply faded away. They didn't want to risk being on the receiving end of the group's wrath."

"Why?" James W. scratched his chin. "What if this I-35 Twenty-Five were mad at them? At you?"

"It's become a very powerful group indeed. Our members are on college boards all over the country, two host separate daily conservative talk show on XM Radio. Heck, we've got a member in San Antonio who preaches on national TV every Sunday. And our most conservative members have no qualms in calling other pastors out from the pulpit."

"What did David Duff do to express his opposition to the group's judgmental beliefs?"

"He called *them* out from the pulpit," Hamlin answered.

"I was not aware of any of this," Matt said. But then again, he'd been a preacher for only seven months before he got part of his skull shot off. He'd had little chance to meet other clergy members around the small town of Wilks.

"Frankly, David is small potatoes compared to the others," Hamlin said. "But that was going to change on inauguration day. When he gave that benediction, he would have had the attention of the entire state of Texas, if not the country."

"His prayer." Matt cocked his head. "Was that what he was supposed to leave with you at St. Gregory the morning of the inauguration?"

"No." At this, Hamlin picked up his briefcase and placed it on his lap.

Lyle appeared in the doorway. "Sorry that took so long. I had to make the tea." Platter in hand, he went over to the brass bar table that held the ruby-red decanter set, cleared a space and set down the tray.

Matt had a sneaky feeling Lyle had been out in the hallway listening in for an opportune moment to bring in the tray. He wondered how much the giant of a man had overheard.

Lyle continued busying himself at the tray. He plated the brownies and turned to the group. "Who wants one?"

James W. sat forward immediately. Matt nodded to his desk. Hamlin was shuffling through the papers in his briefcase and absently said "thank you" when Lyle placed a brownie on the table beside him.

"It looks like you already have drinks, may I—"

"We're good, Lyle. Thanks." Matt said, as Hamlin handed him a paper.

"Delicious brownies," called James W., his mouth full, as Lyle left the room.

Matt studied the paper. "This looks like a draft of the benediction that David Duff was going to give last Tuesday."

"Yes. Those are my markings on the paper. He gave that to me over a week ago to look over."

Matt's eyes rounded as he read on. "He quotes Matthew 23:25. 'Woe to you, teachers of the law and Pharisees, you hypocrites! You clean the outside of the cup and dish, but inside are full of greed and self-indulgence.'" He looked more closely at the paper. "And those are your marks, Bishop Hamlin, that cross out the names of pastors he's calling out, including Reverend Meade?"

"Yes. That's the exact Word file I sent back to David. Along with a note that the inauguration was not the pulpit for this message."

"Did he reply?" Matt put down the paper.

"Yes. If you read the whole prayer, David was praying for God to give wisdom and strength to the new governor not to listen to these false prophets, but instead to the Bible and the words of Jesus. He said he saw nothing wrong with that."

Matt leaned back in his chair. The consequences of that prayer could be devastating to the clergy members Duff called out. If Meade or any of the others knew what was going to be said, to what lengths would they go to stop Duff from giving that prayer?

Finally, Matt thought. A possible motive behind Duff's disappearance.

But would Meade, or any member of the clergy for that matter, go so far as to murder David Duff?

Matt realized Hamlin and James W. were staring at him expectantly. "What was Duff supposed to leave with you on Tuesday morning?" Matt asked.

"The outline for his next ten sermons, right up until Easter."

Then Matt remembered the PDF file Pastor Garcia had sent earlier. Though he'd printed it off at Cop Central, Matt hadn't had the opportunity to read it. He rifled through the stack of copies he'd brought over and found the papers. His phone buzzed. "That's Gage," he said, looking at the caller. "Here, Bishop, look at these," he said, then answered his phone.

"I finished with my meeting early," Gage said. "Both the convention center and Hilton exterior footage have come in. You'll want to see this."

"I'm interviewing Bishop Hamlin—"

"You're going to want to see this," she repeated.

"All right then. We're on our way." Matt clicked off the phone. "I'm sorry, Bishop," he said. "James W. and I have to meet with the police."

Hamlin nodded. "I understand." He handed Garcia's notes back to Matt. "This pretty much confirms what I thought David was going to do. It'll take you some time to take it all in, then we should meet back up."

"When can we do that?" Matt felt the clock ticking.

"I have a huge funeral tomorrow. How about after Evensong tomorrow night in my office? There are some things on my computer I want you to see."

"I'll be there."

James W. had already powered down the computer. "We'll need Lyle to lock up the room," he said as he turned off the lights.

"Good call," Matt said.

As the three men headed out, Matt's thoughts returned to Lieutenant Gage's call. What had she found on the security footage that was so important?

39

HE PARKED WHERE?

He Parked Where?

LIEUTENANT GAGE MET Matt and James W. at the crime lab door. "Lambert didn't park his car at the convention center or the Hilton the morning of the inauguration."

Matt was taken aback. "You already finished going through all that footage?"

Gage led the way down the hall toward the media lab. She pulled open the glass door. "We found it on the second camera we checked."

A tech who looked like he was still in eighth grade worked the playback equipment at the postage stamp-sized office's one desk. "Cue up the parking lot footage, Henry," Gage ordered.

"Sure thing." The kid's fingers played over the controls as if they were piano keys. The screen above the keyboard came to life.

Matt and James W. stepped close for a better view.

"This shot is from the East Fourth Street parking lot, looking north up Red River," Henry said.

"Keep going," Gage ordered.

The tech let the footage play at regular speed, then hit pause and pointed at the screen. "That's your blue Ford Focus turning off of Red River onto Fifth Street. Now, if he was going to park in the convention center overflow parking lot at the Hilton"—he hit play and the car continued forward—"the car should turn south right now into that driveway. But as you can see, it continues east on Fifth."

"Pause it," Matt said. He leaned into the screen. "You sure that's Lambert's blue Ford Focus?"

Henry nodded. "I checked it out. We couldn't get a full shot of the license plate, but the first three letters matched. Now here's what you need to see." He hit play again. "The car passes through the Sabine Street intersection and look here." He stopped the video as the car turned right into a driveway. "It's a dive bar named the Oak and Horn."

Matt turned his head to look at James W. so fast, he felt dizzy. James W., in turn, stared open-mouthed at the screen.

Oblivious to their reaction, Henry hit fast forward on the machine, then slowed it as the figure of a man walked back into view down the driveway. He turned west onto Fifth and headed toward the Hilton's security camera.

"Stop it there," Gage said. "Zoom it in."

Henry obliged. Matt and James W. studied the man's figure.

"Can't see his face," James W. said.

"Agreed," Matt said. "But Lambert had that same slump to his shoulders. What's the time?"

Henry checked his readout. "Nine o'clock. Straight up."

Matt looked at Gage. "And we have him on tape entering the prayer breakfast venue when?"

"Nine-oh-six," she answered. "That's solid. So why did you want to know where Lambert parked?"

Matt nodded toward James W. "The sheriff and I were at the Oak and Horn earlier. I've got a lot to report."

"And I want to hear it," Gage said. "Henry, is there anything else you have for us to see?"

Henry wiped a finger under his nose. "Not yet. I haven't gone through all the cameras."

Gage's brow furrowed. "Preacher, you said Lambert's car was already at Hester's when you got out of the hospital Tuesday night?"

"Yes. When Connor brought me to the mansion, the Focus was already parked in front of the house. Connor said he needed to the move the car into the garage. Something about the neighborhood getting iffy after sundown." Matt tapped a finger to his lips. "But we've got Lambert on tape walking back to the Governor's Mansion after the prayer breakfast."

"All right then," Gage said. "Henry, I want to know when that car left the Oak and Horn, and where it went."

"Yes, Lieutenant."

James W.'s phone rang, and he pulled it from his pocket. "It's Angie," he said and brought the cell to his ear. "Hey, Sis."

Matt could hear Angie's raised voice from three feet away. She was talking fast and her usually lusty low voice was at least an octave higher.

"Slow down," James W. "Okay. Two DPS troopers pulled you over. Were you speeding?"

Her high-pitched response had him pulling the phone away from his ear. "Now, honey—"

Matt snatched the phone from James W.'s hand. "What's going on, Angie?"

"I'm so scared. They're watching me. Us."

"Stop," he ordered. "We're here with Lieutenant Gage. Is this something she needs to hear?"

"I think so."

Matt's danger gauge rocketed skyward. Angie was crying. "If you're in jeopardy," he said, "you need to hang up and call 911 immediately."

"No," she whimpered. "They're gone for now."

Lieutenant Gage touched his arm. *My office*, she mouthed.

"We're going somewhere private, and then I'll put you on speaker phone," Matt said. "Take some deep breaths, okay?"

"Yeah."

ANGIE KNEW Matt was trying to help her, and yes, she knew she had to calm down. But it had been over an hour since she returned to the Fire and Icehouse, and this was her first chance to summon help since she'd come back downstairs from changing out her underwear.

Yes, when that deputy called her Maeve, and she sank to her knees in the kitchen, she'd learned the term "scared the pee out of me" wasn't just a saying.

She'd arrived back downstairs as the Friday happy hour crowd hit the front door. A tech company twenty minutes away let out at two-thirty on Fridays and the Fire and Icehouse had been their hangout since the company opened. Since she'd told Bo to go home and pack up Pearl, Angie was the only bartender on duty. She'd been pouring shots and pulling beers ever since.

Desperate, she'd had Dorothy Jo call Warren Yeck, the retired farmer who'd once been a bartender at the Officer's Club up in Killeen during World War II. He filled in as needed at the Icehouse, and this afternoon, he was definitely needed.

This was the first chance she'd had to make the call to

James W., and all the fear she'd been holding in had festered
into near hysteria. As she waited for Matt to get back on the
phone, she forced herself to take those deep breaths. She was
better than this.

"You still there?" Matt's voice came back over the phone.

"Yes," she said, her voice steadier.

"You're on speaker. You said two DPS deputies stopped
you? What happened?"

"I had just driven through Bastrop—" The events spilled
out of her like a flooding stream. "And I was heading in the
kitchen door when the John Wayne wannabe called me
'Maeve.' The only place I used that name was at the Oak and
Horn. That deputy is connected with someone at the Oak and
Horn."

"Miss O'Day," Lieutenant Gage interrupted. "You believe
the deputies were trying to send a message—a threat—to the
governor?"

"I know it sounds crazy, but yes. That's exactly what I
believe."

There was silence from the other end, then Matt spoke. "I
want you out of there. Now."

"I can't leave," she protested. "Friday and Saturday nights
are my biggest—"

"Angie." This time, James W.'s voice. "You're coming to
Austin. You're gonna stay at the Governor's Mansion with me
and Jimmy. The security there is the best."

"Sure," Angie rolled her eyes. "Guarded by state troopers,
right?"

"And that's another reason you need to come up here,"
James W.'s voice was flat. "Jimmy needs to hear straight from
you the threats that were made against his family if he steps out
of line—whatever that means."

She knew he was right. This whole thing was bigger than a small-town bar on a Friday night.

"We could cut the kitchen offerings down to queso, chips and salsa. Bo did that some nights when I was with Matt after he got shot."

"That's right, honey," James W. said. "And I'm glad you told Bo that he and Pearl need to stay at Jimmy's tonight. Now, here's what's gonna happen. I'm gonna order my deputies to keep their eyes on Dorothy Jo, Bo and Pearl, and Richard Dube will escort you up here to the Governor's Mansion. No arguments."

"And bring Shadow with you," Matt said. "I don't want you in that truck alone."

"All right," Angie said. "I'll bring Shadow. And my gun."

40

FOLLOW THAT CAR!

LIEUTENANT GAGE SAT BACK in her desk chair, her elegant, long fingers steepled. "You're telling me that U.S. Senator William Womack is behind Reverend Duff's disappearance?"

Matt and James W. were seated in the chairs across from her desk. Matt leaned forward. "I don't think I'd go that far. But he's the only person who could've known my fiancée used the name Maeve."

"The bartender could have told him that," Gage said.

James W. shook his head. "Either way, but does a bartender have the power to get two DPS troopers to pull Angie over? To make threats against the governor?" James W. shook his head. "I don't think so."

"I see your point." Gage checked her notes. "And this bar, the Oak and Horn. What part does it play in all of this?"

"I don't know." Matt shrugged. "At least we can say that it's a gathering place for people of interest. We know Senator Womack is a regular because the bartender knew his favorite drink. And Womack's got pull in the place. He's the one who kicked us out of the Oak and Horn. Pastor Lambert went there several times looking for Womack's son. And why did Lambert park there for the prayer breakfast?"

Gage nodded. "Then there's Bishop Hamlin's I-35 Five. Womack's involved in that too. And you think that someone in that group has a possible motive for Duff's disappearance? To stop him from giving that inaugural benediction?"

"Which brings Reverend Meade into the equation," Matt said. "And don't forget, Lambert went to see Meade right before he committed suicide. What transpired in *that* conversation?"

A quick knock came from the door behind Matt.

"Come in," called Gage.

The youthful Henry, his eyes aglow, popped his head around the door. "I've found the stuff you asked for on Lambert's car."

Gage and James W. hurried to the media room, while Matt, his energy waning, lagged behind. This morning, Dr. Ryan had told him his blood pressure was up and he needed to slow down. Perhaps she was right. But he couldn't slow down with Angie in danger.

When he got to the room, Henry was already manipulating the controls on the playback unit.

The security camera's first few seconds showed an empty Oak and Horn driveway and a few cars going past on Fifth Street. Then the front end of a dark blue car edged into view, the bright sun flashing off its hood.

"What time is this?" asked Matt.

"Nine-fifty-seven," Henry replied, checking the time code.

James W.'s brow furrowed. "But Lambert would still be at the prayer breakfast at nine-fifty-seven."

Henry nodded. "That threw me too. So I went back to confirm the time Lambert left the Hilton. He exited the hotel at ten-thirty-two, and never went back to the Oak and Horn. He headed north-west toward the Capitol on foot with some other clergy members."

"So..." Matt rubbed his forehead. "Someone else drove the Focus out of the Oak and Horn parking lot."

"And I think I've got a photo of that driver." Henry hit rewind. "I can't be sure, of course. We don't have a shot of the actual parking lot, but the timing is right, anyway." He hit play.

The video showed an average-sized man wearing a black cowboy hat and carrying a white take-out bag cross Fifth Street and walk right into the Oak and Horn driveway. Less than a minute later, the Focus pulled out onto Fifth Street.

The driver was wearing a black cowboy hat.

"Play it again," Gage ordered.

Henry did and repeated the same thing five more times.

"With that cowboy hat, there's no guessin' what he looks like," James W. said.

Matt agreed. "There's probably a coupla hundred men wearing jeans, cowboy hats, and long-sleeved shirts in down-town Austin every day."

Gage huffed out a breath. "Any chance we can trace where the man came from?"

"I picked out his trail on our traffic cameras." Henry checked his notes, then played piano on his keyboard again. "The cameras at Sixth Street and Red River caught him crossing Trinity Street. Guess where he got his takeout from?" He let the video continue its rewind and stopped it after the man walked backward into a storefront.

"You're kidding me," Gage said.

"Nope. Voodoo Doughnuts. They've got some serious game there."

Sure enough, when the man backed out of the shop, he wasn't carrying a bag.

James W. looked at his watch. "I have to leave for one of Jimmy's events in about a half hour."

Henry looked up. "Want me to back up to where he first appears?"

"Do it," Gage said.

Henry sifted through his notes, then called up another camera. As he manipulated the controls, he said, "Our guy crossed back south when he got to Colorado Street. Took that all the way down to Fourth and"—he hit play—"came out of the Hobby Building parking deck."

Matt's head snapped up, and he grabbed the back of Henry's chair, suddenly breathless.

"You okay, son?" James W. asked.

Matt nodded at the screen. "That's the parking deck where Duff disappeared. He went in, but never came out."

James W. cocked his head. "I thought you said the man that walked out of St. Gregory's wasn't Duff."

Matt turned to Gage. "We need to search that parking deck. Can you get a team out there?"

"What exactly are we looking for?" she asked him.

"A man wearing a blue shirt with a tab collar and matching suit and a Panama hat."

———

BY THE TIME Matt and James W. left the police department, the sky was a deep peach as the sun descended toward the horizon. James W. climbed into his truck and reached for his seatbelt. "Lieutenant Gage didn't waste any time getting a search team out to that parking deck," he said.

"And she remembered Lambert's car had a toll road sticker." With difficulty, Matt hoisted himself into the passenger seat. "If Henry finds out the car headed out the tollway and exited at Lampasas—"

"We'll have a stronger link to the Herne's Hunters out at the Homestead." Matt rubbed his face. "I need to get back to my crime board."

James W. slanted him a look. "You sure you're up to seeing Mrs. Duff right now?"

"I haven't talked with her at all today. I won't stay long. Connor's going to pick me up at five-thirty so I can be at the mansion in time for supper."

Brackenridge Hospital was only a few blocks from the police station, and James W. pulled into its circular drive. "I'll call you when I get back from the dinner."

Matt got down from the truck. "You gotta wear your tux again?"

James W. glared. "Kicking never gets you nowhere, unless you're a mule."

Matt grinned as he shut the truck's door then turned toward the hospital entrance. He realized he was leaning a little more heavily on his cane as he made his way up the sidewalk. And the sinking feeling he had in his gut regarding Reverend Duff's disappearance was zapping every ounce of energy left in his soul.

He headed straight for Shelly Duff's hospital room. The door was open, and he peeked in. Shelly was sitting up in bed, a tray in front of her and an IV stand behind her, its tubes running into her wrist. Mum brightened when she saw Matt in the doorway. "Come in, Preacher."

"As long as you're up to it," Matt said, his eyes on Shelly.

"I am," she answered, straightening the sheets. "I'm so glad you've come. I wanted to thank you for last night."

He hobbled toward the bed, and Mum brought a chair over for him to sit down.

"Your words during communion meant so much to me." Shelly offered a weary half-smile. "I've been repeating them in my mind all day."

"I'm glad you found them comforting." Matt sat down and studied Shelly's face. Her eyes were sunken, but her face was showing some color. Her blonde hair was neatly brushed, her hands steady. "You look like you're feeling better." It was the understatement of the year, but he'd learned it was best to let the patient lead the conversation on how they were feeling.

Mum returned to her seat and took her daughter's hand. "I should say so."

"The doctors said I might even be able to go home tomorrow," Shelly said. "Well, to Hester's, I mean. They don't want me to take that long drive to San Antonio yet."

"I understand a friend came from San Antonio to be with you?" Matt asked.

"I sent Delia off to get a nap and a shower," Mum said. "She'll stay with Shelly overnight." She quirked an eyebrow at her daughter. "My orders are to go to Hester's and get some sleep."

"And you will follow them to the letter." Shelly turned back to Matt. "Have you found David's body?"

The question brought Matt up short. Shelly really was convinced that her husband was dead. He shared the same thought, of course, but still. "We've been working on that all day. But no, we haven't found him yet." A thought came to him, and he cocked his head. "Did your husband receive any death threats?"

"Not in so many words," Shelly said. "But he'd upset a very powerful person."

Matt was still puzzled. "Why didn't you tell us that before?"

"Because I hoped you'd find David alive. But I know after all this time he's gone."

"And who is this important person?" Matt asked.

"Reverend Meade. David was the subject of more than one of his diatribes from the pulpit. Meade called him 'godless,' said he was a leftist militant. That kind of thing."

Matt remembered Hamlin's description of Duff from earlier. "And your husband didn't take that lying down."

"No. He considered it his mission—God's mission—to fight back." Her hands now shook as she picked at a crumb on the sheet. "David said things would get ugly. I'm pretty sure he meant physical. I think he was preparing me for what might come."

"You didn't suggest he back off?" Matt asked.

"Absolutely not." Her gaze seared into Matt's. "David was doing God's will. And like you said last night, David is in heaven along with my daughter—" Her voice broke on that, and a tear slipped from her eye. She wiped it away impatiently. "And I will dine with them every time I have communion and will join them when my time comes to go."

"Shelly, please," Mum said, fumbling with a tissue box.

"I'm sorry, mom," Shelly said. She reached for her mother's hand and squeezed it.

"I'm sorry too," Matt said. "Perhaps we should change the subject."

"I do have a question for you, Preacher," Shelly said. "Why were there firetrucks at Hester's last night?"

Matt shot a questioning look at Mum, who nodded for him to answer. He sighed. "I'm afraid Pastor Lambert committed suicide last night."

Shelly took that in, considered it for a long moment, then nodded. "It makes sense."

Matt sat up straighter in his chair.

"Lambert was Meade's lackey," she explained. "It was his job to keep tabs on what David was up to, whether it be snooping into David's computer files or giving a heads up when David had a speaking engagement. That kind of thing."

"Why didn't your husband ask for his resignation?" Matt asked.

"First of all, a senior pastor doesn't decide who's on the ministerial staff at a church. The congregation offers the pastor a call after prayerful consideration and with guidance from the Holy Spirit. Second, David figured it was better to know who his enemies were so he could protect himself."

Matt considered. "You said Lambert searched your husband's computer files. How is that possible?"

"Lambert's the church's business manager—the administrator for all of the technology. He could get into anything."

"And erase anything," Matt said softly. Which, perhaps, was why Pastor Garcia couldn't find Sunday's PowerPoint on his church computer. "But this doesn't explain why Lambert would've killed himself."

"Perhaps he didn't realize how far Meade would go to shut David up."

"Do you think Reverend Meade killed your husband?"

"That's what you're going to find out for me," Shelly said. "And I want to hear what happened to David from you. Only you. And then I want you to give me communion again so I can be with David and Boudicca."

Matt swallowed hard. "I will."

Shelly closed her eyes and laid back on her pillow. "I'm counting on you."

41

MUM HAS HER SAY

THE RICH SMELL of something wonderful greeted Matt as he came downstairs from a quick shower. He found Lyle in the kitchen, working a pot on the stove. "Whatever you're cooking, it smells delicious," Matt said.

"Scallops and risotto with a corn soup starter. Hester's favorite foods. After what she's been through these last two days, I thought she could use some culinary love. And Mum, too, of course." Lyle nodded toward the kitchen doors. "The ladies are enjoying some cocktails."

Upon entering the dining room, he found Hester seated at the head of the table, with Mum on her right. "I'm sorry I'm late." Matt pulled out his chair across from Mum. Though she'd donned a soft, pink chenille sweater, she didn't look any more relaxed than when she'd ridden silently beside him on the way home. Her face was creased with exhaustion and her smile was forced.

Hester, wearing a navy silk blouse adorned with a simple pearl necklace, waved away his apology. "We both arrived early in search of refreshment." She held up her glass. "We're having vodka martinis, but I also have iced tea."

"Yes, please." No need to tick off Dr. Ryan in the morning any more than he was already expecting to. Matt knew he'd overdone it today. His daily appointment tomorrow might bring quite a scolding.

Lyle entered, carrying a china tureen and ladle. "Corn soup, anyone?"

Mum rested her eyes on Matt. "I'm so grateful to you for helping Shelly. Your words last night made today bearable for her."

"I'm glad I could be of help." Matt leaned back as Lyle placed a cup of soup in front of him.

"And you." Mum nodded toward Hester. "You've been so gracious, inviting us into your home."

"It was the least I could do," Hester said. "I'm glad that your daughter is out of the woods."

"Oops," Lyle said. "I forgot the rolls." He hurried back to the kitchen.

"Shelly will recover. Physically, anyway." Mum picked up her spoon.

Hester's blue eyes were filled with concern. "She's had so much tragedy thrust upon her. But she has you, too. And that's a blessing."

"I'm not so sure."

Lyle returned with the rolls. "Fresh out of the oven," he said.

Matt sipped his soup. It had a kick of spice, but the avocados provided immediate soothing. "What's your special ingredient this time?" he asked.

Lyle's eyebrows bounced. "A jalapeño pepper."

Matt shook his head in admiration.

"Onward to the risotto." Grinning, Lyle returned to the kitchen.

For a moment, the only sounds in the dining room were soup being sipped and rolls being passed. Then Mum put her spoon down hard enough to make a clatter.

"Excuse me," she said abruptly and pushed away from the table.

"Darling." Hester put her hand on Mum's arm. "We're your friends. Let us help you."

Mum grabbed for her napkin, lowered her head and let out a sob.

"Hester," Matt said quietly. "Maybe she needs some time to be alone. She's in mourning, too."

Mum wiped at her eyes, then looked straight into Matt's eyes. "If only that was the problem." Her hands fisted. "I'm so angry."

Matt studied her red-rimmed eyes. Something untold and long-lived was in those depths. "Do you want to talk about it?" he asked.

She worried her lip, then nodded. "I loved how happy my son-in-law made my daughter. He was a good provider. Fun." She breathed deeply. "But I learned—began to understand? He was the most egotistical man I've ever met."

Matt tried not to show his surprise. This was unexpected.

"The longer he served as a pastor—especially after he became head pastor at River Walk Fellowship—the more he became the spokesman of God rather than a mere mortal."

"God's spokesman?" Matt repeated.

"His chosen one. Or God's earthly angel Gabriel. David became a pastor first, a husband or a friend or a son-in-law second." Her anger released, her voice was strong, her eyes blazing. "He wasn't looking for a loving way to spread God's word. He was as bad as Reverend Meade but on the opposite end of the spectrum. Take no prisoners! David Duff's words were the only thing that counted because his words came straight from God."

Hester, her eyes wide, picked up her glass and took a sip of her martini, then followed the sip with a hefty swallow.

"Saying this is probably a sin." Mum's voice shook with anger. "But I think David wanted to be martyred. He didn't care whether he lived or died, as long as he was right. He didn't care about his wife. He didn't care about his unborn daughter. And now, *my* daughter has to live with her dead husband's choices."

She stood. "I'm sorry. I'm fit for neither man nor beast right now. Please have Lyle bring a tray to my room. Though I doubt I'll be able to eat anything with this knot in my throat." Head held high, she left the room.

Seconds later, Lyle appeared, his smile bright, rubbing his hands together. "Are we ready for the main course yet?" He stopped when he saw Mum's empty chair and uneaten soup. "Oh, dear. Was it too spicy?"

"No," Hester said. "Not at all. She's exhausted. Perhaps you could take her a tray of food in a bit?"

"Of course." Lyle cleared Mum's bowl, then saw that neither Hester nor Matt had eaten their soup either. "It *was* too spicy."

"Give us five minutes," Matt said. There was no way he wanted Lyle to feel that he'd failed as a cook two nights in a row. Last night's debacle of turkey flambé and forgotten bananas Foster had not been Lyle's fault. Matt plastered a smile on his face and picked up his spoon. "I want to finish this. It's delicious."

———

DINNER OVER, Matt and Hester headed into her study to enjoy a glass of port. Matt's phone pinged. He looked at the display. Angie.

"I'll be right in," he said to Hester. "I have to take this."

He headed for the parlor's wingback chair. "Hi, honey," he said. "You all right?"

"I made it to Jimmy's. No problems." She sounded tired, he noted, but no longer scared.

"I know we talked about my coming over to Hester's for a little bit," she continued. "But James W. said absolutely not. Not until I tell him and Jimmy exactly what happened."

"I might be able to get Connor to drive me over. My leg isn't up to a coupla blocks walk."

"Absolutely not," she said firmly. "James W. said you looked more tired than a boomtown whore. That's a quote, by the way."

He chuckled. "I hope so. Maybe we can see each other in the morning?"

"You have your doctor thing again at nine?" she asked.

"Yep."

"Surely, James W. will be okay with me getting out in the daytime, for Pete's sake. And in town, no less. How about I pick you up a few minutes before?"

"That would be great." He smiled. "And afterward do breakfast?"

"You're on. I love you, Matt."

"I love you, too. Good night."

Matt ended the call and sat for a moment in the dark, smiling. She was safe. On that he could get a good night's sleep. He shoved himself out of the chair, grabbed his cane and went to the office.

Hester was already nestled in her soft leather recliner. The pot belly stove's flames licked at the open grate, and the scent of pine filled the air. The comfortable setting almost made Matt forget the turmoil that swirled around the missing Reverend Duff.

Almost.

"I take it that was Angie," Hester said, motioning him to the other recliner fronting the stove.

"Yes," he said. "She made it safe and sound to the Governor's Mansion."

"You barely had a chance to tell me what happened that scared her into coming back to Austin. Something about state troopers threatening the governor?" Hester said.

"James W. insisted she come back." He sat down in the chair. "I don't know all the details yet. Only that she's safe and sound for now."

"I hope so." Hester stared into the fire.

Matt liked Hester. Really liked her. She didn't beat around the bush, and she saw things for what they were. And all the while she had a heart of gold.

"I know," he said. "The question is, who would have the strings to sic the DPS on somebody? And to threaten the governor?"

Hester shrugged, as if the answer was obvious. "Senator Womack, of course."

And there it was. Plain as day. And, of course, she was right.

"What do you figure he's up to?" Matt asked.

"Oh, honey. That man's after the presidency. Has been since he first became a U.S. senator."

Lyle entered, carrying a stacked tray. "Time for dessert." He placed the platter on the table between Matt and Hester.

"Wow," Matt said when he saw the crunchy churros and

two small pots of melted dark chocolate. He rubbed his hands together in anticipation.

"I brought some chamomile tea. Or would you prefer port?" Lyle asked as he set out the plates.

"Port for me," answered Hester.

"I'll have the tea." Matt was still trying to toe Dr. Ryan's line.

Lyle made sure everyone was served. "I'll be back to see if there's anything else you'll need."

"Absolutely not," Hester said. "Upstairs you go and say good night to Connor for me."

Lyle looked at his boss gratefully. "Thanks, Hester. Good night, all."

"Good night," Hester and Matt chorused.

As Lyle left, Matt picked up one of the long, tubular, cinnamon-crusted pastries. "Still warm," he said and dipped the churro into the chocolate. He took a bite. "Delicious."

Hester did the same, and for a moment the two sat in silence, munching.

"What's Womack's plan for getting elected president?" Matt finally asked.

"Intimidation. Ruthlessness. Fear." Hester delicately licked some chocolate from her finger. "Just like Hitler."

Matt almost choked on his churro. "Hitler?"

"Of course. That's how you rise to power. You remind everyone of how great things used to be in the good old days. Never mind the fact that the good old days weren't so great—the Depression, the wars, the riots, the corruption. But you get people to believe in the myth that days gone by were wonderful. Then you tell everyone who or what's to blame for things being so bad. 'If only we could bring back this, or if only we could eliminate that.' And then you make yourself the one candidate who can put it all back to rights again." She picked up another churro. "Straight out of Hitler's game plan."

Hitler? "Who or what is Womack blaming for how bad things have gotten?"

"Anything that's progressive," Hester said easily. "Just as Womack's glorifying anything that takes us back to the 'good old days.'" She picked up her glass of port and lifted it toward Matt. "That includes religion, my friend."

Matt felt his head begin to spin, and he held up his hand. "Enough," he said. "I can't process this. Not 'til I get some sleep, anyway."

"Oh, dear," Hester said. "How about we talk about what you owe me after sending me into that pit of backstabbing, bitch-spitting, poisonous pythons this afternoon?"

He laughed out loud. "Hester, you are something."

"You think I'm kidding? My word! Of course, there were some ladies there whose true desire is to promote philanthropy in Central Texas—good, dedicated women. But that Mrs. Meade and Mrs. Womack? My God, they were a piece of work." She reached for her port. "And I don't mean to show you any disrespect, but the governor's mother? How did she raise a decent human being like Jimmy Novak?"

"You have to get to know her, Hester." Matt poured himself some tea and smiled. "How would James W. describe her?" He considered for a moment. "Got it. He'd say she 'can be stubborn as crab grass and can jump on you with all four feet,' but if someone's got trouble? She'd lend you her last pair of long johns."

Hester's brow raised.

"No, really," Matt pressed. "And the two of 'em? Elsbeth and James W.? They've got a deep love for each other. You have to get to know her."

"I *can* at least say she wasn't as bad as the other two. The

Missus Womack and Meade sounded like best friends when they were together, but get them apart? Whew, they had nothing good to say about each other. Or the other's family."

"For example." Matt sipped his tea.

"Their two kids. The Meades have a daughter, the Womacks have a son. You know, Hogg? We talked about him the other night?"

Matt nodded.

"Together, those two mothers mourned the fact that the daughter and son never married. Get 'em apart, though—whoo boy! Mrs. Womack said the Meade girl was as loose as a bucket of soot and drunker than a fiddler's bitch."

Matt raised his eyebrows.

"Her words, not mine. And Mrs. Meade!" Hester rolled her beautiful blue eyes. "*She* said that her daughter would never have married Hogg Womack. The reverend's wife said he was stupid as dirt and barely got into UT, which would be a mortal sin from the senator's point of view. She said Hogg had to go to a trade school out East to get some bogus degree that the senator could use to get him into the university. Sounds like the senator wanted a son to follow in his footsteps, and what he got was a kid who couldn't figure out a seed catalog."

Matt put down his tea. "He went to a trade school out East?" It had to be the Rolfe Evangelical place that Bishop Hamlin had spoken about. "Did she say anything more about that?"

"No. Except he got some sort of pharmaceutical certification—an assistant or something like that. The family figured that would help him get into UT's pre-med program. Reverend Meade's wife thought that was hysterical. Hogg didn't make it through the first semester of that training. So he's a political science major now. Heading for law school. She actually slapped her knee on that one."

"No love lost there." Matt considered. The wives couldn't stand each other, but the husbands were best buds.

Weren't they?

"Did Mrs. Womack say anything about their husbands?"

"Not really," Hester answered. "Only that the two were always traveling together. All over the country. She did make a comment that it was nice for the senator to have a plane at his beck and call like that."

"I wonder if Meade's congregation knows Womack uses their plane as his own private jet."

"Or the IRS. I believe gifts of free plane rides to senators are taxable." Hester picked up another churro, then nodded to Matt. "Better have another one before the chocolate gets cold."

She didn't have to ask him twice. He dipped the churro in the chocolate, swished it around and took a bite. The chocolate dripped down his chin, but he didn't mind. "Delicious."

He finished off the churro. "A wonderful ending to a horrible day. Hester, you're the best."

42

CHIEF AGUILAR

THE ALARM CLOCK on Matt's bedstand went off at precisely eight a.m. He fought to open his eyes as he fumbled to turn off the blaring noise. He finally succeeded at both, then couldn't understand why a mechanical beep still sounded. Oh, he realized. That's my phone.

He pulled his phone from the bedstand. "Hello?"

"Lieutenant Gage here, Preacher. The sweepers found the clerical clothes you described in the parking garage's dumpster."

Matt came wide awake. "That's good. That's very good." He swung his legs out of bed.

"I've got more," she said. "Are you sitting down?"

"Yes."

"Lambert's car got on the 183A toll road at RM 620 and drove all the way through Cedar Park and Leander until the toll ends. Which means the car was heading straight for Lampasas—the town that the Oak and Horn bartender had indicated was the closest cell connection to the Herne's

Hunters' Homestead. Unfortunately, we have no trail to follow once the toll road ends."

Matt thought for a moment. "James W. has a friend who went to that Homestead once when he was a kid. Maybe he could help us out."

"I'm about to go into a suspect interrogation for another case. I doubt I'll free up before eleven o'clock."

"We'll be there at eleven," Matt said. He'd have plenty of time to see Dr. Ryan and breakfast with Angie.

Gage signed off, and Matt pushed himself off the bed. Time to hit the ground running.

Or in his case, shuffling. He chuckled to himself as he reached for his cane.

———

AN HOUR AND A HALF LATER, Matt and Angie sat in Dr. Ryan's waiting room. The doctor was delayed due to an emergency case, and Matt's hopes of breakfast with his fiancée were dwindling.

"We could pick up some doughnuts on the way to see Lieutenant Gage," Angie suggested.

"That might be all we'll have time for." Matt shifted in the hard-shell plastic chair, trying to find a comfortable position. "Or kolaches, maybe."

"I might be able to help you with that," said a voice from behind them. Matt swiveled, to find a compact man with short, peppered hair standing over them. Something about his round face looked familiar to Matt, but...

"Chief Aguilar!" Matt pushed to his feet almost in tandem with Angie. "I didn't recognize you in civvies."

"That's why I like Saturdays." The chief slapped at his

well-worn jeans. "I get to be human for a time. He nodded toward Angie. "And who is this lovely lady?

"My fiancée, Angie O'Day. Angie, this is the chief of the Austin Police Department. Chief Aguilar."

She offered her hand. "Pleased to meet you, Chief."

Aguilar nodded toward a nook in the corner. "Do you mind?"

When the three were seated, Aguilar got right to the point. "Miss O'Day, I understand you had a run-in with some deputies with the Department of Public Safety yesterday."

"Yes." She looked at Matt, alarm in her eyes.

"The governor asked me to chat with you," Aguilar continued. "He and I go back aways. He wanted me to look into what happened. Off the record, of course."

Matt cocked his head. "I take it you're not a patient of Dr. Ryan?"

Aguilar smiled. "No neurological issues as far as I know, though some would debate that."

"And you're not here," Matt concluded.

"Lieutenant Gage said you were sharp. Also said that you've got a nose like a hound dog."

"I'll take that as a compliment."

"You should. She doesn't impress easily." Aguilar turned his attention back to Angie. "Tell me what happened. As many details as you can remember."

Angie explained everything that had happened. Matt's skin crawled as she recited the threats the deputy had made.

Chief Aguilar looked up from the notes he had been taking. "He actually told you to tell James W. that he'd be watching you day and night?" He lifted the paper and read, "You never know when someone might want to hurt the governor or his kin. Especially if the governor crosses a line that upsets the wrong people."

Angie shook her head. "The deputy said *we'd* be watching, not *he'd* be watching. It almost sounded like the whole DPS was in on the threat." Her hands tightened into fists. "The scariest part was when they escorted me to my work."

"Why's that?"

"I never told them where I work."

Aguilar nodded, his pen scribbling furiously. He turned to Matt. "The governor said that Senator Womack might be involved. What would have given him that impression?"

Angie answered. "The night before, I went into a bar called the Oak and Horn down on Fifth Street."

Matt leaned forward. "Pastor Lambert, the man who committed suicide Thursday night? He'd gone to the Oak and Horn looking for Womack's son. I was keeping an eye on Lambert because I felt he had something to do with Reverend Duff's disappearance."

"U.S. Senator Womack's son? Hogg Womack?" Aguilar asked.

"Lambert spent the whole day trying to talk to Hogg," Matt said. "I overheard a conversation between Lambert and the boy Thursday afternoon. Lambert was very upset, even more so when Hogg Womack hung up on him. That's when Lambert went to the Oak and Horn looking for him."

Angie picked up the story. "I went to the Oak and Horn to check things out. I used the name 'Maeve' while I was in there. That's the only place I've used that name. Ever." She swallowed. "That was my mother's name."

"I still don't see—"

"Chief, I'm trying to tell you," Angie said. "When the troopers finally left me at my bar, the John Wayne wannabe called me Maeve."

Chief Aguilar's dark eyes stared hard at Angie. *He's making sure Angie is a reliable witness,* Matt thought. Angie didn't flinch under the chief's scrutiny but met his gaze straight on.

Aguilar nodded, jotted a note on his paper, then folded it and put it in his pocket. He leaned forward and beckoned Matt and Angie to do the same.

"Don't talk about this in the Governor's Mansion," he said. "I don't know what we're up against. But I'll look into this."

"You don't have jurisdiction," Matt whispered.

"I said, I'll look into this." Aguilar's voice was firm. "You wanna talk to James W. or the governor, you do it off the Capitol grounds. You wanna talk to me, tell Hester. Otherwise, keep your mouths shut and your eyes open. Got it?"

Matt and Angie nodded. Without another word, the police chief stood and walked out of the building.

The door hadn't even closed behind him when Dr. Ryan's assistant came into the lounge. "Pastor Hayden? Dr. Ryan's ready for you now."

Angie smiled brightly as Matt stood up. "That worked out great. Time for the chief and then in you go."

"Yes," said Matt. "I'll be right back." As he made his way to the patient area, he gave a slight shake of his head. The timing was too convenient. Too coincidental.

Matt Hayden didn't believe in coincidences.

43

YOU SHOULDN'T'VE DONE THAT

WITHIN TEN MINUTES, Matt returned to the waiting room.

"Done already?" Angie asked.

"Blood pressure was 138 over 86. BPM a nice steady 79," Matt answered. "Dr. Ryan was pleased as punch."

"She said that?" Angie stood to put her coat back on.

"No, but I'm sure that's what she thought."

"Right." Angie pulled her truck keys from her purse. "Today's agenda is figuring out where the Herne's Hunters hangout is, right?"

"They call it the Homestead. Yeah, right."

"I propose we go to the Oak and Horn. If Monica's working, I might be able to get some info from her about where it might be."

Matt stopped in his tracks. "You are not going into that place."

"I wasn't there when Womack came in," she said.

"But he saw you as you left. Trust me. He called you a pretty little filly."

"Still. I looked it up. The Oak and Horn does a biscuit and

gravy brunch on the weekend. They open at ten-thirty, which"
—she checked her watch—"was five minutes ago."

"What about breakfast?"

"I also looked up that Voodoo Doughnut place Henry was
so pumped up about. We can swing by there and pick some up
for our meet with Lieutenant Gage."

"You are not going into that bar."

"Well, I'm driving, and we're going there. If it makes you
feel any better, my gun's in the glove compartment. I'll park
right out front."

"After what happened on your way home yesterday with
the DPS threatening you?"

The argument continued all the way across town and
hadn't ended when Angie pulled the truck to the curb across
the street from the Oak and Horn. "I'll be right back," she said,
shutting the door on his protestations.

"Good thing you already had your blood pressure taken,"
she muttered as she crossed the street. Matt might be her
fiancé, but he wasn't her master. Besides, he should know better
than to argue with her. That only made her more determined to
have her way.

She pushed into the Oak and Horn and was immediately
met with the dank interior's smell of un-showered bodies and
the sound of overly loud men. Apparently, the Herne's Hunters
had returned.

Angie headed straight for the bar. The man tending it was
heavily tattooed and wore a T-shirt that hadn't seen a washing
machine in at least a week. "Yeah?" he asked.

"Is Monica here?" Angie asked.

"Monica Braden? She don't work here no more." He eyed
her closely. "Hey, Decker," he called to the end of the bar.
"Lookie who we've got here."

Angie's heart slammed against her chest. The man who

turned to answer the other's call was none other than the John Wayne wannabe deputy, only this time he was in jeans and a camo T-shirt. His eyes sharpened when he recognized her, then he lowered his gaze intentionally to stare at her chest. When he raised them again, his lips were stretched in a leering sneer. "Hiya, Maeve. What can I do for you?"

The impulse to run out the door was almost overwhelming, but she kept her composure. "Nothing. I just came to see Monica."

"Monica Braden got fired," 'Decker' said. "'Cuz of you and your buddies."

"Fired?"

"Monica broke our golden rule. No strangers in here."

Angie swallowed hard. She'd been responsible for Monica getting fired.

"After the boss heard what happened, she was history," Decker continued. "Probably ran all the way back to Bastrop. Which is what you should do. All the way to Wilks."

A man sitting next to Decker put down his beer and stood. "Sounds like Decker doesn't want you here."

When another bar customer turned to leer at her, fear ran down her spine.

"Of course, if you came in here to be nice and friendly—" Decker started walking toward her. "You're more than welcome to stay..."

Angie was out the door and across the street before she took another breath. She hoisted herself into the truck and locked the door.

"What happened?" Matt asked.

"You were right. Okay?" She started the truck. "I should-n't've gone in there. And Monica's been fired."

"Fired?"

"Deputy John Wayne Wannabe was in there." Her hands

shook as she shifted into drive. "Looks like he's another regular." She pulled away from the curb and hit the accelerator. Only when she was two blocks down the road did she pull into a street parking space to sort herself out.

Finally, she looked at Matt. "I need to settle down. Let's get the doughnuts like we'd planned and then head for APD headquarters. All right?"

"Where you'll tell all of this to Gage, right?"

God, how could she have been so stupid? "Right."

———

WHEN THEY ARRIVED at Austin police headquarters, Matt could tell Angie was still upset. Her skin was pale, and her eyes were...well, she looked spooked. What could John Wayne Wannabe have said to upset her so in the one minute she was inside the Oak and Horn?

"James W.'s already here." Angie nodded to the quad cab parked two spaces away. "Are we very late?"

"Only five minutes." Matt patted the box under his arm. "Besides, these were worth it," he said, trying to cheer her.

The front desk attendant directed them to a conference room. Lieutenant Gage sat at the head of the table; James W. and a gaunt, balding man with a pair of readers perched precariously on his nose took up the two chairs on the far wall. Henry and his freckles had his back to them. When he turned, his eyes immediately fixed on the box that Matt held.

"Voodoo doughnuts!" His voice was almost a squeal.

Matt grinned. "Thought we'd check it out after yesterday." He put the box on the table and removed the top.

James W.'s eyes went round. "Is that bacon?" He pulled out a maple-glazed Long John with two strips of bacon on top.

"Anybody else want the fruit loop one?" Henry's offer was

forced. Matt could almost sense the drool pooling in the kid's mouth.

Even Lieutenant Gage stood to survey the box's contents. "I do enjoy an old-fashioned."

The man sitting next to James W. studied the selection intently through his black-rimmed glasses, then chose a doughnut covered in mini-M&M's. Angie headed straight for a coconut-covered concoction topped with a blue cocktail umbrella.

Matt reached for his favorite. A good ol' yeast doughnut covered—smothered really—in chocolate. At a seven-inch diameter, however, it was like nothing he'd ever eaten before. His jaws could barely open wide enough to take the first bite.

James W. put down his bacon Long John, which was already half gone. "This here's Danny Lee Ashe. When he's not eating doughnuts"—James W. and the man shared a grin— "Danny's the U. S. Attorney for our Texas District. More important for us, he's the grandson of the man who shot the buck standing in the front corner of the Oak and Horn. Danny Lee's granddad took him out to the Homestead when he was a kid. He's familiar with the area, so I asked him to join us."

Danny Lee's thin black hair was slicked back, showing off a high forehead. He had the pallor of a man who sat behind a desk, but his dark brown eyes, emphasized by those thick, black glasses, showed a bit of humor and hinted at the ability to make keen observations.

Danny Lee set down his doughnut. "I need to say for the record that I am not a Herne's Hunter, nor am I associated with the group. It's been over thirty-five years since I was out there, and I only went there the one time. I was a teenager back then. I spent most of the trip with my nose buried in my Game Boy." Danny Lee's lips twitched. "Monochrome screen with insertable cartridges. Times have changed."

"You've been to the Homestead," Gage repeated. Her brows knitted in confusion. "Are you all thinking about trying to find this Homestead?"

Matt leaned forward. "I don't think Reverend Duff is alive, but that's my opinion. Either way, dead or alive, we have to find him. Somehow, I think the Oak and Horn and the Homestead are both involved in this case. The Oak and Horn is where Lambert's car was parked. Where Lambert went looking for Hogg Womack. Where Herne's Hunters meet, including Senator Womack and his son. And the Homestead is where all of the Herne's Hunters went the night after Reverend Duff disappeared. That calls for a look around the place, don't you agree?"

Gage sighed. "I don't have the manpower to go searching for a needle in a haystack. This isn't the only case we're dealing with in Austin, you know."

"Of course not," Matt said. "But if you could loan us Henry for an hour or so, we might be able to narrow down where the Homestead's located. We'd be the ones looking for the needle, not you."

Gage scrubbed at her face. "Even if you do find it—" She broke off. "I'm thinking of the integrity of the crime scene. And yes, I know. James W. is a sheriff and you're a former cop, but..." She shrugged.

Angie spoke up. "I know the governor is very concerned. I spent last night at the Mansion. Reverend Duff's disappearance is weighing heavily on him."

Gage put her hands on the table's edge. She looked at Henry. "You game?"

"Yes, ma'am," he said earnestly. "Especially if I can have the Cap'n Crunch doughnut that's still in the box."

"All right then." Gage stood. "Give it a shot." She narrowed a stern look at Matt. "But you will keep me informed of every-thing you're doing."

Matt nodded. "Yes, ma'am." He looked sideways at Angie. "You gonna tell her what happened to you right before we came here?"

Angie sighed, then stood. "Lieutenant Gage, if I could have one more minute of your time. In the hall?"

Gage looked from Angie to Matt and back at Angie. "Sure."

The two women disappeared out the door.

44

DANNY LEE ASHE

FIVE MINUTES LATER, Matt, James W., Danny Lee, Henry and Angie returned to the APD's video evidence room. While the others gathered around the video playback area, Henry resumed his seat at the console and took charge. "I'll pull up the last shot we have of Lambert's car on the toll road." His fingers did their magic dance over the keyboard, and the video on the screen came to life. The footage showed Lambert's car moving up the Highway 183 toll road, the camera snapping a shot of the car and the license plate as it went through the gate. Henry hit pause. "That's the last shot we have of Lambert's car." He pulled up a road map on a second screen and looked expectantly at Danny Lee.

Danny Lee removed his spectacles and stared more closely at the screen. "I've got nothing," he said finally. "I was only sixteen. That was thirty-five years ago."

Angie watched as James W. stared at the ceiling, Matt studied the floor and Danny Lee looked sorry as could be. They were stumped. How could she help? The only thing she understood about teenage boys was that they were always...

Hungry.

"Did you stop anywhere to eat?" she asked.

Danny Lee folded his arms across his chest and closed his eyes. "Actually, I do remember that we stopped for ice cream."

"A Dairy Queen, maybe?" James W. suggested.

Angie smiled. James W. loved his Dairy Queen. God bless Texas.

"No. It was..." Danny Lee scratched his head. "I got this cup of ice cream that was all smashed up." His face brightened. "With M&M's."

"Like a Dairy Queen Blizzard?" James W. pressed.

"No. It was in a bowl." He made a four-inch circle with his hands. "Maybe three inches tall."

"Okay. So not a Dairy Queen," Matt said. "Did you go into the place that sold it?"

Danny Lee nodded. Angie could see he was beginning to remember. "It was a gas station. But more than that. It had ice cream and..." He snapped his fingers. "Kolaches. That's why we stopped there. Granddad said he always picked up kolaches from there for everybody's breakfast the next morning. Said they were the best in San Saba County."

The teenager of thirty-five years ago was coming to life, Angie noted. "Your grandad was in the car with you?" she asked.

"Yeah. Him and my father." Danny Lee's eyes softened. "Granddad was the best."

Angie heard the unspoken words. Danny Lee loved his grandfather, but his father? Not so much. "You and your granddad were pretty close."

"Yeah," Danny Lee said. "The only reason I went up to the Homestead was because he invited me. Dad invited me plenty, but..." He shrugged. "Dad was a drinker. I wasn't much interested in spending a weekend with a bunch of drunks."

"Did you go inside the gas station to get the ice cream?" Matt asked.

"Yeah. Grandad hadn't even realized they served ice cream. It was in the back of the building. Folks could drive up and place their order." He nodded at James W. "I guess like a Dairy Queen, but it wasn't. The store was kind of big. Had T-shirts and trucker's stuff. And one of those grills with rollers to cook hot dogs."

James W. smiled. "I might be able to make a call and find out where that's at." He kicked the file's bottom drawer closed. "Be right back." He pulled his cell phone from his pocket as he left the room.

"What can you tell us about the Homestead once you got there?" Matt asked. "Hilly? Flat? Were there any buildings on the property?"

"Now *that* I remember." Danny Lee sat up straighter in his chair. "There was a main house. Typical ranch-style. Brick. Yellow brick. Had a barn off to the side. Not like the ones in photos. It was a metal building, painted red for effect. The doors were open and there was a tractor inside. Not like a farm tractor or anything that big. Like the ones that pull a trailer loaded with straw to give kids rides in."

"A ranch-style, one-story building with a red barn beside it," Matt said. "What else?"

"We drove by the house on our way to the bonfire. Had to cross a field where some cattle were grazing. The field ended at a line of trees. There was a path that wound through the trees. My granddad pulled the truck over and parked beside some other vehicles. He said we had to pack in from there. I grabbed my backpack and sleeping bag, and we followed this path through the woods to get to the bonfire. I remember thinking that we were gonna have to sleep outside on the ground and that it was too cold to do that."

FOUR REASONS TO DIE

307

He took a bite of his doughnut, remembering now, then slugged down a gulp of coffee.

"But when we broke through the trees, there was this big, long bunkhouse on the top of a rise. And I was like, thank God. We'll be sleeping inside."

"How long do you figure the walk through the woods was?" Matt asked.

"Not much. About a mile."

James W. walked in, grinning from ear to ear. "Got the name of the kolache place," he said. "Rittenhouse Roadside Filling Station in San Saba County."

Matt quirked an eyebrow. "Now, how the heck did you figure that out?"

"I called around to some of the sheriffs out there. We sheriffs got our own kinda network. And when it comes to food, the network never lets you down."

Henry sat down behind the console. "Okay, then. Let's get to work." He searched the internet for the store's name, then plugged the address into Google Earth. Soon the screen displayed a satellite view of an old building whose roof was a patchwork of steel and shingles, suggesting that it had been added to several times. A set of gas pumps were in the front and what looked like a drive-thru in the back. Henry switched to the street-level view. "Look familiar?"

Danny Lee's smile was broad. "That's it exactly." He read the sign in front of the gas station out loud. "'Come on in and fill up your car, your sweet tooth and your tummy at Rittenhouse Roadside Filling Station.' Yep. That's it. I remember how corny that sounded."

"Okay," Matt said. "Henry, please switch to the map." He pulled his notepad from his pocket. "Anybody got a pen I can use?"

Angie fished one from her purse and handed it over as the overhead view of the Rittenhouse store popped back on screen.

"And zoom out," Matt said.

Henry tapped several times before Matt told him to stop. "There." Matt pointed at the monitor. "There's where the toll ends on 183. If you keep going on the non-toll portion of 183, you eventually intersect with Highway 190. And Rittenhouse is on 190."

Matt was in his element, Angie realized. She'd never before observed him in investigation mode. He was focused. Deliberate. Strong.

She'd underestimated him before. Had it really only been one year ago, almost to the day, that her mother had gone missing? She'd hated the preacher who'd taken the call at that godforsaken Grace Lutheran Church across the river from her bar, and she'd had no idea that Cash Novak had been her father and James W. her half-brother. Matt had been the one to figure out the sad tale behind her mother, Maeve, and Cash's forbidden love story. It was Matt who had enlisted her dog Shadow's to help sniff out the route Angie's mother had taken to her death. In doing so, he had not only solved the mystery of the whereabouts of Maeve's body, but found a family for Angie. And here Matt was again. Finding a missing person for those who loved him, knowing that the news would be devastating, but also realizing the not-knowing would be even worse for those left behind.

In that moment, she loved Matt Hayden more than she'd ever thought possible.

James W. was focused on the screen. "Can you think of anything that would help us identify the bunkhouse from the air? Like in a Google Earth shot?"

Danny Lee put his glasses back on. "Not that I can think of."

"Let's go back to the bunkhouse," Matt said. "What can you tell us about it?"

"The house was wood-sided. Very rustic. It was a one-story, not very wide, but plenty long. Four sets of bunk beds down each side of the building. Kind of a gathering room in the center. Coupla couches around a fireplace. A fridge and an old stove. Bathroom on each end of the building. Had a tin roof, that was for sure."

"Why did that stick in your memory?" James W. asked.

"Because it rained all night. I had to sleep with a pillow over my head, it made so much noise."

Matt looked up from his notes. "Where was the bonfire?"

"Maybe about a quarter mile from the bunkhouse. And there was this huge oak tree about twenty yards beyond the bonfire. That's what they hung the deer from." He made a face. "The thing was dead already—shot by the guy with the pirate gun. But still. They cut that animal open and took out its heart for the guy who shot it to eat. It made me sick. Literally. I had to go upchuck back in the trees. For years, I had nightmares about it. It didn't seem to bother anybody else, though. They all cheered and chugged down a beer or whatever. Then the guy —" Danny Lee shook his head. "He was covered in blood and grinning like a stooge. He got the honor of lighting the bonfire and the party was on. That's the night I swore I would never join that group."

"Okay." Matt checked his notes. "We have a one-story ranch house. A field that's about fifty yards across, then a wooded area about a mile long, then a bunkhouse with a tin roof, a burned-out patch of ground from a bonfire and a huge tree."

"And there's a red barn next to the ranch house," Angie reminded him.

All eyes turned expectantly to Henry. He shook his head.

"I need more than that. There's a lot of country out that way. You at least have to narrow it down to a county."

"Do you remember how long you were on the road between Rittenhouse and the Homestead?" Matt asked.

Danny Lee shook his head. "It was back to the Gameboy for the rest of the trip."

"What about the next day when you came home?" James W. asked.

Danny Lee shrugged. "I slept in the back seat the whole way."

"Okay." Matt stood up. "Time for me to let Gage know of our progress." He patted Danny Lee on the shoulder. "It's all right. We'll head out to the Rittenhouse and see if that'll stir up any memories."

45

HUNTIN' FOR THE HOMESTEAD

AFTER STOPPING at Hester's to pick up some items Matt needed and then again at the Governor's Mansion for Angie's dog, Shadow, the four of them jammed into James W.'s quad cab and headed out for Lampasas.

James W. hit the button for cruise control. "Rittenhouse Filling Station, here we come."

Matt pulled up the map on his phone. "I thought you said this is Loop One."

James W. nodded, his eyes never leaving the road. "That's cuz it is Loop One."

Matt's brow furrowed. "But it's a straight north and south line."

Danny Lee, who was sitting shotgun in the front, chuckled. "Welcome to Texas."

Matt and Angie were in the back seat with Shadow sprawled between them. Matt took her hand and gave it a squeeze. "Since we've got some time here, I suppose we ought to tell James W. about your visit to the Oak and Horn this morning."

James W.'s head whipped around. "What?"

Angie shot Matt a dirty look.

"He needs to know," Matt said.

"Traitor," she mouthed, then said. "You. Please go ahead. By all means."

"On our way over to the police station this morning, Angie —who was driving, I might add, before you take my head off— decided to detour over to the Oak and Horn to see if she could get more information from Monica the bartender about where the Homestead might be."

James W.'s eyes glared at his half-sister in the rearview mirror. "You did *what?*"

"Eyes on the road, James W.," Angie said. "I thought it was a good idea at the time." She held up her hand as James W. started to speak. "And I was wrong. First of all, Monica was fired. Because of us going in there. And second, John Wayne Wannabe was sitting at the bar."

James W.'s response was a heavy foot to the accelerator. After a mile, he slowed to only ten miles above the speed limit. "Dadgummit, girl," he said. "What the hell were you thinking?"

"I was trying to help."

He snorted.

"Who are these Herne's Hunters, anyway?" She asked as she settled back in her seat, and Shadow nudged her hand to pet him. "How did they start? And why would they care about a preacher who was supposed to give a benediction at a governor's inauguration?"

Danny Lee looked over his shoulder. "My granddad told me a group of male students wanted to build a bonfire bigger than the one at Texas A&M over in College Station. Huge rivalry there." He snickered. "The first year, the UT guys almost burned down a house. Two of 'em got arrested, but after they promised to move the event out to the country, the authorities let them go. So they found a rancher out this way who had a plot of land that needed clearing. They've been out here ever since."

"Were they hunters?" Matt asked.

"Naw. If anything, they were a bunch of fraternity rejects who wanted to have their own..." He searched for the word. "Society? Club, I guess."

"Where did the name Herne's Hunters come from?" Angie tousled Shadow's ears.

"A coupla years in, they invited two guys who liked to hunt to join the group. The new invitees offered to shoot some game for the group to barbeque over the fire. Somebody else in this... society...was a lit major. Apparently, Shakespeare wrote about Herne in one of his plays. The name stuck."

James W. shook his head. "Sounds pretty low-key to me. When did they get mean?"

Danny Lee nodded. "My granddad was one of the early joiners. He was probably a freshman to the seniors who originally formed the group. And he was a hunter. More hunters joined. His senior year was when they took the name Herne's Hunters."

"Hold up a second," Matt called from the back seat. "We're getting close to the 190 turn."

"Thanks, son." Sure enough, the sign for 190 West was up ahead. James W. made the turn, then settled back against his seat. "You didn't answer my question," he said. "When did the Herne's Hunters become belligerent?"

"I think things started getting out of hand around the time my father got involved. He was nothing like my granddad. That first generation of the society ended up being successful businessmen. Politicians, bankers. Preachers." Danny Lee glanced back to Matt. "But like anything, even religion, the way things start changes over time. Sometimes a group becomes the exact opposite of what it originally was intended to be. That's what happened to the Herne's Hunters."

"Your father became a member?"

Danny Lee nodded. "By the time he was invited, the group had turned to heavy drinking and perpetuating this folklore about shooting a deer with that ridiculous gun and eating its heart. That was right up my dad's alley." Danny Lee fell silent, and he stared out the window for a long moment. Finally, he turned back to the group. "Sorry."

"That still doesn't answer why they would be interested in Reverend Duff's benediction,"

Angie said.

"Frankly, I don't think, as a group, they are involved with Reverend Duff's disappearance." And now the D.A. side of Danny Lee surfaced. "If anything, maybe one or two members are, but I don't think they would've told the others. Most of the guys just like to party out in the wild and feel like 'real men.' They're misogynists to the core, and literally have a pissing contest off the bunkhouse porch every time they get together. And Lord help you if you're a Democrat."

"Is Hogg Womack a member?" Matt asked.

"I would assume so. His father was. In fact, William Womack was at the Homestead the weekend I went."

James W. nodded out the front window. "Looks like we're coming up on Rittenhouse Filling Station."

James W. pulled off the road into the gravel parking lot. "Okay, Danny Lee, you're on. Play your 'I was at the Homestead with my granddad when I was a kid' bit. You know the drill. Preacher, you go in with him, get the lay of the land."

"I need to walk Shadow," Angie said.

"I figured as much," James W. replied. "I'll go with you. After that stunt you pulled at the Oak and Horn, I'm not letting you out of my sight."

46

THE RITTENHOUSE ROADSIDE
FILLING STATION

MATT CHOSE to leave his cane in the car. He would walk slowly to avoid his limp showing, but he wanted to disappear into his surroundings as much as possible. Beside him, Danny Lee paused to take in Rittenhouse's storefront. He had a smile on his face.

"Good memories here, at least?" Matt asked.

"Yeah." Danny Lee removed his glasses and tucked them into his shirt pocket.

"When we get inside, look for the oldest employee in the store. Keep that smile on your face and let 'em know who your grandfather was. Earle Lee must've had a reputation of some kind here. That stag standing in the Oak and Horn is pretty incredible. Oh! And don't use our real names. The three of us," he nodded toward James W. and Angie, "are persona non grata with the Herne's Hunters."

The two walked up to the screen door and pulled it open. The store beyond was a snapshot from the fifties. The floor was a worn brown linoleum. Splintered barnwood fronted the cash register counters. Vintage signs of Clydesdales and nickel Coca

Colas rimmed the room. To the left were the beer coolers, straight ahead was the bakery, and truckers' paraphernalia was on the right. The place smelled of fresh-baked goods and grease. Matt nodded toward an old geezer at the back of the bakery. Hopefully, Danny Lee could get the old man's attention.

A teenage girl in pink T-shirt and jeans stepped to the counter to wait on Danny Lee. "May I help you?"

Danny Lee smiled broadly. "I'm trying to remember what I had last time I was here," he said, his voice loud.

Good, Matt thought. Trying to catch the old man's attention.

"Musta been thirty-five years ago," Danny Lee continued. "Came here with my granddad on our way to the Homestead."

The old man looked up from the stool he was sitting on. "The Homestead, you say? They've already left."

"I know," Danny Lee nodded. "I figured they'd be finished up with the bonfire by now. I didn't want to disturb them. I'm chasing memories, is all." He continued to study the board.

He's pretending not to notice he's gotten the old man's attention, Matt decided. Good job.

"You say your granddad took you to the Homestead?" The elderly man stood and shuffled to the counter. He leaned heavily against it, out of breath. He wore bib overalls and a brown flannel shirt and looked like he hadn't shaved for days. "What was his name?"

Danny Lee dropped his gaze to look at the man. "Granddad? His name was Earle Lee Ashe." He nodded at the cashier. "I think I'll have two—"

"Your granddad was Earle Lee Ashe?" The old man's eyes brightened. "By golly, that's a name I haven't heard for years. How is he?"

"I'm afraid he passed about five years back. Lung cancer."

Danny Lee held up a hand when the man started to apologize. "He was ready to go. The last year or so..." He shook his head. "But the memories of being with him? They'll last me forever."

"He was a good man," the old man said, extending his hand. "My name's Frank. Frank Rittenhouse."

"I'm Danny Lee Ashe." He shook Frank's hand.

"What're you doin' around these parts?" Frank asked.

"Takin' a ride down memory lane. I saw that deer season was up, and it reminded me of coming out here with Granddad. I brought some friends with me to show 'em what I've been talking about. How are things over at the Homestead?"

"LeRoy passed, of course. He was gettin' old when your grandfather was your age. His kids come and go. Lease the land, get their money, but don't keep it in county."

Matt noted the disapproval in the old man's voice.

Danny Lee held out a hand to Matt. "Come here, John. This here's Frank. He knew my granddad."

"Pleased to meet you, Frank." Matt held out his hand. The man might be old, but his handshake was firm.

"What kind of kolache do you like?" Danny Lee asked. "And Karen?" He turned back to Frank. "Karen is John's fiancée."

Good thinking, Matt thought. Best to have a cover in case Frank looked out the window.

"We'll both go sausage and cheese," Matt said.

Frank shooed away the cashier and pulled out a box.

"Make mine with jalapeño sausage," Danny Lee instructed.

As Frank began filling the order, Danny Lee cleared his throat. "The problem is, I brought my friends out to see the place, and now I can't quite remember how to get there."

"Well, it is out of the way," Frank said. "That's the way the boys like it, of course. You head out 190 toward San Saba and look for County Road 132. Go north..."

47

FINALLY

FORTY MINUTES LATER, James W. steered his truck off the blacktop road, crossed a cattle guard and drove up the dirt road that led to a yellow, brick ranch house with a red, tin barn off to the side.

"This look familiar?" Matt asked.

Danny Lee nodded. "This is it, all right." He sat up in the seat. "See that fence, over there?" He pointed to the west. "I think we drive through that opening, then across the field. The tree line should be right ahead of us."

James W. followed Danny Lee's instructions. When they passed through the gate, which was also offset by a cattle guard, the road stopped. Between the rocks and heavy brush, they endured a rough ride as they crossed the pasture.

Sure enough, the cattle Danny Lee had talked about were all around them, munching on the straw-like grass left after the freeze.

As the truck approached the trees, Danny Lee pointed in excitement. "There! See that tree branch wrapped in red? That's where the trail starts. I'd forgotten it was marked."

James W. headed toward the wrapped oak, pulled up to the tree line and cut the engine. "We walk from here."

Matt retrieved the backpack he'd picked up at Hester's, while Angie put a leash on Shadow. Danny Lee had been pretty accurate in his estimate of a mile walk through the trees. Halfway down the path, Matt stopped. "I want to know how wide this trail is." He swung the backpack off, dug through its contents and came up with a tape measure. "Here." He handed the tape's end to Danny Lee.

"Six and a half feet, give or take," Matt noted when the tape was taut.

"What're you chawing on?" James W. asked.

"Not sure yet."

In another half mile, the path opened to a large clearing. A bunkhouse was on a ridge off to the right. Ahead, the ground sloped down to a burned-out patch of dirt surrounded by a series of logs that circled the dirt. At the burned-out patch's center was a pile of ashes. And twenty yards beyond the bonfire site was a gigantic oak tree, its branches reaching a hundred feet into the air.

"That's where they gutted the deer," Danny Lee said, nodding toward the tree.

Matt wasn't looking at the tree, however. He was studying the grass that ended at the broken ring of logs. "That's where everybody sits?" he asked Danny Lee.

"Or leans against," Danny Lee answered. "Or stands on to howl at the moon."

Matt turned to Angie. "Bring Shadow. The rest of you, stay here."

Angie brought Shadow forward. Matt took the leash. "Stay behind me."

About halfway to the bonfire, Matt found a patch of dried

mud, scarred by a row of angled lines. He sighed heavily. He'd so wanted to be wrong.

"What you got there, son?" James W. called from behind.

Matt didn't answer but swung his backpack onto the ground and pulled out a plastic bag. "Come here, Shadow." He pulled a white cloth from the bag and held it out for the dog with the bloodhound face to sniff. Shadow did so with gusto.

"Never finds a smell he doesn't love," Angie said.

Matt gave the dog's head a pat, then unleashed him.

Shadow took off on a run, then stopped to sniff, then retraced his steps, then ran another few feet—all the time with his nose to the ground. Angie started to follow him, but Matt's hand jerked out to stop her.

"Where'd you get that cloth?" James W. came up beside him. "What is it, anyway?"

Matt stood, his eyes never leaving Shadow. "It's a pillowcase. Reverend Duff's pillowcase."

"You think Reverend Duff—" James W. stopped in midsentence.

Shadow had come to a sudden halt about five feet from the first scorches of the bonfire's black ash. He held his nose an inch above the grass, circled his back end around the spot, then looked at Matt and howled.

"There's nothing but ash left of that bonfire," James W. said.

Matt turned to Danny Lee. "You said they kept the fire going from dusk until dawn."

"Yeah. It was part of the ritual," Danny Lee said.

"And long enough to consume an entire body." Matt carefully picked his way closer to Shadow, then stopped. He bent down and studied the ground closely. "What's this look like to you, James W.?"

James W. carefully made his way over. He bent over for a closer look. "That's a tire print."

Matt nodded. "And not from an ATV. Their treads are much wider."

James W. looked back at the trailhead emerging from the tree line. "Can't get a truck through that."

"But a small car might be able to make it." Matt stood. "Like a Ford Focus."

"Oh, my God," whispered Angie.

"Best get Shadow back on the leash," Matt said. "This here's a crime scene." He pulled out his phone to call Lieutenant Gage.

———

BY THE TIME Lieutenant Gage arrived two hours later, James W. and Angie had returned from driving Danny Lee back to Lampasas, where his wife would pick him up.

Matt, Angie and James W. waved Gage over to the path's opening on the ranch house side. She parked her car next to James W.'s truck and got out. "You found it," she called.

"Danny Lee found it," Matt said. "He had to head home. He'll give you a statement whenever you need."

"A U.S. district attorney?" Gage smiled. "I think he's good for it."

It was decided that Angie would stay behind and show the crime scene crew how to get back to the bonfire.

"And I called the San Saba sheriff. This is his jurisdiction," Gage explained to Angie. "He'll be here shortly. Send him on back, too."

Gage, Matt and James W. headed down the path. During the walk through the woods, the two men gave her their report as well as the careful procedures they had followed not to corrupt the crime scene.

"You didn't go up to the bonfire?" Gage asked as they emerged from the tree line.

"Stayed on this side of the log circle," Matt answered.

Gage carefully made her way to the logs used for seating around the bonfire. She shook her head and returned to the group. "That ash is pulverized."

"Danny Lee said they burned it hot and kept it going from dusk until dawn," Matt said.

"Ain't that some sort of Hindu ritual?" James W. asked.

"Something like that," Matt said.

"Well, there's gotta be something left. Teeth at least," Gage said. "Forensics'll be the only way this one gets solved." She looked back at the path. "You really think a car could get here on that path?"

"I looked up the specs for the Ford Focus," Matt answered. "The small sedan could do it. I'd look for scratches on the side doors from protruding branches. Maybe forensics can do something with that."

As they spoke, Angie and a trio of crime techs wearing protective gear emerged from the path. Gage waved them over and had Matt and James W. repeat their findings to the techs. After a full download, the team set off to begin their work.

"You three have done a lot of good groundwork," Gage said. "We'll take it from here. Time for you to head back to town. I'll keep you posted on what we find."

"Sounds like a winner," James W. said.

"You and Angie go on ahead," Matt said. "I need a quick word with the lieutenant."

"Okey-doke," Angie nodded. She and James W. headed for the trailhead.

Matt turned back to Gage. "You know this is pointing

straight at Hogg Womack. He pretended to be Duff when he went into the Episcopal church. We found the preacher's clothes in the parking garage dumpster—"

"And several of the parking deck cameras had been painted over the night before," Gage added. "That's how he could've changed clothes without being recorded."

Matt took in the information. "That, with the change of clothes, could give us premeditation."

"And puts Lambert in on the whole thing," Gage agreed. "Hogg must've been in or near that garage when Lambert and Duff went out to the car. My hunch is that's when Duff was murdered and put in the trunk of the Focus."

"Then Hogg drove it out here to get rid of the body. So,"— Matt took a deep breath.—"Hogg Womack has access to a private plane, and his father can certainly finance an escape."

"You're asking me to arrest him for murder?" Gage shook her head. "I can't do that. The forensics have to tell the story here. We can't go around arresting a U.S. senator's son on circumstantial evidence. You know that."

"Of course you're right." Matt blew out a breath. "I have this gut feeling he's gonna make a run for it. Could you at least put a tail on him?"

"Maybe." She thought for a moment. "Well, the governor certainly wants this solved. And he's already said he'd back up APD in our investigation." She nodded. "Okay. I'll get that done."

"Thanks, Lieutenant," Matt said.

"You've done a good job here, Preacher," she said. "I hope you can take the night off while we get this evidence processed."

"Actually," Matt said. "I think I'm going to go to church."

48

FOUR REASONS TO DIE

CONNOR DROPPED Matt off at St. Gregory Episcopal Church just as the music began for evening vespers. Matt sat in the back of the towering sanctuary, its arching stained-glass windows lit from outside. Their beautiful hews of amethyst, emerald, ruby and gold mixed with subtle candlelight to create a peaceful, contemplative mood. Matt so wanted to be filled with that peace that passes all understanding. But he also wanted answers.

Bishop Hamlin led the service, which surprised Matt. Usually Saturday evening vespers were handled by an assistant pastor, or even a lay person. But no, a subdued Hamlin quietly led the chants and readings.

The vespers were conducted using the Holden Evening Prayers, a favorite of Matt's. Its music was lyrical and outerworldly, and hit precisely on the struggle within him.

You who made the heaven's splendor, every dancing star at night,

Make us shine with gentle justice, let us each reflect your light.

Gentle justice? How was that possible when it came to murder, especially when the Scriptures were used to fan the flames of hate?

Next came the words of the Magnificat put to song.

You have cast the mighty down from their thrones, and uplifted the humble of heart,

You have filled the hungry with wondrous things and left the wealthy no part.

Left the wealthy no part? A troubling thought for those who solicited money in the name of Christ and lived in mansions and flew on private planes.

Troubling, to be sure. But not as troubling as the phone call he'd gotten from Lieutenant Gage on his ride over to St. Gregory's. *We found several bone fragments, some animal, others not so sure. And teeth. At first glance they're human, but forensics has to verify. Oh, and some rubies and at least one diamond among the bonfire's ashes.* Matt studied the stained-glass window poised over the altar. His eyes zoomed in on the ruby-red blood dripping from the crucified Christ's head, hands and feet. Jesus on the cross.

And Mum's description of Duff's pectoral cross: four rubies at each point and a diamond in the middle.

Matt sat in the hard pew, mesmerized. The blood of Christ and the soul of Christ. Both had survived the bonfire.

Slowly he became aware that people were standing and heading down the aisle. The service had ended, and he hadn't even realized it. Matt looked for the bishop, expecting to see him heading for the sacristy, but instead, Hamlin was walking down the aisle toward Matt.

"I saw you in the congregation, Pastor Hayden. Have you come to finish our conversation from yesterday?"

Matt shook the bishop's extended hand. "I came both for the service and to finish that conversation."

"Please wait here," Hamlin said. "I'll change out of my robes, and we can walk over to the office together."

Minutes later, the bishop and Matt entered the deserted office wing and walked down the short hall to Hamlin's office. After turning on some table lamps as well as the coffeepot, Bishop Hamlin took the seat behind his desk. He picked up a small stack of papers and handed them across to Matt, who had seated himself on the high-backed chair facing the desk.

"What are these?" Matt asked, taking them.

"The notes David Duff shared with me on his upcoming sermon series."

The four main topics were stapled into separate packets. The one on top read, *The Life of Christ*. "This was to be his Lenten series, right?"

"Yes." The bishop nodded for Matt to read through the notes.

The outline began with the Christmas story, then discussed the child Jesus teaching in the temple, then the beginning of his ministry. Each sermon title came with several Bible quotes. Matt's eyebrows rose. "A Camel through a Needle's Eye," he read.

Bishop Hamlin nodded. "Jesus had a cautionary tale for the rich."

Matt read a little further. "Those who live by the sword shall die by the sword." He looked up at Hamlin. "It's not that any of this is new, but to lay it out so explicitly..."

"Christ was a bit of a no-holds-barred kind of preacher." Hamlin chuckled. "That's a David Duff quote, by the way."

Matt picked up the second stack. "The Eleven Commandments," he read out loud. He skimmed through the outline, which covered the ten commandments handed down to Moses on Mount Sinai. On the last page, Matt found Jesus pronouncing the new commandment—the eleventh commandment—in John, chapter 13, verse 34. "A new command I give to you," Matt read. "Love one another. As I have loved you, love one another."

Hamlin put down his cup. "Kinda takes the hate and prejudice out of how folks should treat each other."

"Kinda makes a lot of preachers flat out wrong," Matt nodded, then jumped when he heard a noise behind him.

"And who are you to judge, Pastor Hayden?"

Matt turned to see Reverend Meade glaring at him from the doorway, Senator Womack at his side. As Meade continued into the room, Matt wondered how he'd ever considered Meade a Santa Claus look-alike before. Now all Matt saw was an overindulgent, self-righteous manipulator.

Hamlin rose from behind his desk. "What are you doing here?"

"We came to see if what we heard was true," Womack closed the door behind him. "Apparently you and the preacher here have formed an alliance?"

Hamlin inclined his head. "We were discussing the Bible."

Meade snorted. "You were discussing Duff's upcoming sermon series."

Matt stood, so he could see all three men at the same time. "From what I've read, the two are one and the same." He nodded to the papers he had placed on the front of the desk. "Looks pretty biblically based to me."

"*You* would say that," said Meade. "You and Duff walked step in step."

That took Matt by surprise. "I never met the man."

Meade glared. "Of course not." Sarcasm dripped from his tone. "You gave an almost word-for-word benediction at the governor's inauguration as Duff was going to give with the wise exception of not naming names. If you didn't know each other, how is that possible?"

"I've read the Bible."

Meade's eyes flashed with anger. "I've been in the ministry for over twenty years. You're still wet behind the ears from seminary. How dare—"

"Now, Robert. Stay calm." Womack patted Meade on the shoulder. "Let's all have a seat and talk this out." He pulled a deep, leather high back into a circle with the bishop's desk and the two straight backs fronting the desk and sat down.

Grudgingly, Meade did as he was told, then Hamlin followed suit. Matt shot one last accusatory glance Meade's way, then sat. "That explains what you said to me after the inauguration. 'I know who you are, and I know what you're trying to do.' You thought I was in some plot against you."

"Because you are," Meade snapped back. "What other reason could you have for involving yourself in our business?"

"I'm *involved* in finding Reverend Duff. And today, we might have done just that."

Womack's face blanched. "What do you mean?"

"You've heard of the Homestead? There's a huge bonfire pit on the property. Apparently, they had a big one a few days ago." Matt cocked his head. "Know anything about that?"

"Of course, I do. The guys get together at the end of hunting season and throw a big party." Womack narrowed his eyes at Matt, then seemed to understand something. "*That's* why you were at the Oak and Horn. To find out about a bunch of men who like a long weekend away from prying eyes?"

"No, actually," Matt said. "I was there trying to find out why Pastor Lambert was looking for your son, Hogg, the same day Lambert committed suicide."

Womack's face turned red. "I have no idea what you're talking about."

"Well, I do," Matt said. "Lambert and I were both staying at Hester Honeywell's mansion. I overheard him talking on the phone with your son, who, by the way, hung up on him. Then, what do you know—Lambert headed over to the Oak and Horn to find Hogg, but he wasn't there." Matt turned his attention to Meade. "Where did Lambert go next? Lo and behold, he headed over to your place, Reverend Meade. He was in your church for a while. Came out pretty upset. Then he headed straight back to the Oak and Horn, again, looking for Hogg."

"What were you doing? Following him?" Meade demanded.

"Well, Lambert was the last one who saw Duff alive. Lambert was pretty upset and, as I said, keen to find your son, Senator. Why do you think that is?"

"I have no idea," Womack said between gritted teeth.

"I'm trying to figure out exactly what your plan was, Reverend Meade." Matt paused to sip his coffee. "The bishop knew Duff planned to call you out in his benediction. He tried to warn Duff off. Maybe that worked, or maybe it wouldn't have made any difference to you either way. Maybe you'd already decided his fate. But when you heard *my* benediction, warning the governor of false prophets and power-hungry politicians, you decided I was as bad as Duff. You sent the news media on me like bloodhounds after a rabbit." Matt looked from Meade to Womack. "How am I doing, gentlemen?"

"You think Duff was a saint?" Meade demanded.

"Hardly. Though you and Duff are on opposite sides of the coin, the coin itself is a fake. Hate is hate. Christ preached love. Period."

"And this Christly love is the reason you went to the Homestead today." Womack sat back down, his control returned.

Matt wondered how Womack knew that's where he'd been, but he kept his cool. "Yes, actually. You see, Duff's wife has suffered great stress since her husband went missing. So much so that, two nights ago, she miscarried their child and almost died in the process. Out of love for her, and frankly, love for justice, I went out to the Homestead looking for Duff."

"What does that have to do with my son?"

"We're working on that," Matt said.

"Working on what?"

"Whether or not your son killed David Duff, then put Duff's body into the bonfire pile to burn."

Womack came out of his chair. "How dare you!"

Matt's eyes were flat. "It's a working theory. I'm not accusing him of anything. Yet."

"This is preposterous," Womack spat out. "My son is not a killer!"

Meade blubbered, "Besides, I didn't see Hogg on inauguration day until the ball that night. Don't try to hook me up with that brat."

"My son is not a brat." Womack's voice rose an octave.

Bishop Hamlin finally spoke. "Gentlemen, please. Reverend Duff's disappearance and Pastor Lambert's suicide have put us all on edge. The police will sort this out."

Womack stabbed a finger at Matt. "He's in cahoots with the police. He's put this poison in their heads."

"I've only followed the facts, Senator," Matt said. "The same facts that are in the hands of the police. Can you offer another explanation?"

"I can't, but my son can." Womack pulled the phone from his pocket. "And he'll tell us exactly what did happen." He punched a number into his phone. "Hogg?" His voice was much calmer than a moment earlier. "Can you stop by St. George Episcopal for a moment? I have some questions for you."

Womack paused, then his faced turned grim. "I don't care if you have a test tomorrow. You need to come here. Now."

This time, Hogg's response was much shorter. Matt imagined he'd said something like, "Yes, sir," since Womack ended the call with a smile on his face. He turned to the group. "Hogg will be here shortly."

"In that case," Hamlin rose from behind the desk. "How about I pour us all a cup of coffee?"

49

THE SENATOR'S SON

A SILENT TEN minutes ensued until a knock was heard on the office wing's front door. Womack immediately stood. "I'll let him in."

Matt's brow furrowed. "That reminds me," he said, looking at Meade. "How did you get in?"

Meade shrugged. "The door was unlocked."

Hamlin's face reddened. "Sorry, Preacher. Bad habit."

Womack's large frame filled the door as he entered. The young man behind him was shorter, with lean shoulders. His chin was minimal, a one-eighty compared to his father's square jaw. Matt remembered what Hester had said. *Hogg has his mother's looks and his father's mean.*

Bishop Hamlin hurried from behind his desk. "I'll pull in a chair from the other room." Soon he was back, rolling in a secretary's chair. "Here you go, son."

Matt noted that Hogg moved the chair to the side of the desk opposite his father's before sitting down. Hmm, he thought. Hogg is an outspoken bully when he's on his own, but when his father is around, his bravado disappears. He's a scared little boy.

Womack immediately took the lead. "Hogg, you're here because Pastor Hayden here thinks you had something to do with Reverend Duff's disappearance."

Instead of looking Matt in the eye, Hogg lowered his head.

"Pastor Hayden," Womack continued, "let's get this straightened out right now. Why do you think my son had anything to do with the missing Reverend Duff? The boy is here to answer your accusations."

"More like questions," Matt said. "I overheard you talking with Lambert on the phone the day after the inauguration. You hung up on him. And we have witnesses who say he tried to find you at the Oak and Horn twice that day. What did he want with you?"

"Nothin'. I don't know what you're talking about."

"Did it have something to do with why you were driving his car on inauguration day?"

Hogg's head jerked up. "How do you know about that?"

"We have it on camera." Well, actually, they had it on camera that someone matching Hogg's build drove Lambert's car that day.

Hogg looked at his father, his expression a mix of fear and a plea for help.

"Son. Did you drive Lambert's car on inauguration day?"

Hogg combed nervous fingers through his hair, then glared at Meade. "If I did, it's because he told me to."

"Me?" Reverend Meade's faked bewilderment only made him look more guilty, in Matt's estimation. "Why would I do that?"

Why indeed? Matt wondered. Then he understood. He stood and, grabbing his cane, began to pace, as the pieces began to fall into place. He stopped at Hogg's side. "The plan was never to kill Duff, was it? Just to keep him from the inauguration." He swung around to look at Meade. "Isn't that right, Reverend?"

Meade remained silent, but his hands twitched.

"You wanted to scare the daylights out of him," Matt continued, staring at Meade. "So scared, he'd rethink giving that four-sermon series: the life of Christ, the eleven commandments, Jesus's parables and, finally, the Sermon on the Mount. All because *your* words spewed from the pulpit were the antithesis of what Jesus said and did."

"He made me do it!" Meade slashed a finger toward Womack. "He's the one who told me of his great vision for the future. A return to moral—"

"I don't care about politicians!" Matt cut him off. "They pledge their allegiance to the Constitution and our country, and frankly, that's not my domain. You, however, have supposedly pledged your allegiance to God. Not to money."

Meade jumped to his feet. "How dare you, sir!"

"How dare *you*?" Matt met him toe to toe. "You and your private planes, your fancy, expensive mansion, your multimillion-dollar church in the middle of nowhere. You didn't build that edifice for the poor. There isn't a bus stop near your 'Christian House of Love' for miles. The only people you want in your congregation are the ones who can park Mercedes Benz and Lexus cars in your parking lot."

Meade raised his hand to throw a punch, but Matt stared him down. "The only possession Jesus owned was the robe they cast lots for beneath his cross as he died."

Slowly, Meade's hand returned to his side. He sat down heavily.

Matt breathed deeply, then turned back to Womack's son. "The plan was to dump Duff's drugged body in the middle of nowhere to scare him. But something went wrong, didn't it?"

"Yes!" Hogg looked relieved that somebody in the room understood. "That's it. Mostly."

"Mostly?" Womack exploded. He looked at Meade. "What have you done?"

"Duff was going to out me. On TV! Do you know how many people watch the inauguration?" Meade's face was purple. "And the TV people love that kind of drama. Pastor Duff outs conservative preachers as false prophets. God only knows what he was going to say about you. You and your great plans. You should be grateful!"

"Grateful for what?"

Meade fell silent and looked away. Hogg hung his head.

"Grateful for what!" Womack shouted.

"That's why Lambert went to talk with you, Meade." Matt said quietly. "He must have been in on the plan. More than that, now that I think about it. The only way you would know what Reverend Duff was going to say in his benediction was if you had an advance copy of the prayer." Matt paced again, nodding. "Lambert was the business administrator for Duff's church. He was in charge of the money, human resources, business decisions and..." He stopped pacing and glared at Meade. "...the church's technology, including the computer system. He's the one who fed you what Duff was planning to preach about, pray about, whatever."

"Lambert was a good man," Meade said, his tone defensive. "He worshipped Jesse Duff. Then he died in that car crash, and David took over the church. And with him came all the permissive, socialist, leftist crap that began pushing members out the door. Lambert couldn't stand to watch River Walk Fellowship Church being torn asunder."

Matt shook his head. "On inauguration day, you and Lambert conspired to keep Duff from giving that 'heretical' prayer."

"Exactly!" Meade pounded the arm of his chair. "Why should that garbage be allowed on the airwaves?"

"But Lambert couldn't pull it off alone. He needed someone to help him disable Duff for a few hours. So you hooked him up with Hogg." Matt considered. "Why choose Hogg to help him?"

Meade shrugged. "I told him what Duff was going to say about his father."

Womack elbows were on his knees. "Is any of this true, Hogg?"

"Yes, sir." Hogg's head had been buried in his chest up to this point, but now he looked up earnestly at his father. "I couldn't let him say stuff like that about you. And this was my chance to prove to you that I was a man. That I could take care of my family. Like you always wanted."

"Tell us what happened, Hogg," Matt said.

"It's pretty much like you said. I went to the Honeywell mansion around nine or so the morning of the inauguration. I waited behind the garage for Lambert to let me in. He brought some of Duff's clothes so I could put them on and pretend to be Duff going into St. Gregory's back door." He looked over at Hamlin. "Don't worry, Bishop, I didn't touch anything. Meade said not to."

"Okay, let's go back a little," Matt said, remembering that Lyle had seen Lambert carrying a bag out to the garage before he and Duff left. Lyle had thought Lambert was taking some trash out to the dumpster. "Lambert came down beforehand and handed you a bag full of Duff's clothes. You put them on. Then what?"

"I was in the garage and went over to the door that connects with the house. When Lambert and Duff came into the garage, I jumped out and stuck the needle in Duff's neck. He passed out."

"Then what?"

"Me and Lambert loaded him into the trunk. A tight fit, that Lambert's car is kinda small. Then Lambert dropped me off at St. Gregory's and drove the car over to the Oak and Horn's parking lot. I went into the church like I was supposed to, waited a few minutes, then walked over to the Oak and Horn."

"Where did you change out of Duff's clothes?" Matt asked, already knowing the answer.

"I'd scouted out a parking deck along the way where I could change."

"I don't want to hear another word," Womack said angrily.

Matt's lip curled. "Your son has the right to tell you what he did for you." He put a hand on Hogg's shoulder. "Now's your chance, son. Let your dad know how much you love him," Matt said, glaring at Womack.

"Yeah, so I walked over to the Oak and Horn. I checked the trunk to make sure Duff was still out..." His voice dropped off.

Matt waited a long moment before speaking again. "And what did you find?"

Hogg hung his head, unable to continue.

Matt inhaled deeply. "He was dead, wasn't he?"

"Yes." The whisper was barely audible, but it hurled through the room like a wrecking ball.

Womack covered his face with his hands. All went completely still.

Finally, Matt spoke. "Hogg, what did you put in that needle?"

Hogg broke down in sobs, unable to answer.

Womack raised his head. "What was in that needle, Hogg?"

"It's not my fault." Hogg raised his tear-streaked face. "I didn't kill him. God killed him."

That rocked Matt back on his heels. "*God* killed him?"

"Yeah," Hogg cried, turning to Meade. "It's like you said in your sermon two weeks ago. You said God makes the decision on who lives and who dies. It's divine providence."

Meade looked stunned. "I never—"

"Yes, you did," Hogg insisted. "When you were talking about abortion. You said it was wrong for a woman to have an abortion, even if her life was in danger. You said God would determine which should live, the mother or the baby. Or if either should live. It's up to God to make those decisions. You said it, over and over!"

"But I was talking about abortions," Meade gasped.

"So?" Hogg threw back.

Matt finally took a seat, and it had nothing to do with his bad leg. He felt as if the wind had been knocked out of him.

"Hogg," Matt said quietly. "What was in that needle?"

"Digitalis." Hogg's face was defiant. "After all the things he said about you, was going to say about you, I figured he deserved to die. But I didn't kill him. I left that up to God."

Womack's face turned white. "My God."

Matt managed to sit up a little straighter in the chair. "What happened when you saw that, uh, God had killed him?"

"I knew the bonfire was coming up the next day. And the fire goes all night. I figured it would, like, cremate Duff, and nobody would know."

"You drove him out to the Homestead."

Hogg nodded, finally regaining some composure. "The wood had already been dumped beside the pit. I put some into the pit, then unloaded Duff out of the back of the car and dragged him to the pyre."

His sounded earnest now, Matt realized. Hogg wanted to tell this story. But to whom?

Then I figured the smell of the dead body might be pretty potent when the guys started showing up for the bonfire."

Hogg's gaze focused on his father. "I went back up to the bunkhouse. Got a rifle from the gun safe."

Hogg's voice trembled, but not with fear. With hope. My God, Matt thought, he's trying to impress his father.

"Every member of Herne's Hunters knows the combination," Hogg was saying "Anyway, some cattle were grazing not too far up the hill. I shot a calf, dragged it over, and put it on top of Duff. Covered it all with more wood. I called up the guys who were supposed to build the fire and told 'em it was taken care of. I'd gone out to do some shooting. Said I'd found a dead cow nearby and thrown it on the pile." He brightened. "They were so grateful they didn't have to build the fire, they bought my beer for the weekend."

"And you got the car washed on your way back?" Matt asked.

"Sure did. In Lampasas, at one of those high-end carwashes. Gave 'em a hundred bucks to make sure it was clean as new."

Again silence, then Matt finally spoke. "When Duff didn't show back up, Lambert knew something had gone wrong. He tried to find you, Hogg, and when he couldn't, he went to the man who had conceived the plan to silence Duff in the first place." Matt turned to Meade. "Lambert went to you. What exactly were you going to do with Duff when he woke up, Reverend Meade?"

"Hogg was supposed to take Duff to a field or abandoned building in the middle of nowhere, where he was supposed to wake up. Sore and achy, probably. Disoriented, definitely. But he was supposed to wake up." Meade glared at Hogg.

"That's it?" Matt asked.

Meade shrugged. "Perhaps it would have been made clear that if he continued his hateful verbiage, the next time he might not fare as well."

"You only wanted to threaten him."

"Perhaps."

Womack stood abruptly, as if a switch had turned on in his mind. "There you have it, Pastor Hayden. The whole story. You've done what you felt you had to do. You proved my son is a murderer."

"I am not!" Hogg protested. "God did it!"

"Enough!" Womack's voice boomed across the room. He turned back to Matt. "Now I'm going to do what *I* have to do."

"What does that mean?" Hamlin demanded.

"We're going to reenact Meade's plan. Only with you, Pastor Hayden. Complete with digitalis."

Matt's blood ran cold with fear. He'd cheated death before, but this time he had neither the strength nor speed to escape.

Hamlin pushed f his chair. "Absolutely not!"

Womack turned on the bishop. "You're either with me and Meade or you're with Pastor Hayden and the digitalis treatment. Decide. Now."

"Actually, *I've* made a decision." The distinctly female voice came from behind. Matt turned to see Lieutenant Gage standing in the doorway; two police officers visible behind her. "Hogg Womack," she said. "I am arresting you for the murder of Reverend David Duff." She stood back to let one of the officers by. "Read the Miranda, nice and clear, Officer," she instructed. "We want all the witnesses to hear."

Several officers now swarmed into the room. In the midst of the turmoil, Matt stared at Gage in astonishment. One minute he'd been facing death, and now—"Why are you here?"

"You had us put a tail on Hogg, remember?" Her beautifully sculpted brow rose. "A bit of divine intervention, perhaps?"

The click of handcuffs brought Matt's attention back to the scene.

"Dad!" Hogg cried out.

"Don't you ever call me that again." The senator stepped forward and slapped his son hard across the face. "I'll pay your legal fees, but I never want to see your face again."

Tears streamed down Hogg's cheeks. "But I did it for you!"

"*For* me? Do you know what you've done *to* me? To my plans? How stupid can you be? My God, I'm not sure I *am* your father. Someone musta snuck in there when I wasn't looking."

Matt shook his head. The rage of the father. And the lengths a son would go to earn his father's approval. What a tragedy.

"What are you shaking your head about," Womack demanded. "You got exactly what you wanted. This is your fault."

Matt studied Womack. "I almost wish it were. But this is your doing, Senator. You raised your son without approval, without love, and now you're seeing how that worked out. You raised a son who would go to any lengths to earn that which you could never give. You're so filled with ambition and lust for power that the only person you can approve of, or love is yourself. Look in the mirror, Senator. You are the monster who created this situation."

He turned to Meade. "And you. See what you have created in the name of God?" Matt jabbed a finger at Hogg. "This is what hatred spewed from the pulpit can drive people to. It's blasphemers like you that Jesus drove from the temple two thousand years ago."

"I did not kill Reverend Duff!" Meade protested.

"No," Gage said. "But you are charged with conspiracy to kidnap, and I'm pretty sure the D.A. will consider adding accessory to murder. Officer, please read Reverend Meade his rights."

Matt realized he was shaking, his nerves tangled in a web of emotions. His head began to spin. Oh no, he thought. His blood pressure must be going through the roof.

Gage must've seen it too. She motioned another officer over to Matt's side. "Take Pastor Hayden to Hester Honeywell's. He's had enough of these people for one night."

The officer stepped forward and took Matt by the elbow. "This way, Pastor."

Matt paused to take one last glance around the room.

How sad, he thought. How devastatingly sad.

50

SO SAYETH THE FATHER

So Sayeth the Father

A GENTLE KNOCK at his bedroom door woke Matt from a dreamless sleep. "Pastor?" Lyle's subdued call came through the door.

"Come in," Matt said, but he didn't get out of bed. Instead, he pulled the down comforter closer to his chin.

Lyle entered. Because the curtains were drawn tight, Matt could barely make out Lyle's large frame. "What day is it?" he asked groggily.

"Saturday," Lyle replied.

An entire week since Hogg Womack had confessed to killing David Duff. Or that God had. Matt stared at the coffered ceiling for a moment. He'd moved from the mansion to the guesthouse to gain some privacy and time for introspection. The tragedy of last Saturday night still haunted him. He'd spent many hours the last week searching for that peace that passes all understanding.

Peace was nowhere to be found.

With Duff's disappearance solved, Shelly Duff and Mum had returned to San Antonio on Tuesday. They had a memorial service to plan. Though he'd barely had a chance to get to know Shelly, he missed Mum with her calm countenance and that British accent that always made him smile. Many tears were shed and hugs shared when they left Hester's home.

"I'm sorry to disturb you," Lyle said, his tone apologetic. "But Lieutenant Gage called. She'd like to come over to talk with you and James W."

"James W.'s back in town?" He and Angie had gone back to Wilks last Monday. The day Dr. Ryan had insisted Matt stay in Austin a few more days.

"Yes, and he's bringing Angie with him. Lieutenant Gage suggested it might be a good idea if we were all present to hear her news."

"When is the lieutenant coming over?" Matt asked.

"In an hour. Ten o'clock."

Matt struggled to his elbows and tossed his mop of sandy brown hair out of his face. He sighed. "I'll get in the shower."

———

FORTY-FIVE MINUTES LATER, Matt crossed from the guesthouse to the mansion via the solarium. The late January day was awash in sunshine and greening grass.

Lyle was in the solarium arranging furniture when Matt emerged from the guesthouse. "Make yourself comfortable, Preacher. Hester said it's too pretty outside to meet in the parlor. Be right back."

Matt had barely taken a seat in the nearby wicker chair when Hester entered the solarium.

"Good morning, Preacher," she said.

Matt began to rise in greeting, but she waved him back down. "I'm not sure what the lieutenant has to say. Called at a quarter to nine. I don't usually receive calls until after nine, but she told Lyle it was important."

Connor rolled in a coffee service cart. "Help yourselves, everyone. James W. and Angie just pulled up out front," he said. "I'll send them back."

"They must've hopped right in the truck when you called," Matt mused. "They made good time."

On cue, James W., dressed in his khaki sheriff's uniform complete with wide-brimmed hat, and Angie, wearing jeans and her Fire and Icehouse sweatshirt, walked into the solarium. James W.'s eyes brightened when he saw the coffee cart. "Don't mind if I do."

Hester joined him. "Glad you could get here so quickly."

Matt barely heard the conversation. He only had eyes for Angie. Her golden red hair flamed in waves around her face and shoulders as she crossed to him. She planted a hand on each armrest of his chair and stared into his eyes. "I've missed you, Preacher." She lowered her lips and gently kissed him.

Matt closed his eyes. At least this, this love, was settled in his life. "I was afraid you wouldn't be able to come. A Saturday at the Icehouse?"

"I hired that bartender from the Oak and Horn. Monica Braden? She started yesterday."

Matt came instantly alert. "Can you trust her?"

"She was pretty upset about getting fired." Angie shrugged. "She'd know if any of the Oak and Horn people come in."

"Or let them in the back door."

"Look at it this way. I'll have more time to spend with you." She leaned in for another kiss.

James W. cleared his throat. "Can I get you two some coffee?"

"I'll get it." Angie pushed off the armrests, but not until she offered Matt a flirtatious wink. "Later," she whispered.

Lyle entered, carrying plates and a platter filled with pastries. "A little something to tide everyone over."

Angie detoured from her journey to the coffee. "These look wonderful," she said. "How'd you pull this off in an hour?"

"Talent, my dear. Talent," Lyle said coyly.

"You're the best cook I've ever met," she said. "But don't tell my Icehouse cook I said that."

She filled a plate and brought it over to Matt, then headed for the coffee.

Connor appeared at the mansion's French doors. "Hester, you remember Lieutenant Gage?" He stepped aside to allow the tall, striking woman to enter. To Matt's surprise, Chief Aguilar, shorter and full of brawn, stepped in behind her. Both were in their dark navy APD uniforms.

This was mostly definitely an official visit, Matt decided.

The light mood in the solarium became immediately subdued. "Thank you all for getting here so quickly," the chief said. He turned to Hester. "And thank you for hosting."

"Anytime, Chief," she said.

Lyle and Connor started to leave, but the chief put up a hand. "Please stay."

The two men looked at each other, their eyes wide. They nodded to the chief, availed themselves of the coffee cart, then sat down on the far side of the food table.

Angie pulled a chair over to sit by Matt. James W. and Hester took the seats across from them. Lieutenant Gage and Chief Aguilar stood in front of the coffee cart.

Aguilar nodded to Gage. "Start us off, Lieutenant."

Gage stepped forward and clasped her hands behind her back as if reporting to a superior officer. "I regret to inform you that Hogg Womack committed suicide this morning sometime between three and five o'clock."

Matt felt the blow to his gut. He put down his coffee cup.

"The cells are checked every two hours, which is why we can pin it down that closely. He hanged himself from the cell's bars."

Which meant it would have been a very slow death, Matt decided. And being so close to the bars, he could've saved himself.

If he'd wanted to.

"Yesterday, at 10:30 a.m., we got some of the forensics back from the Homestead," she continued. "The tire print we took by the bonfire matches the tread on Pastor Lambert's Ford Focus. And the soil sample we removed from the car's wheel well the day after Reverend Duff's disappearance matches the Homestead's soil. Additionally, Hogg confessed to throwing away Reverend Duff's laptop and Bible at the car wash. Both have since been retrieved from the car wash's dumpster."

Matt looked at James W., whose lips were pursed. Neither one of them was surprised to hear this bit of information.

"Soon after, I met with the district attorney assigned to prosecuting the case and presented the evidence we had so far. In addition to the new evidence, we discussed the downward spiral of Mr. Womack's mental state. Over the week, Mr. Womack had begun preaching in his cell—"

"Preaching?" Matt interrupted.

Finally, Gage looked at him and nodded. "As if his cell was a stage and hundreds of people were sitting in pews around him, hanging on his every word."

"And that's not all," Aguilar said. "Hogg began fixating on

his beloved, loving father. He talked about his father's plans for a presidential run. He talked about how he had worked so hard to serve his father; to make his father proud. For example, I understand you had a grease fire while frying a turkey a week or so ago?"

Lyle sat up straight in his chair. "Yes?"

"Lambert apparently left several messages on Hogg's phone when he was trying to find him. One of the messages mentioned you specifically, Preacher, and that you were staying at Hester's mansion. On his way out to the Homestead that night, he decided to drive by Hester's to size up the place. He saw the fry pot out on the driveway and threw a match into the boiling oil, just to be ornery."

Matt shook his head. "I never connected the fire with my investigation of Duff's disappearance."

James W. cleared his throat. "You said Hogg talked about his father's plans? Did he mention anything about that Rolfe Evangelical Trade School or whatever up in West Virginia?"

"I'm not free to discuss those details," Aguilar said.

Which meant yes, Matt decided.

Gage relaxed her stance. "In light of this new evidence, the D.A. and I met with Hogg's attorney at 1:00 yesterday after-noon, after which the attorney asked to see Hogg. You see, despite his 'confession' last Saturday night, Hogg Womack had entered a plea of not guilty."

Aguilar broke in. "This, of course, was what his father, the senator, instructed him to do."

"Then the senator did talk to his son," Matt said, feeling relief. "He'd said he never wanted to see Hogg again."

"I'm afraid not," said Aguilar. "The senator kept that prom-ise. He was only interested in putting up a fight to save his reputation. For example, he had Reverend Meade out on bail within twenty-four hours. He refused to pay a dime to get

Hogg out. The senator's only interest seemed to be damage control for his own political reputation."

"Hogg and his attorney met yesterday afternoon," Gage continued. "The attorney apparently asked him if he wanted to change his plea to guilty in hopes of perhaps getting a lighter sentence. Hogg said he'd do whatever his father wanted him to do. The attorney apparently then discussed the matter with the senator, and to that end, Mrs. Womack came to the jail last night around seven o'clock to meet with her son."

Aguilar cleared his throat. "And less than twelve hours later, Hogg was dead."

"My God," Hester whispered.

"That SOB." James W.'s face was red with anger.

"Don't be so harsh on Hogg." Angie said to Matt. "He was a victim, too."

"Not Hogg," Matt said, softly correcting her. "James W.'s talking about the senator."

"I don't get it," Angie said.

"Hogg said he'd do whatever his father wanted him to do," Matt reminded her.

"You mean—?" Her face paled.

Matt sighed. "The message that Mrs. Womack brought to her son was that his father wanted him to die."

"No!" Angie stood abruptly. "No mother would do that!"

"I'm afraid I agree with the preacher," Aguilar said. "He hanged himself with a knitted baby blanket. The baby blanket Hogg's mother presented to the corrections officer on duty for permission to give to her son."

"Dreadful!" Hester said. "Connor, perhaps you'd best bring us some whiskey for our coffee."

But Connor didn't hear her. His hand and Lyle's hand were clasped in a death grip, as they tried to process what they'd heard. The stunned looks on their faces mirrored the horror Matt felt.

"And the reason I wanted all of you here," Aguilar said, "is because I believe the senator will be looking for revenge."

Matt nodded. "He blames me for Hogg getting caught in this mess."

James W. leaned forward. "Son, it's worse than that."

Understanding dawned. "Now he's gonna blame me for Hogg's death, too."

Matt looked at Gage and Aguilar. Their grim faces told him they thought the same thing.

Matt sucked in a breath and let it out slowly. "I can't go back to Wilks."

Angie sat back down with a thud. "What?"

"It won't be safe for you, for the Icehouse, for Bo and Pearl, for Dorothy Jo, for my congregation. Heck, Womack already had it in for our family, for Jimmy. When I gave that benediction at Jimmy's inauguration, I unwittingly quoted some of the same themes Duff was going to say. Womack assumed that meant that Jimmy was against him. Look how he arranged to have DPS pull you over to deliver his warning to Jimmy. That was before anyone even knew Hogg had killed Duff. This is only going to make that situation worse."

"On that note," Aguilar spoke up. "APD has opened an investigation into the situation with the DPS troopers. That's about all I can say right now. But the folks in Wilks aren't the only ones who might need to be concerned."

Hester nodded. "I understand. I've never hidden my disregard for Womack's way of doing things, and now my association with the preacher only adds to my list of sins. Connor? Lyle? You understand what this means."

Matt studied the two men as they took in Hester's words. Their eyes were first clouded with confusion, then they widened with understanding, then narrowed with resolve. "Yes, Hester," Lyle said. "We'll be on the lookout."

"I'll see about upping our security package," Connor said.

"But Matt," Angie's voice trembled. "What will you do? If you can't come home, where will you go?"

"That's simple, my dear," Hester said. "He'll stay here. With us. He's part of our family now, anyway."

Angie looked pleadingly at Matt. "But you have a family already. In Wilks."

Matt took her hand. "Yes, I do. But this settles an internal battle I've been fighting all week. I don't think this is the time for me to return to the pulpit. I've seen how the Word of God can be manipulated by preachers who have their own agenda. Right now, I'm not sure I won't turn into someone who does that same thing."

"Matt, that's impossible," she argued. "You're the most loving, caring—"

He shook his head. "You should've heard me go after Reverend Meade and Senator Womack last Saturday night. I was angry. I was accusatory. I was judgmental. I assure you, no love spewed from my mouth that night. That was wrong of me." He took her hand. "I don't want to be that man, Angie."

"Preacher," Gage said. "For the record, I didn't see it that way. You were confronting men who used the Bible to teach hate. In doing so, they created a murderer. There's no sin in calling out their blasphemy."

Matt studied the tall, efficient cop. They'd never had a discussion about his calling, and he hadn't considered her a religious person. Apparently, he'd been wrong about that, too.

Hester rose from her chair. "Is there anything else you want to share with us, Lieutenant? Chief?"

Gage shook her head no, but Aguilar spoke. "We'll keep you all posted, of course. And sheriff, perhaps we can arrange occasional informal talks with the governor regarding his security. Perhaps your wife would enjoy throwing a party now and then where we could get some private time together?"

"What a wonderful idea," Hester piped up. "Sheriff, you simply must ask your wife if I can assist in planning her social activities. Like right now, it might be prudent to arrange a get-together for your son's highest campaign donors. Maybe at the Bullock Museum on the UT campus? It's a lovely venue."

Matt's brow quirked. Since when did Hester want to spend more time with Elsbeth?

"She's making sure Jimmy won't be harmed by Elsbeth's gaffs," Angie whispered.

"She's sending the message that she's got Jimmy's back."

"And it looks like she has mine too." He reached over to take Angie's hand. "We'll make this work, Angie. I love you."

"And I've hired enough folks so I can come up here more often." She squeezed his hand. "I love you. Nothing's going to keep us apart."

"Ah! Another party," Hester was saying, her smile bright. "And this time, co-hosting with your lovely wife. I so enjoyed her company at the Junior League..."

The End

ABOUT THE AUTHOR

K.P. Gresham, Author

Professional Character Assassin

K.P. Gresham is the award-winning author of the Pastor Matt Hayden Mystery Series as well as several stand-alone novels. Active in Sisters in Crime and the Writers League of Texas, she has won Best Novel awards from the Bay Area Writers League as well as the Mystery Writers of America.

For more information or to sign-up for K.P.'s Newsletter, check out her website at www.kpgresham.com.

ALSO BY K.P GRESHAM

Books by

K.P. Gresham

Three Days at Wrigley Field

The Pastor Matt Hayden Mystery Series

The Preacher's First Murder

Murder in the Second Pew

Murder on the Third Try

Four Reasons to Die

Made in the USA
Columbia, SC
07 November 2021